Whisper Pretty Lies

C.S. BERRY

Author Note & Content List

Dear Reader,

The beginning of a new story is my favorite thing. All the possibilities. Whisper Pretty Lies is a duet meaning the story starts here and ends in Brutal Little Secrets. There is a cliffhanger but the next book is coming soon.

If this is your first read from me, I like my romance smutty, but within the confines of the characters. These heroes are going to come off as assholes at first, but my heroine will be able to go toe to toe with them. Plus she kind of likes it.

So if you like it when the wallflower gets the hottest guys in school and revenge on her cheating boyfriend, this is for you.

This book contains darker themes which can be found on my website csberry.com/lust-liars under content warnings. Your mental health is important. If you're concerned, you can always reach out to me as well.

These guys are definitely sending up red flags all over the place, but I guarantee EvanAnn and them find their happily ever after.

Thank you for reading!!!

XOXOXO

C.S. Berry

Content warning:

Dark themes including bullying, blackmail, stalking, and dubious consent. It also includes attempted sexual assault.

CHAPTER 1

Damon

SCHOOL STARTS in a couple of days. Fuck that shit. I wasn't even supposed to be here. Not this school, not this town, not even this state. My life is a fucking shit show. Stuck at Deimos Academy for another year, senior year, when I was supposed to be off working toward my NHL dream. But that all got fucked by two people.

"If you want to fuck him up, I'll hold back his friends," Hawk Wilker says and hands me a bottle of beer. Conditioning for the season starts next week, so this is it for me. One last fucking hurrah. I take my hockey career seriously, even if my father doesn't.

"Chase Chadwick." Cam shakes his head like someone died and cracks his knuckles. "With a name like that, it's like his parents were begging for their son to get a daily ass whooping."

These two are my ride or dies. We've been friends since grade school and hockey camps. Neither of them is interested in making a living on the ice, but we've played together every year. This was supposed to be our first year apart.

It didn't sit well leaving them behind, but I had to do what was best for my career in the long run. Until fucking Chase Chadwick.

I stretch out my leg, which is still fucked up and aches from the accident. My bike and leathers took the brunt of the pavement along with

1

my helmet. That would have been a mess if I hadn't been wearing one. In the end, it still tore up the skin on my jaw.

"Say the word, man." Hawk takes a sip of his beer while we watch Chase drag his girlfriend over to the beer pong table. She hasn't touched a drop of alcohol and seems so fucking out of place in her jeans and oversized sweatshirt.

The party is outside. It's the end of summer, but it can still get chilly at night. Her blond hair is up in a messy bun. She doesn't fit in here. Not with the other girls in their revealing clothes.

The image of her blond hair in his lap—right before their car slammed into me—plays in my head like an instant replay.

"I'll keep the girl occupied for you two." Cam smirks. From his lecherous gaze, I know he's thinking about what she was doing to her boyfriend that night.

The girl is EvanAnn Ward. A fucking thorn in my side. An ant and theater nerd. She's been in my classes for years, but she's not noticeable. It's odd he's with her, except they're both in the drama program.

The heat inside me will have to wait because, as much as I'd love to beat the shit out of Chase, my hands are tied. Tonight and every night.

"I can't touch Chase. At least not physically. Our dads are business partners." The accident was reported as a hit and run. There are no cameras up in the hills to prove that Chase was the driver. Those fuckers didn't even realize they'd clipped me. They were a little occupied at the time. Though his car probably has scratches and streaks of my bike's paint down the side.

Even if he'd been caught, his father would have made it go away.

Hawk leans back against the house and takes a drag from his beer. For now, all that potential energy has been released. I'm sure he'll find a guy to beat up or a girl to fuck later.

"Your dad still moving the gold digger in?" Cam asks as he relaxes. His beer bottle dangles from his fingers.

I nod and take a drink. The arrangements have all been made. It won't be long now. My life is a fucking shit show.

"Damon!" Olivia Carmichael says my name like she's having an orgasm as she enters our space. Or at least tries to enter our space.

I don't look at her.

Hawk smiles, cutting her off before she can grab on to me. "What's up, Olivia?"

She stops as he steps in her way and shifts so she can still talk to me.

"I was thinking of having a private party later this weekend, Damon. Do you want to come?" She emphasizes the word *come*.

I turn to look at her. She's the opposite of everything EvanAnn is. Her hair is styled to look windblown and natural. Her face is painted to best accentuate her beauty. She's a fucking Barbie doll brought to life, and all the Kens in this school have already used her. Including Hawk, but not me.

That's the only reason the rich princess is interested in me. I'm the one she can't have. But she might be of use to us this year. A plan has been forming, and it's starting to solidify.

I give Hawk a slight nod to let her pass. He steps out of Olivia's way. Moving in close, she smiles seductively as she puts her hands on my arm, squeezing the muscle.

"I have the house to myself tomorrow," she says in a low voice, looking up at me with those baby blue eyes. She glances at my boys, eyeing them up and down like they're on sale at Saks. "You could all come. All three of you. We could have a good time."

"You want all of us to fuck you?" Hawk arches an eyebrow.

"Not at the same time." She glares at him, but gives me an eager look. "Unless that's what you want, Damon."

Desperate is not a good look on Olivia.

"Tell me what you know about EvanAnn Ward." I nod at Evan, where she stands awkwardly to the side while Chase plays beer pong with his teammates. He's on the football team. The teams in our schools tend to stick together. It's something he has right now—and so is Evan.

Evan has her arms wrapped around her center, clearly not a party girl like the half-naked girls dancing around the pool.

This isn't her scene. Wasn't her scene until she started hooking up with Chase.

Olivia's smile falters a little and she turns to look over at them. She smirks and lets out an unladylike snort. "That loser?"

"Yeah, that loser." I brush the backs of my fingers along Olivia's jawline and her eyes light up. She's wanted me for years. I'll let her believe I've suddenly developed an interest if it helps me get what I really want. What I need is information. Information about everything Chase has, including his little theater nerd.

She glances again. "She's been dating Chase since spring, but he never brought her outside to lunch. His ex sits at the Anteros table."

"Abby Baker," Cam fills in, since he knows I don't know. If it didn't involve hockey before this year, I wasn't interested. "Abby's queen bee of the theater department."

"What does that make EvanAnn?" I narrow my eyes on Evan. She shivers and turns to look around like she can feel me hating her.

"One of those good girl types, probably looking for someone to fund their dreams." Olivia laughs. "For the right guy, she spreads them. He's a rich fuckboy. He probably got with her because she's a virgin or something."

"A virgin?" I look the little ant up and down, maybe with too much interest. How many girls in our school make it to eighteen with their virginity intact?

"If she was one, she definitely isn't now," Olivia squeezes my arm. "I doubt she was. She's eighteen and the theater kids get freaky. She's been dating Chase for months. You don't keep a guy like that without giving him what he needs. I don't pay much attention to the Anteros group, but she acts like a prude. She's a real nerd. I don't know why he bothers. Maybe it's because she's talented enough to make it. Not someone that you'd be interested in. She's smart and artistic, exactly what our schools want. But poor."

Olivia says it like it's a disease. To people like us, maybe it is. People want what we have. We were born wealthy, but I won't look down on the girl because she's poor. I have other reasons to hate Evan.

"The only reason he's with that charity case is because she's good at something else, if you know what I mean. Or she can give him a boost to his future." Olivia pets my arm and smiles up at me. "I could be good to you, Damon."

I glance at Cam. I'm done with her. He straightens and moves in.

"Hey, Olivia, where are your friends? If we're going to party, we need more than just you. I doubt you could handle the three of us on your own." Cam wraps his arm around Olivia's waist and walks her away. She glances back as she says something to him. He nods.

"What are you thinking?" Hawk steps in beside me, studying Evan with me.

I glance around at the party and set my half-full bottle down. I have more important things to do than drink tonight. "We need somewhere to talk. All of us."

Hawk nods, getting his phone out and firing off a text. "I have a place in mind."

My gaze returns to Evan, and this time, it's almost like she knows I'm looking at her. Her gaze collides with mine. Her eyes are light, but I've never really paid attention to the color. From here, they're just pale and dull.

But everything is about to change.

Cam manages to escape Olivia's clutches, and we get on our motorcycles to ride up into the hills surrounding the city. My new bike needs repairs from the accident, but my father refuses to pay for them. Fortunately, I own more than one motorcycle.

Hawk signals to a parking area overlooking the city. We come up here often when we need to get away from the noise. It's a pleasant ride, day or night.

We pull in and line up along the overlook, shutting our bikes off. The city lights shine bright in the night, but up here it's dark with only the sounds of nature—crickets, the occasional owl. It's peaceful.

Cam reaches into his saddle bags and pulls out a cold beer for each of us. We're not going to get shitfaced, but it's cold and tastes good.

"What's the plan?" Hawk sets his helmet in front of him and leans back on his bike.

"Yeah, if we can't fuck up Chase, what can we do?" Cam leans forward, elbows on his handlebars, staring down into the city lights.

"We can fuck up his life." My words hang in the air between us for a moment while they let that settle in. "Take away his future. Every piece of it."

Hawk smirks. "He does have a girlfriend."

"So, what?" Cam tilts his head as he looks over at both of us. "One of us is going to go for his girl?"

I take a sip, because Evan is more than a game now. "What was that big speech you made after I found out I was locked down here for another year?"

Cam rises from his bike and steps back like he's about to give the speech of his life. "The three of us."

"Fuck, this again?" Hawk shakes his head. But there's a small lift to his lips. He secretly loves this shit.

Cam holds his beer out to Hawk like he's giving him a toast. "We're fucking eighteen years old. We've got one more year before Damon goes off to play hockey in the big leagues. Hawk goes off to Columbia and makes a name for himself. And me, fuck, I'll probably go to Crowne Mawr and rule Delta Psi Lambda, because once a devil, always a devil."

"Are we going to listen to the whole thing?" Hawk rolls his eyes and drinks his beer.

"Yes," Cam says. "Because we're brothers. This is it. After this year, no more partying together. No more hockey together. Yeah, we'll go see Damon on the ice, but it won't be the same. So let's do this right and not fuck it up. We have one more year together."

"Then we take her from him, together." I smile.

"Exactly what are you proposing?" Hawk straightens.

Cam grins and thrusts his hips. "Girl's got three holes. Pretty sure they've been used. Even if she acts all innocent, like a goody two-shoes."

"My point." I tip my beer to Cam. "We show the school and Chase how big of a slut Miss EvanAnn Ward can be. We ruin his little good girl for him. We take away all of the good things in his life, until he's left miserable. Everything that gives him his future. And we make sure my father's gold digger finds her living situation unacceptable, which should coincide nicely with our first objective. Two birds with one stone."

"Together!" Cam steps in and clinks his bottle against mine.

"Together," I say and take a drink.

Cam clinks his bottle with Hawk's. Hawk meets my gaze. "Together."

CHAPTER 2

EvanAnn

Iᴛ's the start of my senior year and my life couldn't be better. I'm one of two student directors being showcased this fall, and I have a boyfriend this year. He would have driven me to school, except I had to come in early to get some copies of sides for auditions this week. So I drove myself today. But that's okay. Chase has football after school anyway, so having my own car makes sense instead of him taking me home and then coming back.

But he did offer.

We're ready for this year. Chase and I had a good summer... when we got to spend time together, getting to know each other outside of school. We didn't hang out as often as I would have liked.

But he had a job and some football camps. We saw each other when we could. Mostly at parties and he brought me around to meet his parents. They're super nice.

Now, with school starting, we'll see each other every day. Then there will be the dances. The parties.

The shows. I can't wait for the shows. Theater is my life.

This year is going to be my best yet. I know it.

I grab my bag and books from the passenger seat and stand, straightening my skirt with a grin. It's so peaceful at this time. I love getting to school early, before all the other students get here. The parking lot isn't a madhouse. The halls are quiet, calm like the moment right before the curtain lifts on stage. It's perfect.

The distant roar of motorcycles ricochets off the buildings, capturing my attention. I stop at the crosswalk and glance both ways. Three motorcycles careen down the road toward me, but they'll pass.

The lead motorcycle slows to a stop in front of me, blocking the crosswalk. My arms tighten around the books against my chest as my heart tries to leap out of it.

Oh shit!

It doesn't matter that I can't see his face behind the black helmet. I know who he is. Every girl in school knows who he is.

My cheeks flush with heat and I step back, holding my books like a shield. Two sleek, black motorcycles pull up behind him.

What is happening? *They* should have gone by. I'm not the kind of girl *they* stop for, which means I must have done something wrong. What the hell did I do?

My mind spins with possibilities, which are fairly limited because I haven't interacted with them at all. Not even in passing over the last three years of high school.

Damon Storm leans back on the lead motorcycle. The engine growls between his legs. His gloved hands rest casually on his thighs. He doesn't remove his helmet, but I can feel those sharp blue eyes on me. A little shiver works through my body.

The other two are Hawk Wilker and Cam Warwick. I don't need them to take off their helmets to know who they are. They're gorgeous, wealthy, popular, and every girl in both schools wants them.

Hockey legends in the making, according to the gossip. The Devil's trio.

Our schools are unique. It's a dual setup. Mine is Anteros Conservatory, an art conservatory school. Theirs is Deimos Academy, an academic school. We have all our regular classes with them. Both require talent or money to get into. If you want to mix art and sports, everyone is allowed to try out for the teams and extracurriculars at either school.

Generally speaking, the students don't mix. Even though a lot of our socials are for both schools. The art kids stick with the art kids and the academy kids stick with their own.

The guys in front of me go to Deimos. They're called the Devils, the school mascot. They have no reason to stop and talk to me. I bounce lightly on the balls of my feet while I wait for whatever they need to say, so we can all move on with our lives.

It's not like they need me to do their homework. In fact, Hawk and I are both competing for valedictorian. Maybe they're trying to scare me into throwing a few tests to give him an edge.

I arch an eyebrow at Damon. That won't be happening. I need my grades and rank to help get a good scholarship.

Movement from the guy on the right draws my attention away from Damon. Hawk pulls off his helmet and tilts his head, looking at me with a smirk. Those green eyes are captivating, but they've never looked at me before. A little rush goes through me at the sudden attention.

His thick black hair is cut short, to make it almost look like a soft layer of velvet.

"EvanAnn, right?" His voice is like satin, too smooth for my liking. There's no reason for him to know me, except for my class rank. I'm not the kind of girl these guys pay attention to. But being in their presence stirs something hot and wild in me.

Which it shouldn't, because I have Chase. Fuck. I need to get this shit under control.

"Yes." I swallow and glance toward the school doors. Maybe I should just walk around them. It's not like they'll beat me up and steal my lunch money. It isn't that kind of school.

He smiles and leans his arms on his helmet in front of him. His green eyes twinkle, but not necessarily in a good way. They're decidedly wicked. "You're dating Chase Chadwick?"

It's almost a statement, but also a question, so I nod. Does this have something to do with Chase? Part of me relaxes, while a small part of me is disappointed. That small part is a little vexing to be honest. I shouldn't crave their attention.

His eyes narrow on me as he takes me in. I left my blond hair down today, and the wind lifts it off my shoulders. For a second, I stand there and let his gaze run from my head to my toes.

It sends sparks through my system like a physical caress. I wonder what he sees. I don't wear much makeup, if any at all. While my hair is naturally blond, I don't do much with it for school. I have classic features, but I'm by no means beautiful. Not by their standards.

Damn it. What am I doing standing here?

"Excuse me." I walk around the front tire of Damon's bike. Cam revs his engine, jerking forward with a wicked laugh like he might run me over. I flinch a little and stifle the urge to scurry away. Of all of them, he would be the one to do something dangerous for the hell of it.

Cam's laughter follows me as I make my way up the stairs, not sure what to make of the interaction. Maybe it's about Chase. I've been in classes with Damon, Cam, and Hawk before, but none of them have ever talked to me. Honestly, none of them even looked at me.

Why would they, when there are cheerleaders and dance squad girls offering themselves on a platter to those guys? There are always popular girls surrounding them in the hallways or sitting close to them in class. Those guys definitely won't waste their time on a theater geek like me.

Their engines roar behind me as I reach the doors. I don't turn to look as I slip into the building and drag a breath into my starving lungs. I shake off the weirdness. Maybe it was intimidation to make sure Hawk gets valedictorian.

I should probably mention it to Chase, though. In case it's about him.

When I walk into the office, there's a tall blond girl waiting at the counter. Her hair is up in a ponytail with the ends curled. We're wearing the same uniform, which makes her one of the Anteros like me, but I don't know her. She turns and her blue eyes meet mine.

"Hey," she says with a smile. "I hope you're not in a hurry. I'm not sure anyone actually works here."

I look around, but yeah, the office is currently abandoned. "Normally, it isn't like this."

She's got on the uniform, but her skirt is a little short. I notice the waistband is rolled once. A lot of girls do that. Mine is naturally short from washing and age, but I haven't gotten a replacement yet. Mom hasn't noticed, and I'd rather her not use her money.

I put my books on the counter next to the girl and smile at her tie, which hangs undone around her neck.

"First time in a uniform?" I ask.

She smirks. "Yeah. Is it obvious? I kind of want to blend in a little."

"You'll fit right in with the rolled skirt." I reach my hands toward her tie but stop myself. My fingers twitch to make it right. I'm so used to fixing costumes. "May I?"

She grins and turns to face me. "I'll be your best friend if you do."

"Deal." I take the ends and work the knot. "I'm EvanAnn, by the way."

"Mia Lewis. Evan?"

"EvanAnn. Mom had a brother who passed away when he was a child." I shrug because I've had to explain this my whole life. "I went by Evan for a while, but it confused teachers."

"Well, Evan." She glances toward the door behind the counter where voices drift through. "I'm serious about the friend thing. I don't know what I was thinking, transferring senior year."

"It's a really great program and school. Which art is your focus?" I straighten her tie and cinch it up before loosening it a smidge.

"Performing arts. Acting." She strokes her fingers down her tie with a smile. "Thanks."

"Any time." I lean on the counter. "I'm in the performing arts program too. Directing."

Her grin grows. "I knew we were going to be besties."

"I'm happy to show you around."

The door to the back office opens and one of the administrators, Ms. Davis, peeks her head in. "I'll be with you girls in a minute."

When she closes the door, Mia turns to me and leans her elbows against the counter behind her.

"You'll have to show and tell me everything. Including the guy situation." Her eyebrow lifts, suggestively.

"Oh." My cheeks flush remembering Damon, Hawk, and Cam in the parking lot. This is the kind of girl they'd notice. Not me. I'm still flustered they even know my name.

Her lips curl into a smile. "What's that look for? A crush? You can tell me."

"No." Definitely not. "I have a boyfriend."

"Nice. I'm a free agent. I don't think I want a boyfriend to spoil my senior year." Mia releases a breath and spins to face the counter again.

She wiggles her eyebrows at me. "I'm excited to get away from my old school. There was definitely a hierarchy."

I laugh lightly. "Trust me, there's one here too. Depending on which school you belong to."

"And that's why I'll have you to show me everything." She nudges my arm with hers. "Besties."

I can't help the wide grin on my face. My awesome year just got a little better.

I FINALLY GET MY COPIES MADE. WITH HER NEW LOCKER number and schedule in hand, Mia and I leave the office. Students are now trickling in. When we step out, someone grabs my waist from behind and pulls me back into him. His cologne surrounds me.

"Chase," I chastise and pull away to turn and face him. My cheeks burn. We're so not *that* couple.

He pushes his hand into his dark hair and smirks down at me. "What? I can't hug my girlfriend?"

I shake my head like he's a naughty child, but he's far from a child, taller than me and broad. Built for the football team and handsome for acting. He has an all-American look that's perfect for the industry. His blue eyes meet mine. I still can't believe we're officially dating, even though it's been four months.

Mia clears her throat.

I turn to her. She watches the two of us carefully. Maybe she's not sure what to make of him grabbing me. Mia and I really don't know each other well enough for me to read her yet. I hope that changes over this year.

"Mia, this is Chase. Chase, Mia. She's new."

Sliding his hands into his pockets, Chase gives her the nod guys give people. "Nice to meet you."

"I'm sure we'll see a lot of each other." She threads her arm through mine. "Evan is my new best friend."

Chase raises an eyebrow at me. "Really?"

I shrug. For me, this is new. I haven't had a new friend since grade school. Angie goes to my old school. We didn't keep in touch. When I started at Anteros, I tried to put myself out there, but I didn't really click with anyone. I'm willing to try with Mia, because it would be nice to have a friend.

I've never had a boyfriend before, but Chase and I are doing well, so maybe this friendship will be the icing on the cake.

"Mia's in performing arts with us. I'm sure we'll be seeing each other all the time. Especially with auditions coming up. Then rehearsals."

He gives me a smile that used to make my heart flutter when he first noticed me. He's so handsome. "You're already casting her, aren't you?"

I shrug and he wraps his arm around my shoulders, pulling me closer to him and away from Mia.

"My girlfriend is a big deal." His voice is filled with pride.

"I'm not," I assure her.

He keeps talking, like I didn't say anything. "She's one of the student directors this year. All of the final calls come from her. She only picks the best."

He kisses the top of my head. For some reason it always makes me feel like I'm a pet to him and not a person. But he doesn't seem to notice my tension at being held like this. It was one thing to be affectionate this summer, but this is school.

"Obviously." Mia smirks. "That's why she picked me for her friend. She knows the best when she sees it."

I move away from Chase and hug my books to my chest, stepping next to Mia. "I'm going to show her around."

"We're set for dinner with my parents on Wednesday?" He smiles down at me.

I nod. His parents are really nice. They make me feel at home, even though their house is a freaking mansion.

"We still have second together, right?" Chase gives me a look like I might have opted for a different class. "You'll save me a seat."

"Of course." I give him a soft smile. Most of his classes at Deimos are less advanced than mine, but second is one of the classes that's a requirement for all seniors to graduate.

"Good. You're my secret weapon. Have fun with your new friend."

He glances over at Mia before winking at me and heading down the hallway.

"Pardon me, ma'am, but your boyfriend is hot." Mia smirks.

Heat floods my cheeks and I release a sigh. "Yeah."

"All right." She pulls me down the hallway. "Let's see what other guys might be available while you show me around this monstrous school. I want to know if everyone else is as hot as your boyfriend."

"The school isn't so big once you get the hang of it." Ignoring her comments about hot guys, I lead her to my locker and point out hers across the hallway. "Let's put our bags away and then I'll walk you through the building."

A guy rushes down the hall and almost runs me over. Mia pulls me out of the way at the last moment.

"Watch it, ant!" The guy keeps going.

"Hey!" She glares at the guy's back. "Ant? What the fuck was that?"

I sigh. "It's what the Devils call us Anteros. Ants. Real original."

"Well, sounds like they're a bunch of dicks." Mia scowls after the guy.

I let out a little chuckle. "They kind of are."

"Devils?" With her attention back on me, she cocks her head to the side.

"It's the mascot of the sports teams." I shrug. "They call us ants and we call them Devils."

She heads over to her locker while I put my stuff away. I really want to go hide in Mr. Watson's room. He's one of our theater teachers. He's everyone's favorite. It's easier to hide, work on my play, and avoid running into anyone, than to maneuver through the social network of our school.

Mia will soon learn I'm not popular. Yes, I go to parties, but only so I can be with Chase. He loves to party. I didn't attend them until we started dating. I wasn't really invited before he began to bring me. But I also wouldn't miss it if we never went to another one.

Mia crashes back against the locker next to me and grins. Her fingers rub the end of her tie. Her eyes are almost predatory as she stares across the hallway behind me. "Okay, who are they?"

I don't even need to turn to know who's caught her eye. It's almost like my body knows they're nearby. The air practically sizzles.

Every girl watches them when they strut down the hallway, because every inch of them is perfection. Deimos also has a school uniform, but those students are much more relaxed about the dress code.

I close my locker and hold my first period books against my chest as I lean back against it. Mia wraps a lock of hair around her finger as she takes them in.

Damon, Hawk, and Cam.

The cream of the crop. The teenage hotties who slip into my dreams to do naughty things to me. It's not like I can stop my brain from doing that. I've tried, but they still end up in there.

Their top buttons are undone. Cam has his sleeves rolled up, showing off his powerful forearms. Hawk is the most put together.

Damon... His tie hangs loose. There's a red scrape on the side of his jaw. What is that? I narrow my eyes on it, forgetting myself for a moment. Maybe it's the lighting. Did he get hurt? Maybe a fight?

Fuck, that's none of my business. I clear my throat.

"Damon Storm, Hawk Wilker, and Cam Warwick," I say in a hushed tone, so they don't hear me saying their names. No need to draw their attention for a second time this morning.

"I wouldn't mind being the meat in that particular sandwich." She makes this low noise to indicate they're hot. Wouldn't we all? But I don't say that. My cheeks are burning.

"They don't date Anteros students." I shrug.

She laughs softly. "I wasn't thinking of dating them."

The fire in me grows even hotter, and I give her my attention.

"I'm sure you'll have them in at least one of your academic classes this year." I smile. "You never know. You could give some of the girls they hook up with a run for their money."

She grins like I made her day. "Okay, show me around, bestie."

As we head toward the Anteros building, the hair rises on the back of my neck. I turn to see Damon watching me. Or maybe us? He leans against the lockers, talking to the others, but his gaze is solidly on my back.

A shiver of apprehension races through me. It's not the light. He definitely has an angry red lash across his jaw. What happened? Was it hockey? His jaw tightens when I stare a little too long trying to figure it out.

His eyes narrow as they catch mine. I spin to face forward. His attention on me doesn't make sense. I've never done anything to him or his friends. Today is the first time any of them have even spoken to me.

"Okay then, who are the hotties in Anteros?" Mia drags my attention back as we make our way through the hallway.

I don't look back, even though my skin still prickles like Damon's watching my every move.

EvanAnn

MIA and I share first period, but when I head into second period alone, I don't see Chase. Biting my lip, I try to decide where to sit. He likes to sit in the back row, so he can talk and fuck around with his friends during class. I'd rather sit up front where there are fewer distractions and it's easier to learn.

Besides lunch, this is our only class together outside of our senior theater class. He has acting blocks while I have directorial blocks in the afternoon. It won't kill me to sit in the back for him. It's only this one class.

I take a seat one row from the back so Chase can sit behind me. Maybe then I'll be able to pay attention to the teacher.

Light chatter surrounds me as students fill the seats. I pull out my phone and check to make sure Mom hasn't texted me. She's seeing a new guy. Has been for a few months.

I text her to remind her about our lease. Our lease is almost up on our house, and I'm not sure if she finally signed the new one. It's been nice to have a house instead of an apartment, but I wouldn't be surprised if she wants to move again. I hope we don't.

I'm worried she'll forget to do it because of the guy she's seeing. It's almost about the time when she usually blows up the relationship and wants to spend all her time with me until she gets a new man. It's a pattern that has repeated since my father died eight years ago.

What she had with my dad was something special. I don't blame her for looking for him in every guy she meets and finding them all lacking. Though it feels like she dates to have someone, rather than to find something special again. I'll admit Chase isn't quite the man my father was, but the potential might be there. Maybe?

I don't think Chase and I will last. We're young. It's not like we're getting married. We haven't even had sex yet, just made out a little. He's being patient with me and I like that about him.

"Daydreaming, EvanAnn?"

My gaze shoots up to Hawk's green eyes. Smirking, he walks past me to sit at the desk behind me. He can't sit there. I turn around in my chair to face him.

"I'm saving that seat."

He leans back with his hands behind his head. His black hair is the length I loved when Chase's was that short last year. My hands tingle wanting to run them over it, but I would never. Not that Hawk would let me. Hawk is the definition of gorgeous. Add to that his out of this world body, plus his golden boy status—and he's perfect. He can do no wrong in anyone's eyes.

Except take my boyfriend's seat.

I raise my eyebrow when he doesn't move.

"I didn't know we could save seats, Annie." He leans forward, invading my space.

Okay, technically it's his space since I'm talking over his desk.

My jaw tenses at the name, but one battle at a time. His gaze travels down to where my shirt gapes slightly. I loosened my tie and undid a button because it was too hot in my last class.

He wets his lips and meets my eyes. "Maybe I saved that seat."

I straighten so my shirt sits flush against my skin and redo the button. "Don't be ridiculous."

"Exactly." He smiles like he has me backed into a corner. "You can't save a seat, so this one is mine."

What the hell is going on? I'm arguing with Hawk about a desk when there are so many more to choose from.

I can fix this. The bell hasn't even rung yet. *Sorry, Chase, but we're moving into my territory.* I turn to grab my things so I can change seats.

Cam sits down in front of me. His dark brown eyes meet mine with a smile. "Hey there, EvanAnn."

"Hi?" This feels like I'm in an episode of *Black Mirror.* They've never even said my name before. When I reach for my things, Cam puts his hand on them, startling me.

"Where are you going?" he asks it so reasonably, like I'm doing something wrong.

"I'm changing seats." When I try to move my books, he holds them down.

I puff out a frustrated breath and his smile grows.

"Do I smell bad?" He arches an eyebrow and sniffs his armpit. His arms are thick and his shirt strains against the muscles. "Bad breath?"

No, he smells really good, like sandalwood and leather. It makes my insides soften. I'd love to find his cologne so I could spray it in my room. Even his breath smells good, minty fresh.

"I just want to move." I give him a look that's bordering on pleading. What is going on today? My brain is not dealing with these alarming developments.

My words make a mischievous gleam light in his eyes. "What will you give me?"

"Excuse me?" I don't know how to play this particular game. I don't know how to play any games. This is out of my depth.

"See, I chose this seat because you're here. So if you move, there's no reason for me to sit here."

My mouth opens and closes. Because I'm here? What is going on? I'm pretty sure my brain is oozing out of my ears by now. People keep glancing our way and whispering to their friends.

The heat in my cheeks grows more intense.

"It only makes sense you give me something as an exchange." He runs a hand through his thick brown hair, never losing his smirk. "If you move."

"I don't know what you want from me." I give up. The classroom is filling up and if I want to find two seats together, I need to go now.

His smile lightens and he leans in. "You could give me a kiss."

I rear back.

"I have a boyfriend." The shock in my voice isn't fake. "What are you playing at?"

"Your loss, goody two-shoes." He turns to face forward.

Goody two-shoes? What are we, seven? My mouth drops open, ready to defend myself, but I don't think I can win this. Reengaging would be a mistake. Better to admit defeat and scurry off to another location.

When I turn to slide out of the desk, Hawk's legs block me in. Ugh. I've had it up to here with these boys and their little game. When I lift my head, figuring I'll step over Hawk's too long legs, my gaze collides with Damon's sharp blue eyes. Frozen in place, I swallow.

"Going somewhere, Evan?"

Fuck, the way he says my name should be illegal. Everything about Damon should be illegal. His blond hair is an unruly mess of curls, like he just climbed out of bed and sauntered into the classroom. His voice is so low it resonates in my chest. I'm caught like a butterfly on a spiderweb. Helpless.

The bell rings and Mr. Ridgeway walks to the front of the class. "Calm down. I know it's the first day of school, but can we pretend we aren't heathens for the next ninety minutes and learn something?"

Damon arches an eyebrow at me. I slide back into my seat and look around. The class is almost full.

Chase still isn't here. Where the hell is he?

Mr. Ridgeway begins his lecture, discussing everything we'll be covering this semester during his class, while I try to ignore the hockey players surrounding me. The Devil's trio. It's a fitting name for these three.

Halfway through the class, the door opens and Chase walks in.

"Mr. Chadwick, so nice of you to join us."

Chase smirks and runs his hand through his disheveled hair. Where was he? "Sorry, Mr. Ridgeway. Nature called."

Mr. Ridgeway gestures to the only empty seat toward the front of the class. Chase nods and looks around the class as he heads to it. His eyes lock on me and he gives me a questioning look.

I shrug. I'd gladly trade him seats if I could. But Mr. Ridgeway isn't that kind of teacher.

Chase looks at the guys filling the chairs surrounding me and his brow furrows. But he takes his seat.

Something brushes my hair and heat closes in on me from behind.

"Doesn't look like your boyfriend likes you sitting here, Annie," Hawk's words are so low, only I can hear them.

A shiver courses through me at his closeness.

There's nothing I can do except ignore them and try to focus on class.

"Babe."

I close my eyes. I really hate that pet name.

As soon as the bell rang, I sprang from my seat and raced out of the classroom before any of those three could touch or talk to me more. There must be a reason for the trio's sudden attention. Something I did or... They asked about Chase. Something Chase did?

I stop to the side of the hallway and wait for Chase to catch up to me.

He drapes his arm over my shoulders and I resist the urge to shrug it off. It's like he's trying to prove a point. Claim me. I don't know why, but I don't like it. He knows I'm not big on public displays of affection. This wasn't an issue last year.

Maybe this is him trying to take our relationship to the next level.

"I thought you were going to save me a seat." He glances to the left as Hawk walks by me on the other side.

"Yeah, Annie, that's rude of you not to save a seat." Hawk winks.

What the fuck! He's the one who took that seat. But before I can get out anything beyond a self-righteous squeak, he takes off down the hallway.

"Annie?" Chase pulls me to a halt in the middle of the hallway. His gaze follows Hawk as he walks away.

My cheeks flush red as students surge around us. "We're in everyone's way, Chase."

"Why is Hawk Wilker even talking to you?" Chase looks down at me like I've done something to warrant this unwanted attention. Like it's somehow my fault.

I shrug. Frankly, my whole body is tense and anxiety races through my veins. "I have no fucking idea. Can we get to our next class now?"

"Such language, goody two-shoes." Cam tugs at a strand of my hair as he passes. The pain makes me rub my scalp a little.

"I'm in the fucking twilight zone," I mutter and check to make sure Damon isn't lurking anywhere nearby, ready to pounce. So far though, he's barely said a word to me. Mostly just looked at me.

It's all alarming.

"Are they fucking with you, babe?" Chase puffs up his chest like he's going to do the manly thing and protect my honor.

Fuck that. "Calm down. They're just messing with me. Or maybe you? Maybe you did something?"

My tone is hopeful, because I don't know how else to explain this sudden interest. Maybe they lost a bet? It would make more sense than the three hottest guys in school suddenly wanting to talk to me because... Seriously, I can't think of any reason.

Chase shrugs and looks away. It's a guilty look, but it's gone when he returns his gaze to me. Is he hiding something? "It could be a foot-ball-hockey thing."

"Maybe." I don't know much about sports, but I know rivalries exist. Maybe the guilt I saw was because they're targeting me to get to him.

"I wouldn't worry about it if I were you." He throws his arm around my shoulders and pulls me forward. "They'll give up soon enough."

I bite my lip and glance around for Damon. I saw the other two go by, but not him. I can't imagine him teasing me like the others, but the hair on the back of my neck stands to attention again. I don't dare turn around and meet those eyes.

Best way to defeat a bully is to ignore them. Right?

———

I'm still wondering what's happening when third ends and I head to lunch with everyone else. I really need to put it out of my mind. Our cafeteria mimics a college campus with different restaurants to buy food from and a main area for seating. There's also an outdoor area for when the weather is nice.

When I walk in, I'm not paying attention, too deep in my thoughts about classes this afternoon. I'm hosting auditions in a few days and I need to mentally prepare to select my cast. The showcase at the end of the semester is one of the most important of my life.

It will help determine what schools I'll be able to get into, and possibly secure me an internship on a film set over the summer with one of my favorite female directors, Alexis Bloom. It's the type of boost I need to help me in my career.

As I head toward the line to get food, I don't bother searching for Chase. He'll find me here. He always does.

Will Mia find me? Will she still want to be my friend? Or has she already found a clique to hang out with? There's a group of hot, rich girls in the theater group who she'd fit in with.

While I'm friendly with most of the students in the theater group, I wouldn't call anyone my best friend. Maybe that's because we all had to audition for a spot at this school. It makes it feel more competitive, even though we're already here. Maybe that's because we still have to compete for spots in productions.

Since you never know who will be able to help you later in life, it makes it hard to know who's truly trying to be your friend and who's using you to get ahead in their career.

People are friendly with me this year because I'm one of the directors making the casting decisions. Of course, I'm not the only student director in the showcase. I'm going up against someone who is popular, rich, and has friends.

Brandt Stanwell. We're in this showcase because we're both great at what we do. The school always chooses the best to show off the talent our school produces. Brandt is more of the meet-and-greet type director who knows everyone in the field already, thanks to his semi-famous, wealthy parents.

People suck up to him because of his connections. I may have talent, but no connections.

I glance around again, thinking about Mia. It'd be nice to have an actual friend to talk to. A friend to bounce ideas off and share my dreams with and discuss what's going on in my life. Just someone to talk to, period. This day has been crazy.

I really need some advice about Chase. I don't know if I should take that next step with him or not. He's been pushing for more. It doesn't feel quite right, but I'm eighteen and I should get some real-life experience under my belt. Besides, a disappointing first time is character building, right?

I'm almost to the salad bar, my first choice, when an arm settles over my shoulders.

"Cha—" I stop because that isn't Chase's cologne. No, it's something much more devastating. Leather books and citrus. My heart thumps.

"Hey, Annie."

Fuck.

CHAPTER 4

EvanAnn

I LOOK up at the smile on Hawk's face as he walks with me through the cafeteria. I'm so fucking shocked, I don't stop or brush his arm off. The weight of it isn't oppressive like when Chase does it. But it's still not appropriate for a guy who isn't my boyfriend.

I lift my gaze from his smirk to his dancing green eyes. "What are you doing?"

His smile grows and he draws me into a hug. Like literally into his chest, almost smothering me in that intoxicating scent. He's warm and solid. Something inside me hums to life, like he's the jolt needed to get this party started.

I wrench away and stare up at him in horror. Nope. That's not right. Sure, he's attractive and is basically the whole package, but I don't *want* him. Maybe the dream version of Hawk, but not this Hawk. This Hawk is nothing like dream Hawk.

"What's wrong, Annie? Cat got your tongue?" He doesn't look fazed by my public rejection of his hug. Very public.

I swallow down the fear surging through me. The attention of the cafeteria is solidly on my person. I can feel their eyes on me. Sweat trickles down my back. Being on stage and pretending to be someone else is easy. Being the center of attention in real life is something I've been working on, but always as a persona—EvanAnn, the director, sometimes actor. Never just me.

But I can't drop my gaze from Hawk's green eyes. I'm not really well-known on the Deimos side of school, except as the student who ruins the curve for everyone else.

Well, one of the students. The other is currently watching me with an amused expression.

I narrow my eyes and close the distance between us. His eyes widen like I've surprised him. My finger pokes his chest, which is hard as a fucking rock. "Why are you messing with me?"

"Messing with you, Annie?" He gives me this innocent look that doesn't touch those eyes. No, those green eyes are downright wicked. A little shiver goes through me as I realize I might have poked a bear.

Literally.

I drop my hand back to my side and shake my head. What am I doing? I'm not confrontational.

"I was going to offer to buy you lunch." He sounds so sincere, like there's nothing wrong with what he's doing. I'm dating someone else. It's not like he doesn't know that.

"Why?" I give him a quizzical look. I've always studied other people at lunch, including Hawk and his friends. It's a habit, a quiet one that doesn't hurt anyone, but helps me figure people out.

Aberrant behavior doesn't really exist. Everyone has a pattern, a motive. When the pattern changes, that's part of what makes a story. If the actor doesn't know the character's motivation, they can't perform the scene the way it needs to be acted. And it's on me, as the director, to help them discover that motivation.

But right now, standing in front of arguably one of the hottest guys in school, who's saying he wants to buy me lunch? I've got nothing. I'm not suddenly the most attractive girl in school. There's been no makeover or body changes. Nothing has changed since last year except their behavior toward me. It's ludicrous. There's no reason for it, unless it's all a big joke or a con.

There are two things I truly hate: being laughed at and liars.

I straighten. No, the Devils don't get any more of my time. I glance around the cafeteria at people whispering behind their hands while surreptitiously watching us. Yeah, this doesn't make sense to them either.

I meet his green eyes and say calmly, "I don't want to be your punchline."

Without another word, I turn and walk away. Today seems like a good day for pizza, which is on the other side of the cafeteria. I'm sure I can make it there without running into his friends.

After all, they always sit outside at lunch. Most Deimos students do.

I shake off the encounter and refocus on the script I'm working on. I spent most of the summer cutting and editing the play to fit my time slot. What I'm looking for in auditions are strong leads and equally strong supporting roles. Every role matters and must be cast perfectly for the whole story to come together.

To live up to my vision, I need the best actors in the ensemble.

"Hey, Evan."

I turn at Mia's voice and release the pent-up breath I was holding in preparation for the next altercation with the Devils. I probably could have handled Cam, but I don't think I'll ever be able to handle Damon.

He's more... intense than his friends.

I give her a relieved smile as she joins me on the way to the line.

"How have classes been?" I ask as we reach the end.

"Interesting." She smiles and glances over at a guy from Deimos who gives her a kissy face. She gives him a coy look. "You definitely have a nice-sized population of hot guys. I can't wait until theater class this afternoon."

"Have you met other Anteros students?" I showed her the differences in the uniforms this morning so she could tell us apart. Not that it's hard, but if you aren't used to uniforms, it could be confusing. Each uniform has a few different options, and while the colors are the same, the patterns are different.

"A few." She glances at me out of the corner of her eye, but then turns to me with a huge grin. "I met one of those hot guys in third."

She grabs my arm and bites her lip. I laugh lightly. They're a lot and I'm used to seeing them in passing. Not so much with the interactions like recently though.

"Which one?" I ask. Probably Cam. He's the most outgoing of the three. Always looking for a party or being the party.

"Hawk. Fuck, even his name is hot," Mia groans.

I stiffen, but she doesn't notice and drags me forward in line.

"He's so fucking gorgeous." She leans in. "And I swear, he gives off big dick energy. Do you know what I mean?"

Technically. "Yes."

In real life, not really. I mean those guys are dicks, but I've never seen their—I cut off that train of thought real fast. I do not want to think about Hawk's dick. Size, or how he uses it, or anything else.

I swear I get a waft of his cologne as we step forward. When I glance around to make sure he isn't about to pounce again, I relax when I find he isn't in the vicinity. I'm pretty sure his scent clings to me. My insides still buzz like he's nearby.

I need to check my mental health, because these involuntary reactions to them are upsetting. They shouldn't be happening. Not while I'm in a relationship.

"He was talking to me about maybe trying out for the plays this year." Mia hugs my arm tight. "That would be amazing, wouldn't it? It's like the dream to fall in love on set."

I clear the sudden lump in my throat. "I don't think he'd be able to make practices. He's on the hockey team."

She pouts, but then smiles. "Maybe I should try out for cheerleading. Do they have cheerleading at hockey games?"

"I don't know." When we reach the front of the line, I order a large slice of veggie pizza and a drink.

"Hmmm." Mia orders her pizza before turning to me. "I really need to focus on my acting, so maybe not cheerleading. But we'll go to the games, right?"

"I don't really go to games." I pay for my pizza and head for the table I've sat at for the past three years. I have a pattern, just like everyone else. The same table. The same people. Chase was new last year, but now it's the same boyfriend.

I don't go to hockey games. Hawk doesn't talk to me, sit near me, put his arm around me, and pull me into his solid, warm chest. Fuck, why was he so warm? And the way he smells...

Mia catches up to me. "We should go. It's our senior year. If you haven't been to a game, that's even more of a reason to go."

I shake myself out of it.

"I plan to go to the football games." It seems like the right thing to do, to support my man and all that. "Chase is on the football team."

"Aw, that's sweet. Football was a big deal at my last school." Mia takes the chair next to mine and continues to talk as she sits down. "The quarterback and his friends were the big guys on campus. I haven't really noticed anyone quite like them here."

She glances around the cafeteria.

I chuckle. "The popular kids sit out in the courtyard. They're mostly Deimos kids and a few kids from Anteros who have wealthy parents."

That's where Brandt sits, schmoozing with the other wealthy kids. That's the real dividing line in our schools. First, Deimos over Anteros, then the Haves and the Have-Nots. I'm definitely in the Have-Not category. I'm not sure where Mia falls.

Everyone at Anteros had to audition for their spot. Everyone at Deimos had to meet a minimum grade requirement. Our uniforms are meant to show unity, but even then, you can tell who has money and who doesn't.

Chase is a Have, but he really likes me. Hawk, Damon, and Cam are in the Haves. They practically rule the Haves.

"You mentioned football at your old school?" I need a distraction because I don't want to think of Hawk, Damon, or Cam. I lift my pizza and take a bite. It's not bad, but I prefer the salad bar.

Mia blushes and her ponytail swishes. "Honestly, I was lucky to get transferred. The guys there were next-level shit. Bullies if you aren't one of their favored people. They went a little crazy on my twin brother, Tanner. Got him kicked off the football team. He still goes there. They really are a nuisance. Though I did have a good time with a couple of them."

My eyes are wide as she tells me all about when she hooked up with two guys at the same time. Apparently neither of them were average-sized either. She includes positions, which I do not need to think about. My face is still hot when Chase sits down next to me.

"You feeling okay, EvanAnn?" He pulls away a little, like I might get him sick.

I take a drink of my water and fan my face. "Just a little hot."

Mia winks at me before glancing at Chase. "So, are you one of the head guys on the football team?"

Chase sets his lunch down and nods. "Starting defense this year."

"Is that good?" Mia twirls her blond hair around her finger. She arches her eyebrow at him like she's daring him to lie.

"One of the best." Chase gives her a quick, cocky smile before turning his attention back to me. "Are you all set for auditions Thursday, babe? Do you need any help?"

He's kind of thoughtful that way.

"I'm good, but thank you for offering." I glance around the cafeteria. Even though Chase and Mia are new, nothing has really changed for me since the beginning of last year except the new faces of the first years. Even the rest of our table are the same people I've sat with since we were the new students.

A few students wave when they notice me looking their way. I wave back, but I never really got on with anyone. We're all nice and talk at school, but no one seeks me out. I was too busy keeping my grades up and working to make a name for myself in the theater department. Parties weren't my thing. I never had a boyfriend until last year, when Chase and I were partnered for a scene in theater class.

I glance at Mia as she asks Chase about the football team. Will she remain my friend after she gets to know everyone in the drama department? The seniors will all be in the next class with Mr. Watson.

The theater clique of pretty girls will be there. They sit outside for lunch with the Deimos students. Mia would probably fit in with them better than she fits with me. They would probably share a sex story in return because they would have one.

Chase was dating one of them last year, but they broke up months before he started talking to me. Abby, his ex, doesn't like me at all.

It's a shame because she's really talented and would be great to have in my cast. Having her talent might not be worth the real-life drama she likes to stir up.

"I told Evan we should go to the hockey games." Mia smiles when I give her my attention.

"Why?" Chase touches my waist and slides my chair closer to his. "EvanAnn is coming to all my football games already."

"Evan hasn't ever been. It's a good experience. It's not like we're asking you to go with us." Mia laughs. "Besides, some of the guys on the team are hot. Maybe I want to get with one of them."

Chase shakes his head. "Why would you want to get with a hockey player? I bet half their teeth aren't even real."

That can't be true. I mean, Hawk's teeth look real. His smile is a really good smile. Warmth slides through me.

"Maybe I want to go because they're single, and Evan wants to go because she's my new best friend." Mia smiles at me, snapping me out of thinking about Hawk. "It's not like she'll be shopping for a boyfriend when she has you."

This conversation is getting weird, but I do want to keep Mia as a friend.

"I'm sure it will be okay. It's only one game, Chase." When I turn to him, his eyes are narrowed on Mia, but he smiles and looks down at me.

"Whatever you want, babe."

"Great, it's a date." Mia smiles. "When's the first hockey game?"

CHAPTER 5

EvanAnn

"THIS IS the part I've been waiting for," Mia whispers as we settle into the chairs in the black box of our theater department. The chairs are off to the side like they would be if someone was performing. The room is painted black from the floors to the walls to the ceiling. The curtains in the back are black. It's perfect.

This is where everything starts.

No costumes. No stage. No props. Only actors and their raw talent to make us believe.

It never fails to send tingles down my spine.

Chase sits on my other side with his arm over my shoulders. I resist the urge to lean forward, away from his touch. I should want to lean into him. Shouldn't I? We've been together for months. This should be comfortable. He should be comfortable. Instead, it's like pinpricks where we make contact.

I don't know what's changed since this spring. I would never say we were hot and heavy. But his touch gave me goosebumps, and the first time we kissed was better than I could have imagined. His attention was flattering at first, but when he asked me out, I was shocked. Of course, I said yes. A hot guy asked me out.

The first guy to ask me out since Billy in kindergarten. What girl wouldn't want Chase Chadwick?

"Good afternoon." Mr. Watson walks in, sets his things on a chair in the front row, before grabbing a different chair and walking it to center stage. He turns it so the back is to us and straddles it, lowering himself to sit. "Are we ready for our senior year?"

"Yes," we all say back to him.

"We're not actors because we want to be in the audience. Grab a chair and bring it out to our stage for the year." Mr. Watson gestures around him.

"He's hot," Mia murmurs as she grabs her chair and walks out to the floor with me.

"He's almost thirty." I really look at him, but yeah, he looks like an adult to me. He's handsome, but I wouldn't call him hot. Not when you have guys like Hawk, Damon, and Cam walking around school.

"I don't know, maybe it's time to give an older man a try." She grins and winks before setting her chair close to Mr. Watson's.

"Great!" Mr. Watson looks around the circle and zeroes in on Mia. "We have a new student this year. You must be Mia Lewis."

"Hi." She smiles at everyone and gives a little wave.

"Why don't you perform your monologue for us?" Mr. Watson leans back to study her.

"Now?" It's a fake shyness that doesn't suit her, but she pulls it off well.

"All of us have spent years together." Mr. Watson gestures to the rest of us. "We've seen what the others can do. Picked it apart and broke it down into pieces, only to rebuild it again. So, show us how you got into our school. You're an actor. Act."

She nods and stands.

We settle in to watch her perform. It's a simple monologue. One I've seen a couple students butcher before they grasped the concept that, in performances, sometimes less is more.

Mia acts with a simple beauty. She captures the pain of the character perfectly. I can't help watching her and thinking about *Othello*, the play I've been tasked with directing for the season. She would make a beautiful Desdemona.

She'd capture the subtleness that defines the character in my mind.

Chase has been after me all summer to cast him as Iago. It's practically the lead role. It's Iago's machinations that drive the whole story. I don't know though. Iago is evil and petty. He causes the deaths of multiple people because of jealousy when he didn't get the promotion he wanted.

Chase assured me he's up for the task.

Honestly, he can act and takes direction well. It would make sense to cast him because we can spend even more time together. Maybe being together more often will help our sparks a little. Mia wasn't wrong about people falling in love on sets.

When Mia finishes, everyone claps.

"Well done, Mia. You've earned your place at the table." Mr. Watson doesn't give praise easily, but I can tell she impressed him.

She bows dramatically. "Thank you."

When she sits next to me, she squeezes my hand.

"You were really good," I whisper.

"Thanks!" She crosses her legs. "It took years of pleading with my parents to even allow me to audition. I'm living with my aunt while I'm here."

"You definitely belong here." I squeeze her hand back and release it as Mr. Watson continues with the expectations for this course.

By the end of class, I'm feeling even more energized for this year.

"Don't forget, auditions are Thursday for the plays. Everyone in this class is required to audition unless you're directing." Mr. Watson stands and clearly delivers his statement. "It will count as part of your grade. There are two directors and two plays. Anyone in the school can audition. If you don't get an onstage role, you'll be expected to help backstage to participate for your grade. Any questions? Good. See you tomorrow!"

Everyone stands.

"Oh my god, I hope I get a part." Mia grabs her things and turns to me. "You're directing?"

I nod and smile. "*Othello.*"

"Shakespeare, sweet." She looks around at the emptying classroom as people take advantage of the fifteen-minute break before intensives. "You probably already have a full cast in your head. I mean, these actors are amazing."

She's not wrong. I've been eyeing Mark Green as my Othello, though there are a few others that impress me if he ends up taking a different role. It's tricky to start casting when you're vying for the same pool of applicants.

The audition process has the actors perform in front of both directors. Afterwards, we pick our ideal cast, and the teacher checks against their preferred parts. Meaning if I cast Mark for *Othello*, but then Brandt casts him in his play and Mark's preference is Brandt's character, I'll get my second choice.

My problem is I have to have a strong cast for *Othello* to work. Meaning my actors must be able to handle Shakespearean dialogue without tripping over their tongues.

"Hey."

I lift my head at Brandt's confident voice. We rarely talk outside our directing classes, but it's not me he's talking to. He's a good-looking guy with dark brown hair and brown eyes. Average height, not really built for sports. He's always well put together with his hair perfectly styled. He glances at me in acknowledgement before turning to Mia.

His smile oozes charm. "Mia, right?"

She takes him in. "Yes."

I'm curious what her initial thoughts are of Brandt. It would help me understand her character better. In my opinion, he leans too heavily on his famous parents. He's talented enough, but sometimes he comes off a little too smarmy.

"I'm Brandt Stanwell." He pauses, waiting for her to recognize the last name. When she doesn't immediately start gushing about his famous dad, he smirks. "I'm Alexander Stanwell's son and the other director this year."

"That's cool." She's not gushing over him, which puts me at ease. She's being polite, which is a good way to play this meeting. No one wants to be seen as too eager to get in with someone. "What play are you doing?"

"*The Crucible.*"

It has some amazing female roles. Will Mia prefer to do his play? It means we wouldn't spend as much time together. She'll probably make friends with that cast and I'll be back to the status quo.

"You'd make an amazing Abigail. I hope you'll try out for me." Brandt gives her another smile.

Mia nods. "Of course. *The Crucible* is one of my favorites."

Brandt holds his smile and turns to me. "EvanAnn."

"Brandt."

When he turns and walks away, Mia steps closer to me and watches until he's out the door.

"What's his deal?" Mia asks.

"Rich, famous parents. He's talented too. Great at getting people to do what he wants." I shrug. "*The Crucible* will be good."

Chase wraps his arm across my shoulders above my breasts and pulls me back into him. "He's not as good as you, babe."

"Thanks." I blow out a breath. Should I tell Chase I'm not comfortable with how much he's touching me at school? I don't remember him being like this in the spring, or even all summer.

"I'll make sure to wow you at auditions tomorrow, so I get chosen for a part in *Othello*." Mia smiles and my heart warms. "After all, us girls gotta stick together."

"I have to get to class." I gesture toward the door. "You two are in here next period?"

"I think so." Mia looks down at her schedule while Chase releases me and steps in close.

"Are we going to get together after practice today?" He brushes his knuckles against my jawline and smiles. "I'd love some alone time."

Warmth floods my face but it's not the same anticipation that welled in me when Hawk touched me. Maybe it's just because Hawk is unpredictable while I know Chase. His touch is familiar, comfortable.

"I'll text you when I know." I turn around to escape. At the door, I look back. Mia is still looking at her paper but her lips are moving. Chase smiles and turns away from me.

A weird feeling writhes in the pit of my stomach, but I push it away.

MY CLASSES GO WELL IN THE AFTERNOON. THERE ARE TEN OF us on the director path this year. Only two of us were chosen as student directors, which means both Brandt and I have to choose an assistant director from the remaining eight.

My stomach churns. The decisions I make must be for the best of the play. My assistant director has to be able to help me make those crucial decisions. What if Chase isn't the best for Iago? What if I'm only putting him in that role because he wants it so badly, and I want to make him happy because he's my boyfriend?

I spent all of class trying to figure out who to pick for my assistant director. There are three remaining seniors and five juniors. This could be the seniors' last chance to really shine while at Anteros. We'll all have smaller plays in the spring. It would make sense to help one of them, but the juniors need the opportunity too.

Last year, Erica Bartlett chose me, a junior, as her assistant. I really want to pay that forward. It would be easier to decide if I knew who Brandt was picking. Though one of his followers would make sense. I'm no closer to a decision than when it was announced I'd be the fall student director at the end of last year.

I've had all summer to figure it out, but I just can't. There's no one I really connect with in the director program. At least not any seniors.

As I head to my car, I get a text from Mia. We exchanged numbers earlier. My stomach buzzes.

MIA:

OMG I'm so happy to be here and can't wait until we can hang

ME:

I'm excited you're here too

The dots appear, but before she sends her message, my phone rings. Mom's calling. I draw in a breath, ready to handle whatever she is about to throw at me, but also bracing myself, because Mom is fully engaged after a breakup until she finds a new man. And she always finds a new man.

"Hi, Mom."

"Are you on your way home, honey?" Mom sounds harried.

"I'm about to get into my car." I open my car door and throw my backpack on the passenger seat. "What's up?"

"I have some exciting news to share with you!"

Okay, wasn't expecting happiness. Maybe she hasn't quite decided to pull the trigger yet with the latest guy. I figured the honeymoon phase had finally ended when she spent most of last week at home instead of out with her boyfriend.

"I should be home in ten," I say. Maybe she's excited to see this one go. That would be a change. Or maybe she has the next guy already lined up.

"Great." She disconnects the call.

I don't like this any more than all the other changes in my life. Mom's acting weird and happy. Chase is clingy. The Devils are paying attention to me. None of this makes sense.

The hair on the back of my neck stands on end again. If I turn, will Damon or one of the others be standing there watching me? Or is it just all in my head?

It's probably all in my head. I'm psyching myself out. Fuck, I need to know.

I hold my breath and turn, scanning the parking lot. Over by the doors to the ice rink, I can see three figures. It's too far away to tell who they are, especially since they're geared up for hockey practice.

A shiver works through me. Maybe this year will be a little more complicated than I initially thought, but I'll figure out why they've suddenly taken an interest in me. One way or another.

I get in my car and head home. Well, to our rental house. We haven't had a real home since Dad passed away. For all I know, that was a rental too, but we'd been there for a while. Mom moved us into apartments until two years ago, when she found this house for rent.

I know it's only a rental, but it feels like home. It's safe. My room is decorated the way I like it. I even got to paint the walls a pale blue. It's like we finally have a place of our own. We know all the quirks. We're settled.

As I pull up, I notice the truck in front of our house. A worker steps out the front door, and Mom follows, thanking him.

He doesn't look at me as I get out of my car. Mom turns when my door shuts. Her grin spreads across her face.

"Evan!" She walks down the steps and crosses the yard to reach me. We're about the same height now. I share her blond hair and light blue eyes, but I have my grandma's smaller nose and dimpled chin. Not main character energy. Maybe best friend energy, but definitely behind-the-camera energy.

"What's going on, Mom?" I sling my backpack over my shoulder.

"I've got bad news and good news." Mom doesn't look devastated, so maybe this won't be as hard as last time she ended things with a guy. She rarely tells me the guys' names, sometimes the first, and then in passing like they aren't important enough for me to know. I stopped trying to remember them after guy number five.

In my head, I'm already queuing up a few romantic comedies we can watch over the next few nights while I do my homework. We have a few favorites that always help pull her from her slump.

"Okay, let's have the bad news."

She turns to walk with me back toward the house. "Our house is being sold."

Whoa. I stop and turn to face her. I must have heard her wrong. "I'm sorry. What?"

"The owners are selling our rental." Mom links her arm with mine and pulls me toward the house. "I know it's crap timing, but they already have a buyer with a cash offer who wants to terminate our lease. And since I hadn't renewed yet..."

"Uh, we need somewhere to live." My head is spinning. There's always open apartments at the last complex we were in, but the main reason we moved away was neither of us felt safe there. It had been time to leave.

"That's the good news." Mom squeezes my arm. "We're moving in to my boyfriend's house."

My brain goes into a fog. Her boyfriend. They've barely been dating, maybe the summer, maybe a little longer. And she'll probably dump him soon. This is a bad idea. She could blow it up within a week of moving in, and then we'll be even more desperate for a place to live.

Maybe we have time to find someplace else. Time enough to not end up at those apartments again.

Mom's still talking to me, but I blanked it all out. I clear my throat to get her attention. It's better if I take this easy.

"Do you think that's a good idea? Do you want to move this fast?"

Mom laughs. "Haven't you been listening, Evan? Adam has more than enough room. Besides, we've been dating for a while and we're ready to take the next step. You're only around for one more year. Then it will be only me when you go off to college. I need to move on with my life."

"What happens if it doesn't work out, Mom?" I've never known my mom to be an optimist when it comes to guys. Normally, she has one foot out the door.

"We can at least try, Evan." Mom opens the front door. "We're having dinner with Adam and his son tonight. We'll get a lay of the land and figure out how to move forward."

His son? This is such a bad idea. What if the son gets attached to my mom and then she does what she always does? She hasn't said this time is different. What makes this *Adam* different than the dozens of guys she's dated before?

I hear what she says, but I just can't believe this. I walk into the cozy living room that's been home for two years. Dammit. I'm not ready to leave, but what choice do I have?

"Please, honey, give it a try for me." My mom's eyes are more hopeful than I've ever seen them before. "If it doesn't work out, we'll find somewhere. Adam says it would be fine for us to stay with him while we look, but we both really want this to work."

"I haven't even met him, Mom. How do you know this will be a good fit?" I set my bag on the chair and turn to face her with my arms around my waist. This house has become comfortable. The years of moving from apartment to apartment weighed on me. I didn't even realize what I was missing until we moved in here.

The stability I needed.

"You'll adjust. You always do. We're survivors." Mom smiles and brushes my hair behind my ear. "One step at a time. We're meeting them at their house for dinner. Adam will give us a tour, and then we'll sit down and answer any questions you might have."

She smiles, and it's so hopeful I don't know how I can say no. In all these years after my dad passed, she's never been this happy. Maybe she's jumping on this opportunity because we don't have a lot of other choices. Or maybe this guy is the real deal.

I'm still wondering how to say no when we pull up in front of a house three times as large as the house I grew up in. There are multiple garages off to the side. When Mom holds out a controller and presses a button, one of the doors lifts.

"Who is your boyfriend?" I don't hide the skepticism from my voice. Will he even realize we're living with him? There must be at least twenty rooms in a place like this. I don't like it. Is this why she's staying with him?

I dismiss that idea as soon as it enters my mind. He may be rich, but that can't be all there is to him. That's not my mom.

Mom laughs. "Come on. You're going to love it here. You'll never want to leave."

I *will* want to leave. This all feels wrong, and after the day I had where something unusual happened at every turn, I'm not looking forward to even more changes. Mia was a good change. A new friend.

But Damon, Hawk, and Cam's attention was alarming and disturbing. Chase suddenly being all touchy-feely made me uncomfortable. This change might be too far for me.

Mom never introduces me to her boyfriends, claiming she's overprotective of me. But not only is she introducing me to this guy, but we're apparently moving in too.

Mom leads the way across the driveway to the front door, where a man stands in the shadow of the doorway. Her smile is so genuine, so pleased, I stumble a little.

I don't know what I was expecting. But I think she really likes him.

"Adam." She reaches out both hands and he takes them, pulling her in for a hug, before moving her to his side with his arm still wrapped around her.

I follow a little slower, dragging my feet. When I climb the steps,

Adam looks vaguely familiar. I can't place why though. I don't think I've ever met him before.

"You must be EvanAnn." He holds his free hand out to me with a warm smile.

I take his hand and shake it like I've been trained to do. "It's a pleasure to meet you, sir."

"I'm Adam Storm. You can call me Adam." He gestures for me to follow him, but my feet are rooted in place.

Storm? It can't be that common of a last name, right? It could be a coincidence. Maybe it's not even spelled the same. Mom glances back at me with this hopeful smile that somehow gets my legs moving, following her into a foyer straight out of a movie.

Luxurious marble floors with a beautifully crafted round table topped by a vase brimming with fresh-cut flowers centered in the space. I swallow as my gaze lifts to the two-story ceiling and the crystal chandelier lighting the entryway.

A door opens somewhere in the house.

"Oh, good. My son says you know each other from school." Adam's tone is all pleasantry.

Son? Mom said it before, but I didn't think about what that would mean. That it could ever be...

My heart is going a mile a minute. I need to run away.

Now.

I'm not supposed to be here. This shouldn't be happening. But my feet are glued to the floor, knowing no matter what, this is a horror I'm going to be forced to face.

"Damon, come meet EvanAnn."

CHAPTER 6

EvanAnn

I'M FROZEN as Damon Storm saunters into the foyer. His smile is knowing, but not nearly as welcoming as his father's. His eyes narrow on me. My knees suddenly feel weak like they aren't going to hold me up.

"We know each other." Damon's voice is rough and low. It captures the butterflies wreaking havoc in my stomach and crushes them.

That's a lie.

We don't really *know* each other, but the way he says it makes it sound like we do. I know *of* him. Everyone in both schools knows of Damon Storm. Before this year, I would have said he probably didn't know my name or what I looked like. I'm insignificant. Not even a blip on his social radar.

Now I'm invading his space. Is this why they invaded mine at school today? What has my mom gotten us into?

"This is Heather, who I've told you so much about," Adam says, oblivious to the underlying tension between his son and me. Sounds like Damon is more prepared for this meeting than I am. I bet he didn't find out an hour ago I was moving in with him. Has he known all day? Did he assume I knew?

Mom smiles like this is the best day of her life and holds her hand out to Damon. "It's such a pleasure to finally meet you. I'm so sorry about your accident, but your dad says you'll still get to play hockey this year. That's a good thing."

What accident? Damon shakes my mother's hand briefly before releasing it. Is that where the redness on his jaw came from?

"I've got dinner in the dining room for all of us to sit down and discuss how this is going to work. I know you're both teens and need your space, but from what Heather says, EvanAnn is rarely home due to theater, and with hockey, Damon is always busy." Adam's smile is a little strained. Maybe he's picking up on the tension. "I doubt you'll even see each other."

Or maybe this whole thing is stressful, meeting the kids and introducing them. Even though we're both eighteen and technically know each other, this wasn't exactly well thought out.

"Shall we eat?" Adam nods toward what I guess is the dining room, before heading with my mom in that direction.

I'm still frozen in place though, because my mind hasn't caught up to the fact my mom is dating Damon's dad and hasn't said anything about it in the past few months. Not to mention, now my mom wants to move in with Damon's dad. Meaning, I'm moving in with Damon.

Fuck, I'm moving in with *Damon Storm*.

I don't have a choice in the matter, because she's all I have left.

And if I pitch a fit, we'll end up in that apartment complex. I can't go back there, not after what happened.

Though maybe Damon doesn't really live here. I don't know anything about Damon outside of school. Maybe he actually lives with his mom and only visits his dad. Maybe he's only here on weekends or every other day, which should give me a break.

My gaze takes in this palace around me. It's not cozy like our house. It's a little cold and sterile. If it's this or the apartments...

This is by far the prettier cage. I drag a breath into my lungs. It's only one year. How bad could a year be?

Can I live with Damon? He's never noticed me before today, but since he has, my life has been chaos. What will my life become if I live with him? What will people at school think? I can't tell them. It's not an option.

"Come on, Evan." Damon hasn't followed his father, but stands there watching me cope with this new development. His lips twitch up into an almost-smile, but it's not pleasant. "It's only dinner. What could possibly go wrong?"

Famous last words. Does he know that? How could he *not* know that? I cock an eyebrow at him. But his words unlock the part of me that was frozen.

When he turns, I follow him into the dining room. What else am I going to do? This is happening whether I want it to or not. I doubt we have the money to make a counteroffer on the house we're in.

Mom has a good job, but not that good. We get by week to week.

Pouting in the car won't help anything. Neither will pitching a fit.

The dining room is modern with light gray walls and sheer drapes on the tall windows. The mahogany table is large enough for twelve, but the place settings are all down on one end. Silver utensils sparkle, cloth napkins lay on the white plates, and a mix of glasses shine next to everyone's setting.

Is this normal here? A special occasion? Or is this what they call casual? Anxious energy flows through me. This is what my mom wants?

Adam sits at the end with my mom beside him on the side with two place settings. Damon lounges in the chair on his father's other side, and I take the chair next to Mom. I lift the napkin off the plate and drape it over my lap.

I don't know what to do in this situation. I mean, I know enough etiquette to eat a fancy meal, but this isn't really what my life looks like. I stare unseeing at the plate in front of me. Is this the reason why he and his friends focused on me today? Did he know this would happen?

How long did Mom know about this before springing it on me? I don't believe this was a *today* decision. Was she afraid I'd try to talk her out of it? Or did she not tell me because she knew I'd roll with the change and not make a fuss? Because that's not who I am.

I do my homework without being told. I keep my room tidy. When my dad got sick, I took care of myself so she wouldn't have another person to take care of. After he died, I kept on taking care of myself because she was grieving. Then she got busy with work and dating, and I just kept rolling with the changes.

"Your mom says you're a vegetarian, EvanAnn."

I lift my gaze to Adam's blue eyes and see the resemblance to Damon. He's handsome, just like Damon. My mom holds Adam's hand on the table. It's easy for them. They've gotten over all that awkward getting-to-know-you phase. They probably told each other about their kids.

Did Adam tell Damon about me? Because Mom said nothing to me about him. Other than she was dating another man.

"Yes, I am." After I get through this meal, I can figure out what the hell I'm going to do. I mean, obviously, my only option is to come with my mom, but I have to figure out a way to deal with this so it doesn't blow up my life.

Telling anyone at school is a huge no. The rumor mill would be rampant. Me? An ant? Living with the Devil's king? We're not even adjacent in social status. He's at the top and I'm down on the bottom.

I can't tell Chase. He'd throw a fit. He was weird when they all sat around me in second period. Then to find out I'm sleeping in the same house as Damon?

Oh shit, I forgot to text Chase about not being able to hang out tonight.

My phone is in my pocket, but I don't reach for it. What would I even tell him? I'm out with Damon Storm, but don't worry, I'm moving in with him soon so...

Yeah, that's a hard pass.

Besides, Chase won't show up at my house and find it empty. It should be fine. I'll text him later that my mom and I went out to dinner, which is not really a lie. We are out and we are at dinner. Even if I don't like lies, I just won't mention it. Omission is better than lying.

"Honey?" Mom's voice draws me back in.

"Yeah?" I blink a couple times to focus on her.

"Are you feeling okay?" She reaches out and touches my forehead with the back of her hand and frowns.

"I'm okay." I draw back. I'm so not okay. "Why do you ask?"

Mom's smile is tense. "Adam was telling you about the meal and you seemed to space out for a bit." Her smile turns apologetic when she turns to Adam. "I meant to tell her sooner, but she's been busy with her boyfriend and school."

Adam nods in understanding, lifts my mom's hand to his lips, and kisses her knuckles. I've seen my mom every day this week. Chase was busy with football. When did she not have time?

"I wanted you to know everything tonight is vegetarian. I've talked to our chef to make sure there's always an option available for you." Adam's eyes soften. "I want you to feel at home here."

Our chef? I must be dreaming. Or having a nightmare. This isn't how things happen. I focus on school. I work hard to get what I want. No one cooks for me, with the exception of Mom, and that's rare. I'm good with a jar of peanut butter, some jelly, and a loaf of bread.

"Heather says you're in the drama program at Anteros Academy and you've been selected to direct for the Fall showcase. That's quite the honor."

I clear my throat. This, I'm used to. Telling someone about what I'm working on at school.

"Um, yes. I'm directing *Othello* this fall." I stop when a plate is put in front of me. I glance up and see a young woman who smiles before serving my mother.

They have a server.

In their house.

Forget the twilight zone. Frankly, this is too much. I don't know what to make of any of it. Maybe Mia wouldn't be opposed to me hanging out at her aunt's house with her all the time. Is that too much to ask of a new friend?

"That's great." Adam glances at Damon. "Damon's playing hockey this year at Deimos."

Damon's lips tighten but he doesn't say anything. As soon as his plate is set in front of him, he grabs his fork and begins to eat.

Is that not what was supposed to happen? Because as far as I know, that's the standard for sports. You play them through high school, then head off to play them in college, and then you get to go pro. If you're good. And from what everyone at school says, Damon is one of the best.

I don't dare show any interest. What must Damon think of me? And my mom? We're not these kinds of people. I don't even associate with the truly rich people at Anteros or Deimos. Chase is the exception. But that's different, he's my boyfriend and he asked me out.

This feels like an invasion of privacy. An invasion I didn't plan, but I'm definitely an accessory to.

I lift my fork and push the pasta around on my plate. Any appetite I might have had went out the window as soon as my mom told me we had to move.

For a second, everyone eats quietly. I do take a few bites. It's a lovely pasta dish with garlic, butter, and small pieces of veggies in it.

Adam clears his throat. When I glance up, I meet Damon's eyes. My breath catches. I'm so not ready for any of this.

"We know this isn't ideal." Adam steeples his fingers in front of his lips, resting his elbows on either side of his plate. "We'd planned to continue dating for a year before moving in, since both of you are seniors. But with your rental home being sold, it makes sense to do it now and only have Heather move once."

Mom turns to me and puts her hand over mine. "Think of it as a temporary place, Evan. You'll be off to college next year. This will be somewhere to sleep this year. Anyway, I'm sure you'll spend all your free time working on the play and with your boyfriend."

I don't think she realizes how often I'm actually home. Even dating Chase, we go out once in a while, but I have homework and things to do. He has football and likes to hang out with his friends. It works out because we both have just enough time to be together.

"You can always have your boyfriend over here too." Adam gives me a smile like he's trying to win me over. "We have a pool and tennis courts in the backyard. There's a rec room in the basement we'll show you on the tour."

It's almost like I can feel the intensity pouring off Damon. When I glance at him, his eyes are narrowed on his father. Not only would I be invading his space, but his father told me to bring my boyfriend into his home, who Damon and his friends might have something against.

My whole insides feel twisted into knots, but I push the pasta around on my plate so I don't have to look at anyone and force out, "I don't think he'll have time. He's on the football team and if we hang out, he usually likes to go out."

"The offer stands," Adam says. He seems nice. I can see why my mom likes him.

After a few more minutes of tense silence while eating, Adam offers us dessert. My mom declines, which is what she does when she wants someone to believe she's watching her figure. She typically has a serious sweet tooth.

"EvanAnn?" Adam asks. "Dessert? Chocolate cake? Heather said it's your favorite."

"No, thank you." I place my fork on my plate and take a drink of water.

"Okay, well maybe after the tour, when you work up an appetite." Adam stands and helps my mom to her feet.

I notice the server waiting in the corner to clear our plates. It feels wrong to not wrap it up and save the leftovers for another meal. Or at least put the plate in the dishwasher.

I lay the napkin on my plate and rub my hands together as I stand. This is going down as the weirdest day ever. But I don't think anything about this year is going to be normal.

Adam takes the lead with my mom and talks about the architecture and designer like he's personal friends with them. Maybe he is. I don't really know anything about this man, except he's dating my mom and Damon is his son. We walk to the kitchen first, where a few people are working. They stop when we enter. After we exit, the noise resumes behind us.

Damon follows us a few paces behind with his phone out.

"This is my office when I work from home." Adam opens the door, but we don't go inside.

The wooden desk is massive with a comfy chair behind it. Some shelving holds books and files.

"What do you do for a living?" I figure it's better to get to know him than to fidget.

"I'm a contracts lawyer." He gestures for me to follow him farther down the hallway. "In here is the conservatory. Beth, my late wife, used to spend a lot of time out here, especially during her time in hospice."

My stomach twists. I didn't know Damon's mother had gotten sick and died. I don't dare turn to look at him. Something tells me he wouldn't want my sympathy. Or to know I understand that kind of pain. I guess he doesn't have anywhere else to live either.

It's a huge house. Our rooms might not even be in the same wing.

"We both lost our spouses to cancer." Mom turns and looks at me. "It's something we bonded over."

I don't think Damon and I are going to have a similar experience. But I give her a nod to let her know I heard her. The first floor is enormous with too many rooms to keep track of. I'm pretty sure I'm going to need a map to get around it without getting lost.

When we go down to the rec room, it's massive. Plenty of seating. Billiards. Poker tables. A humungous television with surround sound speakers.

"There's this television, but the theater room is on the second floor if you want to watch movies with friends or play games." Adam remains pleasant. It really seems like he genuinely likes my mom.

Were all her boyfriends like him? Did she dismiss perfectly nice guys? I don't know because I never met them. What makes Adam so special?

When he mentioned having friends over, Mia comes to mind. I don't know if she'd be used to this type of wealth. I didn't really ask about her socioeconomic status. She went gaga for Hawk though, and if she knows I have access to Damon—forget about it. She'd be here and want to...

My brain stalls out because I would have thought *date* him, but that's not what Mia was talking about doing with the guys. No, she wants to fuck them. My cheeks heat.

Maybe I can't have Mia over, either. Not that it will be a problem this semester. The play will devour all my time. I'll practically be living at school. By spring, I'll be used to living with Damon Storm, and we won't have any issues avoiding each other.

Adam leads us upstairs. "In this direction is the primary bedroom and the children's rooms are this way."

My stomach lurches and I'm glad I didn't eat much for dinner. Adam goes to a door and pushes it open.

"Beth always wanted a girl." He walks into the bedroom.

It's a light purple with white-painted furniture. The room is massive. Even the bed is a king. I've been in my twin since I was a little girl.

While it isn't overly fussy, the bedding looks soft and inviting with so many pillows.

"We never really use this room. There aren't any paintings or wall art, but your mom assures me you have plenty to decorate a room." He crosses and pushes open one of the two doors. Does he know where we live now? Has he seen it? "Your closet. The shelving is perfect for film equipment."

My whole closet in our rental is filled with everything I need to direct. But the contents of my closet would barely make a dent in this extra room. No windows though. It could be a darkroom. I glance up at the light fixture and consider changing it to a red lightbulb. I've always wanted to experiment with film.

"Will it work, Evan?" Mom smiles.

I nod. I mean, what else am I supposed to do? Complain about the massive upscale of a room?

"I hope you don't mind sharing a bathroom." Adam opens the other door to a large bathroom with a separate shower and soaker tub. It has a dual vanity with a marble top.

Mom and I have always shared a bathroom, so sharing isn't a big deal. Until I hear a snort from behind me. Oh, why would I share with my mom here? I freeze as I look at the only things near one of the sinks. There's a razor and a bottle of cologne.

"We do have cleaners, so you don't have to worry about scrubbing." Adam smiles. "You'll have a few drawers to keep your things in."

My gaze fixes on the other door in the bathroom. Maybe it leads to the hallway? Adam walks through and pushes open the door into what can only be Damon's bedroom. It's almost a replica of the purple one, except in a navy blue with dark wood furniture.

His bed isn't made. Pillows and blankets are strewn all over it.

My stomach flips like someone pushed me off a ledge and there's nothing I can do to catch myself. This is going to be a long year.

CHAPTER 7

EvanAnn

WHEN WE RETURNED to the foyer, Mom said we needed to head home. Or at least what will be home for a little while longer. I asked when we were moving in, figuring we had at least a month for me to get used to the idea.

Nope.

Friday. We're moving this week. At least I don't have to worry about packing. Oh, no, Adam is taking care of everything. Apparently, Mom has known for a while we would need a place. Not that she told me when she saw me yesterday.

Or the day before that. Or the day before that.

I can't even make a stink about it. I have no control. I may be eighteen, but I'm still in high school and still financially dependent on my mother. Besides, I haven't complained any other time we moved. So why didn't she tell me?

Now, I sit cross-legged on my bed. How the hell did my life go off the rails so fast? I'm sorting through the scripts for casting, trying to keep my mind off all the other things plaguing me. My phone buzzes on the bed next to me. I stare at it like it might bear some tragic news.

After the day I've had, I wouldn't be surprised. Maybe news of the zombie apocalypse. That would be in line with what my day's been like. Hmm, would I survive a zombie apocalypse?

When I turn my phone over, it's Mia calling. My shoulders relax and I put it on speakerphone.

"Hello to the only good thing that happened today," I say.

"I will take that." Mia sighs. "Is there always so much homework on the first day?"

I cringe. Yeah, she probably wasn't prepared for that. Even though we're a conservatory school, our academics are rigorous.

"Yeah. Deimos is a really well-ranked private school. Everyone wants their kids to funnel into an Ivy League school from here, so they make sure we're prepared."

Mia scoffs. "I'm not going to anything ivy-covered. I might take a year to live in New York or LA and see what I can do."

I chuckle, because that's almost every actor's plan if they don't plan to attend college. "That's the dream. To be discovered."

She laughs. "Yeah. To make it big without spending a ton of money on college or acting school."

She's not wrong. It would be awesome to get a job out of high school. If I had connections, I could, possibly. So I need to make it into the best college I can afford that can introduce me to the people who can help me in my career.

"That would be amazing," I say and lean against my wall.

"I have nothing to go on, but I'm sure you're awesome at directing and Hollywood will snatch you up as soon as you graduate." Mia sounds sure of herself.

If only it were that easy. Someone like Brandt might. He has connections and money. He can dabble and enter short film contests. Hell, his parents could put him to work on a real set as soon as he graduates, giving him real-world experience.

Not me though, I need college. A good college with lots of industry connections. Which is why I need to focus on what's important this year. Not the Devil's trio.

"Honestly, I'm excited about college. I've got a few conservatory schools and film schools I'm looking into." The problem isn't desire or even ability. The problem is cost. Wherever I go, I'll need a scholarship if I don't want to be saddled with mountains of debt.

"Oh, the best thing about college—the college boys." Mia sounds excited. "Seriously, college boys are the best. Last year, I fucked a few at parties. Usually better than high school boys."

I hear a guy call Mia's name in the background. Somehow I'm not surprised given how many sex stories she's told me so far today.

She covers the phone and yells back, "Just a minute."

I'm impressed though. Did she seriously snag a guy on day one, while it took me over two-and-a-half years *and* working on a project together to find a boyfriend? Of course, I'm me. If I looked like Mia, maybe I'd have a bunch of guys going after me too.

She could probably get one of the trio everyone wants. Maybe even all of them.

"Hey, Evan, I have to go. My brother is here this week to help out. Not that we don't get on each other's nerves, but since I'm not going to see him all year, I should go hang out with him."

"That's nice. Do you like having a brother?" I stare at the ends of my hair. I've always been an only child. Seems like Damon has too.

I don't know how any of this is going to work. I get that my mom is ready to move on. It's been years since my dad died. But Adam Storm? Damon's dad? I don't think she's thought this one through. If all they have in common is being widowed, is that enough for a relationship?

I try to figure out how long they've actually been dating, but I was too busy with Chase to be her sounding board on this one.

"Having a brother is okay, but I'd kill to have a bathroom to myself." Mia laughs. "Which I'll have as soon as he leaves, so that's exciting."

"Yeah, I've had to share with my mom." And now I get to share with the hottest boy at school. Somehow, that doesn't make it any better. How does that even work? Do I have to lock both doors before using the bathroom? What if I forget to unlock his side? Will he have to come through my room? I guess I'll figure it out.

"I can't wait for tomorrow. Different class schedule, right?" Mia asks.

"Yes. New classes, new teachers. I think we have third together though—American History." I try to remember her schedule, but so much happened today.

"Yup." She pops the *p*. "I'm so excited to learn more about our school and those guys."

"The guys in the acting classes?" I ask, hopefully. But I'm intentionally being dumb. There's only one set of guys the whole female population are obsessed with. Yes, there are some good-looking guys in acting as well, but most of them are in relationships.

Damon, Hawk, and Cam have always been available. None of them have ever had a girlfriend. I doubt that will change this year.

"The hockey guys." Mia laughs. "I'm going to tear through that team, starting with the guys on top. Oh, or maybe I'll be on top."

Even more reason to not tell her I'm sharing a bathroom with Damon. Part of me wants Mia to like me for me, and not who I can get her close to. At our school, it's hard to tell who is being friendly to use you and who is honestly a friend. It can be really cutthroat. Which is why I don't have many friends.

An impatient, muffled voice comes through the phone again.

"Oof, my brother won't leave me alone. I have to go, Evan. See you tomorrow."

"Yup, tomorrow." I hang up. Fuck, what will tomorrow even be like? Will the trio be in any of my classes? Will Hawk offer to buy my lunch again?

And what about moving on Friday?

I glance around my room and sigh. I have a few more nights in my room before I have to live in that castle. Part of me wishes I could hold onto this moment forever. I don't want to leave.

Our house is a one-and-a-half story, meaning I have this floor to myself. The bathroom is downstairs, outside my mom's bedroom. It's been a nice home and there are even some trees outside my window. So much better than the apartment complex we left that was basically a concrete block.

Movie posters and theater tickets litter my walls, along with fairy lights and a few shelves to hold the equipment that doesn't fit in my closet. Little things I've been able to accumulate because we stayed in one place for more than a year. My twin bed and desk would look like children's furniture in that huge room.

Not that I'll need them. The room comes furnished. That bed is big enough for at least four people. My cheeks heat. I haven't really considered sleeping there yet. Sleeping in the next room over from Damon?

Will I really have any privacy? Will I ever feel safe to sleep in that house with Damon Storm sleeping a few doors away from me? I didn't notice if there was a lock on the bathroom door inside the bedroom.

That would be weird, right? But it would need one. Otherwise, he can walk into my bedroom and I can just walk into his. It's not like we're real siblings who wouldn't think of crossing that line. Not that either of us would cross that line.

My brain stalls, but my heartbeat starts again.

I don't have to worry about Damon sneaking into my room. Guys like him don't want girls like me. I'm a nerd and he's a jock. He has hot girls falling over him all the time. The only reason he even knows I exist is because of my mom. He must be angry that my mom and his dad are shacking up. That must be it.

Or maybe it's Chase they're mad at? Or me?

I can't think of anything I could have done to get on their radar. My summer was spent at home working on *Othello* until my eyes wanted to bleed. I took in everything I could to distill the story to its essence. Nothing that would suddenly make those guys interested in me.

I stare out the window, wishing Mom had given me more time to get used to the idea. Now I have to adapt and roll with the punches. Of course, this will be a much cushier move than we've done before. I don't even have to load up my car with all my things.

Fuck, I don't know what to think. I can't begin to process this.

What was my mother thinking?

I don't have anyone I can talk to. Mom is too happy. The whole way home, it was *Adam this* and *Adam that*. And how happy we were all going to be in that house.

Maybe she's in love. Maybe she really believes money can buy happiness. I don't believe that's the case, but it can definitely make us more comfortable.

She wants this so badly. I don't want to be the squeaky wheel and ruin it for her. All she's done since my dad died is work and date. What if this is the one that works out? Or maybe this is just the one she *wants* to work out, because he's filthy rich and she won't have to work as hard if it did.

I check my messages and notice Chase hasn't responded to my text about going out with my mom for dinner. He could be busy. Or he might be mad I blew him off tonight. Sending off a quick text to see what he's up to, I set my phone aside.

After failing to focus on the scripts, I eye my phone. I could call him. Maybe talk to him about this move. Isn't that what boyfriends are for?

What would he think of me moving in with Damon Storm? He didn't seem happy about me sitting near them or them talking to me. Now they'll have access to me he doesn't. Fuck, I don't want to add any additional animosity between him and the Devils. I glance at my phone. Why hasn't it buzzed?

Chase and I don't talk constantly, but he usually texts me back. Eventually. It's not like I'm a needy girlfriend. I don't always answer his texts right away either.

He's a big deal and has a very active social life. I try to participate when I can, but I don't have the same social battery level he does. I need my alone time, and that doesn't seem to bother him.

Normally, being alone wouldn't bother me. I have things to keep me occupied, but knowing I have to move into that mansion makes it hard to concentrate.

Focus, that's what I need. I want to study *Othello* more. Auditions are closing in on me. Decisions will have to be made, like whether to pick people I like or people who are best for the part. Hopefully, they're the same people and the decision will be easy.

Mia wants to be my best friend, even after meeting everyone else. But will it last? Does she actually want to be my friend or was I just the first person she met? She did text, and that's what friends do.

Maybe I'm underestimating Mia. Maybe she could be the sounding board I could talk to about this move. To help me not stress out about all the awkwardness of sharing space with Damon. Except she was busy with her twin brother tonight.

"Evan!" Mom calls up the stairs.

"Yeah?" I'm still surrounded by scripts, so I don't move from my bed. In a perfect world, I could tell Mom my concerns, but I haven't seen her this happy in a long time. Who am I to ruin what might be a good thing for her?

She's right. In less than a year, I'm gone. It might be uncomfortable living with them, but the alternative isn't better. In fact, it could be far worse. Iciness floods me.

"I'm going out for a little while." Meaning she's going to go back to her boyfriend's where we're literally moving Friday.

"Okay." I wait a few minutes and the door shuts. Her car starts outside my window and she drives away. My stomach sinks.

So basically, I have no one to talk to about this.

Maybe there's some anonymous website I can post on and wait for people to comment. I wouldn't trust anyone outside of our school to understand what's happening. I'm moving in with the hottest boy in school, and he and his two friends made it a point to *see* me today.

They'll probably say stop whining and enjoy the high life. Or worse, they'll say I should try to hook up with my future stepbrother.

My insides grow warm thinking about Damon.

Ugh. Nope, random advice from strangers is not for me.

The house is very quiet tonight.

I shake my head, select my playlist on my phone to block out my thoughts, and focus on working on the scripts again.

I'm usually okay being alone. Prefer it actually. But tonight I need someone rational to bounce this off of, because it feels like my life is falling apart. Which is ridiculous because my life is going awesome.

I'm one of the top students at an exclusive conservatory school. My play earned a spot in the showcase. My boyfriend is being attentive, not clingy. I haven't had a boyfriend before and need to get used to it.

I made a new friend who seems nice. My new room and house will be a step up from this house. Which should make me happy for me and my mom because she really seems happy this time. Maybe I'm misjudging everything and she and Adam have a lot more in common.

Maybe I should give this a chance and not worry about what happens when things fall apart and we have nowhere to live.

I rub at that ache in my chest.

The doorbell rings. I straighten, suddenly alert, and turn off my music. I'd been so lost in my thoughts I didn't hear someone pull up. When I check my phone, there aren't any new messages from Chase or anyone else. Careful of my scripts, I slide off the bed and head downstairs, straightening my t-shirt and brushing off my pajama bottoms. I don't bother with socks. I'm sure this won't take long.

DAMON

There are few things I'm sure of in this world: hockey is my future, Heather Ward is a gold-digging whore, and EvanAnn is a lying little cunt, along with her boyfriend. I'm going to enjoy breaking her.

She opens the door without hesitation. Her eyes go wide when she sees it's not only me, but Hawk and Cam too. I use her disorientation to take her in. There's not much to her. She's average height for a girl, blond hair and blue eyes that are almost gray.

Her current outfit doesn't show off her legs or that tight little body like her school uniform does. Though her pink toes peek out from under the legs of her pajamas. I honestly didn't know she existed until the end of summer. Now she's all that's on my mind.

I want to destroy her.

Her mouth opens but no sound comes out.

Hawk steps up to her and taps her chin. "What's up, Annie?"

Cam chuckles as he slips into the house while Hawk has her distracted. I follow Cam's lead. Hawk is the seducer. He knows how to get what he wants. I'm not surprised he's into this. Evan is a challenge and Hawk loves a challenge.

"What are you doing here?" She backs away from Hawk and wraps her arms around her center, drawing the t-shirt tight against her tits. Pretty sure she isn't aware of that.

Though maybe she is. Maybe everything she does, from this cute, little shy act to drawing my attention to her breasts, is one giant game to her. She's not as innocent as she acts. I have to remember that.

"Only seems fair, Evan," I bite out. "You got to see my place. Seems I should get to see yours."

"My mom's not home." Her tone implies we're not welcome.

I know exactly where her whore of a mother is. Where she always is, making my father lose his goddamned mind. Playing on his grief from losing my mother. She's another con artist trying to get with Adam Storm. He may be blind to it, but I'm not.

She won't be the first or last gold-digger I have to drive off, but this time I get to have revenge at the same time. Something I intend to savor.

I need to do something with this rage brewing inside and Evan is the perfect target. Having Evan under my roof will be perfect for what I want to do.

I walk into her house like I own the place. Honestly, I could probably buy it and everything in it—including EvanAnn—with my monthly allowance. The living room is tiny, with a small flat-screen TV and a couch that's seen better days. An armchair that looks like it came from the turn of the last century sits next to it.

I shudder to think they'll bring those things with them. Dad already cleared out a guest bedroom for them to store their belongings in. A room that might have been perfect for Evan, if I hadn't convinced Dad we already had the perfect room for her.

I want Evan close so I can keep an eye on the traitorous bitch.

The carpet is worn in a path from the door, so I follow the trail.

"You shouldn't be here." Evan finds her voice again. That voice and that body are designed for sin. And we all know she's not as righteous as she sounds. How far will she let me push her? I'll find out when she has nowhere else to go.

"Is that any way to talk to your future stepbrother?" I walk into the kitchen. Fuck, this is tiny. My father is so far out of Heather's league.

No wonder she's moving in after only a few months.

"Come on, Annie. Show me your room. I want to see where the magic happens." Hawk chuckles. He slides his hand against the small of her back, causing her to scurry away. The only thing she might have going for her is she seems loyal to her asshole of a boyfriend.

We'll fix that.

Cam opens the refrigerator. I glance toward it and see there's barely anything in it. Not surprising given they're moving in Friday. My fucking dad is blinded by the mother's pretty blue eyes. I won't fall for the same trap.

I close in on Evan and she takes a step back into Hawk. Her blue eyes go wide. They're a clearer blue in this light, but they won't tempt me to go easy on her. She makes a delightful little squeak and steps away from both of us. "What are you doing here?"

It's like she's stuck on repeat.

"I showed you mine. Now show me yours." I don't hide the innuendo. Even give her a little wink.

She bites her lip. Fuck, they're full and pouty. On any other girl, I'd have her pressed against the wall, nibbling my way over every bit of them, but not Evan. No. That's not the goal here. The goal tonight is to put her in her place before she lets her ego take off. Moving from this dump to my house is enough to make any girl think she's fucking special.

The only reason Evan is getting our attention is because of what she and her fucking boyfriend did. I'm going to tear them to pieces for it and enjoy every minute of their downfall.

But to do that, I also need her to trust me. Can't get ahead of myself.

"There's not much to see." She purses those lips and crosses her arms again, trying to protect herself from us.

I want to laugh at the effort. No girl has ever told us no. Evan won't be any different.

"Don't sell yourself short, Annie." Hawk's been the most aggressive but he's used to leading, to being the front man. After all, he's our team captain. He's also everyone's favorite. He can do no wrong. Except deep down, he wants to.

He's as fucking dark as I am, but he hides it better. Will he let his darkness out to play with our little revenge plot? Fuck, I hope so.

"Be a good girl and show us your room." Hawk gives her that soft look all girls seem to trust.

"Fine, but then you have to leave." Like she can make demands.

I don't laugh at how naive she is. Or is it all an act? From what I know about Evan, the type of girl she is, she's not fucking shy. Blowing her boyfriend in a convertible where anyone can see. His hand hiking up her skirt to dip below it. She definitely isn't shy for him.

Not a single inch of her delectable little body.

CHAPTER 8
EvanAnn

It's like being surrounded by wolves. I don't know who to keep my eyes on. But I can't keep my eyes on all of them. Cam is in my kitchen rummaging in my fridge while Damon glares at me. And Hawk stands there acting nice.

They tower over me, making me feel even smaller and more insignificant than I am.

I don't trust Hawk's nice act. I don't trust any of them. But I also don't know what to do to get them to leave. Mom probably won't be back until much later, if she even comes home. How many nights have I stayed alone in this house and felt safe?

I don't feel safe now.

"I didn't know my mom was dating your dad." I turn to Damon. Maybe if I put my cards on the table, he'll know I had nothing to do with our current situation. "She doesn't usually get attached to her boyfriends."

His lips press together and those blue eyes turn hard. Maybe that was the wrong thing to say. But it's the truth. I don't like feeding people lies. I mean, it's part of my job, but that's storytelling, not real life.

Lies only end up hurting.

"Unless you want us to go through your house without you, I'd lead the way, Annie." Hawk gestures for me to get on with it.

I squeeze my hands together. He keeps calling me *Annie*, but I don't feel the urge to correct him. Changing from Evan to EvanAnn required a lot of correction so it's almost instinctual, but he isn't calling me Evan. Though Damon does and I don't correct him.

I don't want to think too deeply about either of them.

"Come on, goody two-shoes." Cam comes out of the kitchen with a slice of leftover pizza. He takes a bite and says, "Give us the tour and we'll go."

More lies? Telling me what I want to hear so I let down my guard? Maybe. Or maybe I should trust them until they prove they can't be trusted. Hawk really seemed perplexed when I turned down his offer for lunch. But there's no way to embarrass me in front of everyone here. Unless they film me.

But that would be obvious.

Besides, I'm not ashamed of where we live. It may not be what they're accustomed to, but this has been my home and I'm proud of what we made of it in the two years we've lived here. Unfortunately, unlike Damon during his tour, I can't sullenly look at my phone.

"Fine." Besides, this shouldn't take long. "The living room."

I step around Cam, but he shifts so our bare arms brush. A little jolt of electricity shocks my system, but I ignore it as I step into the kitchen. Yes, the attractive guys are attractive. Thank you, body, for reminding me.

"The kitchen."

I don't turn to see if they're still with me. Pushing open the door to the one bathroom, I try to ignore the bras hanging to dry on the rack and turn on the light.

"Our bathroom."

"Just the one?" Hawk asks as he puts his hands on the top of the doorframe, blocking me in as he leans in to inspect it. His arms bulge with muscles.

That scent of leather and books overwhelms me for a moment and draws me like a moth to a flame. I close my eyes and inhale. Fuck, why is that so intoxicating?

Fingers brush my cheek and my eyes pop open. My breath catches. Fuck. I take a step back from the touch, but the wall is right there. I can't get away. Hawk's green eyes have darkened as his gaze follows his fingers over my cheekbone and down the side of my neck. My insides shimmer beneath his touch.

My pulse goes crazy.

I can't suppress the shiver that works through me or the goose-bumps rising in the wake of his fingers against my skin. He seems mesmerized for a second as I'm frozen in place. His touch isn't bad. Just the opposite, and that's what's so alarming.

When he touches me, I forget myself.

He shakes himself out of it and steps back. "Nice."

I'm assuming he's talking about the bathroom and squeeze by him to get out of there. I drag a breath into my starving lungs. My cheeks feel warm and that same overwhelming feeling deep in the pit of my stomach strikes me. I have a boyfriend, but I'm in my house alone with three guys.

This can't be good, but I can't exactly call the police on my future roommate? He's not my step-anything yet. If my mom does end up marrying his dad, that would start our relationship off on the wrong foot.

Remember that time you had me arrested. Somehow I don't think that will ever be funny, no matter how many Christmases down the road. Besides being annoying and invading my space, they haven't really done anything that would warrant a call to the police.

Nope, I need to get through this.

I hurry to my mother's room and push the door open wider. "Mom's room."

I breeze past Cam and Damon to head up the stairs. Only one more room. It's not a huge place, but it's ours. Or was ours. It's home and I've been happy here. My heart squeezes. I hate to leave it.

They're right behind me as I stop outside the door to my bedroom. I left it open so I gesture toward it. "My room. Tour over. You can go now."

"That's not very nice, goody two-shoes." Cam steps into my room and Damon follows him.

"Going through my things is not part of the tour." I cross my arms over my chest again. Maybe I should call my mom and tell her what's happening. But if Damon's house is the only place we have to go, what will that accomplish?

A shudder goes through me remembering the apartments. I'd rather deal with Damon than the apartments.

"Should be, Annie." Hawk smirks and drops his gaze to my chest.

I follow his gaze thinking I spilled something on my t-shirt, which wouldn't be a surprise. Instead, it's just my breast... that I've hoisted up. I drop my arms.

"I have work to do, so if you could go..." This isn't my strong suit. I had trouble getting my friends to leave even when I was a kid. Even Chase has overstayed his welcome on more than one occasion.

Hawk walks over and lifts one of the scripts off my bed. Cam is already at my dresser, opening drawers. Damon sits at my desk and rifles through the papers.

They look ridiculously huge in my tiny room.

"What's the end goal here, guys? I have no control over where my mother takes me. I didn't even know about any of this until a couple hours ago." They have to listen to reason, right? "If you're trying to intimidate me to get her to change her mind, it won't work."

Damon lifts his gaze to mine. It's clear he doesn't like me. What I don't understand is why.

"Is it because Chase is on the football team?" I lean against my door-frame with my arms crossed.

Cam chuckles. "Why would we care if Chase is on the football team?"

I shrug. "Hockey-football rivalry."

"Not a thing." Hawk winks at me before he goes back to reading over the script.

"Is it because we're both up for valedictorian?" I'm grasping at straws, but that's all I've done today. My brain can't find any reason why they'd suddenly be interested in me. I'm no one at school.

"Nah, you can have it, if you want it, Annie. I've already got my future planned out." Hawk doesn't even look up this time, but flips the page.

"Then what?" I almost whine, because this is a lot. "I don't want your attention. If I didn't do anything—"

Damon is quick. He's suddenly right in front of me, glaring down at me with those piercing blue eyes. "If you didn't do anything, Evan, you have nothing to worry about, do you?"

My breath catches in my chest, but not before breathing in Damon. Something dark and earthy swirls in my lungs as I wait for him to shift away, to give me the space to breathe again.

He takes all the air when he's near me, like his aura wants to suffocate me. From the look in his eyes, he might enjoy watching me die. The others are fucking with me, but there's some real intense hate coming my way from Damon.

"I don't understand," I say softly.

His eyes narrow. He reaches out and I flinch. I don't know why. Maybe I'm afraid he'll touch me and I'll feel what the others make me feel. How wrong would it be if a guy hates me and I want him? What kind of cliché is that? But maybe I'm afraid he'll hurt me.

He tucks a strand of hair behind my ear. Sparks light beneath my skin where his fingertips brush. Fuck. My heart sinks into my stomach.

"You'll figure it out, Evan." He drops his hand. "Time to go."

He turns and walks down the stairs. For a second, I can breathe again. Then Cam stops in front of me.

He's tall and broad. His light brown hair is untamable. And he always has an easy smile, but it doesn't reach his eyes. I've wondered if the party boy persona is a mask he wears.

He gives me a once-over that makes me blush.

"Later." He smirks and makes a kissy face at me before following Damon down the stairs.

Hawk stands and sets the script down on my bed, almost reluctantly. When he crosses the room, he lifts his green eyes to mine and holds my gaze. His eyes are truly pretty. My heart thumps a little faster and harder.

"I wasn't trying to make a fool of you in the cafeteria." His words are quiet as he closes in on me.

My heart beats in triple time. My mind goes blank with him so close. "What?"

His fingers trace over the back of mine. I'm so shocked at the sparks he lights I don't pull away.

"I wanted to buy you lunch and get to know you better." His smile is soft and tempting. Everything about Hawk is tempting.

My breath catches. "I have a boyfriend."

Am I reminding him or me?

He smirks. "You've said, but he's not here tonight, is he?"

I don't say anything, because he's obviously not.

"If you were mine, you wouldn't be alone in a house with three guys forcing you to give them a tour." His words are soft, but they make absolutely no sense to my brain. His?

What does that even mean?

He puts his hand on the doorframe above my head. "Think about it, Annie."

He leans down like he's going to kiss me, but I turn my head to the side. He chuckles.

"I'll know for next time." He starts down the stairs.

"You'll know what?" My voice is breathy and my heart hurts from pounding so hard.

"Not to give you notice." He turns and winks, before leaving me standing there. I hear the downstairs door open and the three of them are gone.

I slide down the doorframe and put my head in my hands. What am I going to do?

WHEN MY ALARM GOES OFF, IT FEELS LIKE I JUST FELL ASLEEP. I locked the doors after my little pity party. Then I went back to my scripts and thinking about auditions. I could have tried to figure out what that was with Damon and Cam, but I'm not even going to think about Hawk.

It would have been more spinning of my wheels anyway. Better to not think about any of them.

I'm at school the same time as the student body this morning, so there would be no run-ins with the Devils. At least not the specific Devils I'm trying to avoid. Of course, I won't be able to avoid Damon forever. We'll be living under the same roof starting Friday.

How is that going to work?

"Hey, bestie." Mia bumps her elbow into mine.

"Hey."

"Rough night?" Her brow furrows as she takes me in.

I didn't bother with makeup this morning. Most mornings I only do a little light makeup, anyway. Anything that takes longer than five minutes is too long for me. I didn't even attempt to hide the bags under my eyes.

"I didn't sleep much."

She glances around and drags me into the nearest girls' bathroom.

"Friends don't let friends walk around with bags under their eyes." She sets her books on the counter, which are blessedly dry because it's early in the day. She opens her purse and pulls out some makeup. "Fortunately, you and I have about the same coloring, so I should be able to fix you up."

"Thank you." Tears choke the back of my throat at her kindness, but I swallow them down. When I tried to go to sleep last night, I went over every word Hawk, Cam, and Damon said, trying to dissect them and figure out why they were even at my house. What do they want from me?

"Do you want to talk about it?" Mia applies some concealer under my eyes. "Is it Chase? Did he do something wrong?"

I shrug. "He didn't respond to my texts, but he had a busy day."

"Boyfriends are supposed to respond to texts." She arches an eyebrow and steps back to study her work. She digs in her bag and pulls out an eyeliner pencil.

"It's okay. I mean, we don't talk every day." Besides, he's not the one bothering me right now. I stare into her blue eyes. She has experience with guys. A lot more than I do. "How do you make a guy leave you alone?"

"Are we talking about a specific guy or one in general?" She finishes with the eyeliner and pulls out a small container of blush. She applies it to my cheeks and eyelids before putting it away.

"In general?" I wish I could talk to her about this, but she's new and I want her to like me. I don't know how she'd react to the guys barging into my house last night. Would she be jealous? She wants them.

"Okay. In general." She pulls out a light pink lipstick. "You could let him know you're not into him."

"What if that isn't true?" My words are quiet. That's the problem. I think I might be into those three, but I also know none of them are right for me. Chase is the type of guy I want. He doesn't push at my barriers. And I'm definitely not right for any of them. They like girls who are willing to do anything to be with them. But how do I say *no thank you* and mean it?

"Well, then you need to ask yourself why you're pushing him away?" Mia puts her makeup back in her purse and then turns me to look in the mirror. "Because you could get any hottie you wanted, Evan."

I do look better. More alive and less like a zombie. "Thank you, Mia."

"If this is about Chase…" She picks up her books.

"No. It's not about Chase. I just…" I could tell her. She might have a different perspective that could be helpful.

The door opens. Abby Baker, Crystal Taylor, and Becca Anderson walk into the bathroom. This is the popular clique of the drama school and Anteros. They're the most popular, richest, beautiful, and talented actresses. Abby is tall and thin with dark hair and dark eyes.

Crystal has strawberry-blond hair and striking green eyes. She attracts attention wherever she goes. And Becca is who every girl wishes they could be—blond, blue-eyed with curves that normal high school girls don't have. These girls are the cream of the crop and they know it.

They stop laughing when they notice us, settling into plastic smiles. Their eyes skim over me and focus on Mia. My heart squeezes. They'll ask her to join them. She'd fit in perfectly with their group.

It was only a matter of time before I lost her.

"Hi, Mia." Abby gives her a fake smile. "You were amazing in class yesterday. So talented."

"Thanks." Mia's smile is almost as fake as Abby's. "I can't wait to hear your monologue today. It's one of my favorites."

Abby turns to look at me. "EvanAnn, how are the roles coming for *Othello*? I thought it odd you got *Othello* and Brandt got *The Crucible*. I would have thought you'd want to do a strong, female-led cast and not the other way around."

I arch an eyebrow. "The female parts in *Othello* are as important as the males. The casting has to be balanced so Desdemona can be thought an equal to Othello in all ways."

"But Shakespeare." Abby shakes her head and pouts. "It doesn't exactly roll off the tongue. I think you'll have trouble casting your play when the juicy female roles are in *The Crucible*."

"Yeah, I don't understand why anyone would pick *Othello*." Becca leans into the mirror and reapplies her lipstick. "It's not like *Romeo and Juliet* or *A Midsummer Night's Dream*. It's so boring."

I disagree, but it's pointless to argue with them.

Crystal glances at Abby, then looks at me. She may be a follower, but she's not stupid when it comes to her career. "My uncle took me to see *Othello* at Shakespeare's Globe last summer. It was amazingly done. I wouldn't mind being cast as Iago's wife."

I could see Crystal in that role. I give her an encouraging smile. "I look forward to your audition."

"Isn't Chase begging you to cast him as Iago?" Abby's looking to stir trouble. He is her ex after all.

"Chase would make a fine Iago." I edge my way toward the door. "If he gets the part."

Abby arches her eyebrow at me like I'd be stupid not to give him the part. Mia walks with me. Yes, he wants the part, but he has to earn it like everyone else. Just because he's my boyfriend doesn't mean he automatically gets a part.

"Oh, Mia, you should sit with us today at lunch." Abby smiles but it doesn't reach her eyes. "We sit out in the courtyard with the cool kids."

I swallow hard because that's a tempting offer for a new student. To get in with that crowd is to get invited to all the parties and be seen by the most attractive guys, like Damon, Hawk, and Cam.

"I'll think about it." Mia looks at me. "Evan can come, right?"

Abby's eyes narrow on her, but then she laughs. "Of course."

Yeah, Abby doesn't want me there any more than I want to be there.

CHAPTER 9

Cam

THIS YEAR WAS GOING to be boring as hell. All I wanted was to fucking party with my friends and enjoy our senior year, but they had other plans. Damon was supposed to head off to a junior hockey league so he could get into a top tier NCAA college with a pro team already signed on. Hawk swore he needed to focus on his college applications.

This summer changed their plans.

The counselor encouraged Hawk to seek out something to balance out his fantastic grades and hockey for his college application. And Damon is stuck here with us because of his father and the accident. I can't wait to make the most of it.

I mean, every guy needs a little project. And thanks to Chase Chadwick, which is a stupid fucking name, we have ours. EvanAnn Ward.

Not the hottest girl in school, or the wealthiest, or the prettiest, or the most popular. Fuck, this girl falls pretty far down in the rankings of girls at Deimos and Anteros, which is saying something. She's not ugly. She's pretty enough and she'd probably be considered hot at a normal school. But she's also super geeky. Theater nerd and top of the class.

My first class today is English Literature. When I walk in, I immediately catch sight of EvanAnn, sitting close to the front of the class with no one around her. The tables are large and have two chairs each. Usually, you end up partnering with your table mate for the semester.

Most girls travel in packs to avoid being paired up with some rando. Not little miss goody two-shoes.

I ignore the girls batting their eyelashes at me and flaunting their cleavage like I haven't seen tits before, and head over to snag the chair next to EvanAnn. She glances toward me, completely blasé about whoever was going to sit at her table.

Until she recognizes me. Her eyes widen and there's that hint of fear in her gaze as she reaches for her books.

I release a huge sigh. "Are we going to do this dance again?"

She tilts her head like I'm speaking a foreign language.

"I'm going to sit here. But if you move, I'm going to follow you to that spot. So can we chill with the dramatics and accept the fact I'm going to sit next to you for this class?" I flash her my smile. "I'd hate to start rumors when I have to kick people out of their seats because you sit with them."

Her lips purse like she wants to say something, but decides not to. She pushes her books back where they were.

"Looks like I have you to myself." My hair falls into my eyes and I blow it out of the way before giving her that smoldering look girls love.

She looks at me like I've grown an extra head and it isn't as attractive as the first one. What the fuck is up with this girl?

Sure, she's got a boyfriend, but that's never stopped girls from talking or even flirting with me. A few of them even blew me or fucked me despite their relationship status. Don't know if they told their boyfriends, but if a girl's down to fuck around, who am I to say no?

EvanAnn pulls out her phone. That's cute. She's going to try to ignore me. She's definitely not like most girls. I've seen her at parties, but only since last spring when Chase decided to date her.

Gotta admit, I didn't think she was his type. He's almost as loud and gregarious as I am. And a fuckboy to boot. That guy was swimming in pussy all the fucking time. But now he's with EvanAnn. Shy, little bookworm Evan.

Damon thinks that it's all an act. From what he's seen, she knows how to be a bad girl. I could see her being a little wild beneath that innocent facade. I'd love to get a taste of her wild side.

I lean back in my chair and study her. Her cheeks are pink. She's got her blond hair tied back into one of those messy buns girls like to do. I prefer it down around her shoulders, but back means I don't have to gather it in my hands to watch her suck my cock.

My gaze lingers on her lips. Her pink, pouty lips would look good stretched around my dick, which rises to the occasion like I'm calling the fucker out of hibernation. I usually have some control, but the more I focus on those lips, the harder I get.

I need to move on to her other assets, because English Lit isn't exactly the best place to pop a boner. Her breasts aren't the biggest, but they're big enough. My cock twitches and I reach down to adjust.

She glances over at the movement and her eyes widen before she looks away like she didn't see my hard-on for her. I'm tempted to grab her hand and let her feel what she does to me. What would she do if I shoved her hand in my pants?

Her skirt is short like the other girls', showing off those long legs. Fuck, maybe I'll slide my hand beneath it and see what I can do for her. Her skirt isn't rolled at the waist to make it shorter. I don't think she's wearing a too-small skirt to be slutty though. After seeing her place yesterday, I'm pretty sure she's just poor and uniforms are expensive.

Not that she can't be slutty and poor. Some of my favorite slutty girls are poor. But EvanAnn doesn't strike me as the slutty type. I think I'm going to have to disagree with Damon on this one.

I know what he saw, but I don't see it when I look at the girl next to me.

Though I'm willing to see how far I can get with her. Sometimes the shy ones do like to get wild.

I put my arms on the desk. "What's the plan, goody two-shoes?"

She blows out a breath and turns to face me. Those eyes of hers are huge and blue like the summer sky. She's not classically beautiful, which doesn't bother me. She's cute and sexy in that uptight way of hers.

"What do you mean?" she asks.

I mean, fuck, I can't wait to hear her ask me to make her come in that voice. It's low and a little rough. I move closer and wet my lips.

"I mean, when are the two of us going to find some place to have alone time?" I give her a wink and I swear her brain short-circuits.

Her mouth opens and closes, then opens again. Her knees press tight together as she turns to face the front of the classroom.

"Come on, EvanAnn, aren't you tired of doing what everyone expects you to do?" I scoot my chair closer to her and inhale her scent that makes my balls ache. It's like cedar. Most girls smell sweet or flowery, but not EvanAnn, like her name, her smell is unique and makes my cock rock hard.

"What does everyone expect me to do?" she asks. She sounds genuinely confused.

"Be a good girl and sit in class all day. Make the best grades. Be the best little director. Never let your hair down and feel the wind in your face." I lean in a little closer. Her eyes darken slightly. I affect her. Good. "Feel a motor purring between your legs as you squeeze those thighs around my hips."

Her brow furrows. "Are you talking about riding your motorcycle?"

I smirk. "It's a start. I have other things you could ride, goody two-shoes."

Her gaze drops to my crotch, which, fuck, makes my dick pulse. Maybe not that innocent, after all.

***

EvanAnn

I need a cold shower. Seriously, what is wrong with me? The image of Cam on his motorcycle and me straddling him was a little too vivid for my liking. Especially inhaling his leather and sandalwood scent.

I'm not that kind of girl. I don't like when things go fast.

The teacher comes in and gives us the typical first day lecture before sending us off to second period. As soon as the bell rings, I hurry away from Cam as fast as I can. Why would his offer even begin to tempt me?

It doesn't make sense. Chase is my boyfriend. He's all I need. He's respectful and kind and considerate. He doesn't push me beyond where I'm comfortable. I don't need to ride a motorcycle or feel anything between my legs. Especially not while uncomfortably wet. This is ridiculous.

I shouldn't be reacting to these guys at all. They shouldn't even be noticing me, because I'm not on their level. Not even close. I'm so far beneath them, it's laughable.

I shouldn't be on their radar. But now that I'm on it, I have no idea how to get off it.

And I can't deny part of me wants to stay on it. That part is so damned curious. Why can't I be curious about Chase? My actual boyfriend? He's everything they are. Attractive, wealthy, athletic.

He should be the only one on my mind and making my panties damp. He's helping me break out of my shell. We date and go to parties, when I was all about school before.

I walk into second period and almost walk right back out. Damon sits in the back. His blue eyes fire daggers in my direction. How am I supposed to live with this guy when he so clearly hates me? And why does him hating me not turn me off?

The only good part is, he's already seated, so I can sit as far away from him as possible. Unfortunately, there aren't many seats left in the class to take. I head to the front of class. Before I set my things down, a Deimos girl takes one look at me, plops her backpack on the chair, and says, "This seat is taken."

Fair enough. There are still more chairs.

A few people came in and filled in the gaps while I was trying for that chair. There's one right next to Damon or one in the far corner. He's watching me. Is he wondering if I have the balls to go for the chair next to him?

For a second, I want to prove to him I can be bold if I need to be. I make decisions all the time for the plays I direct.

Instead, I go to the corner and sit down. I don't know what's going to happen over the next year, but I need some space. And I'm going to need space from Damon, especially if I'm going to be sleeping twenty paces away from him for the rest of the school year.

For the most part, teachers let you sit where you want at Deimos. On occasion, a teacher will put us alphabetically, which puts me near Hawk or Cam, but not Damon.

Mrs. Conrad comes in. She's young for a teacher at Deimos, still in her twenties. She wears pencil skirts and blouses, which means most guys barely concentrate in her classes. Her dark hair is pulled up in a tight bun. Her blue eyes scan the room.

"Welcome to Calculus. If you are in the wrong room, get out." She picks up a dry erase marker and starts writing on the board. "If you think this is an easy A... what the fuck were you thinking? Get out. I don't have time. If you think you need extra help, find the smartest student in this room and make them your friend. We will be going fast. There will be quizzes, tests, and homework. So much homework, you'll wish you'd signed up for basic math. If you can't handle that, get out."

She turns to face the class. "Who's going to be bold enough to solve this equation?"

She steps out of the way. It's a complex equation we learned last semester.

No one moves.

"Okay, let me sweeten the pot. Whoever gets it correct starts the semester with ten points of extra credit." She leans against her desk. "If someone doesn't at least attempt it, everyone loses ten points."

Brad, a Devil, stands. "I'll do it."

She holds out the marker to him and he takes it. He walks up to the equation and stares at it. When he starts to write, she makes a buzzer sound.

"No. Next."

Brad sits down. Renee stands. She's in the visual arts program at Anteros. She takes a crack at it.

"No. Next."

Most of the front row has made an attempt, when Mrs. Conrad walks to the back of the class. She glances at the back row. "You."

She points at me. I stand and take the marker. I'm self-conscious of the length of my skirt as I walk to the front of the class—this is one I should really replace or at least stop wearing. But the equation on the board doesn't intimidate me. I quickly write down the answer before returning to my seat.

"Interesting." She clears the board and writes another equation. When she holds up the marker, a few students raise their hands. She ignores them. "You. Damon Storm. Come up here."

He stands, stretching to his over-six-foot height, and walks to Mrs.

Conrad. He has at least six inches on her, even though she's wearing three-inch heels. He takes the marker and has the answer in seconds.

"Very nice." She takes the marker and erases the problem. She adds another problem.

This goes on for a while until everyone has gone up to the board once.

"Grab your things and stand against the wall." Mrs. Conrad goes to the front seats and calls out. "EvanAnn, you're number one until someone beats you. Damon, number two. Gareth, number three. Cadence, number four."

She calls out each of us and we fill the seats, meaning I'm sitting next to Damon after all. I release a breath, but don't look at him while the rest of the class gets sorted.

Brad now has my seat in the far back corner.

"Take note. We rearrange weekly based on scores. If you're sucking, you'll be in the back. If you're a winner, you'll join me in the front." Mrs. Conrad smiles. "You want to be a winner."

When the bell rings, we all rise and grab our books.

"Homework is in the portal. Grades will be published on the home page. You'll see your ranking in the class as things are turned in. It resets every morning. Don't disappoint me."

I head out into the hallway. Everyone says to avoid Mrs. Conrad's class, but she also gives the best recommendations. I need a stellar recommendation from her for college.

My next class is next door. I know I have this one with Mia, and I'm looking forward to having someone to sit with. American History is one of those classes that has multiple sections and every senior must take it to graduate.

So, I'm not surprised when Damon follows me in. I head away from him and he takes a seat near the door. Mia comes in and glances at Damon before heading over to me with a grin.

"I'm so glad to see you." She puts her books next to mine on the four-top table. It's a weird setup, but discussion is a big part of the history classes here. "Oh my god. My first class I have with Chase and Hawk. It was an interesting hour. How have your classes been?"

"Uh, good." I honestly don't know what to say about them since the one with Cam had me uncomfortable the entire class and the one with Damon had me uncomfortable in a different way.

Brandt walks in with Drake, his friend. They look around the room and I see him zero in on Mia. Fuck. I really don't want to spend the class discussing things while Brandt flirts with Mia. As they start our way, I look down at my book.

"Oh, good." Mia seems really happy when the guys join us.

I cringe. Brandt doesn't actually do his classwork. So if we end up having to do a paper together, we'll be doing all the work.

But it's better than sitting with Damon. I lift my head and meet a set of familiar green eyes. My pulse jumps.

"Hey, Annie." Hawk smiles like we're best friends.

Damon sits next to him at our table. I look around, wondering if I could get Brandt instead. He's sitting at the table behind Mia. Close enough to chat or to catch her on the way out of the classroom.

"I was telling Evan you're in my first period class." Mia twirls her hair and purses her lips at him. "With her boyfriend."

My stomach falls, because she's not attached to anyone. If she wants Hawk, Damon, Cam, or all of them, she can have them. Not that I want them, because like she said, I have a boyfriend.

That doesn't stop the twist in my gut, which doesn't make sense.

"I don't think we've met yet." Mia smiles at Damon and holds her hand across the desk. "I'm Mia Lewis."

"Damon Storm." He takes her hand and gives her the smirk I've seen him give other girls. Not me though. No, he hates me.

"I can't wait to come to the first hockey game to cheer you guys on. I never went to a hockey game at my old school." She smiles at me. "Evan and I are going to come watch."

Hawk leans his arms on the table, angled toward me. "Are you, Annie?"

Mia turns and nudges me.

"Of course." I already agreed to it, anyway. I catch Damon's glance. Fortunately, the teacher comes in and we don't have to make any more small talk.

The teacher announces that there will be a group project this semester. And of course, my group is my table.

CHAPTER 10

Hawk

DAMON WANTS to fuck over Chase Chadwick, who is a pretentious asshole and deserves fucking over. The best way to fuck with a guy is to fuck with his girl. And the best way to fuck with a girl is to fuck the girl.

I may be captain of our hockey team and used to leading, but this particular boat is steered by Damon. And add Annie's mother happens to be a gold digger creeping in on Damon's dad, and the target on poor Annie grows bigger.

Of course, she's not innocent in any of this. She was there that night. It takes two to party like that.

Unfortunately, Annie isn't like other girls. Most girls are crawling all over me the second I give them any attention. Not Annie. Fuck no, she practically told me off yesterday at lunch. And even though her eyes were screaming yes at me last night, she turned away when I leaned in to kiss her.

When I saw Brandt heading to Annie's table in history, Evan sat there and accepted the inevitable. She obviously didn't want him at her table. He's her fucking nemesis for the showcase. But she was just going to take it. Fuck that.

Besides, I like the idea of having to complete a project together. I plan on seeing a whole lot more of Annie this year anyway.

Her new friend though...

Mia's a wannabe puck bunny. She's already laying the groundwork to make her way through the hockey team. I would say Annie is an odd choice as a friend for Mia, but then again, Annie is dating a manwhore.

When class is dismissed, it's easy enough to follow them to lunch. Mia keeps up a running dialogue with both Damon and I, keeping us attached to her and therefore Annie. She looks mortified we're anywhere near her.

I should have kissed her last night. Would she have gone running to her boyfriend? How far would she have let me get? We were in her bedroom. The others would have waited for me, or they could have taken off and I would have had Annie to myself.

If she told Chase, I don't think he'd have the balls to call me out. If Annie were mine, I'd knock his teeth down his throat for daring to come near her.

Okay, that thought gives me pause. We don't do girlfriends. It's too fucking messy. We don't even fuck anyone on the regular. When girls try to claim us, it only ends in catfights, which, while entertaining, are not fun when you're the cause.

The student body watches us move into line. Annie picks the salad bar again. I know better than to ask to pay for it, so I head with Damon to get something with protein and carbs.

"What's the plan?" I ask Damon.

Annie's moving in, but not until Friday. How long before she's in his bed? He's not particular about keeping a girl to himself. We've shared on more than one occasion. Not at the same time, but we've fucked the same girl in the same night. Damon wants us all to take her, and I can't say I'm opposed. I'm attracted to Annie and enjoy a challenge.

"Nothing." Damon glances toward Annie and Mia as their line moves faster.

"I thought you wanted to crush him." We haven't played this game before. But I want to take Annie from Chase. I want to make her crawl for me and have her obey me. Something about that innocence she wraps around her so tightly makes me want to prove to everyone how dirty she really is.

I'm usually all about the seduction, but Annie gets under my skin.

"It's going to take time. She's going to take time." Damon shakes his head as he grabs his food and heads outside. I follow behind. "Rushing this will cause us to crash and burn too fast. Her fucking walls are up and she's on guard. We need to wear her down."

What he says makes sense, but I don't want to wait. I'm fucking drawn to this girl. I want to fucking ruin her, over and over again.

The courtyard is full today. The Deimos royalty is already present, picking at their lunches. Gemma Florence, Megan Baron, and Olivia Carmichael. Popular, rich, beautiful. I've fucked them all, and they've fucked half the school. They were born knowing their place in this world is on top.

I try to imagine blond-haired, blue-eyed Olivia in Annie's house. The carpet was so old it was worn from traffic patterns. It was clean, but everything looked dated. My mother would have thrown out the whole lot and started over. Olivia wouldn't even make it into the neighborhood before turning her Bentley around.

"Damon, love, come sit. I need to tell you something." Olivia flashes her smile at Damon and pats the seat beside her. She's confident she can have anything she wants. She's been trying to get Damon for years. He's been avoiding fucking her.

Maybe he likes the game. Or her desperation. Whatever the reason, he doesn't mess with her.

Damon almost got away. But since he's still here, I'm pretty sure he's Olivia's game plan for this year.

Damon walks her way. The rich and popular Anteros students have another table filled with people like Brandt and Abby Baker. I fucked her once, but she tried too hard.

Maybe I'm bored with girls like Abby and Olivia. Maybe I want a challenge like Annie. She doesn't want to want me and I find that shit fascinating.

The doors open, and I'm shocked to see Mia leading Annie out into the courtyard. Mia acts like she belongs here as she makes her way over to Abby and her friends.

Poor Annie looks like a frightened rabbit. She knows she doesn't belong out here. Not with these sharks. She's never been out here. I give her five minutes before she scurries back inside.

"Hey, Mia." Abby scoots over, making enough room for only Mia to join them. Mia doesn't hesitate to sit, but then looks for a space for Annie. The table is full, but if each of the girls moved a little or put a purse on the table, there would be room.

Annie's smile doesn't falter, but that light dims in her eyes. It's like watching someone lose their friend. Fuck.

I stand before Annie can turn and run back inside, because that's exactly what she should do. But I'm faster than she is. When I drape my arm over her shoulder, she tenses.

"There's room over here, Annie." I pull her to where I was sitting.

Annie is too intent on watching her feet, but Mia's eyes narrow as jealousy sparks in them. She flirted with me yesterday and in class this morning. If I wanted her, I could have had her already, just one day in.

But instead, I want this timid girl who looks like she'd rather bolt than follow me. But she's aware of how it would look to these people if she left me after coming to her rescue. She already made a scene yesterday, but that was inside. So, she lets me lead her to my table and sits down next to me.

Cam comes out of the cafeteria to shouts of *Cam!*

He smirks, notices Annie next to me, and heads our way. Damon stays next to Olivia, but his attention is on Annie until Olivia says something.

Mia's smile stays fixed as she talks with those other girls, but her eyes say she'd rather be over here. And I don't think Annie is the draw.

"Stepping outside the lines, goody two-shoes?" Cam sits on her other side, straddling the bench to face her.

"I should go back inside." She's pale and glances toward the other table. When she sees Mia laughing, her gaze falls to her tray.

"Nonsense." I pick up my burger and take a bite. "You're already here and you have a seat."

Her cheeks flush with warmth, but she doesn't lift her eyes to look at me. Fuck it, I want to put her at ease. I'll torment her later.

"*Othello,* that's the play you're directing for the showcase?" I keep my attention on her, hoping it will make her relax to talk about something familiar.

She nods and picks at her salad with her fork.

"What's your focus for your production?" I need to get her talking.

"I find the machinations of Iago to be fascinating." She takes a small bite, like she's afraid.

"How so?"

Cam lifts an eyebrow at me, but we all go to an excellent school. There aren't a lot of stupid people here. We've been dissecting Shakespeare for three years now. I think I can have one discussion with a theater nerd.

She lifts her gaze and narrows her eyes. "Are you really interested?"

Cam chuckles, but coughs when she glances at him.

"Yes, Annie. I want to understand your take on *Othello*."

She starts off slowly discussing how Iago manipulates and lies to get what he thinks is justice and touches on the blatant racism in the piece. As I ask questions, she slowly opens up and gets into the discussion.

"You're familiar with the work?" she asks. Her blue eyes focus on mine. This is where she's confident, talking about theater.

"I've read through it and seen it on stage before," I admit.

She bites her lip and looks down. "Mia said you were thinking of auditioning."

It's not a question, but I take it as such. "My college application could use some rounding out. It's a little late to start playing an instrument. The best I can draw is a stick figure. Most clubs take up too much time and I already have hockey."

"The play is going to take up a lot of time." She cocks her head to the side.

"But some of the practice is during the school day."

She smiles like she caught me. "You'd have to miss class."

"I have a free period at that time."

"It's not only during that time though. Have you ever acted before?" Her blue eyes search mine, and they aren't shy this time. She's genuinely curious.

I kind of want to crack open her brain and see how it works. What is she thinking? Does she honestly wonder if I could be in her play or is she figuring out ways to dismiss me?

"Can you keep a secret?" I ask.

Cam snort laughs.

Annie's eyes light up and she practically beams. "Yes."

I lean in and reach to brush her hair away from her ear. She draws back before I can touch her. I arch an eyebrow. "It's a secret. I have to whisper it in your ear."

She gives me a worried look but tucks her hair behind her ear and turns so it's facing me. Cam rolls his eyes. I give him a gloating smirk. She's so fucking proper sitting between us, but the way she talks about Shakespeare and directing is with passion.

It makes me want to taste that passion.

I lean in and my lips touch her earlobe. She lets out this shaky breath that makes me want to slide my hand between her legs and see if she's wet. Does Shakespeare turn her on? Do I?

I wet my lips and my tongue flicks against her ear. This time her breath catches.

"I spent a summer doing *Shakespeare in the Park* on a dare." My lips brush her skin with every word.

"On a dare?" Her voice is soft and breathless, like it will be after I make her come.

I smile and she shivers because my lips are still brushing her ear. I slide my hand against her neck. "I do a lot of things on dares, Annie."

"EvanAnn!" Chase's voice makes her bolt to her feet.

I lean back and smirk as Chase walks over to us. His eyes are narrowed, but he doesn't seem worried that I had my mouth against Annie's ear and my hand almost around her neck. I ignore the way my cock aches.

I can't wait to sink it into her. It's only a matter of time.

"Chase," she says. She's still a little breathless from my touch.

My smirk gets cockier. So close. I can still taste the salt of her skin against my lips, and the woodsy scent of her lingers in my nose.

Chase looks confused, but he doesn't say anything until he closes in on her. "Hey, what are you doing out here? I was waiting for you at our table."

Annie looks down at her hands and her tray with what looks like guilt. "Mia wanted to sit outside. Sorry, I forgot to tell you."

Chase glances at me and then Cam. "Where's Mia?"

"There wasn't room at her table." Annie sinks back into her seat and offers, "I can go back inside with you. I'm done with lunch anyway."

Whatever light was on in Annie is off now. She's going through the fucking motions with this asshole. Why? Because he's rich and attractive? Because he could be a name some day? What is she using him for?

I didn't take her as a gold digger like her mother, but maybe the apple doesn't fall far from the tree.

What does he have that I don't? I'm probably worth more than that asshole. Definitely smarter. More attractive.

When he holds his hand out, she stands and grabs her tray. Before she leaves, she turns and looks at me with those blue-gray eyes. "I look forward to your audition."

He walks her back into the school. The thing he has that I currently don't is Annie.

But that's going to change.

CHAPTER 11

EvanAnn

"Why were you with those guys, EvanAnn?" Chase asks as I get rid of my tray.

He's right behind me as I turn around and look up into his blue eyes. My ear still tingles from Hawk's lips. The way he grabbed the back of my neck sent sparks flooding my system.

"I went out there with Mia." I shrug and turn to leave the cafeteria. "She found a spot, but there wasn't room for me. Hawk offered a place at his table, so I took it. I don't see what the problem is."

But I do. It shouldn't have been a problem, but Hawk and Cam sat close to me and talked to me the whole lunch period. That's not the problem though. They're attractive and I enjoyed being around them. What Chase wouldn't understand is that Hawk actually helped me out.

When the popular girls snatched Mia up, I stood there feeling lost.

Hawk saved me the embarrassment of turning around and going back inside. Chase doesn't know what it's like to be a lowly ant. Yes, he's Anteros too, but he's part of the in-crowd.

Chase belongs. If he wanted, he could have any seat out there. He did when he dated Abby. The only reason he sits inside is because of me.

I never should have gone out there with Mia. Should have told her I don't belong, but they made it so obvious I don't. There wasn't room. There's never room for me at their tables. It's a reminder.

Maybe in the future when I've earned the space by being a note-worthy director, I'll be included. But not right now. Not while I'm a lowly ant.

"I would have come out and sat with you if I'd known, babe." Chase wraps his arm around my shoulders and squeezes me against his side. "I don't mind sitting outside. I thought you liked sitting inside."

"I do." I glance up at him, feeling awful for soaking up the attention from those guys when I have this one who actually likes me. "I like sitting inside with you."

He grins and we head to our acting studio. Mia catches up to us.

"Hey." She glances at Chase before her blue eyes settle on me. "Are you okay? I'm really sorry about lunch. I didn't realize those girls would do that after clearly inviting both of us."

"It's okay." I shrug, because I don't really have any way to express to her that it's the social system. I knew better. She'll be part of the in-crowd because she's beautiful and talented, while I'm not talented in the same way. She'll be in front of the camera, while I stay behind it.

"No, it's not okay." She straightens. "I should have gone back inside with you. After all, you're my bestie." Her eyes meet mine and there's a little uncertainty there. "Right?"

I nod. For as long as she wants me. I may not be able to tell her about my future roommate, but she's still the only friend I have. Chase is always busy with his friends. And while I should spend more time with him, it isn't feasible with our schedules.

"Good." She releases a breath. "I'd say we should do dinner, but my brother is still here. This week only though. So next week make sure to pencil me in for whatever we should do around here after school."

"Practice for the plays will begin next week. Which means if you end up cast in my play, we'll see each other all the time." I give her a weak smile. "Until you get sick of me."

She smiles and hooks her arm in mine. "I won't get sick of you, Evan. Besides, I found out the first scrimmage for the hockey guys is on Saturday afternoon. It's not a real game, but it should be fun to watch. We should go."

"If it's Saturday, I can go with you guys." Chase squeezes my shoul-der. "I haven't really sized up our hockey team this year."

I smile even though I don't know how to feel about going to see the trio. By then I'll be all moved into my new room that's adjacent to Damon's. The Devils will be distracted with the game, so obviously it'll be me and Mia time. And apparently, Chase.

"We're still on for dinner with my parents, right?" Chase asks. When Mia goes into the classroom, he holds me back in the hallway.

Mia glances back at us before smiling and heading to her seat.

"Yeah, tomorrow." I look up at him. He really is classically handsome. His looks will take him far in an acting career. But when I look at him, there's no buzz of energy like when I'm around Hawk, Cam, or Damon.

Did I ever feel that same buzz with him? Maybe my anxiety around them is working overtime.

Chase cups my jaw and brushes his thumb over my cheek. It's nice, but it's nothing like when Hawk touched me last night or when Damon brushed my hair behind my ear. It's probably because I'm more familiar with Chase's touch now. It's comfortable.

He leans down until his lips are almost on mine. My instinct is to turn away. We're at school. This isn't the right time to kiss, but I don't move. Because I need to know. He touches his lips to mine and it's pleasant, but not earth shattering.

He lifts his head and smiles. "We definitely need to find some alone time this weekend, babe."

That could be all we need, some time together.

DAMON

It's late. The house is quiet, but I know Heather went to bed with my father. This woman has way more sticking power than the previous women my dad has brought home. But I've seen her house, and if I had her life, I'd do anything to keep a guy like my dad on the hook.

The only time I haven't seen her around the house was last week, when Dad was on a business trip. I don't think this one will run away if I look down on her or make snide comments. There's hunger in her eyes when she looks at my father.

Maybe it's for my dad. After all, he's in good shape and handsome. But it could be the lifestyle upgrade he offers her. It doesn't matter. She isn't like my mom, who was the partner my dad deserved. Anything less than her is caving to lust, which isn't acceptable.

Lust dies after it's slaked.

I go down the back stairs and out the door to the garage. I'd grab a motorcycle but they're too loud. While no one in this house will hear it or even care I'm out this late, when I drive up to Evan's, it might alert her, which I definitely don't want to do.

My black BMW M4 will be perfect for my late-night mission. When I get in, I set my black gloves and mask on the passenger seat, along with the cameras I intend to plant.

A slut like Evan should provide something for me to blackmail her with. Whether she's giving her boyfriend head or fucking him, it doesn't matter. A sex video spread around school would be social suicide for someone like Evan. And if her mom is at my place, I can almost guarantee Chase is at Evan's.

Pussy without having to be quiet. He should be all over that.

I admit she plays her role of the good girl perfectly. If I didn't know better, I would take her for a tight-lipped, little virgin. But no, there's definitely something naughty about EvanAnn. I'll never forget the image of her head in Chase's lap.

Maybe she's only giving it up to him.

I should have called the guys to come help with this, but fuck, I want this done without Evan even realizing I've been there.

Besides, they might not approve of cameras in her house. It might be the most boring video ever of her studying and packing. She is a straight A student, after all. But if there's a show, I'll make sure to loop them in.

I pull up beside her house, turning into the driveway to park toward the back, and shut off the car. Chase's car isn't here. Only Evan's beat-up Honda. The lights inside the house are all off. The street is noisy, even at this time of night. There's a highway not too far away, providing a steady stream of cars driving by. A truck that needs a tune-up pulls into the driveway a few doors down.

My car sticks out like a sore thumb. Fortunately, this neighborhood isn't the kind where someone would try to jack it. Still, I shouldn't leave it out here for long.

That's the part I don't understand. If Heather is at my house right now, why not bring her daughter? Why wait for Friday? Why leave her here all by herself where anyone can get to her? Is it so Evan can adjust to the thought of moving in with me?

I shake my head and slip on my black leather gloves. Yes, I'm dressed in all black and will look like a fucking criminal if I try to break in. But I had the forethought to grab Heather's keys.

She's not going to miss them until the morning when they'll already be returned to her purse. I slip out of the car and walk with confidence to the back door.

The cameras are in my pocket. All I have to do is install them where they aren't obvious, so Evan doesn't take them down right away. I slip into the tiny kitchen and wait to see if Evan is awake enough to hear someone come in. Hopefully, she'll assume it's her mother and return to sleep.

There's no sound anywhere in the house as I creep in. There's not much to Evan's house. Honestly, we could probably fit this house in our garage. Yes, I realize this is a lifestyle upgrade for both of these women, and they'll cling to it with both hands, but I'll manage to shake them loose.

I was a little surprised Evan didn't use her new status at school today. The new girl doesn't even seem to know. When they came out for lunch, I figured Evan would have spilled the good news to everyone, and assumed she'd be accepted now that she was rich-adjacent.

But it was Mia those bitches wanted to join them. Not Evan.

Instead, Evan looked like a puppy that had gotten kicked. Olivia nudged me and chuckled softly like I should watch the show. Evan kept her chin up, but even I realize how humiliating it would be to have to turn around and go back inside.

I sat back and waited to be entertained. But Hawk swooped in and rescued her. Fucking savior complex. I love my friend, but if he doesn't get over that shit, she's going to run right over him.

I move quietly into the living room and determine the angle I need to get most of the room with the camera, checking on my phone. It takes me a few more minutes to find somewhere to hide it before settling it into place. It's programmed to upload to the cloud where I'll get notifications when something is moving on the video feed.

The stairs to her bedroom are right there. Moonlight and streetlight pour through the windows, just enough to illuminate the way. I hesitate. It's a risk to go upstairs, but I can't seem to resist. Putting a camera in her room would be better than downstairs.

Though the single bed makes it difficult to have company over, I'm sure they manage. My friends are excited over the prospect of fucking the good girl, but I'm all about ruining her, ruining her boyfriend, and ruining her mother.

I want to prove to everyone she isn't who she pretends to be. I climb the stairs silently. Her door is shut and I don't know if the hinges will squeak when I open it. Holding my breath, I turn the knob and push the door open slowly, carefully.

I stand in the open doorway and breathe in her woodsy scent. She's asleep, her blond hair spread out on her pillow. Her blankets are kicked down by her feet, leaving her long legs bare, glistening white in the streetlight creeping through the curtains.

I'm not immune to her curves or how pretty she is. Not pretty enough to be popular at our school. But I'm not opposed to fucking her.

Her nightgown barely covers her white panties. Her eyes are closed. Realizing I'm standing there staring, I move toward her dresser. I need to get the camera placed before she becomes aware I'm here.

She's going to be packing soon. Or maybe she won't, since my dad is funding their move into our house. I set the camera. Part of me wants her to find it when she's packing, so she knows whoever planted it has pictures of her.

It's an invasion of privacy, but fuck, she's invading my life. She can handle a little intrusion. I walk toward her bed and glance back at the camera. It's hidden enough from this angle.

She lets out a little noise and shifts on the bed. Freezing in place, I turn to see if she's awake. I'm close enough that when her arm falls off the edge of the bed, her fingers brush against my jeans. But she doesn't wake up.

How deeply does she sleep? It's a curiosity, because she'll be sleeping next door to me soon. I've already made sure she won't have a way to lock me out. Will she not be able to sleep, worried I'll creep in on her, or will she sleep like the lamb she is? Ripe for the slaughter.

I study her face, soft and unaware. None of the usual worry shows on her face. I drag my gaze down her long neck to her breasts rising and falling in time with her steady breaths. Her nightgown shifted higher with her turn, showing off her white cotton bikini briefs.

Always playing the virgin. I shake my head, but my cock is hard. How long until I can have her under me? I have to play this carefully, so she doesn't misinterpret my intentions. But we need more information.

The cameras are only the beginning. I need something to hold over her, so she'll do whatever I want. I don't care if it's not fair or right. She and Chase took my future from me. Maybe I can get my future back on track, but I'll be a year behind now.

So I'll own her year to make up for my loss, and at the end of it, I'll make sure she's as broken as I am right now.

CHAPTER 12

EvanAnn

"EVANANN!" Chase's father reaches his hands out to take mine. "How wonderful that you could take time out of your busy schedule to come see us."

I smile and take his hand, while Chase holds my other. "Mr. Chadwick, thank you for having me over for dinner."

His grin grows as he releases my hand. "Please, call me Tom. Jess is on her way. We can wait for her in the sitting room."

I smooth my hand over my summer dress. It's a little worn because it's a favorite, but it's nicer than jeans and a t-shirt. I always feel like I need to dress up when I have dinner with Chase's parents.

Chase and I follow him into the sitting room. Unlike Damon's house that's covered in cold marble, Chase's house is full of rich wood paneling and comfortable-looking furniture. It puts me at ease.

"Have a seat." Tom sits on a chair and gestures to the loveseat. Before Chase sits, Tom adds, "Why don't you go grab a drink for your lovely girlfriend?"

Chase squeezes my hand before he heads out of the room.

Tom smiles and leans back in his chair. "So how has the first week back to school been? Are you ready for the auditions tomorrow for *Othello*?"

There's something easy about Chase's parents. Yes, they're ridiculously wealthy, but they seem genuinely interested in what I'm doing. Like they actually care about me.

"Classes seem reasonable. My calculus class is going to be a challenge and we're reading Shakespeare in English Lit to start. I'm excited to finally choose actors for my cast."

Chase walks back in with two glasses of soda. "I'm hoping I'm the best for Iago. I've been working on my audition piece."

Tom's smile grows. "If you're the best, then I'm sure EvanAnn will cast you. She knows when she has a good thing."

Chase hands me my drink and sits next to me. My cheeks flush at Tom's praise. Chase has been good to help me break out of my shell a little more. To help me be a little more confident with people my age, like Mia. I don't know if I would have been bold enough to try to make friends with her before Chase chose me to be his girlfriend.

"EvanAnn even made a new friend at the beginning of school." Chase takes my hand and threads our fingers together on his thigh. "New girl. Of course, EvanAnn wanted to take her under her wing."

"She must be a pretty lucky girl to find a friend like you." Tom stands as Jess comes in.

When I start to get up to greet her, Tom motions for me to sit. "Don't get up. We'll talk in here a little longer while they set the table next to the pool for dinner."

Chase invited me to come use the pool over the summer. I was able to make it over once. It was nice and relaxing. His parents were here then, so I didn't have to restate my boundaries to Chase.

"I'm so glad you were able to join us." Jess sits next to Tom.

"How could I resist, when you always have the best meals?" I say. Chase's parents are wealthy, but they don't look down on me.

We talk for a little while longer before someone comes in to say that the meal is served. When we stand, Chase takes my hand to lead me out to the table and even pulls out my chair.

I touch his hand lightly as he joins me. The conversation starts with school and the play, but then shifts to Tom's upcoming birthday party.

"I can't wait to introduce you to Sandra Cox." Tom sets his wine glass down.

My heart picks up pace. He can't mean... "The director?"

Tom glances at Jess as if he wanted it to be a surprise. "Yes, she's a dear friend and I want to introduce you to her. She's always looking for bright young minds to mentor, and I think you would be the perfect fit."

I'm literally speechless. My teachers do what they can to help me get connections for college, but Sandra Cox is in the industry. Having her as a mentor could open doors that would otherwise be closed to me.

Chase covers my hand on the table. "She's beyond thrilled."

Jess chuckles a little.

"Yes," I finally get out. "She's one of my favorite directors."

Tom grins. "Good. It should be a great party then."

I glance at Chase and he gives me a smile. I can't believe this is happening. Everything I've done has been to grow within my field. And Sandra Cox is someone I never thought I'd meet until I had a career, let alone be introduced to.

***

CAM

"Hey, man." I grab my teammate Fletcher's hand and we do our handshake as he holds the door to his house open for me.

"Where's your entourage?" Fletcher looks behind me into the dark night. It's only my bike parked out there with the cars.

"Riding solo tonight." It's Wednesday night. The others are busy.

"Nice." Fletcher bobs his head up and down.

He steps back and I walk into the house. He leads me down to the pool where there are about twenty other teens hanging out. It's a school night, and most students at Deimos can't afford to skip the work required to get good grades.

"Cooler's over there. Bathroom's on the first floor. No using the bedrooms." Fletcher winks.

I nod. "Just looking to chill tonight."

My dad's been on a tear about my grades. How do I expect to attend Yale with grades like mine? I can't tell him Yale's not my priority. It's his. Instead, I took off. Hawk has homework and Damon has extra strength training tonight, so I'm on my own.

Fletcher grabs a beer out of the cooler and hands it to me. I thank him and head toward a handful of teammates where they're spread out around the fire pit. It's a great angle to watch the girls in the pool from.

"You good, Cam?" Liam asks as I take a seat.

"Yeah. You?"

Liam smirks. "Been eying the candy and hoping to get a piece tonight."

His gaze strays to the pool which is filled with mostly girls in bikinis. But not the one that's been on my fucking mind. I don't know if it was Damon putting it into my head, but now that we're going after Evan-Ann, I'm all in.

Tonight I needed somewhere to relax and to not argue about my future and the poor choices I'm making. If I wanted a piece, I'm sure there would be a willing chick, but I'm going to hold out for the main event with EvanAnn. After all, I've already messed around with most of these girls. Fucked a few of them.

"You got one picked out?" I ask, taking a pull from the bottle. It's cold, refreshing, and exactly what I need. I might not have my future all plotted out like Damon or Hawk, but I also don't have to miss out on shit like this. Relaxing and hanging out with my friends.

Fletcher takes a seat and scoffs. "He was going after Bristol, but Chadwick beat him to it."

"Fucking Chadwick." Liam shakes his head.

"Chase?" I ask, sitting up and looking over the couples making out on the couch. Not that there's another Chadwick in the school. Is that fucker cheating on his girlfriend? Or did they already break up?

Because if it's the first one, I'll make sure EvanAnn finds out and blows him up. Then I'll offer to be her revenge sex because there's nothing hotter than revenge sex. And if they already broke up, I'm going to lobby the others to accelerate our plan. Because this is fucking dragging.

"Yeah." Fletcher points to where Bristol straddles Chase. Her long, manicured fingernails poke out of his hair as she grinds on him while they mouthfuck.

"You didn't offer them a room?" I ask and sit back. This makes things interesting. I'd take a pic to send the others, but it's kind of a code not to take pics at parties. There are too many future senators and judges in this school. Everyone wants to let their hair down and not regret it later in life.

"And miss the show?" Fletcher laughs and I hold my beer to him. He taps his against mine and we both take a drink.

Chase fumbles between them for a moment and Bristol lifts before sinking down. Her skirt covers them enough, but it's obvious what they're doing. Fuck, it's free porn. Much better than arguing about how I'll be an embarrassment to the family if I go to a state school.

"The guy has a type." Liam leans forward. "Blonds. What's the name of the girl he hangs out with at school? The cute nerdy girl?"

"EvanAnn." Her name slips from my lips, but I watch Liam. Is he looking to make a play for her? He called her cute.

He snaps his fingers. "That's right. She's got a tight little body. I bet she's a fucking wildcat in the sack. It's always the quiet ones who surprise you."

"I doubt he's seeing much action from her though." Fletcher leans back and adjusts his cock. His eyes never leave Bristol and Chase, fucking on the couch.

"How do you figure?" I ask.

"Chase spends most of his time at parties without her. He only brings her around once in a while." Fletcher shakes his head. "But he's always goofing off with his friends instead of paying attention to her. And anytime he's at a party without her, he's getting his dick wet by some other girl."

What a fucker. I was all for getting revenge by taking EvanAnn away from him, but now it's my mission to make him regret being a dick to her behind her back. Maybe I'll have her ride my cock at a party where he can watch what he can no longer have.

I stop paying attention to them fucking and get my phone out.

ME:

He's still a manwhore

HAWK:

What the fuck are you talking about?

ME:

Chase. He's fucking Bristol right in front of me

DAMON:

Take a pic

ME:

That's a fucking party foul

HAWK:

Don't make it obvious

Fuck. I flick over to camera and start recording. I lift my phone enough to get Chase and Bristol in the shot before stopping and changing back to the text messages.

ME:

Did my best

DAMON:

Good

ME:

She there?

DAMON:

Fuck yeah. She's always here

I close out and slide my phone into my pocket. EvanAnn's mom. She spends most evenings at Damon's, even though that leaves EvanAnn all alone in that house. I know her prick of a boyfriend isn't over there keeping her company. Which, what the fuck, man.

He could be over there without an audience, having her give him everything he needs. I don't understand this asshole.

"They coming out?" Fletcher asks.

I shake my head. "Nah."

I hang out for an hour before I get tired of watching others fuck and talking shit about people and sports. When I get on my bike and strap on my helmet, I don't want to go home.

Fuck it.

I ride over to EvanAnn's house. Her mom's car still isn't here. I park and lift my helmet off. Her light is on up in her room that smells like her. Nothing quite smells like EvanAnn. How can that asshole have access to her and fuck someone else?

The steps to her porch creak beneath my feet. This place isn't great, but the neighborhood is okay. I ring the doorbell and run my hand through my hair. I have no fucking clue what I'm doing.

Part of me needed to see her, so I'm here. I could stand outside like a creeper and wait for her to step in front of her window, or I could fucking knock on the door like a normal person.

She opens the door and her blue eyes widen when she sees it's me. When she doesn't open the door all the way, I smile. She's learning.

"What are you doing here, Cam?"

I shrug. "Was at a party and got bored."

"You were at a party on a Wednesday night?" Her eyebrow arches.

That's pretty judgmental. I bet she doesn't know her boy is at that party right now. I should show her the video. Tell her what her boy's been up to.

"You still dating Chase?"

"Had dinner with him and his parents tonight. Why?" She gives me a suspicious look.

I'm not the suspicious fucker here. But she apparently doesn't know.

"Can I come in?" Fuck, say yes.

"I don't think that's a good idea." She glances behind her at what I know is an empty house.

"Come on, goody two-shoes." I move closer to the door, and she tips her chin up to meet my eyes. She's so tiny, I could probably lift her out of the way. My fingers itch to move her exactly how I want her. "Live a little. Let me in."

She bites her lip in a way that makes me want to kiss it better.

"Your mom's not home. You've got to be sick of being alone." I lean in the open doorway. "I promise to behave."

"I actually like being alone," she says, and it sounds like she means it. Fuck, maybe she does.

"Maybe I'm lonely."

She narrows her eyes. "Didn't you come from a party?"

I grin. "You weren't there."

"What does that have to do with it?" She straightens.

"The only one I wanted to see tonight is right here." I shrug, like it doesn't matter. "So here I am. A guy. Standing in a door. Hoping the girl I like will let me in."

She makes a face. "That's not the quote."

"I improvised." My hair slips down over my eyes. Girls always fall for my sweet act. "You got something better to do than hang out with me for..." I glance at my phone. "Thirty minutes?"

"I have a boyfriend."

And he was fucking some other girl and doesn't deserve your fucking loyalty. But I can't tell her. Damon wants to wait until the right time. We're all pawns in Damon's game.

"All I want is to talk or hang out while you do whatever you need to do." I blow out a breath. "I don't want to go home."

She opens the door a little more. "Why don't you want to go home?"

"My dad's on me about college and his big plans for my future." I reach out for the door. "So what do you say, goody two-shoes? Wanna let me in?"

CHAPTER 13

EvanAnn

I SHOULD SAY NO. I should say no and close the door. But then he gives me this look like he's a little lost, which makes me open the door and step back. He straightens and I forgot how fucking tall he is as he steps into my house and shuts us in.

I swallow, suddenly feeling more vulnerable than when all three of them were in my house.

"Thanks." He keeps walking and heads into my kitchen. He opens the refrigerator and sighs.

It's pretty bare. I walk over and open the freezer. I grab a frozen pizza and set it on the counter before walking to the oven to preheat it. Even though I ate earlier, I could use a snack.

"You gonna cook for me, goody two-shoes?" He grins as he rests his hip on the counter beside me, looking down with those brown eyes. His flirting is easier to take than Hawk's touching and Damon's scowling.

"It's not really cooking." I shrug. Not sure why I thought feeding him would be a good idea. Or why I even let him into my house.

He's right though. I am lonely. Mia's with her brother. I'm not sure what Chase is doing, but he didn't even ask to stay when he dropped me off after dinner. Mom's always at her boyfriend's. And I'm still freaking out about having to move in with Damon Storm in a few days. Not to mention, auditions are tomorrow.

My stomach is a mess of butterflies that don't seem to know how to fly straight.

"So, what are we doing while we wait?" Cam gives me this smoldering look.

"I was going over my homework for tomorrow." I could have offered him anything. Maybe watch a movie or an episode of some show, but I honestly don't know what to do with Cam Warwick.

"Mind if I sit with you?" He gives me a half smile. "I promise I can be quiet."

I shrug. He definitely surprised me by showing up, but I could have kept him out. He wasn't forcing his way inside and maybe that's why I let him in.

He didn't barge in. He asked.

I walk into the living room, pick my book up from the coffee table, and return to my seat on the couch. Cam sits on the other end and pulls out his phone. When he doesn't try anything or even start a conversation, I read through the next few pages of my textbook before the oven dings to let me know it's preheated.

I walk into the kitchen and unwrap the pizza, sliding it in the oven before setting the timer. Will I even be able to do this at Damon's house? They had a staff of people in the kitchen. I doubt they even have frozen pizza.

I glance toward the living room. Fuck it. I need to talk to someone. I can't tell Mia or Chase about what's happening. I thought about talking to Chase on the way home, but he had the music turned up loud. Mom is still floating on cloud nine, and I don't want to bring her down.

When I return to the couch, I drop my book on the coffee table. Cam lifts his gaze. When he realizes my attention is on him, he sets his phone on his lap.

"Have you been to Damon's house?" I ask, picking at the strings of my sweatpants.

"Of course." He's waiting for me to ask another question.

I lift my gaze to his. "Is your house the same?"

"In size?" He shrugs.

"Do you have a kitchen staff?" I blurt out.

He chuckles and leans in. "No, but we do have a cook. I don't think they ever buy frozen pizza though."

"Probably not." I pull my knees into my body, wrapping my arms around them and putting my feet on the edge of the couch. I'm used to doing everything for myself, to being left on my own to figure things out. What will it be like to have others to do everything for me?

"You worried about living there?" Cam asks. His eyes are soft. He's not being cruel. He seems genuinely curious.

"A little." When he raises an eyebrow, I admit, "A lot. This is the nicest house I've lived in." I gesture to our house.

He glances around. "It's definitely going to be an adjustment. Are you afraid of change, goody two-shoes?"

I shrug and look away. "All we had was change until this house. My dad died and we moved into one apartment after another. A couple years ago, Mom managed to rent this house. It felt like we were finally settled and now everything's changing again."

He makes a humming noise.

God, I enjoyed being settled. I'm not ready for the change. I'm comfortable. This is home.

"Your mom didn't talk to you about it?" Cam's brown eyes search mine.

A little laugh bursts out of me and everything pours out. "I found out Monday and then suddenly I was at dinner with Adam Storm. Before that night, I didn't even know the name of the guy she was dating or that he was Damon's dad. How the hell did my mom land Damon's dad? And then they're showing us around, and he looks like he really likes her and she really likes him, so what am I going to do? Complain?"

I take a breath, but Cam doesn't interrupt.

"It's not like I can tell Chase I'm moving in with Damon Storm. He didn't even like when I sat near you in class, and then yesterday at lunch..." I stand and begin to pace. Suddenly, I have way too much energy flowing through me. All these things I've bottled up inside are spilling out. Because Cam knows. Yes, he's the enemy, but right now, he's the only one I can talk to. "And I have a new friend, Mia. But she wants to sleep with you guys, so I can't tell her I have access. I want her to like me for me, not because I can get her close to Damon."

I cover my eyes. "It's all too much."

Cam rises and I drop my hands to look up at him. "That's a lot, EvanAnn."

I smile and shrug. "And I have the play, and all the decisions I have to make for it, and everyone I'll disappoint if I don't do a good job."

Cam reaches out and puts his hand on my shoulder. "We should go for a ride. That's what I do when I need to clear my head."

The timer rings in the kitchen. I step around him to get to the pizza. What am I doing? I can't believe I spilled all of that to Cam. He must think I'm insane.

He comes in while I'm cutting the pizza.

"Plates are over there." I gesture to the cabinet.

He doesn't say anything but grabs two plates. When he stops beside me, he holds them out. I put a few slices on his and one slice on mine. I lead the way back into the living room.

Setting the plate on my lap, I lift my gaze to his as he resumes his seat and takes a bite of the hot pizza.

"I didn't mean to unload all that on you," I say quietly and look at my pizza. "I guess I'm a little lonely."

"I was surrounded by people tonight and never felt more alone." Cam's words make me look up to see if he's making fun of me. His eyes are sincere. "My dad wants me to go to Yale. It's all he talks about anymore. And that's all good for him, but I don't want to go to Yale. I don't want to go someplace exactly like Deimos where, if I don't study twenty-four seven, I'll fall behind. It's too much pressure. I want to go to Crowne Mawr where maybe I'll be able to play on their hockey team and join a fraternity and actually enjoy college. It's the last time in my life I'll be free to just be. After that, I'll have a job and responsibilities."

I take a bite and chew thoughtfully for a minute. "Do you think he'll understand your decision?"

He shrugs and finishes his slice. "When I don't get into Yale, he won't have a choice but to let me go where I want."

"How do you know you won't get into Yale?" I ask, glad to have someone else's problem to listen to. Mine aren't going away. I know we're moving on Friday, but it's not something in my control. It just *is*.

Cam smirks. "Trust me, goody two-shoes, I'm not Yale material. Everyone knows it except my dad."

We finish the pizza in silence. After I finish my slice, he goes and gets me another and fills up his plate with the remaining. When I've had enough, I set my plate on the coffee table and pick up my book to read a little more.

"You done?" Cam asks after a while. I look up from my book and he's reaching for my plate. There's still half a slice pizza on it.

"Yeah, I'm done."

He nods and takes his plate and mine into the kitchen, setting them on the counter. When he comes back in, he puts his hands in his pockets and looks at me. Those butterflies start rioting again at the soft smile on his face.

He gestures with his head toward the door. "Walk me out?"

Somehow, I thought the thirty minutes wasn't so much a deadline, but rather a way to convince me to let him in. It doesn't feel as lonely with Cam sitting near me. I set my book down and follow him to the door. He opens it and looks down at me.

"Thank you for the pizza," he says.

"Sorry for dumping my issues on you." I wring my hands in front of me. "You aren't going to tell Damon what I said, are you?"

He shakes his head and smirks. "Nah, that's between you and me."

He reaches out with his hand and tips my chin up with his knuckle. Sparks light beneath his touch, and I'm too shocked to back away. He searches my eyes and gives me a smile that makes those butterflies drunk little bastards.

"I mean it about the ride, goody two-shoes." He steps away and I miss the warmth of him as he walks down to his bike. "Anytime you need to let loose. You call me."

"I don't have your number." It's not what I should say, but it's the only thing my brain thinks of.

Smirking, he straddles his bike. "I'll make sure you get it then."

CHAPTER 14
EvanAnn

"Are you ready for auditions?" Ms. Murphy asks as I enter the auditorium. She's one of our instructors for the directing seminars.

My fingers shake a little, but I'm ready. "Yes."

It's a school-wide open casting call, but we rarely get students from outside the theater department, especially for plays like *The Crucible* and *Othello*. Musicals will generally draw some of the vocal students, and every now and then a Deimos student will wander our way, but it isn't often.

Ms. Murphy nods and guides me toward the table in the black box theater room. Brandt sits there with his laptop open. I sit in the other chair at the table and take out my notebook and a few pens.

"You know, I can pretty much have my pick of the actors who are about to perform for us." Brandt leans back and glances at me. "You'll get Chase because he's your fuck buddy."

I glare at him. Fuck him and his misogynistic crap.

"I've been kissing up to Mia. She would have been perfect as your Desdemona, wouldn't she?" Brandt gloats and looks at his screen.

There are a lot of things I wish I could say to Brandt, but we'll see where the players fall after casting. If Mia decides *The Crucible* is better for her as an actress, there isn't anything I can do to change her mind. I hope she'll want to stay friends.

"Are you two ready?" Mr. Watson comes out and stands in front of us.

I nod and Brandt says, "Yes."

"We're hoping to cast tonight and not have to do callbacks." Mr. Watson turns to look at the door where the actors wait in the hallway to be let in one at a time. "Everyone has a monologue prepared as well as the sides to read for each director. We have a great turn out, meaning this is going to take some time. So if either of you needs a break during, let us know between actors. We start in two minutes."

I draw in a breath, like I'm the one about to audition, and center myself. Each of the characters I have to cast float through my head. The critical ones are Othello, Iago, Desdemona, Cassio, and Emilia. The problem is any actor at this school could step into these roles and make them their own.

But I need them to lose themselves in the part until I can't separate them from their character. And to have that chemistry to play off each other. That's why I'm hesitant to cast Chase as Iago, the most manipulative, gaslighting villain of the play.

I don't know if I want to think of my boyfriend like that. But if he performs and I can visualize it, I'll give him the part. But not because he's my boyfriend. He has to earn his spot like everyone else.

I inhale and open my eyes.

"Do you want my list ahead of time, so you don't embarrass yourself and pick my actors?" Brandt slides a sheet of paper my way. "Might save you some time tonight."

"No, thank you." I look Brandt in his eyes and smile. This is my night to cast and I'm not going to let him under my skin.

He chuckles. "Your loss. You'll be up until midnight trying to recast, but you do what you want, EvanAnn."

The door opens. The first person walks into the room. The first audition is Abby Baker. She performs her monologue and then switches to my sides for *Othello*. Her delivery is flat, like she isn't even trying. I'm honestly not surprised. On *The Crucible*, she takes on the hardest part of Abigail Williams, the villain, and makes it her own.

Brandt winks at her as she leaves the stage. That one I expected, so it doesn't surprise me. Abby doesn't want to work with me any more than

I want to work with her. But honestly, if she'd tried, she could have had a shot at a lead. None of the women in my play are villains, so I put her down as one of the supporting cast if she doesn't get a part in Brandt's play.

It may not be what I want, but there's an understanding that we're encouraged to cast seniors in our plays when we can.

Crystal and Becca go next. While it feels like they're both trying for *The Crucible*, Crystal actually gives an excellent audition for *Othello*. I might be able to cast her for Iago's wife, Emilia, or Bianca.

The other students come in and I continue to fill up my sheet with potentials, moving people down or adding alternatives. Mark Green is my lead. When he performs Othello, people will stand up and take notice. He's brilliant. I hope he chooses my production over Brandt's.

Then Mia comes in.

Brandt smirks and crosses his arms as he watches her deliver her monologue. The sides she chose are for Desdemona. She hits it out of the park, and when she finishes, she smiles.

We've talked the past couple nights on the phone. Her brother Tanner is still in town and I don't know what to tell her when she wants to come over next week. It's not like I can keep that I'm living at Damon's a secret from her, but I can try.

She gives an equally stunning performance of Elizabeth Proctor. Two very different characters.

My guess is she'll have her pick between the roles. I hope she picks mine.

A few auditions later, Chase walks in. He gives me a smile and a wink. Will Brandt even try to cast him as a lead, or has he figured Chase would go for mine over his?

Chase chose to do one of Iago's monologues for his main monologue. I have to admit, he's good. There's a devilish delight in his tone that makes his eyes light up.

After his performance, Mr. Watson gives us a ten-minute break. I hurry to the bathroom, having flooded my body with caffeine to stay alert during auditions. It's been hard to sleep, knowing I'm moving in days. I'm about to flush when some girls walk in.

"Did you see who's auditioning?" Crystal's voice rises in pitch.

"Calm down," Abby says. "Hawk Wilker can have whatever role he wants from me."

"You have a better chance with Cam." Becca laughs. "Besides, didn't you fuck Hawk sophomore year?"

"Yeah, so?" Abby sounds nonchalant. "I could have him again. All I need to do is get Brandt to cast him. Maybe some nobody role."

"He could just stand on the stage and smile." Becca's voice is dreamy.

The girls giggle.

I wait until the door closes behind them before coming out of the stall to wash my hands. Hawk said he was going to audition. I didn't really believe it at the time because it sounded like another way to mess with me. He did say he performed *Shakespeare in the Park* on a dare. I shiver as I wash my hands and look up into the mirror.

Dark smudges rest under my eyes. Mia tried to help me cover them up again this morning. My hair is pulled into a hasty bun. My whole current look says frumpy, sleep-deprived teen.

It's not like he hasn't already seen me today. We had history together where we had no time to talk because we had to take notes.

I shake off the dread creeping over me and return to the black box theater. Hawk can't be better than the actors who have been studying for years. There's nothing to worry about. He'll come in. Brandt will find a way to cast him, which will fulfill Hawk's need for an extracurricular. And we'll all be happy.

When I sit down, Brandt is talking on his phone. "I mean, I might end up the laughing stock of the theater department if I cast him, but think of all the girls he'll attract opening night. The guy doesn't even need to be good. Maybe I can cast him as an extra. He could stand on stage as a guard or something."

Brandt glances at me dismissively before he returns to his phone call. "I'll talk to you about it later."

I roll my eyes. There are no guards in *The Crucible*. Of course Brandt wouldn't consider the actual performance over the draw of the actors in it. What if Hawk is awful? Would Brandt still cast him? Better him than me.

I already see too much of Hawk. If I cast him, I'll see him so much more. Of course, he's not the problem in the trio. Damon is the real issue, and starting tomorrow, I can't get away from him if I want to.

"Ready to start?" Mr. Watson steps in to ask.

We both give him a thumbs up.

The door closes and opens again. Hawk walks into the room like he owns it. He nods to Brandt and gives me a smile. My heart flutters. I can almost hear him calling me Annie.

"I'm Hawk Wilker and I'll be performing a monologue from *Romeo and Juliet*."

I clasp my hands together as he lowers his head for a moment. When he looks up, his expression is a little lost as he begins, "'Tis torture, and not mercy: heaven is here, Where Juliet lives; and every cat and dog, And little mouse, every unworthy thing, Live here in heaven and may look on her; But Romeo may not."

My heart clenches as those green eyes lock with mine. It's not the part I thought he'd do. He holds me captivated by his words, his voice, his whole being. The despair.

"More validity, More honorable state, more courtship lives. In carrion-flies than Romeo: they may seize on the white wonder of dear Juliet's hand and steal immortal blessing from her lips, Who even in pure and vestal modesty, Still blush, as thinking their own kisses sin; But Romeo may not; he is banished."

The pain he projects over Romeo finding out he has to leave his love is so enrapturing, I truly forget he's playing a part. It could be the intimacy of his constant eye contact with me.

"Flies may do this, but I from this must fly; They are free men, but I am banished; And say'st thou yet that exile is not death? Hadst thou no poison mix'd, no sharp-ground knife, No sudden mean of death, though ne'er so mean, But 'banished' to kill me? 'Banished'? O friar, the damned use that word in hell; Howlings attend it: how hast thou the heart, Being a divine, a ghostly confessor, A sin-absolver, and my friend profess'd, To mangle me with that word 'banished'?"

He lowers his head and I release my breath. I squirm in my seat. Fuck, he's good. And he did *Shakespeare in the Park* on a dare?

I barely noticed when Brandt straightened about halfway through the performance, clearly impressed. Now that Hawk's proven he's actually a performer *and* a potential draw for the audience, Brandt wants to sink his claws into him. Hawk clears his throat.

"I only prepared the sides for *Othello*." He looks at Brandt. "I can read yours from the pages if you'd like."

Brandt smirks. "Sure, man, whatever you need."

Hawk nods and when he recites Cassio's lines, I can see him as the young lieutenant who Iago is jealous of. It's not a large part, but it would fit Hawk. He's everything Cassio is. Smart. Handsome. Privileged.

With a smaller part, he would be able to miss practices without compromising the production schedule. I'll have to keep his schedule in mind when deciding when we rehearse certain scenes.

Hawk reads the sides Brandt hands him.

Even reading, Hawk is good. He probably could have tried out for Anteros and gotten in if he desired. He wants this for his college transcript, to help round him out. And now that I've seen him perform, I can't think of anyone I'd want to cast more for the part.

Which sucks, because it means I'll see more of Hawk.

I'd written down a few possible actors during the auditions, but they don't compare. Maybe someone after him will be better.

I wish I could have brushed him off, but as the rest of the auditions proceed, my mind keeps coming back to his performance. There's a junior, Sofia, who I write down next to Crystal for one of two parts.

After the last person leaves, Mr. Watson approaches us. "Do you need more time?"

"I'm good." Brandt pulls out his list with a name scratched off and Hawk replacing it. I want to roll my eyes, but I don't.

"I could use a moment." I don't lift my head from the list I'm putting together. In my mind, I can see them all still standing in front of me. I try to put them together in my head. The way their performances might complement each other.

"Take your time," Mr. Watson says.

"I'm heading out. You'll email us any changes?" Brandt stands.

"Yes."

The door closes as he leaves. And then it's only me and Mr. Watson.

"What are you deliberating over?" Mr. Watson takes Brandt's seat.

I sigh. "How do I know I've picked the right person for the parts? How do I know the chemistry will be there when they take the stage, and it won't fall flat?"

Mr. Watson smiles. "You don't. That's part of being a director. You have to take the actor's jagged edges and smooth them out so they fit together."

"Do you think it would be crazy to cast Hawk Wilker as Cassio? Maybe I should give it to Jason instead?" I tap my pen on the paper in front of me.

"You want to talk it out?" It's something he says in class. It's a way to work through the problem verbally, without judgment.

I sit back and stare at the doors. "Hawk is..."

"A lot?" Mr. Watson laughs. "You aren't as familiar with him as an actor as most of the students in the program."

"Exactly." I turn and meet his brown eyes. "What if he really isn't as good as I think? What if I cast him, and he doesn't take it seriously because he's only doing it to pad his college resume?"

"It's always a possibility." Mr. Watson leans back in his chair. "But what if he does?"

I almost groan because remembering his performance makes me more inclined to cast him. If he does get up on stage, he will own Cassio. I know it.

"He's perfect for Cassio. It's like he was made for the part." I sigh. "But he has hockey and school..."

"And those are his problems to work around. Sometimes we have to take a chance on someone, but we don't need to put all our eggs in one basket. For him, I would cast an understudy. He could get injured during hockey or have a conflict. But if he's who you really want..."

Something warm flutters in my stomach. That's part of the problem, but I'm not about to tell a teacher I want Hawk. It's confusing and weird, and I'm already dating someone so it's completely illogical and never going to happen.

But I know what's best for the play, and honestly, he's the best Cassio. And given Chase's reactions to Hawk already, the bite of jealousy Iago feels for Cassio might be easy for them to feed into. I'll also take Mr. Watson's advice, and give the understudy role to Jason, a senior, who would need a part in the performance.

"Thank you, Mr. Watson." I finish writing on my sheet and hand it to him.

"Anytime, EvanAnn. Honestly, I was pushing for you to be a director this season. You've come a long way from where you started as a freshman. You have the potential to go far in this business."

My cheeks flush with heat. His words mean everything to me.

I take a breath. "Now what?"

He sets our lists out side by side. "Now to make sure we don't have any conflicts. You can go. I'll call if I find something that needs to be resolved. Otherwise, I'll email you both the list in the morning and post it at lunch."

I bite my lip. Part of me wants to stay, but I'd just hover nervously. I grab my backpack.

"Good night, Mr. Watson."

"Night." He waves and I head to the doors leading out into the hall-way. It's late, so I'm not expecting anyone to be here. The lights are bright, reflecting off the white tiles. I walk out and the doors shut behind me.

"Hey."

I shriek and turn to see Hawk leaning against the wall. He holds up his hands and smiles.

"Didn't mean to freak you out."

I put my hand over my racing heart. "What are you still doing here?"

There's no one else here. The hallway is empty. If he's here, there should be a few stray girls hanging around to get close to him.

He shrugs. "I get a little rush when I perform. I wasn't ready to leave. When I saw Brandt head out, I figured you'd be on your own in the parking lot. So I stayed to walk you out."

"Oh. That's nice of you." I don't know what else to say. It's unex-pected, but actually a nice thought.

"Come on. Let's get out of here." He walks toward the door and I hurry to catch up. Outside, it's dark and the lights are on in the parking lot, but I feel safer with Hawk beside me.

As we get close to my car, I can tell something is off. My Honda is listing to the right.

"Flat tire? Do you have a spare?" Hawk walks over and squats next to the tire.

Fuck. When he looks up at me, I press my hands to my eyes.

"Pretty sure that is the spare."

ANNIE NIBBLES ON HER LIP. "I can call my mom or go ask Mr. Watson for a ride home."

"Nah, I've got you." I back away from her with a smirk because this means I get to have Annie on my motorcycle. It wasn't my plan, but I can't see anything wrong with her wrapped tight around me. Which was my plan, but not likely to happen.

"That's probably not a good idea." She glances at her bare legs. The skirt isn't ideal for riding, but I've given other girls rides home from school.

I pause and shrug. "Why? I have a means of getting you home. I promise to take it slow and bring you straight there."

"Did you ride today?" she asks and starts toward me. "Do you even have a spare helmet?"

"Of course, Annie."

"My name is EvanAnn." She sounds a little disgruntled.

I smirk, loving how I get under her skin, and wait for her to catch up before draping my arm over her shoulders. "I think Annie fits better."

She doesn't shrug me off, but she tenses beneath my touch. I don't tell her the real reason I waited for her, because she definitely would run back inside and not go anywhere alone with me.

All this energy needs an outlet, and the only girl I want is currently walking with me to my motorcycle. I won't do anything she doesn't want me to, but I'm willing to encourage her in any way possible.

Other girls were waiting with me at first, until they realized I didn't want any of them. I could have slaked my lust with my pick of those girls, but it wouldn't be as fulfilling as fucking Annie.

Unfortunately, what we've discovered about Annie this week is she's loyal to her fucker of a boyfriend who isn't loyal to her. We've asked around, and multiple people have confirmed he's fucking around behind her back. We double-checked with the actual girls people said he fucked, and confirmed he hasn't given up his fuckboy ways.

Does Annie know? Is she okay with it? Is that part of their deal as a couple? That's what we don't know. Because if it's a secret and she has no idea, we can blow that shit up at the right time.

Will she be broken up by it? Or will she want revenge? Because revenge sex is awesome. I'd vote for revenge sex.

"So, Chase Chadwick," I say.

She tilts her face up to study me, but doesn't say anything.

"How'd that happen?"

"What?" she asks. Her eyes narrow.

"How'd you two become a couple?"

She shrugs and looks away. "We were paired together in an acting class in the spring. He said he liked me for a while and we kind of fell into a relationship."

We get to my bike and I unlock my bag from it. When I take my spare helmet out and offer it to Annie, she hesitates.

"What are you going to wear?" She looks up at me with those big blue eyes. Fuck, everything about her screams innocence, but we know it's a lie, a front she puts on. Chase holds onto her for a reason. Maybe it's her time of the month. Maybe she makes him work to get a taste of that pussy.

She's a fucking temptress dressed in lamb's clothing.

How long will she keep up the innocent act? How long before she gives in to that heat in her eyes and burns with me?

I tap my helmet, where I have it locked on the handlebars.

She still looks skeptical. I turn my spare helmet over and show her the padded inside.

"It has Bluetooth, so you'll be able to talk to me during the ride. We'll stay on side streets. I won't go fast." I reach out and brush a strand of hair behind her ear. I want to feel her wrapped tight around me. Her thighs clenching the outside of mine. If I don't get to have sex with her tonight, this will be a good substitute. It will have to be enough. "Your house isn't far."

She shivers and her eyes widen. "On second thought, I could go ask Mr. Watson or call my mom to come pick me up."

That's the last thing I want.

"Never ridden before?" I ask.

She shakes her head and my cock twitches. I'm more than willing to be Annie's first ride on a motorcycle.

"It's not difficult. If I could get up on stage and perform for you and that asshole Brandt, surely you can do this, Annie." I lean in and she sucks in a breath, but doesn't move back. She searches my eyes. "You aren't afraid, are you?"

Some resolve strengthens inside of Annie. "I'm not afraid."

"Good." I step in close and smile when she holds her ground. If nothing else, Annie has been able to keep me on my toes. I lift the helmet to put on her head. When she reaches for it, I say, "It needs adjusting and it can be tricky the first time."

Her blue eyes are wide as they look up at me. For a moment, I think she's going to back out again. Instead, she gives me a nod.

Before I lower the helmet onto her head, I need her to know some safety rules. "Don't lean with me on the curves, hold on tight, and stay centered on the seat."

There's a little worry in her eyes, but her lips press together and she gives me a tight little nod.

"Help me settle this on you, Annie." I slide the helmet on her head, and she reaches up to help me guide it down. I have the face shield open. When it's down over her face, I lean down to fix the chin strap.

She draws in a harsh breath as my fingers brush her neck. When I glance up at her eyes, her gaze is fixed over my shoulder, but her lip is caught in her teeth. I take my time to make sure the strap is in place, maybe a little longer than needed, before backing away to grab my helmet.

She shifts on her feet, tugging a little at her skirt like that'll somehow turn it into pants, while I put on my helmet. She's adorable. But easily overlooked in these schools filled with gorgeous girls who are born to be future influencers, models, and actors.

"Be careful not to rest your legs on the metal." I meet her eyes. "I'd hate to burn your skin."

I'd promise to kiss it better, but she's a skittish doe, ready to bolt at the first sign of danger.

She nods, not used to the additional weight of the helmet. I palm the side of her helmet. That worried look enters her eyes again as she searches mine. I make sure the Bluetooth is on in our helmets and close the face shield on hers.

"Can you hear me?" I ask.

"Yes," she says.

"Good. I'll get on first and then you climb on behind me." I show her where she can put her feet.

"Okay."

I straddle the bike and raise the kickstand. "Your turn, Annie."

She glances over her shoulder like her tire will suddenly not be flat. Things are going my way and I didn't even need to do anything to make it happen. Tonight, Annie's mine.

Evan Ann

My stomach twists in knots as I wish things would go my way for once. But maybe they are. After all, I would have had to call my mom or ask Mr. Watson for a ride if Hawk wasn't here. Both would have taken time.

I'm not at all convinced riding Hawk's motorcycle in my school uniform is a good idea. He watches me, I think. As much as I can tell with his helmet swiveled my way. The black visor is practically reflective.

I could back out. I could call my mom. Maybe even Chase could come to pick me up.

Thinking about Chase makes those knots twist even more. I'm

about to ride with another guy. Maybe I should call Chase, but he didn't wait for me to make sure I got to my car. Hawk did.

"Come on, Annie." His words are in the helmet, surrounding me.

I'm already burning up from him being close and having his fingers on my neck were like fire on my skin. I'm about to climb on the back of his bike, where there's barely a seat for me, wrap my arms around his waist, and breathe him in.

His voice and scent surround me, and soon I'll have his warm body pressed against mine. This seems like a horrible idea, even as sparks tingle inside me.

"You can be in control, baby girl."

Fuck. The way he says that makes my knees weak. How can I like it when he calls me that, but when Chase calls me *babe*, it irritates the crap out of me? I shouldn't be anywhere near this boy. He messes with my equilibrium.

"If you want me to slow down, I'll slow down. I want to get you home safe and sound."

His words are meant to calm me, and they do, in a way, but they're also keying me up. Something about him makes everything in me sit up and pay attention.

I can't stand out here all night. Besides, it would be cool to know what it feels like to ride on a bike. Especially after what Cam said the other day. It's definitely a main character moment and not a quirky best friend moment.

I step in close and look at what I need to do. Which isn't easy in the helmet.

"Do you see the footrest?" His voice in my helmet makes me feel like he's in my head instead.

A shiver runs through me. I put my left foot on the footrest.

"Hold onto my shoulders, baby girl, and swing your other leg around."

I think I liked Annie better, because fuck, those words make me want things I can't have. Things I don't want to want. This is all a bad idea, but I'm in the middle of it now.

I put my hands on his shoulders and swing my right leg over the back of the bike. Hawk's hand catches my left hip to help steady me, and my breath catches when his thumb brushes my bare thigh.

"You're doing so good." His words are low and soft, making my insides melt. "Almost there."

I settle on the seat, trying to keep some distance between his back and my front, but there isn't much room. I tuck my skirt under my ass as much as I can, but the front can't be helped. My panties are exposed, but not so anyone can see them. My breasts brush his back and I inhale as they tighten and grow heavy.

He chuckles darkly and straightens. When I try to lean away from him, he brings both hands to grip my hips and slides me forward on the seat until I'm pressed tight against his ass. My legs spread around his hips in a way that shouldn't feel as good as it does.

I bite back a little whimper as my pussy clenches.

"Trust me, Annie. You're going to want to hold on." He takes my hands and wraps them around his center. His hard abs tighten beneath my fingertips. I want to explore the dips and rises beneath his shirt. I don't ever think this way about Chase.

I shouldn't be doing this. Hawk is dangerous. Maybe not only in the sudden, fiery, motorcycle-death way, but in the sanity department.

The helmet is unwieldy, but when he starts the engine and the motorcycle rumbles to life beneath us, I turn my head to press against his back, squeezing my eyes shut and tightening my hold around him.

"I'm going to take it slow, baby girl. Don't worry." He touches my clasped hands. "You doing okay back there?"

I nod before I realize he probably can't see me or feel me through his jacket.

"Yeah." My voice is breathy, but I can't help it.

He chuckles. "Hold on. We're going to ride in the parking lot first so you can get used to it."

The motorcycle moves, and I cling tighter to him, trying to remember what he said—not to fall off, and not to press my legs against the bike even though it feels weird and hot, sitting spread open behind him. The only thing between me and his slacks are my panties.

He sticks to his word and rolls the bike slowly through the parking lot, taking a turn.

"You feel that?"

"Feel what?" I ask because I'm feeling a lot of things I shouldn't about a guy who isn't my boyfriend. My heart is racing. My stomach dips. I'm warm all over.

"I'm going to turn again. All you have to do is hold on and stay straight." He does and I do my best to stay still and not do anything to tip us over.

"Good girl," he murmurs. His hand rubs over my knee.

Again, this shouldn't be doing anything for me, but it's like I'm being overwhelmed by all things Hawk. His warm, solid body pressed into mine. His scent filling me. His voice in my ears. And the nervous anticipation of the ride ahead of us.

"You ready?" he asks.

"Mm-hmm." I squeeze my eyes tight as he speeds up. The growl of the motor rumbles through me. My arms tighten around him, as fear begins to overwhelm the desire he stirs in me. We roll down the ramp to the road, then he increases the speed. My stomach dips in a decidedly not sexy way. The wind hits my legs, chilling me as I snuggle into Hawk's warmth.

My helmet bumps against his as the motorcycle rumbles beneath us.

When he rolls to a stop, putting his feet down on the ground, his hand touches mine. "How are you doing, Annie?"

Freaking out probably isn't what he wants to hear. "Good."

We fly down the streets, and it feels like he's speeding even though he's probably going the speed limit or slightly below. I'm afraid to open my eyes to see the pavement rolling beneath us. Tension winds through me, and not in a pleasant way. My muscles are stiff and my thighs and arms clench tight around Hawk.

I'm afraid to loosen my grip and open my eyes. To acknowledge how vulnerable I am right now. Anything could happen and I'm not wearing enough to protect my body from a fall on pavement. My head, yes, but the rest of me is squishy too. I try to keep the panic down.

True to his word, he takes us the back way to my house, which isn't far from the school. But the fifteen minutes feel like an eternity. My heart pounds. Inside my brain is only flashing warning signs and screaming *oh god, oh god, oh god.* Such a bad idea. I don't want to die.

He pulls up to my dark house and relief pours through me. It's okay. So, I'm not going to be an adrenaline junkie anytime soon, but I probably didn't need to ride a motorcycle to figure that part out.

The motorcycle slows to a stop and he turns the engine off. The constant buzz beneath me ceases and the rumble of the motor silences. We're safe. We're here.

Fuck, I don't know if I can let go. All my muscles are stiff. I should release him, but I'm curled around him so tight. I need to stagger away from the death machine.

"You okay?" He strokes his fingers over mine.

My hands are clasped together, but little sparks light beneath his touch.

"I just need a minute for my soul to catch up to my body." I lean into his warmth and let it seep into me. My legs are trembling. I don't know if it's from the cold or the release from fear.

"Take as long as you need, baby girl." His chuckle sends heat pouring through me. "I've got you."

I take a deep breath and sit up, putting a little space between me and his tempting warmth. I don't let go of him though.

"I'm going to lean the bike on the kickstand, okay?" he says.

"Okay." My pulse is calming down. I can breathe.

He shifts the weight of the bike under me, and I return to full-on koala mode. He chuckles, but then he grabs my legs and draws them around his waist. "Put your arms around my neck, Annie. Piggyback style."

I carefully move my arms to link around his neck.

"Good girl." He shifts and lifts us both off the bike.

A squeal escapes me. His hands are under my knees and the shock of skin on skin finally hits me. All that fruitless energy swirls into a pit of desire low in my belly, shocking me.

"Put me down, please." I don't dare let go as he climbs the steps on my porch.

"It'll be easier inside." He holds a hand out to the side. "Keys."

Mine are in my backpack on my back, but there's a hidden one. I guess it doesn't matter if he knows where it is, because tomorrow this won't be our house anymore.

"Under the mailbox."

He slides his hand under the mailbox and finds the spare key held by a magnet. "Sweet."

After he unlocks the door, he ducks to bring us inside and flips on a light. He closes the door and walks over to the chair before sitting in it with me behind him.

"Are you able to let go now?" he asks.

I release my hands and for a second, he squeezes my knees before releasing me fully. When he stands, I quickly fix my skirt to cover as much of me as possible before he turns. He undoes his helmet and sets it on the coffee table before lowering to one knee in front of me.

His dark hair is too short to be ruffled, but my palms itch to smooth over it. To feel the soft texture teasing my skin. The smile he gives me lights me up on the inside. He's pleased with himself.

When he lifts my face shield, our eyes meet. My breath catches. His green eyes are darker than normal. I've had every inch of me pressed against him. I don't know that I've ever gripped anyone tighter in my life.

"I need to undo your helmet." He tips my chin up. One hand wraps around the back of my neck with his thumb right under my upturned jaw. His other fingers work on the strap. That rush winds through me, but I try to ignore it.

It's pretty hard to ignore a hockey player kneeling at my feet and touching me though. Especially this hockey player. He releases the strap and lifts the helmet off my head. Unlike him, I'm sure my hair is a mess. My hand automatically reaches up to fix it.

"Don't, Annie."

My hand stops on his command. His hand is still around the back of my neck. His fingertips press into the soft muscles there. Anticipation buzzes through my system. Back on high alert. His thumb brushes back and forth against the corner of my jaw and I can't seem to look away from his green eyes. My thighs clench together against the aching pulse in the center of me.

"Do you know why I really waited for you, baby girl?" His wicked scent, citrus and leather books, weaves around me. Those words make that ache grow.

"No," I say softly, but I don't pull away from him. There's something brewing inside me I can't seem to push down. It's wrong for him to touch me.

But it feels so right.

He smirks. "All that emotion and energy acting stirs up inside me? It needs somewhere to go."

My pulse jumps against his hold. Can he feel it? "Kind of like runner's high?"

"Yeah, but the thing I want to do isn't allowed." He's so close I can feel his breath against my lips.

"Why not?" My eyes search his.

My heart trips over itself. I should stop this. I should pull away. Like last time, I need to turn my head. But I'm snared in his trap before I realized it was too late, knowing I'm the prey, he's the predator, and there's nothing I can do to avoid this.

Part of me is so fucking curious and doesn't want to escape.

"She belongs to another."

His mouth crashes down on mine before I can even think to get away. He drags me to the edge of the chair as he kisses me as if I'm his lifeline. As if I'm his Juliet. That death would be preferable to leaving me. It's intoxicating, and for a moment, I give in to the feeling.

No one's ever kissed me like this before.

He groans at my surrender and his hand tightens on the back of my neck. I gasp at the sensation, and he takes advantage of my open mouth, sliding his tongue against mine. Everything inside me wants more. So much more.

CHAPTER 16

EvanAnn

Fuck.

It takes everything in me not to completely surrender. To push down the part wanting to stay in his arms. I put my hands on his chest and push him away. He doesn't release me fully.

"Fuck, baby girl." He kisses my jaw. "Don't push me away."

It's like sinking into a warm pool. I can't seem to resist. I don't want to resist, but I need to.

"No, Hawk." My words are soft, almost meaningless. They come out almost as a plea. Like I don't really want him to stop, because I don't.

His lips trail down my neck, making everything inside of me tingle. I don't belong to this man. I need this to stop. It's already gone too far.

"Hawk," I say it more forcefully and push against his chest while trying to pull away.

His hand tightens and his green eyes lock on mine. His eyes narrow. "Why?"

My breathing is harsh, and my body agrees with Hawk. But I can't.

"I have a boyfriend."

He closes his eyes and a growl fills the room. "Chase."

I should be afraid, right? Something in me should be throwing up all kinds of warning signs, but instead, I want him close to me again. I want to feel those lips pressed to mine. I want to be his.

He searches my eyes and I try to firm up my resolve. I tighten my lips and give him a nod.

"Annie." My name is part plea, and part agony.

"Please let me go," I whisper.

He releases me and stands, pacing away from me before turning. "Why are you loyal to him?"

A chill flows over me without his warmth. My brow furrows. What kind of question is that? "He's my boyfriend. That means he's the only one I kiss."

His eyes narrow on me as he closes the distance between us. I get to my feet, even though my knees are still shaky. He towers over me. Part of me wants him to kiss me again.

"Is he loyal to you?" he asks.

"Of course." I tilt my head. What kind of question is that?

"What if he wasn't?" His gaze falls to my lips. They still burn from his kiss.

I fight back the urge to lick them and catch the taste of him again. He's dangerous. He even tastes dangerous. Cam in my house was simple and pleasant. A little unnerving, but he put me at ease. Hawk is more like a hurricane threatening to destroy everything.

Cam respected my boundaries, but Hawk wants to burn them to ash. And I want to burn with him in a way I've never felt before.

I wrap my arms around myself protectively.

"Chase is my boyfriend. If he was cheating on me—and that's an *if* —then we would need to talk about it." I don't know why Hawk's persisting with this. What purpose does it serve? "But I still wouldn't cheat on him. I'd break up with him first."

"You kissed me back, baby girl." His voice lowers.

My knees grow weaker, but I have to hold my ground. "I was surprised."

"You were into it." His eyes take in every inch of me. "I could take more."

A little shiver goes through me. "But you won't."

Fuck, I hope those words are true. Because I don't know if I'm strong enough to hold off a sustained attack on my senses by Hawk. Part of me wanted to say *prove it*. I don't know what's going on with that.

"Break up with your boyfriend, Annie." Hawk's eyes meet mine.

I open my mouth and close it. He's not offering to be my boyfriend. What the hell am I supposed to say to that? He wants me to break up with my boyfriend so I can make out with him?

His reputation speaks for itself. He flits from girl to girl. No commitment. Just a night or two of sex before moving on to his next conquest. I don't want to be another conquest.

"I won't."

DAMON

It's late when I finish my cardio. Once Evan goes to bed, I'll watch what she was up to tonight when she got home from auditions. But as I drink my water, I sit at my desk to pull up the live feed to Evan's living room.

I got an alert earlier when she got home, but I made myself wait until I finished working out before checking in. She's become an obsession I can't resist. Watching her live her boring little life settles me in a way nothing else does right now.

I justify watching her because I'm learning her patterns. I need to know what makes her tick to ruin her. The lights are off downstairs, so I move to the camera in her bedroom.

Her small body is sprawled across the bed. I glance at the time. It's a little early for her to go to sleep. She tosses to the side with a huff and hugs her pillow to her.

But she's alone. She kicks off the sheets in frustration and tosses the pillow on the floor. Her pale eyes are open and glare at the ceiling. I wish there was a way to know what she's thinking. To slip into her mind and know everything about her.

Her hand comes up and touches her lips.

My cock twitches. I've watched her all week, with the exception of Wednesday while I was working out, which I still need to watch. She's a creature of habit. She studies. She putters around that small house all on her own. And she sleeps.

But tonight, it looks like sleep is eluding her.

She sits up. Will she pull out the book she's been reading? Or go to her desk and work more?

"What boring thing will you choose to do next?" I muse out loud. The video has some definite highlight reels, but so far nothing with her and her boyfriend. Nothing I can use to lure her into my trap.

She flops back on her bed and spreads her legs. I arch an eyebrow and anticipation floods me. Her hands slide down her body to the hem of her nightgown and she edges it up over hips.

I lean back in my chair and glance at the door to make sure I locked it. If we're going to get comfortable... I smirk. After all, a girl's got needs. It was only a matter of time before she decided to flick the bean. But why tonight?

Her fingertips slide over her pale stomach and beneath her nightgown until she cups her breast. My cock hardens painfully. I've jerked off to her studying, changing, and sleeping. But she's never touched herself.

I wish this thing had audio. That I could hear her little sighs and moans. Or is she quiet, like the little mouse she is?

Her lips part as she toys with her breast. I can't see what she's doing with her nightgown in the way. I draw my cock out of my shorts and stroke it. Her breasts are better than advertised. I want her to show me them.

I could text her and tell her to take off her nightgown, but I'm pretty sure that would be the end of my show. Getting her number was easy. Not using it when I want her to think of me is fucking annoying.

Who does she imagine touching her?

Is it Chase?

Her other hand comes up and touches her neck, sliding along the sensitive skin. My cock throbs in my hand, but I keep my strokes steady. If she's going to come tonight, I want to come with her.

Her hands slide down her body again and her knees fall out to the sides. Eyes closed, she slips her hand beneath her cotton panties. Her chest catches on a breath. Fuck.

"Are you wet, Evan? Show me those fingers."

I make the screen as big as I can as her hand shifts beneath her panties. Her hips roll slightly against her touch. Her head tips back and her lips part.

I can imagine sliding my cock between those full lips. Her mouth warm and hot as she suckles on me.

Shivers course through her and some precum spills out of the tip of my cock. I stroke it down my length as her other hand slides between her legs. The fabric stretches as she thrusts a finger into her pussy.

How wet is she? Who does she think about? Whose face floats into her mind when she touches herself? Whose dick does she wish was working that sweet pussy?

Someone she's already had or does she imagine someone else? Hawk, Cam, me? What gets her off mentally?

Her hands shift beneath the fabric. I want to rip those panties off so I can watch her fuck herself. Is she teasing her clit or burying so many fingers in that cunt so it stretches out to feel like a cock working in and out? One more night alone, Evan.

Smirking, I fall into pace with her rhythm, stroking my cock, knowing she'll be mine soon enough. And when I fuck her, I want her eyes open and on me. Her hot cunt swallowing me down as I thrust into her. I want her to see who's making her lose her fucking mind.

Her body arches into her touch and her mouth falls open, and for a suspended second, she remains like that. I stroke myself harder as my release pounds through me, spilling over my hand.

My breath is heavy as I continue to watch her. She slides her hands out of her panties. Her fingers glisten with her wetness. Fuck. Such a waste. I wet my lips, longing for a taste.

She heaves a sigh before sitting on the edge of the bed. Her gaze lifts and it's almost like she looks right at me. I straighten and narrow my eyes, but then she stands and leaves the room.

I grab some tissues and clean myself while I switch to the living room feed. She walks past the camera and into the kitchen, disappearing from view. Two cameras aren't enough. I glance toward the bathroom we'll be sharing.

Even though she'll be under my roof, I want to know everything she does. She walks back through the living room and climbs the stairs.

I switch back to the bedroom camera. She climbs into bed and pulls the covers over her.

Cameras. I need more to set up in her room and the bathroom. I need ones that will give me sound too. On my other monitor, I pull up a store and drop what I need into a cart.

When she turns, her eyes are shut and the tension is gone from her face. I can't wait to have her under my control.

I get up to take a shower. While she sleeps on one monitor, I'll review the times I missed. All I've learned is Evan has a boring life, and she flushes pink when she comes. I smirk. Her life won't be boring for long.

EvanAnn

The day I've been dreading is here. It's Friday. Move-in day. I also haven't decided whether or not to tell Chase about what happened with Hawk last night. It was a kiss. A very hot, panty-melting kiss, but I stopped it.

What happens if I tell him and he goes after Hawk at school? Any physical altercations on school property could end in suspension or expulsion for them, and it would be my fault.

Chase pulls his truck up in front of my house and honks twice. I grab my backpack and head out. He unlocks the doors as I approach, and I climb in. Turning, I take in the house that's been my safe haven. One last look at the closest thing to home I've found.

My heart aches. It feels like the end of something good. But maybe this is the beginning of something good for my mom.

"Morning, babe." Chase grins like nothing's changed since I saw him yesterday at school. My stomach ties in knots.

I should come clean.

"Thank you for picking me up," I say.

"I wish I'd known about your tire last night. I would have given you a ride home." Chase runs a hand through his hair and gives me a smile that says the world is his for the taking.

"It's okay." I put on my seatbelt and cross my legs. I don't even know what to say about last night. Do I tell him I cheated on him? I kissed Hawk back. Granted, he kissed me first. But after he stormed out last night, I lay in bed replaying every moment on a continuous loop. Until I'd worked myself up so much I gave in to the temptation to get off.

"Did you get the cast you wanted?" Chase asks, glancing my way.

"I won't know until Mr. Watson emails me."

Chase pulls up to a stop sign and turns to me with a devious smile. "You could tell me if you cast me."

I shake my head. "I'm not allowed. You have to find out with everyone else."

"My little rule follower." He smiles. "Fine, I'll wait. I have time to grab dinner after school before the bus leaves for the game." Chase starts driving again.

The roar of a motorcycle has me turning back, but I don't see anything.

"Did you hear me, EvanAnn?" Chase glances my way.

"Yeah," I say, kind of disappointed Hawk didn't show up to take me to school. He didn't offer. Not that I want to ride to school on the back of his motorcycle. That would have been a disaster.

Showing up with him after casting him in my play?

"Dinner tonight? Yeah? We haven't seen much of each other this week." Chase turns down the next street.

"Yeah, we can do dinner." Maybe then I can tell him about my secret kiss. My gut twists. I shouldn't have kissed Hawk back. It was almost instinctual. It was epic, but it was still wrong.

Will Chase dump me? Do I want him to dump me? I still like Chase, and Hawk isn't offering to date me. He's not even asking me out on a date. I don't want to be just another notch for him.

If Chase does break up with me because I kissed Hawk, how will that work for the play? I didn't get any texts from Mr. Watson last night, but he'll email this morning and then post the list around noon for everyone else. There must not have been any conflicts between my list and Brandt's, but that doesn't mean I got my first picks.

I texted my mom last night about my flat tire. She said she'd take care of it.

I haven't seen her since Monday night. Hopefully I'll see her more once I move into her boyfriend's house. I glance at Chase. He has the music up, so we really can't talk unless I shout. Should I tell him about my mom and me moving in with her boyfriend?

If Damon didn't live there, would I still be hesitating to tell Chase? I glance down at my hands in my lap. I don't feel like a good person right now. Maybe I should get it over with.

If I tell him and he breaks up with me, what will I have left? Can I go back to being alone? Will Mia even stay my friend? As long as I have Chase, I seem more interesting. Without him, I might have nothing.

He pulls into the parking lot and the space where my car was is empty. Guess Mom had it towed?

"Meet me here and we'll go out tonight." Chase smiles as he turns off the truck. "I've missed seeing you this week."

He leans across the console. He's going to kiss me. Nerves flutter in my stomach, but I lean in and touch my lips to his. I can't lose him right now. I feel nothing except nervous energy. Nothing like the tsunami of Hawk's kiss.

"Mmm." Chase leans back with a smile. "We're going to the party Saturday night, right?"

"Is it okay if Mia comes with us?"

Chase rolls his eyes. "Are you serious about being her friend?"

I nod because yes, I want a friend my senior year. Maybe I want it all in my senior year. A friend. A boyfriend. A guy who secretly wants me. My cheeks heat.

"Fine. We'll go to the hockey scrimmage on Saturday, have dinner, then go to the party. All with Mia, if it pleases you."

I smile and lean in to kiss him quickly. "Thank you."

We get out of his truck and walk toward the school. Hawk, Damon, and Cam pull their bikes into their spots. I can feel them watching me as Chase takes my hand. I want to shake him off, but what would that look like? I drag in a breath. No, I'm with him.

He's my boyfriend. I'm his girlfriend. We're together.

I try to ignore them. And I manage to do that in the early morning hallways and in first period with Mia. My message from Mr. Watson comes through, and I got my first choice in my leads. A couple of the extras went to Brandt's production, so I got my second choices for those roles, but overall, I'm very happy with my cast.

"Are you going to tell me what that smile is for?" Mia asks, leaning on her desk toward me.

"I got my dream cast for *Othello*." I'm practically bouncing I'm so excited. But then I remember last night and that kiss. It can't happen again, and if I want to make sure my play goes off without a hitch, I can't tell Chase about it. He has to play off Hawk in a lot of scenes, and whatever grudge they have might already affect that.

If Chase knows Hawk kissed me, what would he do? I can't lose one of the only two people in this school who care about me.

"Hey." Mia touches my arm, bringing me back to class. "You were happy and then you got this far-off look. Everything okay?"

I glance at the front of the class where the teacher is going on about something I should probably pay attention to, but I really want to talk to someone about everything that's happened. Mia is so new to me. If I hadn't been burnt by other girls, maybe I could trust her more.

She's not those girls, but I also don't know her very well yet.

"Maybe we can talk Sunday?" That seems like a good amount of time to get to know her. I'll be spending most of Saturday with Mia at the game and the party. I should know her well enough to determine her character by then.

Right?

Mia smiles. "My brother heads home then, so yeah, we can go out shopping or grab a coffee or something. It might be cool to hang out in something other than schoolgirl chic for once."

The teacher pulls our attention back to the board. My pulse quickens because I'll see Hawk in my next class. I don't know what to say or how to act around him. It's not every day I have to turn someone down.

It's never happened before. Not until I pushed him away last night. It can't happen again.

And I'll also have to face Damon. He glares at me like everything is my fault. Like my mother consulted with me about moving in with his dad. Like we plotted together to get into his house. Like whatever Chase did has anything to do with me. Next he'll be mad at me because Mia wants to bone him.

It would make the same amount of sense.

The bell rings and we head to our next class. Dread makes my steps heavy. Will it be all over my face when Chase sees me with Hawk? Will he believe I didn't lead Hawk on? I sat with Hawk for lunch and I enjoyed our talk.

Hawk called me Annie in front of Chase, and I didn't correct him. I didn't shrug off his arm when he put it on my shoulders. What if this is all my fault? What if, by not discouraging him, I encouraged him? Maybe I should have discouraged him from the beginning.

I take my seat and brace myself for the inevitable.

Damon is the first of the trio to walk in. At least he doesn't usually engage with me, preferring to let the others do their thing. At this point, I'll take his glares. It's easy to ignore him when he glares at me.

He sits and leans back in his chair. When I turn, he's giving me a contemplative look. My cheeks heat. Did Cam tell him about coming to my house? Or did Hawk? Maybe both of them.

Hawk walks between us, breaking our stare-down. I glance up at his face, trying to get a read on him. After all, we're about to spend the next few months working on a play together.

He takes his seat and pulls out his phone, ignoring me.

Oh.

Somehow that hurts worse than anything else he could have done. I turn forward in my desk and try to control my racing heart. Obviously, it was just another night for him. Just another kiss. I doubt I even register on his scale of kisses.

What if I'd told Chase and he broke up with me over a kiss that meant absolutely nothing?

Cam sits in the chair in front of me. "What's wrong, goody two-shoes?"

I meet his dark eyes and see the concern in them. I want to laugh, because when did this become my life? Last year at this time, I had a few acquaintances I would talk to occasionally at lunch or in class, but nothing outside of that. I didn't have any sort of romantic interest or whatever the fuck is going on with these guys.

Studying and directing were my life. I lost myself in the theater. It was easy, and I didn't have to worry about feeling left out. My mom spent her evenings with me after breaking up with her most recent boyfriend. But otherwise, I kept my head down and did what I needed to do to get into a great college and win a scholarship.

I open my mouth, but honestly, I don't know what to say to any of these guys. I shouldn't be talking to them at all, because they shouldn't know I exist. Instead, I shake my head.

Cam's brow furrows like he's going to poke more, but thankfully, the bell rings.

I need to go back to basics. Keep my head down and focus on school.

CHAPTER 17

Cam

IF THERE'S one thing I can't handle, it's tears. And EvanAnn looks like she's about to cry when she leaves second period. Damon watches her, but Hawk ignores her. We walk down the hallway to third.

"How'd auditions go?" I ask.

"Fine." Hawk doesn't look at me. He was fucking excited about this yesterday. Figured it'd be a good in with Evan and the whole college thing.

Damon glances at Hawk with what looks like a glare.

"What the fuck is going on with you two?" I keep my voice low, because we aren't about to duck into a room to work out our feelings. No, if we need to work out some aggression, we take it to the ice.

"Nothing." Hawk breaks away and heads for his next class.

I shake my head. "That's not nothing. Fuck, does this make me the chick who wants to know what everyone is feeling?"

Damon laughs. "Nah, but I'll show you why he's pissed tonight after practice."

"We're partying at yours tonight?" I smirk, because tonight is Evan-Ann's first night in the mansion.

"I've got some things I want to make clear." Damon smirks as he breaks off to go to his class. "Don't worry. Evan will fall in line."

I'm all in on this. Revenge. Taking the girl. Damon wants the gold digger out of his house too. That's going to be complicated, because forcing her mother out will likely lose us the girl.

EvanAnn

Mia squeals as she reads the list posted on the board. She pushes her way out of the crowd of students around the cast lists and rushes over to me. Her arms fling around me and squeeze me tight against her.

"You are the absolute best!" she says.

My chin is against her shoulder but I manage to get out, "No, you're the best. Which is why I cast you."

She pulls back and her grin is contagious.

Crystal squeals, "Oh, my god."

She turns, finds me, and hurries over. "You cast Hawk as Cassio?"

"Turns out he's really good at Shakespeare." I keep his background in theater a secret just in case he doesn't want anyone else to know. I don't know what to think about Hawk today, so I'm trying not to think about him.

"Oh, my god." She squeezes my arm. "I have scenes with him, right?"

I nod. She grins and squeals again. Maybe I won't have any problems with Hawk wanting me when half the cast will want him. He should have no trouble finding someone single to kiss.

Crystal is playing Emilia and I cast Sophie as Bianca. I hope Sophie won't be too awestruck by Hawk to play his courtesan.

"This is going to be amazing." Mia is all grins as she pulls me with her to the cafeteria.

I nod, but swallow down the bitter pill that I need to keep what Hawk and I did a secret to maintain unity amongst the cast. Mia wants Hawk. Sure, she wants them all, but it's definitely against girl code to go after someone else's crush.

Besides, it's not really a lie, right? Just something I'm not telling anyone. If someone asked me directly if I kissed Hawk, I could say no. After all, he kissed me. It's semantics, but I have to do what it takes to have a successful production.

Besides, no one would ever guess Hawk decided to kiss me. It was probably a mistake. He said he was practically high on auditioning. Maybe he regretted it as soon as he left my house. Which is why he's ignoring me today. That makes sense.

Mia parts from me as I head to the salad bar. I should be walking on air. I got my dream cast for *Othello*, but the rock in my stomach remains. Maybe I should come clean to Chase.

"Babe!"

I cringe as Chase wraps his arms around my shoulders from behind. I force a smile.

"You're the absolute best. We're going to have an expensive dinner tonight to celebrate." Chase kisses my cheek and walks away.

Dinner, and then I have to move into my new room at Damon's. Maybe it would be easier to think of it as Adam's house instead of Damon's. It doesn't negate the fact Damon lives there, but it might be easier to tell people we're moving in with my mom's boyfriend.

But then they might ask who's the new boyfriend...

I grab a salad and head to my table inside. There's no way I'd step outside into that courtyard today, not even if Mia and Chase go out there. Nope, I'm accepting my lot in life and running back to safety.

Mia joins me first, still bubbling about being cast. Chase also has high energy when he joins us. They chat over me about the cast, the production, and how great the show is going to be, but all the energy I would normally have is sucked dry because of what happened last night.

It was a mistake. As long as I keep telling myself that, eventually I'll believe it.

Later, after acting class, I walk to my directing classes. As I approach the classroom, a tentative touch on my arm makes me turn.

"Hi, EvanAnn." Keira Fox stands with her books held against her chest. She's a junior in the directing program. Her dark hair is pulled into a low bun, and her bright green eyes are fixed on me.

"Hi." I keep walking because we're both going to the same class.

"So, I know we haven't talked much." Keira tucks her hair behind her ear and glances toward me as she falls in step beside me. "But from the projects in the directing class we've done, I know we have similar visions. It's your decision, of course, but I wanted to say I really respect you as a director and as a student, and would love to work with you on *Othello* or any other future projects you have."

I don't think she took a breath during that sentence. I stop to look at her. The seniors are probably all trying to convince Brandt to let them be his assistant. Most juniors look up to the seniors and only hope one of us will pick them.

She stops with me and sighs. "I know I'm coming on too strong, but honestly, when I look at you, I see me. We're both here because we auditioned and made it in. We're smart, but we don't have the money or connections most kids do. We're lucky this school is in the same town as our parents, or we couldn't afford to do this at all."

I release my breath. "I loved your take on *Sally's Gone, She Left Her Name* last year. It was different from the other takes on it. Original."

She smiles and tucks her hair. Nervous tick? "Thanks."

I have to decide today who I'll work with. "I'll definitely consider you for my assistant director spot, but I have to think about it."

She beams. "Really? Thank you. I won't let you down if you pick me."

She goes up on her toes and turns to walk with me to class. When I take my seat, I consider the other people in our class and how I might rank them. At least it distracts me from thinking about seeing Hawk at play rehearsal and seeing Damon at home every day.

In the end, I let Keira know between classes I'm choosing her. She practically walks on clouds, and I wish I could have that feeling today. The rest of the day is hectic with arranging the production schedule, now that we have the students' schedules to work around. Fortunately, hockey isn't in full season yet, but football is.

Working around both is going to take me time to figure out, but Cassio is in the play a lot less than Iago. It's our last block of the day and the teacher has given us free time to work on the schedules or the project the other directors have for this semester.

Keira and I sit at a table with the schedules in front of us. I've already blocked out what scenes to work on together to optimize the time I'll have the actors. I spent most of the summer working on it, knowing people's time would be limited to practice outside of school. I don't want people to hang around for only a few lines.

"Thank you again," Keira says as she labels Post-its with the characters and actors' names.

I nod. "Honestly, I probably would have chosen you if you hadn't said anything. Like you said, our work is very similar. We'll have less conflict than if I'd chosen someone who has a very different aesthetic."

And right now, I need something easy in my life to rely on. But I don't tell her that. We work the whole time and put together a feasible schedule, including the two hours every other school day where we'll have the full cast in the afternoons.

I have everyone's email to send them the schedules. The first practice will be the read-through on Monday during the afternoon time slot. Keira walks with me out the front door and heads off toward her ride.

I release my breath and look around the parking lot. Chase isn't at his truck yet. He usually drives his car, especially when he picks me up. I assume, with a scrimmage tomorrow, the trio will have hockey practice today.

The scrimmage I'm attending with my boyfriend and my best friend, who has a crush on the guys. Fuck. Who decided I needed a shake-up in my life? Because I so didn't. I liked my little world where the most stressful thing would have been picking my assistant director.

That was the easiest part of my day.

An arm drapes over my shoulder from behind, and for a second, I forget to breathe. When I inhale Chase's cologne, I relax. Turning, I look up at his wide smile.

"Let's go get dinner."

He leads me to his truck and even helps me in, which is a first. He must be super happy to be cast as Iago. When he climbs in the truck and starts it, I turn to him.

"You know you earned your part, right? I didn't give it to you because you're my boyfriend."

He winks at me. "It doesn't hurt to kiss up to the director though."

I shake my head, because I hope he's kidding. He turns the music up as he pulls out of the school lot and heads downtown. We're still in our school uniforms, so we can't go anywhere super fancy, but he picks a nice sit-down restaurant.

"Anything you want. It's on me." He sits back in his chair and looks over the menu.

I still look at the prices and choose something on the cheaper side. When the waiter walks away, Chase sits forward and takes my hands on the table.

"We're going to have such a great year, babe. You're going to knock this play out of the park, and people will be lining up to have you come work for them." Chase rubs his thumb over my knuckles. He smiles sweetly, and I remember why I decided to date him. He can be a really nice guy when he wants to be.

"I don't think it works that way, Chase." I pull one of my hands back and tuck my hair behind my ear. "I need to get into a great college and make the connections I'll need to have a great career."

"My dad can get you connections. You know, we could be a power couple. Your brains, my looks, your smarts, my money." The way he looks at me is different than how Hawk looked at me last night. Almost like I'm something Chase wants to buy. Hawk looked at me like he wanted to possess me, like it was a physical need.

Cold flows through me, but I push away the thought that maybe Chase isn't with me because he wants me. We've kissed and he's pushed for a more physical relationship, but when I told him I wasn't ready, he backed off.

That's completely normal, right? He's introduced me to his parents. They seem to like me.

"EvanAnn?"

I focus on Chase. "I'm sorry. What?"

He smiles softly. "You thinking about us in the future? We could go far, babe. You wouldn't even need to go to college with me by your side."

My brow furrows. "I want to go to college, Chase."

"Why? We could do films together straight out the gate. Who needs college when you can have a career?" Chase sounds perplexed.

"Me. I need college. I know I'll learn a lot on the job, but the types of connections I can make at a good university will be invaluable as I progress through my career." We've talked about the future together. I thought he knew this was what I wanted.

"Of course, babe. Whatever you want." He smiles. "College will be great. You can go somewhere in New York City or LA, so we can stay together while I work on my acting career."

"Do you really see us together after high school?" I mean, sure, we've talked about it, but I don't know if I'm going to stay with my high school boyfriend forever. It happens, but what I feel for Chase is respectful and nice.

"You don't?" He straightens like I said something wrong.

I shrug, because I don't have the answer to that.

He reaches for my hand. "Let me take you somewhere after we eat. I'll show you how good we can be together."

"You have a game to get to," I remind him.

"Tomorrow, then." He rubs my hand. "I want to make sure you know how much I value you."

Value?

"We have the hockey scrimmage, the dinner, and the first party of the year tomorrow. You said we shouldn't skip it." Usually, I'd rather skip it, but not this time. This time I'll have Mia and I'll be able to talk to her when Chase is hanging out with his friends.

"You're right." He releases a breath. "Sunday. It'll be our last time to be together before everything takes off."

Be together? Is he talking about sex? Because I'm *definitely* not starting a physical relationship with him when I'm sneaking around with other guys. Not sneaking, per se, but... Fuck, what am I doing? "I'm still not ready—"

"Your filet, sir." The waiter sets Chase's steak in front of him, then puts my pasta in front of me. "Miss."

I don't say anything as we start eating, but if Chase wants to have sex, we're going to have to talk more. Even if I was ready, I can't have sex with him while I have stronger chemistry with other guys.

"Hey," Chase says softly, bringing my attention to his blue eyes. "I'm willing to wait for you, EvanAnn. You take all the time you need to be ready. I'm in this for the long haul."

CHAPTER 18

Damon

CAM SITS down as he puts on his socks. Hawk leans against the lockers, looking pissed. We're done for the day, but we're far from being finished.

"What's the plan with Evan?" Cam asks.

I smirk because he isn't calling her EvanAnn like he used to. I didn't tell them about the cameras, but I enjoyed the footage from the week and plan to show them all of it. It should give me the leverage I need over Evan to make her fall in line with my plans.

"You got cast?" I ask Hawk.

He's been quiet all day, but I know why. Rejection stings. But my plan will take that pain away. He's going to know how affected Evan was by that kiss.

He nods. "Practice's scheduled. Read through on Monday."

"What do we know about Mia? The new girl she's been hanging out with?" I ask Cam. She's also been absent from Evan's outside of school life.

Cam always has his finger on the pulse of what's going on at school. I focus on hockey. Hawk focuses on academics. And Cam focuses on the social network of our combined schools.

"New girl. Acting." Cam meets my gaze. "She's been eye-fucking the guys on the hockey team. Pretty sure she's going to make her way through the team, given the chance."

I'm going to have to consider how I can use that.

"The good thing is that means she'll be dragging Annie along with her to games." Hawk rubs his jaw. "But Mia can cause issues if our girl thinks her friend has dibs. If Annie's loyal to that fuckboy, she'll be loyal to the whore too."

"What makes you think she's a whore?" I stand and grab my jacket and keys. I haven't paid much attention to the new girl, but I've caught the look in her eyes when she glances my way—the one that says she wants me. But I'm used to that from girls.

"She offered to blow me on day one." Hawk shakes his head. "Turned her down, but now I'm thinking I probably should have let her. Shown Annie what kind of friend she really has."

"A slut, like her." I shrug.

Cam makes a non-committal noise. He looks doubtful, but I'll prove him wrong. I know what I saw that night on the road. And I know she hasn't told her boyfriend about what happened with any of us. If Chase was half the man he pretends to be, he would have at least come at Hawk for kissing her. Maybe Evan wants to keep her claws in the rich prick. Maybe he's her meal ticket. Like mother, like daughter.

"Are we going to show her the video of her boyfriend fucking another girl?" Cam looks up at me. He wants her to be free to do whatever we want. He wants to fuck her as badly as the rest of us do.

I don't understand what it is about her. Maybe it's this plan or maybe it's just a game I want to win. This girl is under my skin already, and I want to show the whole school who the little wallflower really is.

"I have a better idea."

Evan Ann

I didn't think this through. I don't have a car. When Chase offers to drive me home, I'm not about to admit I've moved in with Damon. That he might be my future stepbrother if our parents decide to get married. Even if they don't and they stay together, we'll be spending breaks together during college.

Does Chase know where Damon lives?

Even if he doesn't know it's Damon's house, pulling up to a mansion is going to make Chase ask a million questions I don't want to answer.

"Why don't we just go to the high school?" I turn in my seat to Chase. "You need to catch the bus to the game. I can ask Mia to give me a ride home."

"You think?" Chase glances at the time on the dashboard. "It would save time."

The restaurant took a while to get the bill to us, so we didn't have time to go somewhere to make out like Chase wanted. I wasn't really thrilled with the idea, but maybe that's what we need.

Some time to reconnect.

Dinner was nice. He talked about his thoughts on Iago and then about the team they're playing tonight.

"I'll text her right now." I pick up my phone and panic for a moment. I can't call Mia. I'm not ready to tell Mia who I'm living with, either. If she knew about my living situation, would she use me to get closer to Damon, Hawk, or Cam?

My stomach twists uncomfortably and I resist the urge to put my hand over it. Even if I wanted to be with them, I can only be with one of them. So why does it hurt to think of her with any of them?

There's a new text message on my phone. Curious, I open it.

> UNKNOWN:
>
> How are you getting home, Annie?
>
> Need a ride?

Fuck. I hate how I know it's him without him saying, but no one else calls me Annie.

Hawk didn't give a damn about me this morning or all day, but now... Dammit. I hate the little thrill racing through me that he texted. Part of me wants to tell him to shove his ride up his ass. But I don't have a lot of options.

I don't have the money for a car service to pick me up and I don't know if my mom is even home.

It's Friday night, and that's typically her date night. She doesn't know if I'll be home because it's football night and she hasn't been around for me to tell her it's an away game.

Fuck it. At least, Hawk can solve one problem right now. My heart skips a little and I tamp it down.

ME:

Can you pick me up at school?

UNKNOWN:

I'm still here

Fuck, I glance up at Chase, but he's paying attention to the road. I don't really want Chase to run into them. Not before I can tell Hawk I'm not telling anyone about our kiss. Fuck.

UNKNOWN:

I can't wait to get between your legs again

What the fuck? I flip my phone over on my lap. My cheeks flare with heat, but that's not the only place that grows heated. My phone vibrates, but I ignore it as Chase pulls into the parking lot. He drives around the back to park near the bus loading area.

When he shuts off the engine, he leans toward me. "If we win tonight, I could come over so we could celebrate properly."

He kisses me, but I pull away before he can deepen it. I'm so confused right now by all of this. But I need to make sure Chase doesn't drive to my old house.

"My mom is going to be home tonight and we're watching a movie. I'll see you tomorrow though." The lie flows out of me before I can stop it.

I smile as panic floods me. If he goes by my house, he'll see we're not there anymore. Then there will be the questions of where I've moved and why I didn't tell him? And then I'll have to tell him about Damon sleeping a door away from me at night. Which I shouldn't be afraid to tell my boyfriend where I'm living when it's not something I can control as a teenager.

I haven't begun to process being that close to Damon Storm all the time. Or how I'll sleep knowing he's right there.

"I'll miss you." He kisses me softly. "Wish me luck, babe."

"Good luck."

We get out of the truck and he heads toward the locker room. I have no idea where Hawk is, and frankly, I'm a little scared to read whatever he sent me after the last text.

I walk around the side of the building and toward the front of the school where the main parking lot is. I glance over my shoulder to make sure Chase isn't following me. I don't think he would, but I already feel guilty about not telling him about the kiss and now I straight up lied about how I'm getting home.

What am I supposed to say when Mia mentions that she didn't give me a ride home? It shouldn't come up, but the potential is there. Fuck.

I open my phone and ignore the new message. Instead, I pull up my text with Chase.

ME:

Mom is coming to get me instead

Have a great game tonight

Go, Devils!

CHASE:

See you tomorrow

I breathe out and open the message from Hawk.

UNKNOWN:

Out front where we park

My footsteps falter. Fuck, I didn't even consider it might be all three of them. Or someone might see me leave with them. Someone who might tell Chase. This is why I hate lying.

The truth always comes out.

If it weren't for everything riding on this play, I could be truthful with my boyfriend. I could tell him his costar kissed me, and while I did kiss him back, I did push him away.

Eventually. Even though everything inside me wanted to keep going. That means something, right? My insides churn.

I should be able to tell my boyfriend that I'm moving in with the costar's friend who might be Chase's enemy for some unknown reason. Or maybe Damon's mad at my mom and me for encroaching on his space. Though in a house that big, we shouldn't have to run into each other.

Except we're sharing a bathroom, so I will be in his space. I don't think our parents really thought that through.

I lift my gaze to see all three motorcycles and three guys waiting for me. I'm not ready for this. Not ready to be with all three of these guys off school property, but I don't have a choice if I want to keep Mia and Chase in the dark about my strange association with these three.

Part of me wants to turn around and run as far away from this as possible. But the other part accepts this is what my life is right now. Like everything that's come before, we'll get through this. I drag in a deep breath and steel myself.

Another part of me is so fucking curious as to be a pest.

DAMON

It's amusing to watch Evan walk as if she's a death row convict on her way to the electric chair. Knowing she left her boyfriend's truck to come home with us is the icing on the cake. It won't be long now before I have her under my thumb.

She'll do everything I say if she wants to keep her house of cards from falling down around her. I know Cam wants her to be free of her asshole boyfriend, but I don't. No, I want to bask in the knowledge I led his girl to ruin and she'll help us ruin him.

And when the time is right, he'll find out.

But right now, I'm confident this girl who prides herself on her loyalty will do anything to keep her boyfriend from finding out what she's been up to. I've watched her carefully.

Everything she does at school and at home—none of it strays outside the boundaries of her little world.

Except when she let Cam into her house and fed him pizza. And when she let Hawk bring her home and kiss her. I hope she enjoyed it, because I'm going to be watching the live show as soon as I show her what's at stake.

Her gaze lifts to mine like she can feel me watching her. Can she? What will she think when she discovers there are no locks on the bathroom doors? I left the ones on our doors to the hallway. Can't have mommy or daddy coming in to disrupt whatever show I decide I want to watch at any given moment.

Evan hesitates and I arch an eyebrow at her. Come on, little devil, I know you want to come out and play. Every move she makes leads her closer to her ruin.

Hawk already has her helmet out and ready for her. We're all connected to the same Bluetooth setting so we can communicate while riding. Now we'll have access to Evan too.

And soon we'll have an all-access pass.

Evan's gaze drops from mine. Maybe it's the knowing smile on my face making her shy. Because I know exactly what my little devil has been up to.

"Thank you for offering me a ride home." Evan's voice is soft as she steps up to Hawk. "I'm sorry about last night."

"Don't mention it." Hawk presses his lips together. He lifts his spare helmet, and she helps guide it down onto her head.

Cam's eyes narrow at the exchange, but he'll know what it means when we get back to my house. I made sure to tell my dad I'd help to get Evan situated so he can take her mother out on their date.

Fuck, that woman spent every night this week at our house and left poor, little Evan all alone. I know because as soon as I got home from hockey, I turned on my new favorite show while I went about my evening.

Evan may not know it, but we spent every night together this week. Eating, studying, getting ready for bed. I wished the camera went both ways, because watching her sleep with her nightgown riding up around her hips made me horny as fuck. Those cotton panties shouldn't be sexy, covering every inch of her and hiding her from my view.

Part of me wants to go through her drawers and throw away every pair of those panties. The other part wants to rip them off her body and take what's going to be mine. I don't care how many fuckers she's had before me. From now on, there will only be three. I'm willing to share her, to watch the others fuck her, but no one else.

That means I need her to cut off Chase with whatever lie she has to tell him. She can tell him she has a STI or a fucking yeast infection, but once I get my dick wet, he gets cut off.

She may not like the terms of our agreement, but I will. And that's all that matters. After tonight, she's mine.

I DON'T KNOW what the fuck is going on. Damon said he's going to get everyone in line, but the way he looks at Evan is like he's already cornered her. If he has, he hasn't shared with the rest of the class.

Hawk doesn't say much as he helps Evan with the helmet, adjusting the strap.

She shivers beneath his touch. He makes sure her helmet's Bluetooth is connected before he climbs on his bike. Evan takes a deep breath and then climbs onto his bike like she's done it before.

"You ridden before, goody two-shoes?" I straddle my own bike.

"Hawk gave me a ride home last night. I had a flat tire and no spare." Her voice is soft. "He stayed to walk me out after auditions."

"Convenient." Damon's voice is loud. "We ready?"

There's an edge to Damon's voice. Hawk didn't mention he took Evan home last night. Or that he got her on his bike. He said Chase drove her to school, and we saw her get in his truck at the end of the day, too.

But knowing Evan, she hasn't told anyone about her new living arrangements. The question is, would she let Chase take her home? Because Chase has been to Damon's house for business dinners with his father.

Apparently, she wasn't ready to tell Chase about her new digs.

I glance over at Evan. She's wrapped around Hawk tight. Her skirt hiked up enough I can almost see the edge of her panties on her thigh. Does she have her eyes squeezed shut too?

Hawk rubs his hand over hers that are clutched at his abs. "Easy, Annie. Just like last night. It's a little farther to ride, but don't lean with me. Keep your center above the bike. Okay? You with me?" His tone is softer than I've ever heard him with a girl before. It makes me straighten.

This is supposed to be revenge. A conquest. Something to bond over for our senior year. Maybe he's just making sure she's comfortable going with us.

"Yeah," she says.

Damon gestures to follow him. He drives into the parking lot and then turns toward the back of the school. It's a little out of our way, but Damon is nothing if not calculating in his movements.

We rumble by the school buses parked there while the football players load onto them for the away game. If Chase sees us, he won't know it's EvanAnn on the back of Hawk's motorcycle. Her backpack is the only thing that might give her away.

It's a dangerous game to play, because I don't know what kind of guy Chase is. He cheats on his girlfriend, but he presents as this nice, popular guy. Why date at all if he wants to fuck around? How is Evan special to him? What does she give him those other girls can't?

Damon revs his engine, and it echoes against the building. Fuck it. I pop a wheelie and land hard before gunning after him. We ride out of the parking lot and onto the road.

I slow down to fall back beside Hawk and Evan. With the face shield down, I can't tell if she has her eyes open. But she's stuck like Velcro to Hawk's back. Gotta admit, I'm low-key jealous.

"How are you doing, Evan?" I ask.

"She probably won't answer you," Hawk says, glancing my way. "Riding a bike terrifies her."

"It's not as bad today." Her voice is barely audible over the engines.

Hawk chuckles. "You'll get used to having all this power between your thighs, baby girl."

It sounds like she whimpers, but I can't tell. Damon leads us through the streets. But we stick to the side streets instead of going down Main. People will be out and about at this time, and there's a possibility someone could see us with her.

Most people won't believe it's Evan, but the speculation could get back to Olivia or the other girls who ask questions they've got no business asking. They'll want to know who was on the back of Hawk's bike. It's a hassle we don't want yet.

Evan wants to hide that she's with us. She hasn't told anyone at school she's moving in with Damon. That's fine for now. It works to our advantage. But at some point, I'm going to do exactly what her fucker of a boyfriend did with that girl—fuck Evan at a party where Chase can watch what he can't have anymore.

My cock twitches at the thought of her riding it. Of everyone seeing her take me into her with her skirt covering us, but they'll know. Her hands tangled in my hair. Our foreheads touching, our breath mingling as we fuck.

But first, we have to get through the revenge part. This is in Damon's control because what happened with his dad and the accident were out of his control. He needs his revenge. He needs payback for losing this year.

I get it. If I had my future mapped out and it was taken from me because some asshole was getting road head, I'd want to fuck up his life too. Damon can do what he needs to do, because in the end it means I get to fuck my little goody two-shoes.

Damon is quiet on the way, which is typical. I can't keep quiet. I hate the silence more than anything else. It's why I don't stay home most nights. Because if my father does talk to me, it's about college.

The need to speak is almost overwhelming. If I talk, no one will respond. I'm used to it, but the quiet is too much for me most days. Hawk occasionally interacts with me, but something's bothering him.

And I'm confident that something is EvanAnn. I would have offered to let her ride on my motorcycle, but I'm glad Hawk took her. With the way I ride, she probably wouldn't have wanted to get on a bike ever again. I like the thrill. The danger.

"When's the first play practice?" The words burst out of me. It's a reasonable question Hawk might answer.

"The table read is Monday," Evan answers but doesn't lift her head from Hawk's back.

"How did you decide on your cast?" I figure she might give me a quick answer. Besides, I like hearing her in my helmet.

"Auditions, but I've been watching most people for years. It's kind of a nervous habit."

"Watching people is a nervous habit?" I chuckle. "I do it because I find people fascinating."

"Me too," Evan says. "I've been in the same classes with these people for the past three years. I know how they perform and what they're capable of."

"You didn't know about me." Hawk's voice is harsh.

"You surprised me." Her voice sounds like she's perplexed. "You could have easily been an ant."

He chuckles. "I'll always be a devil, baby girl."

We pull up to Damon's house and he opens the garage for his motorcycles. We pull in and turn off our bikes. His damaged bike sits off to the side. A silent reminder of how bad the accident could have been if he hadn't been wearing his helmet, now broken and scratched on the floor beside the scraped up bike.

Damon could have died that night. If the two of us hadn't been with him. If he'd been riding on his own. If someone else had hit him on the blind corner once he was down. A thousand what-ifs. I'm not ready to lose my best friend. Either of them.

When Hawk straightens and lifts his helmet off, Evan doesn't move.

"Better this time, Annie?"

She nods, but doesn't release him.

When Damon takes off his helmet, he shakes his head at them. "Come on. We have things to discuss."

I leave my helmet on my motorcycle and walk over to Evan. I hold out my hand to her.

She looks at it and releases Hawk with her arm to take my hand. She seems unsure how to proceed to get off the bike.

"Just pick her up." Hawk sighs. "I'm never going to be able to take you out in public, baby girl. Not until you figure out how to get off the bike properly."

I reach for her waist and she turns to hold onto my shoulders. When I lift her off the bike and set her on her feet, her hands go to her skirt to tug it down into place. She still has the helmet on.

I meet Hawk's eyes over her head, and he shakes his head. How does Damon think this girl is a huge slut? Maybe she's just loyal. I've asked around, in the locker room and in class. No guy stepped up to say he's fucked or even dated her. It sounds like Chase might be her first boyfriend.

That doesn't mean she hasn't been with guys outside of our school. She went to school somewhere in this town before high school.

I know what Damon saw in Chase's car, but I'm beginning to wonder if he saw Evan or if it was some other girl? I can't tell Damon that. He's convinced, and I didn't see the girl with Chase.

It doesn't matter who the girl was though. Even if Chase was cheating on Evan that night, taking Evan away from Chase is the only way Damon can punish him without fucking up Damon's father's business. Because Chase is a little bitch who wouldn't take the ass-whooping he deserves. He'll go crying to daddy if Damon makes a move against him directly.

I tip up Evan's chin and undo the latch on the helmet before helping her take it off. She blinks up at me owlishly with those huge, silver-flecked blue eyes of hers. Her golden hair is a halo around her head. She's pretty and has a nice body.

Someone has to have tapped that before. Granted the metric at our school for beauty is skewed because of the wealthy elites and actresses who attend, but Evan isn't a girl you overlook. Most guys do, however.

Need shifts through me. The need to feel her lips against mine. My fingers dig into the helmet. My other hand fists at my side, as I resist the urge to slide it behind her neck and draw her into me.

She takes a step away and looks down at the concrete, breaking the spell. "Thank you for helping me. And for bringing me... home."

"We were coming here anyway." Hawk touches her hip and her head jerks up to look at him. "Come on. Let's go inside."

She sidesteps from his touch, but follows him inside. I take her backpack to carry for her. She gives me a little smile in thanks. Poor thing. She has no idea what she's walking into.

A lamb to the slaughter.

When we step into the house, she turns and holds her hand out for her backpack. "I should go sort out my room. Thanks for the ride home and for carrying my bag."

Damon chuckles, drawing her attention. "I've got something I need to show you, Evan. Promise it will only take a few minutes."

She bites her lip, and I can see how much she wants to flee. It won't work. She and Damon have been on a collision course no one can stop. It's better to get it over with now so we can move on to the fun stuff.

I slip her bag off my shoulder and set it on the steps. She starts for it, but I block her.

When I tip her chin up, her eyes are wide and wary. "We want to talk, goody two-shoes. You're going to be around this house. We need to establish the rules. Besides, don't you think you should get to know your potential stepbrother?"

I lift my gaze to Damon and Hawk, letting them know I'll handle this. I can handle Evan.

Damon scoffs and heads downstairs. Hawk follows him, leaving Evan and me alone. That urge to kiss her startles me again. I'm attracted to Evan. I've known from the second Damon put her in our sights, but the strength of that attraction is what confuses me.

I don't want to just fuck this girl. Sitting with her while she fixed me something to eat was unexpectedly pleasant. She's easy to talk to, and I want to be around her. With most girls, I fuck them, and I'm done. They're useful to satisfy the itch.

With Evan, I want to spend more time with her. I need to convince her to spend time with us.

"What do you plan to do in your room anyway?" I glance up the stairs. "I guarantee everything's unpacked. This place runs like a well-oiled machine. The only reason Damon's bed isn't made every day is because he told them not to."

I hold my hand out to her and give her the smile that says trust me and gets me out of trouble with older women. "If you feel uneasy and want to leave, tug on your ear and I'll get you out. But you don't have anything to worry about."

She searches my eyes doubtfully. She should be concerned. Damon's done waiting and he thinks he holds the key to make her do what he wants. I'm curious what will happen honestly. Will she shed the good girl act, or is she truly as innocent as she seems?

"Tug on my ear?" Her blue eyes are so wide and trusting. For a second, I forget myself and step closer, tucking a stray strand of hair behind her ear. It would be so easy to kiss her. No one would stop me, except her.

Would she? Stop me? Her gaze drops to my lips before looking away.

"Yeah. It'll be our code." I let my hand drop to my side, though I long to slide my fingers into that thick blond hair and tilt her head back. I want to claim that plush little mouth with mine and find out what she tastes like. But I want her trust.

For now.

She swallows. "Okay."

EvanAnn

This is stupid. This is so stupid. I walk with Cam down into the rec room. I don't know if my mom or Damon's dad are in the house, but I'm convinced even if our parents were, they wouldn't be able to hear anything we do.

This house seems even bigger now that it's supposed to be my home. It feels like it will gobble me whole. Cam is familiar. Even Hawk and Damon are familiar. They're all I know here and am a little comfortable with. Though my heart is racing, and all I can think is that I'm alone with them.

This whole plan of my mom's sucks. But I get it. She's been lonely for years.

Adam is handsome and better off than most men his age. I'm going to college next year and won't be home. I still don't understand what happened with our rental house, but if they've been dating for a while, it was probably inevitable they would move in together. It's better I move in too instead of being left alone all year, while Mom basically lived with her boyfriend anyway.

I can't fault my mom for wanting to move on with her life, but she has no idea how this has already disrupted mine. That's on me. I don't want to spoil her future because I'm uncomfortable.

Damon sits on the couch with his phone in his hand. The television is on, but not displaying anything.

He leans forward and his blue eyes lock on mine. "Come here."

My steps falter, but Cam puts his hand on the small of my back and guides me forward. This is a fucking trap. I know it. I can feel it in my bones. But Cam's right, it's going to happen eventually. Maybe Damon will finally tell me what I did to grab their attention.

I need to know what I did wrong so I can apologize and we can get back to normal. I glance at Hawk. His green eyes are hooded and he's not showing me anything. I almost touch my lips, remembering the feel of his lips against mine. Cam's fingers burn my back. And Cam, is he as lonely as I am? That night he wanted company, and fuck, did I need someone to be there with me for a little while.

Do I want to go back to the way things were before?

Do I want them to look through me like I don't exist? Because that's the way it was. I swallow. It's what I should want, but it's time I face the truth. I like their attention. They make me feel alive in a way I've never felt before.

I thought my life had changed when Chase noticed me and worked to bring me out of my shell, but it was nothing compared to these guys. I don't know what that means, and I'm trying not to look too closely at it. I cheated on my boyfriend with Hawk. I've spent more time talking with Cam in the past week than I have with Chase.

And Damon. Nervous butterflies riot in my stomach at his attention. Those piercing blue eyes seem to see all the way into my soul. They measure me to see if I'm worthy, and fuck, I really want to be worthy. My fingers twitch to rest my hand over my stomach to try to calm it, but there is no calming it when it comes to Damon Storm.

When I stop in front of Damon, Cam sits next to Hawk.

"Will you tell me what I did wrong now?" I ask softly. Maybe he'll finally tell me and get this over with. His sly smile makes me swallow and the butterflies inside me crash into each other.

"Evan, Evan, Evan." He shakes his head and pats the spot on the couch next to him. "Sit down."

CHAPTER 20

EvanAnn

THIS IS THE MOMENT. I could run, or I could stay here. It's a choice. Two rather sucky options, but it's *my* choice.

I have no idea why these guys are suddenly interested in me. Maybe they're fucking with me. Maybe I did something they think needs to be corrected. I could leave right now and never find out. Things will remain the way they are.

We'll keep circling each other, or they'll give up when they don't get whatever they want from me. Chase and I will continue as we are. My play will move forward. Everything I want this year will be in my grasp.

Or I can sit down and find out some version of the truth. At least, Damon's truth.

I'm so fucking curious about him. I've watched him for years. The pattern rarely changes for most people. But it does for him. His moods fluctuate.

Maybe that's why I've always been fascinated with him. I can't read him. I can't figure out his motivation, what drives him. Yes, hockey, obviously. His friends. Girls, there have been plenty.

But there are things that don't follow the pattern. That make me question everything I think about him. He's an abnormality. Sometimes, a girl will approach him and he'll give her the attention she seeks, and other times he'll push her away. He's brilliant, but he doesn't always do well in classes, but not because he doesn't understand or isn't interested.

What does he want? Does he even know?

"Come on, Evan." He smirks like he knows I'm going to run away. "Aren't you curious?"

With every fiber of my being. And maybe that will be where all of this goes wrong. Damon draws my attention when he's in the room. I can feel him like a buzzing in my skull.

I'm aware of the other two. They're not simple either. And the more I learn about them, the clearer the shape of their character becomes. But it also muddles my brain because the curiosity grows as I learn more about them, like I'm ravenous and everything I learn makes me hungrier. I want more.

I take a breath and sit, leaving some space between us, determined to unravel the truth.

"That's it, little devil," Damon says it so softly I barely hear him.

Before I can question him, the TV springs to life. The footage is grainy and green, like it's a night camera. Damon's face is the focus of the camera. I'm captivated, but as he steps back, my living room at our old house comes into sharp focus behind him.

My heart stops. I suck in a breath. He was in my house? And planted a camera? When? How long ago?

My heart pounds, but I'm frozen in place. The footage ends, then there's another view of Damon as he turns a camera on. He backs away with a smirk and my bedroom comes into focus—including me, asleep in my bed.

"What the fuck?" A tingling sweeps up my neck and through my head, leaving me light-headed. I move to stand up.

Damon's hand clamps down on my thigh, branding me with his heat and holding me in place on the couch. "Don't worry. I didn't do anything to you."

"You put a camera in my room and saw me sleeping." My cheeks are hot as I return my gaze to the television and the image of me with my nightgown hitched up around my hips and the sheet down around my ankles. This is so invasive. My heart claws up my throat.

My whole being is on fire. I can't take this away from him. He's seen this. He was with me when I was at my most vulnerable.

Not when I was in this house, but when I thought I was safe from him.

He was in my room and I didn't know it. He could have done anything to me. I register he's still touching me now.

My pulse pounds like I'm already running away. The heat of his hand on my bare thigh pulses through me. But I'm spinning so hard I can't focus on his touch.

I turn to look at Hawk and Cam. "Did you know?"

"No," Cam says. His attention stays on the TV and part of me wants to get up and cover my image. It's bad enough Damon saw me like that, but he's sharing it with Hawk and Cam. Who else does he intend to show this to? My heart stops.

Hawk runs a hand through his hair. His green eyes meet mine and he shakes his head.

Oh, fuck. The kiss.

"When is this?" I turn back to Damon and grab his wrist to try to remove his hand from my thigh, but he grabs tighter, not budging. I'm not strong enough to move him.

"Worried, Evan?" He leans into me. His blue eyes the only thing I can focus on as my body loses its fucking mind. His scent is overwhelming, dark and earthy. My insides soften as my gaze slips to his lips before returning to his eyes.

Heat pulses through me, making my pussy ache and grow damp. My thighs clench together against his fingers. His gaze drops to where I'm squeezing his fingers. He wets his full lips and lifts his eyes to mine.

Fuck. His blue eyes have always drawn me in. They never looked real. Up close, I can see the flecks of gold and black mixed in the pools of blue. I could drown in them. His fingers squeeze my thigh, making me gasp. Not in pain or fear, but something much more primal.

He smiles and his gaze drops to my parted lips. Some of my common sense returns. I snap my mouth shut, pressing my lips together into a thin line.

"Let me go," I say as sternly as I can. He ignores my request.

"This has been my favorite show." He turns back to the TV and I follow his gaze. It flicks to a new scene. I have a towel around me as I walk through the living room and it cuts to me in the bedroom, pulling things out of my drawers.

No. Oh god, bury me now.

I want to take his phone and throw it at the TV. Stop this from happening, but he's already seen it all. My god, he's seen all of me. No one has seen me naked before. That should have been my choice.

"Stop!" I lurch to grab at his phone or charge the TV to block it or turn it off, but he holds me in place.

When I drop the towel on the screen, I close my eyes, humiliated. He filmed me in my home. And now he's sharing these private moments with his friends. No one's laughing, but they must be making fun of me. How could they not, when those beautiful girls throw themselves at them? I'm nothing compared to them. I want to run away, but my legs feel weak beneath his touch.

He has a show to put on, and I'm captive until he decides to release me. I just want this to end. But I know it won't. I try to steady my breathing and to stop the tears burning at the back of my eyes.

Damon's breath against my ear startles my eyes open. "I wanted you to know that I saw everything, little devil. Remember when I made you show me yours, because I showed you mine? I believe in equality."

The horror of this moment is intensified by the lust pouring through my veins. How can I even want to be in the same room as this guy? He hates me and I want him. How fucked up is that?

On the screen, I'm mostly dressed now. He's watched me most of this week. Every second of my life documented for him. It's been edited, but there must have been hours of me sitting and working.

"Don't worry, little devil. They haven't seen this yet." His hand squeezes my thigh and his thumb strokes over the sensitive skin on the inside of my thighs. I gasp as sparks light beneath his touch, shivering through me like an earthquake. "They haven't seen you like I have."

I can't look away from the screen. The scene changes thankfully. It's me studying in the living room.

"To be honest, I was hoping you'd have your boyfriend over." When he says boyfriend, the word is filled with hate. "Give me some good footage of the two of you to convince you to do whatever I want. Imagine my surprise..."

I swallow, remembering this night as past me rises from the couch and heads to the door. After a few minutes, Cam follows me in.

"What the fuck, Cam?" Hawk asks. He sounds surprised. What does he think I did with Cam?

"You guys were busy. I didn't want to go home."

I turn to look at Cam and he shrugs.

"Nothing happened," he adds.

Damon's hand slides higher on my thigh and I try to hold it back, tightening my hands on his wrist. On the screen, Cam and I sit on the couch as I work and he plays on his phone. I disappear into the kitchen, and when I come back, we talk for a few minutes. We go into the kitchen and return with pizza. I'm glad there isn't sound.

"How fucking domestic." Damon's still right next to my ear. His breath is warm, caressing my skin.

His face is so close to mine, if I turned my nose would brush his. I don't dare turn. My skin buzzes with his closeness.

"What would your boyfriend think?" He tsks in my ear and a little shiver runs through me. Not of dread. No, that would be better. That would make sense. This shiver is warm and makes my body soften. When I think about Chase, I know I'm not a good girlfriend. That guilt has been eating at me all day.

I know what Damon has to show us next. But no one is laughing at me, so I tamp down the wild need to flee and realize I have an opportunity. The kiss has already happened. Damon has watched me kiss Hawk. Only Cam doesn't know about the kiss. It's recorded. I swallow, but I'm curious how it all went down.

The replay in my mind of the kiss with Hawk is clouded by my emotions. As someone more comfortable behind the camera than in front of it, I want to see how it looked from an observer's standpoint. Because frankly, that kiss wrecked me.

"I'm not ashamed of what I've done." I wish my voice hadn't trembled.

"Aren't you, Evan?" Damon's other hand brushes my hair away from my ear, sending sparks cascading through me from every brush of his fingers against my skin. "I don't think Chase would like this next part."

The scene changes to Hawk carrying me in piggyback style. I try to ignore the presence of Damon's dark energy surrounding me and focus on the scene unfolding with the critical eye of a director. Ignore the fact that this is a weak moment, one Damon could use to blow up my life, because I never confessed to Chase.

Past Hawk sits with me and then stands. Takes off his helmet before dropping to his knee before me. He takes off my helmet and then he's kissing me. It lasts both longer and shorter than I remembered.

I pull away first, but it's obvious I was kissing him back. My stomach knots.

I should have told Chase what happened and asked him for forgiveness, but then what would have happened during play rehearsal next week? The tension between Chase and Hawk could overwhelm the whole production.

I don't think either man would fight over me, but there's the sense of honor when someone makes a move on your girlfriend that might come into play.

"Should I show them what you did later that night, little devil?" Damon's words make my skin flush hot, but those words are also enough for me to snap out of this.

I push him away and he finally releases me. I hurry to the television and turn it off. He watched me. Fuck. Fuck. Fuck.

I press my hands to my forehead unable to turn around and face them. What do I do now? What can I do now? I'm ignoring what Damon saw me do later that night. I can't handle knowing he invaded my privacy like that.

"Here's what's going to happen, Evan." Damon stands and closes in on my back. He doesn't touch me, thankfully.

I don't think I could handle that right now. I drag in a breath. How did I get here?

"Why?" The word rips out of me. Because none of this makes any sense. Tears sting my eyes. They annoy the fuck out of me, because I can handle this.

This could blow up my life or I can get ahead of it and figure out what the fuck he wants. Because if he wanted to blow me up, he wouldn't have shown me this. He would have sent it to everyone in school, or just Chase.

No, he wants something from me. He caught me on film because he thinks he can control me with it.

I swallow that bitter pill and force down the tears. My arms drop to my sides. When I turn and look up at him, he watches me like I'm a feral animal he's backed into a corner. And damn, do I feel like prey trapped by the predator.

"You wouldn't have shown me this if you didn't want something." I don't dare look past him at Hawk or Cam. Nothing in the video would blow up either of their worlds. There's no audio.

Hawk might be embarrassed by my rejection, but it could be edited to not show that part, leave it up to the viewer to decide what happens next. I lift my gaze to Damon's, tipping my head back since he's so much taller than me.

I try not to think of him seeing my hand in my panties later that night. I won't be embarrassed by relieving a need. Because I know he probably masturbates more than I ever have.

I raise an eyebrow. "What do you want, Damon?"

He smirks. "Everything."

"Evan?" My mom's voice breaks the spell like cold water drenching me. I step away from Damon, like coming up for air. He backs up, but I'm sure this isn't over.

"Down here, Mom." I glance at the others before heading toward my mother's voice. Cam and Hawk both seem content to let this play out.

Damon's voice echoes in my head. *Everything.*

CHAPTER 21

EvanAnn

MOM WALKS WITH ME UPSTAIRS. "I know this is a lot, but I think this will be a good change for both of us."

I grabbed my backpack on the way up the stairs. Now I drop it inside the door to my new bedroom. What am I even doing here? How is this our life? How is this going to be a good change for me, when Damon's already invaded my privacy even though I wasn't living with him yet?

Mom's gaze takes in my worn uniform. Her lips purse.

"I'll get you some new uniforms. This one's color is all faded." Mom puts her hand on my shoulder. She's never noticed when my uniforms are worn out or too small. Usually, I have to tell her. "Maybe a new backpack too. You'll see, this will be a good thing."

"I don't need new uniforms, Mom." I adjust my skirt. Mom doesn't have the money to throw away on new uniforms. Maybe if I don't take anything from Adam, Damon won't take anything away from me.

His scent lingers in my nose. My ear still burns from the warmth of his breath.

My skin feels tight and part of me is nervous that as soon as she leaves, Damon will return and explain what *everything* entails. Why that thought doesn't terrify me more is something I'll have to contemplate later, when I'm alone.

"Nonsense, Evan." She touches my hair. "You're such a beautiful girl. We should get your hair trimmed."

"I don't need anything, Mom. What I have is fine."

The bed is as obnoxiously large as I remember, but like Cam said, there isn't a box in sight.

"Where are my boxes?" I glance around. The things that were on my desk at home are now arranged neatly on the desk here. Not exactly how I left it, but someone took the time to arrange things.

Mom goes to the closet and opens it. "The staff put it all away."

I walk over and see my things hung from wooden hangers. My camera equipment is lined up on the shelves. I open a drawer and find my bras and underwear.

Mom keeps talking, but I can't focus on her words. She's saying something about how much we're going to love living here.

The back of my neck pricks and I glance up in the corners. Does Damon have a camera in here? Or my room? Or our bathroom?

My stomach churns, remembering how humiliating it was to see those moments that were supposed to be mine displayed on his TV. What are his plans with those files? My skin crawls, imagining the whole student body laughing over those images.

When I asked him what he wanted, he was pleased I figured it out. I wish that didn't make me proud. I'm as smart as he is. It doesn't take a neurosurgeon to figure out that if he's showing me the video, he wants to use it against me.

The feel of his hot hand is branded on my thigh. My body is still keyed up. All that potential energy brewing between us didn't vanish at my mother's voice, but it definitely cooled. The fire was banked, but I'm sure it's going to burn me whole.

"I thought you'd be gone tonight because of the football game. Is everything okay with you and Chase?" She gestures to my backpack. "I saw your backpack and knew you were here. It's so unusual for you to leave your stuff out."

Thank fuck, Cam left it out. I could still be in that basement, staring down the god of our school. Me, a lowly ant.

I focus on her question. "Everything is good between me and Chase."

At least for now. I still don't know what Damon's intentions are. Will he show it to Chase? If he wants Chase to dump me, he would, but how does that help Damon?

It really seemed like Cam and Hawk were surprised by the videos, but what if this whole thing was a setup? What if Cam didn't do what he was supposed to, so Hawk made sure I had to ride with him that night, knowing he'd be able to get his leader something good to blackmail me with?

It doesn't matter who's at fault. I fell for it. I'm the one who will have to face the consequences.

"Oh, that's good." Mom smiles and touches her necklace, which glints in the room light. I noticed she wasn't wearing what she normally wears around our house. It's date night though. But now I clue in to the way she's dressed. Her clothes aren't anything I've seen before.

"New clothes?" I ask.

She touches the pants and smiles softly. "Adam likes to spoil me."

I swallow. Maybe my mom and I are the real problem Damon wants to deal with. Our only option now would be the apartments we had to leave before. I swallow down the bile that rises thinking about what happened there.

I don't want to go back, but we may not have a choice.

"Maybe we should have an option in case this doesn't work out, Mom." I sit on the edge of my new bed. "Just in case. I really hope you and Adam work out, but—"

"Honey." Mom walks over and sits next to me, taking my hand. "I know you don't want me to replace your father. I will always love Jason and there's no one who could ever take his place, but I don't want to be alone anymore."

"You have me." I blow out a breath. It's a weak argument, but it's the only one I have. "This feels like a lot. This house is… a lot."

"You have your whole life ahead of you, Evan. This is barely a year of your life." She takes my hand between hers and squeezes it. "How did auditions go?"

She's changing the subject, and honestly, I don't blame her. I'm worried about what will happen when she leaves me alone. Are the guys going to stay tonight or will I only have to deal with Damon?

I don't know which would be worse. But for now, I have my mom's undivided attention. So, I tell her about the play.

———

Mom leaves me alone after talking about going shopping this weekend. I don't like any of this, but I'm happy for her. I don't want to bring her down by telling her my new stepbrother might be trying to blackmail me.

For what? I don't know. *Everything* isn't a real clear statement of intent.

Things I don't have are money, status, or beauty. I have nothing he can't get somewhere else. My cheeks burn, thinking about the weight of his hand on my thigh. The way his heat seeped into my being, making me uncomfortably turned on and anticipating his next move.

Fuck. I run a hand through my hair. I can't think of him like that. He's my enemy. He broke into my house and planted cameras to watch me. Maybe he hoped for something more than he got. But what he has is enough to take me down.

If he wanted to get back at Chase or drive us out, all he'd have to do is show others those videos of me. Fuck, if he spread them around school I don't know if I'd be able to finish out my senior year there.

Yes, they aren't salacious, but he has one of me masturbating. He threatened to show the guys, but didn't. At least not in front of me. My chest tightens. At least my thoughts are my own.

He doesn't know what I was thinking while I touched myself, but I'm sure he could use his powers of deduction.

I glance at the door to the bathroom. I've searched my bedroom and closet for hidden cameras, but I don't really know what I'm looking for. Really tiny cameras exist, ones I may not be able to find. I haven't searched the bathroom yet. It's weird to approach the closed door, but I knock just in case he's upstairs already.

When there's no response, I open the door. I didn't notice a lot about the bathroom when Adam showed me. Now I walk in and hold my breath for a moment.

Okay, it's a bathroom, except now my things surround the other sink and my bath supplies are in the shower with Damon's. It feels weird, sharing this space with him.

Personal. Intimate.

Especially knowing he's seen everything. My cheeks heat.

The door to his bedroom is closed. The toilet is in a water closet. I breathe a little easier and slip inside, locking the door to use the facilities before coming out to wash my hands.

When I turn off the water, the doorknob captures my attention. It's smooth. There's no obvious lock.

I dry my hands on a towel. Walking over, I shut the door to my room and try to figure out how to lock it. There's no lock. Wait. I turn and go to his door. It's the same knob. And there isn't a way to lock it. I leave it open.

What the fuck? Panic flutters through me.

Neither door locks on the inside or outside of the doors. It's not like Damon hasn't seen me naked. My stomach churns. Him seeing an image of me naked when I wasn't aware is very different than standing naked in front of him. Vulnerable, within touching distance.

I'd love to think it's a fail-safe to make sure I don't accidentally get locked out of my bathroom, but it seems intentional.

Everything.

His dark voice haunts me. A shiver runs down my spine. What does *everything* even mean? I glance at the open door to Damon's bedroom. I bite my lip.

I shouldn't. But he was in my room when I wasn't aware. He invaded my inner sanctum and watched me for days. Like he said, he showed me his. Well he saw mine...

Fuck it. I walk into his room.

His earthy scent makes my head spin. I don't know what it is about Damon that captivates me. His desk draws my attention. His calculus book is out on it and it looks like he was doing his homework. Unsurprisingly, all the answers are correct.

The surface of his desk is otherwise clean. I glance at the closed door to the hallway. He went through my room. And more. He stood over me while I slept, and what? Studied me?

It's only fair I get to creep around his room. I have no idea where he is or when he'll come back. Instead of fear, a thrill works through me.

I've never done anything like this before.

I'm sure his desk drawers are like mine, filled with supplies. Fuck that. I want to know what's in his nightstand. I walk over and sit on the edge of his bed, with another quick glance at the door.

It's shut and when I don't hear anything, I pull open the top drawer of his nightstand and look up at the door, totally expecting the act of violating his sanctuary would have summoned him. When the door remains closed, I focus on the drawer and its contents.

There's a bottle of something. I lift it. Lube. Makes sense. I set it back in the drawer and shift through the condoms lying on the top. Also makes sense. I slide it shut. With a quick glance at the door, I open the next drawer down.

My mouth falls open at all the sex toys. I don't dare touch anything and disrupt the positions, but there's a lot of what looks like anal plugs and vibrators. Cock rings, maybe? Some silky straps.

Does he have sex in his room? Is he going to have sex in there while I'm in my room? My insides twist. Fuck, I don't like the idea of him with someone else, which is insane. I don't have any hold over him or the other guys. I slide the drawer shut. It's not like he's a monk. The Devils have sex. That's a fact.

I open the next drawer down. There's only a framed picture in it. I lift the frame out and look at the gorgeous woman holding a toddler. They both look so happy. My fingers trace over it.

I have a similar picture with my dad that is always on my dresser. Why is his in a drawer?

"What are you doing, Evan?" Damon's voice startles me. My heart pounds. My hands shake as I set the picture on his bed and stand to face him.

I shrug with an air of nonchalance I don't feel at all. "You saw inside my drawers."

He glances at the picture and steps in, closing the door behind him. The lock snicks in place and my already frantic heartbeat goes crazy.

Run, my instinct yells at me. Running from a predator is rarely a good strategy. I don't want to back down from him either.

I'm trying to calculate how long it will take me to reach the bathroom. Because I did this to myself. Trapping myself with the devil himself.

"Where are Cam and Hawk?" I ask.

He glances down before lifting those piercing blue eyes to mine. "They headed out to a party. My father didn't feel comfortable with them staying here on your first night in our house."

"Oh. Were you going to the party? I'll let you get changed." I back up and gesture to the bathroom. "I should go to my room."

His chuckle is dark and captivating at the same time. "Are you going to try to hide now, little devil?"

He hasn't moved from the door, but he crosses his arms as he shakes his head, like I'm the one doing something wrong. Fuck that, and fuck him. My breath shudders in and out. Anger swirls through me at his intrusion into my life. The humiliation of watching those videos with his friends.

"You had no right to invade my privacy." I step toward him.

He smirks and drops his head to the side, scratching the back of his head. "Why not? We practically live together. We're going to share everything, Evan."

I swallow. He moves quickly, like a predator, and I stumble back away from him. Before I know it, I'm against the wall with nowhere to go. His hands land on either side of my head. I flinch. I have no survival instinct when it comes to him.

"Do you know what you've done, Evan?"

I stare at his black shirt hanging away from his abs. My heart pounds in my ears.

"I haven't done anything," I say softly. "None of this is my fault. My mom didn't check with me to see if I wanted to move in with her boyfriend and his son. If this has something to do with Chase—"

He grabs my chin and tips my head back, so I have no choice but to look him in the eyes. My breath catches and I don't know if I'm even breathing. His heat and scent surround me, suffocating me in all things Damon.

He tsks slowly. "I can see why they like you."

"They?" I ask, a little lost in his intense gaze. The heat of his body seeping into mine. Those firm lips moving when he speaks.

"Cam and Hawk." He lowers his head toward mine, and I can't look away. I'm frozen, waiting for the inevitable. Hoping for it. Needing it. "They want to protect you, but I know the truth, little devil."

"What truth?" I ask.

"You crave our attention." His thumb swipes over my lips. Sparks flood through me. Is he going to kiss me?

"I'll scream." My voice is shaky.

His chuckle is dark. "Go ahead, little devil. Scream. Bring your mother and my father rushing into my room to find us kissing. Or maybe you need to scream to be aroused?"

His eyes light with interest as he rubs a strand of my hair between his fingers.

"Is that what you need, little devil?" His fingers slide into my hair, sending a cascade of sparks through me so powerful I can barely think.

"Let me go." My words are a whisper.

"No."

A gasp parts my lips before his mouth crashes down on mine. The room disappears as he brutally takes my mouth with his. My lips part for him, unable to resist. I've never been consumed in such a way before. Like he craves me more than his next breath. It unlocks something inside me I'm helpless to resist.

My fingers press against the wall. The only place we touch is our lips and his hand on my chin to keep me there, but he didn't need to bother. I can't turn away as I fall into the brush of his tongue against my lips before it slips inside to tangle with mine.

He tastes of mint and darkness. I'm drowning in the feel of him. Wanting, needing more.

He lifts his mouth, and for a moment, his darkened eyes search mine like he's unsure of what he's doing. My knees tremble and everything in me wants to press up into him again. I shouldn't be here. I should have stopped him. There's this knot of need and knowledge warring within me, telling me to pull away from him. I should scream.

"Run away, little devil."

CHAPTER 22

Damon

I SLEPT LIKE A BABY, knowing Evan is probably freaking the fuck out. I woke up early to run and left my door open into the bathroom, so she'll know I'm not there. She needs to get comfortable with our living arrangement.

I shouldn't have kissed her last night. But I can't regret it.

Kissing isn't my favorite thing to do with a girl. Not when I can bury my cock into their tight cunt or warm mouth. I prefer fucking. But I could see getting lost in Evan's taste for hours, just kissing.

But Cam is right, the girl is loyal to her boyfriend. We have no fucking clue why. I could have pushed for more last night, but at some point she would have come to her senses.

Even now, the memory of her makes me hard. She tastes like cotton candy, and I've always had a sweet tooth.

I head into my bedroom and notice the door to the bathroom is closed. I smirk. By now she realizes I won't have any locks between us, but I have every intention of making her feel at home.

I go into the bathroom and the separate toilet room door is closed, with the light shining under it. I close the door to her bedroom before turning on the shower. I strip down and step under the water.

There's no door, just a piece of glass and an opening. The mirror hangs directly across from me, giving me the perfect view of the water closet door. The water warms as I duck under it, rinsing the sweat from my hair.

The toilet flushes, but Evan still doesn't come out. I shampoo my hair and soap my body before stepping back under the stream to rinse. She'll have to come out eventually, but maybe she thinks she can wait me out.

Thinking of her so fucking close has me hard.

"Little devil, come out and play," I say, loud enough to be heard.

"You're in the shower." The door muffles her voice. "I can wait."

"I'm not getting out of the shower until you come out." I rinse all the soap from my body and hair. I slide my hand over my cock. "Come on, Evan, I've seen you naked already. Now's your opportunity for payback."

That gets her to open the door. It's why she was in my room last night. If I hadn't invaded her space, she never would have ventured into mine.

She doesn't come out of the doorway next to the shower. I meet her gaze in the mirror, challenging her. Her gaze rakes over me. She's got on pajamas, a little top and shorts. Her lips part when she notices my hand stroking my cock.

"It's only fair, little devil." I try to coax her out. "I watched you come all over that hand. Don't you want to watch me come all over mine?"

She swallows, but somewhere in that little, tight-strung body she finds the courage to step out of the only place she can hide from me. I want her to feel safe, but there's a key on the door frame if I need to pry her out of it.

"Want to give me the live show?" I smirk. The memory of her hand moving beneath those panties is burned in my mind.

"No." She steps out to the counter and washes her hands before turning around. Her ass rests against the edge of the countertop and she crosses her arms below her breasts as she blatantly watches me stroke myself.

I reach over and turn off the water. When I step out of the shower and onto the shower mat, her lips part. Fuck, I want to know what those lips will feel like wrapped around my cock.

"Tell me what you thought about when you touched yourself, little devil."

Her blue eyes spark as she lifts them to mine. "No."

My gaze drops to her breasts.

"Show me your tits." I arch an eyebrow in challenge.

Her brow furrows. "I'm not helping you."

"But you want to, don't you, little devil?" Precum leaks out of my tip and I spread it down my cock. I've worked on my body to make it a masterpiece for hockey. I tower over Evan. Every girl who's ever seen me wants to fuck me. I doubt Evan is any different. "Do you want a taste? I won't tell."

"Is that what you want?" Evan lifts her gaze to mine. Her blue eyes have darkened with desire. Will she be wet if I slide my hand into her panties?

"It's a start." I squeeze my base to keep from coming.

"What do you want from me?" She drops her arms to her sides but she presses her thighs together.

"Are you turned on, little devil?" I step toward her and watch her breath catch.

She's trying to be so fucking brave. So certain I won't take what I want from her. I could have her, but she might cry foul. And while I want her and her mother gone from my house, I need time with her first. I want to take advantage of her stay here.

"I have a boyfriend." She's not offended or telling me off. It's a statement of fact.

"And you're loyal to him?" I step closer.

She lifts her chin. "Of course."

"Except you kissed both Hawk and me."

"You both kissed me." Her cheeks flush redder. Semantics. Poor little devil.

"And you kissed us back." I brush my hand over her jaw and she shivers.

Her eyes grow wary. She never should have let me get this close. My dick grows harder.

"You should have pushed me away like you did Hawk."

"Are you going to finish this little demonstration so we can move on?" She raises an eyebrow like I'm beneath her. "After all, you saw mine. Show me yours."

It's not a bad image. Her riding my hard cock. Those breasts rising and falling with her movements. I groan as my release claws at me.

I smirk and close the distance between us before she can think of getting away, wrapping my hand behind her neck and dropping my mouth to hers. Her hands go to my chest, probably to push me away. But her lips part beneath mine with a whimper.

Her surrender makes me come all over my hand. I groan into her mouth, wishing I'd spilled it inside her instead. Soon. Because fucking cotton candy. My cum-covered hand slides to her ass to draw her against me. She gasps and her hands press against my bare chest.

It's too fucking late to protest, and she's not even really trying to get away as she matches my tongue and lips, following my lead. Her kiss is intoxicating.

My still-hard cock rests against her stomach. The hard tips of her breasts brush against my chest. Fuck, if I slide my hand into her panties, how wet will she be?

Before I can back away enough to slide my hand between us, there's faint knocking. It's not on the bathroom door.

"Evan?" Her mother's voice is muffled by the two doors.

Evan pushes a little harder. I bite down on her lip and she moans like I shoved my fingers into her pussy. Fuck, what is it about this girl?

I back away. She stands there for a moment. Her blond hair wild from sleep and my hand in it. Her blue eyes wide with mortification.

"Your boyfriend doesn't deserve your loyalty, little devil."

"What do you mean?" She presses her trembling fingers against her lower lip. It's swollen from my kisses and my bite. There's a spot of my cum on her top.

I want her to question everything. "Do you think you're the only one he's fucking?"

EvanAnn

I'm not proud. I fled that bathroom. Payback sounded like a good idea. Make him feel how I felt. Exposed.

But it was a double-edged sword. I've never watched a guy jerk off in real life. My pussy pulsed and clenched watching his fist work himself. Imagining what it would feel like if he pushed inside me, filling me. My breasts felt tight and achy. And even though he was the one getting off, I was breathing hard.

My panties are damp, and I'm decidedly rumpled when I answer the door. My lip aches from where he bit me. I never should have let him kiss me. I never should have stayed for his little demonstration.

"Yes?" I open the door only a few inches.

"Did I wake you?" Mom smiles. "How'd you sleep?"

Like crap. "Good. I'm not dressed, Mom."

"Oh, okay." She touches my forehead. "Are you getting sick? You seem flushed?"

"I'm good." I blow out a breath. "Just hurried to get the door is all."

"Do you have plans today?" she asks. She knows things get busy with rehearsal. Maybe she wants to spend time together. Or she might be checking to see if she can go out with Adam again.

"I'm going to the hockey scrimmage, dinner, and a party with Mia, her brother, and Chase." My brain stalls on what Damon said. Chase doesn't deserve my loyalty? What does he mean I'm not the only one Chase is fucking? He's not even fucking me. We're dating, so he shouldn't be fucking anyone else.

Is Damon trying to get into my head? Mission accomplished. He's been living there rent-free for years and now, he's moved in permanently after that kiss. Why didn't I push him away? I could have turned my head. Why did I stay in there at all?

"Oh, good. I was worried. We're going to the city to have dinner and might be back late. We may decide to stay there, depending on traffic." Mom smiles and tucks a strand of my hair behind my ear. "But it sounds like you'll be busy."

I nod. Pretty sure there's cum on the back of my shorts. Fuck, what was I thinking? That I could go toe-to-toe with Damon Storm? I'm not experienced enough to deal with someone like him.

"Morning." Damon nods to my mother as he passes her in the hallway. He's dressed in jeans and a black t-shirt that stretches across his chest. His blond hair is as unruly as ever.

Mom brightens. "Good morning."

His blue eyes flick up to mine, and it's like I can still feel the heat of him pressed against me. All of him.

"Shower's all yours, Evan." He winks.

My cheeks flare with heat. "Thanks."

Mom smiles in approval and watches him walk down the hallway. "I'm glad to see you two getting along."

"Did you need anything else, Mom?" I'm suddenly exhausted.

"Oh, Adam said you can use one of his cars while yours is being fixed." She smiles and holds out a set of keys.

I take them and turn them over in my hand. BMW? "But my car only had a flat."

"Adam had them take it in for a tune-up. He doesn't want you to get stranded again. He'll take care of everything, honey." Mom glances down the hallway. "I'm sure it won't take long."

I can't drive this, unless it's a beater. Fuck.

I'M STILL NOT SURE HOW I'M GOING TO GET TO THE scrimmage. My brain's been turning over the problem since I took the fastest shower known to man. I worried about the door opening and Damon coming back in to finish what he started.

I'm trying not to focus on seeing him naked and stroking his cock in front of me. Because part of me wants him to finish what he started. Every inch of me ached for his touch. If I felt half of this with Chase, I wouldn't still be a virgin.

Damon is potent. And all I feel now is guilt for how much I want him.

I put on some light makeup and pull my hair up into a ponytail. My lip is sore from Damon's rough kiss. After eating some breakfast, I go out to the garage to find out what car Adam thinks is a good replacement for mine.

With a heavy sigh, I stare at the black BMW. It's sporty, and when I open the door, it smells like Damon. Raw and earthy. My insides stir with longing. Fuck.

I can't have Chase pick me up. Not without admitting who I'm living with. I want to trust Mia, but I've barely known her a week. Maybe next week I'll be able to handle her knowing this.

Before it wouldn't have been an issue. I was proud of our little house. It wasn't a big, professionally decorated mansion, but it was ours.

If I show up in this car, there *will* be questions. I might as well announce I'm living in Damon's house. Fuck, I don't know how long I can keep it a secret.

Probably for a long time, honestly. It's not like I have people over to my house. But this shit always gets out.

I doubt most people in the school even know where I live, but if my mom gets me new uniforms and I have to drive this car, someone will say something. I rest my head against the cool metal roof of the car. I'm so fucked.

"It's my favorite."

I lift my head at Damon's voice. My eyes widen, but I don't turn around. I can't take more of his teasing and touching. I should jump in this car and lock the doors.

"You need a way to get around, little devil." He chuckles darkly. "I told Dad he could offer you my car, since I'm riding to school. Unless you want to ride with me."

I turn to see him leaning in the doorway of the garage with his hands in his pockets.

"Up to you. You could always admit to other people you live here." Smirking, he leaves me alone.

CHAPTER 23

Hawk

THE ICE IS where I rule. The scrimmage doesn't usually draw a huge crowd, but today, there's a decent number of students in the stands. Especially with Damon back on the ice.

He can skate circles around the Kentwood Prep guys. His whole life has been focused on hockey. Achieving the next level.

Being back at Deimos is hard for him. The plan was to go to the Junior League, get noticed by the big division one schools on the East Coast and by the NHL. Instead, he's here. Some of these guys will play in college, but for most, high school is the end of the line for them with hockey.

They may play in rec leagues when they're older, but they will never be on this level again. And never with someone who will be drafted to the NHL.

I've loved every moment I've had on the ice, even when the coach forces us to bag skate, skating drills without the puck. But this is probably my final year. I have to focus either on my studies or on hockey. I'm good on the ice and could play in college, but I'm not at the level Damon is.

Cam glides up next to me. "She's here."

My gaze goes to where he indicates in the stands. Annie sits between Mia and Chase who's talking to some blond guy.

Annie looks happy, but when her gaze collides with mine, the smile freezes on her face. I can't get the feel of her lips against mine out of my mind. I don't want to. I want to do it again.

The rejection stung, not going to lie. I'll take whatever Damon gets her to offer, but no girl has ever rejected me before. It makes me want to make her beg for it. And she will.

"Scoping out the puck bunnies?" Jackson Riordan slides to a stop next to me. We played together when we were younger. He's on the Kentwood Prep team on a scholarship. He's good, but an asshole. "Who's the blond?"

"Mia Lewis." Cam skates backwards, leaving me with Jackson. He's not a fan. None of us are.

"She looks promising. Blonds are my favorite." Jackson smirks. "Is that who you were looking at?"

"Fuck off, Jackson," Damon says as he skates over to us.

"Feeling territorial?" Jackson sneers at him. He's always hated Damon. Maybe because Damon is better than him on the ice, or has more money, or gets more pussy. It doesn't matter what Jackson is good at, Damon will always be better.

"Warm-ups are over, Riordan." I know better than to let Jackson and Damon talk for too long, because the hate goes both ways. We don't need a fight before the game even begins.

Jackson skates back to his side of the ice.

Damon's gaze goes to Annie in the stands. "What did he want?"

I'm not surprised he's already locked onto her. Last night was fucked up. But we've all gotten to see Annie naked, and fuck, does it make me want to make her beg me for it even more. I don't know what she brings out in me, but I'm ready to explore it.

"Nothing. We should head to the coach." I gesture with my head.

Cam assumed Jackson was talking about Mia, but his gaze seemed intent on Annie. Something about that focus set off warning bells in my head. Damon doesn't need to know that. Not before going into a game.

He needs to focus. We need this win.

EvanAnn

The hair stands on the back of my neck. I turn to meet Hawk's gaze. He's standing on the ice with Cam and both are looking in my direction.

"Oh my god, I think Hawk's looking at me." Mia straightens and smiles.

My cheeks heat. I haven't seen Cam or Hawk since they saw me naked on video. I don't know if Damon showed them the other footage, but it seems like something he would do. Did he tell them about us kissing?

Fuck, that kiss in the bathroom with him naked and exposed. I was the one coming undone. He may have been naked, but he had complete control over me, making me the vulnerable one in that situation.

"I didn't pay attention to the hockey team at Sherman." Mia cranes her head around to check out the entire team. "Do you think we could move closer to the ice?"

"These seats seem good," Chase says. He reaches over and takes my hand.

It's chilly in here and my hands are cold, so I appreciate it. I turn to thank Chase but get caught in his blue eyes and his classic smile. The trouble is, my brain can't stop thinking about someone else's blue eyes. I didn't touch Damon, but he touched me. If I thought Hawk shook my foundation, Damon shattered it.

I couldn't have pushed him away even if I wanted to. But Chase doesn't know. He doesn't know I've kissed two guys behind his back. Sure, they kissed me, but that's semantics. I know what I felt. It's how I should feel for Chase, not Hawk or Damon.

Chase turns away from me when Tanner mentions something.

Do you think you're the only one he's fucking? Damon is in my head and I can't seem to shake him out. What if I'm not the only one doing things behind closed doors? A stone sinks in my stomach.

I turn back toward the ice. Mia's focused on the guys, leaving me stuck in my thoughts.

Chase had a reputation before we started dating. He definitely got around. He also hasn't really pushed me hard on the physical side, claiming he's willing to wait for me to be ready. But what if he isn't waiting? What if the reason he's willing to wait is because he's getting sex on the side?

He's introduced me to his parents and talks about a future, so why would he be with me if he's having sex with other girls?

Maybe Damon is fucking with me to make me doubt my boyfriend. But for what purpose? Why did he kiss me? It took everything in me not to reach out and touch him. To slide my hands down his solid chest and feel his cock pulse in my hand.

Fuck. My cheeks flush with heat. Definitely need him out of my head.

I don't know what the purpose of Damon's attention is yet, but it can't be good. A shiver rolls through me.

"Look at Damon." Mia draws my attention down to the ice where Damon skates on the ice like he owns it. "Fuck, he's so hot. Can you imagine what he'd be like in bed. Do you think he'll be at the party tonight?"

My lip aches from his bite, and I resist the urge to reach up and touch it. What would have happened if my mom hadn't interrupted us again?

I've never seen a naked guy in person. Every inch of Damon is sculpted to perfection, including his cock. Although I have nothing to compare it to, he definitely seemed larger than the ones I've seen online.

Heat floods me. I'm trying not to focus on him and what happened in his room and the bathroom, but fuck, his lips on mine are enough to set me on fire. His heart, beneath my palms, had been beating as rapidly as mine.

"You okay?" Mia asks.

"Sorry, what?" I tear my gaze from him and look at Mia.

"You seem distracted. Is everything okay?" She gestures to the ice. "I know this is distracting, but you seem distant."

"Just thinking." I can't tell her what I'm thinking about. I don't know if there's some girl code about guys your friend wants to fuck. Besides, I can't tell her about Damon with Chase here. I don't even know how to explain what's happening without giving it all away.

I'm a mess.

"Okay, but if you need to talk, I'm here for you." Mia's look is concerned.

I give her a smile. "I appreciate that."

"Did you see the guys on the other team?" Mia looks down at the ice with hearts in her eyes. "I might have found my new favorite sport."

I shake my head with a smile as the guys line up for the face-off. Then they're a blur on the ice. It's difficult to follow who's who and where the puck is.

"You want something to drink?" Chase leans in to ask.

"I'm good. Thanks." I search his eyes. Is he cheating on me? Is that why he isn't pressuring me for sex after months of dating?

He leans in to kiss me and something loud hits the boards, startling me. I turn with wide eyes and see Damon glaring up at us before he skates away from the guy he pushed into the boards. My heart is in my throat.

Did he just… ?

I cough to cover my distraction and Chase rears back.

"You getting sick, babe?"

"It's just a little cough. I'm sure it's nothing." If Damon didn't do it on purpose, it's a weird fucking coincidence. Fortunately, Chase is a bit of a germaphobe, and I haven't been enjoying his PDA. What's the point of kissing me here, anyway?

He stands. "I'll get you some orange juice or something. Gotta stay healthy for the play."

Tanner stands with him. "You need something, Mia?"

"No, I'm good." Mia doesn't take her eyes off the guys on the ice.

Tanner chuckles, shaking his head, and follows Chase. They've been talking about football and something about horsemen, which I didn't follow.

As soon as they're out of sight, I turn to Mia. "Can I ask you something?"

"Sure, bestie." Mia turns to me. Her cheeks are pink. From the cold or the excitement?

"Do you know how to tell if someone is cheating on you?" I glance toward the ice and the three guys who are making me question everything. Is it wrong of me to ask since I technically cheated on Chase? It's not a tit-for-tat situation though. I don't have any evidence of his cheating and I don't think he's aware of mine. Besides, if Chase is fucking someone else, that's different than me getting kissed and not immediately pushing the guy away.

My stomach churns. It doesn't excuse what I've done. It's always possible Chase isn't cheating at all, and Damon wants to fuck with my head. That seems to be his goal in life right now. I should come clean to Chase and tell him everything.

Mia straightens her skirt and keeps her eyes on the ice. "I haven't really been in a relationship for someone to cheat on me. But I'm sure there would be signs. Are you worried about Chase?"

I shrug and try to put it out of my mind. "This is my first relationship. I feel like I'm winging this and it should be harder."

Her eyes meet mine and she smiles. "I'm sure you're doing fine."

Except I've cheated with two guys. When my gaze lingers on Cam, I know it's only a matter of time before I cheat on Chase with a third. Maybe I shouldn't be in a relationship. But then I imagine sitting alone at lunch and having no one to talk to.

Maybe Mia would stay, but Damon doesn't want me to be his girlfriend any more than Hawk or Cam do. I shouldn't let them tempt me. I should stay with the guy who values me, dates me in the open, introduces me to his parents, and talks about the future, no matter how far-fetched.

CHAPTER 24

EvanAnn

DINNER IS AWKWARD. Maybe not for anyone else, but I can't seem to get out of my head. Did Damon seriously stop me from kissing my boyfriend, or was I projecting? Do I not want to kiss Chase?

We've made out. We kiss. We haven't done more than that. It shouldn't feel wrong to kiss my boyfriend. I *definitely* shouldn't feel guilty about kissing him. Fuck, my head is so screwed up.

Mia keeps up a running dialogue about the hockey game, the guys, and how they won. She found a website with all the guys' names, positions, and stats. Hockey is, after all, her new favorite sport.

Tanner participates in the game talk, but turns to talk to Chase when Mia begins cataloging the guys and which ones she's planning on going after at the party. Seems like Liam Massery is top of her list, along with Fletcher McIntyre, if she can't have the Devil's trio.

My stomach turns when she talks about the Devil's trio. They could fuck a different girl every night, and I have no right to tell them not to. They aren't my boyfriends.

"You don't mind if I make some moves tonight, do you?" Mia asks. "I need to work my way into their beds."

I shrug. "I'll be fine."

I'm used to being on my own at parties. Even when I'm around

Chase, he usually focuses on his friends. Occasionally, I find another ant to talk to.

Tanner gets Mia's attention, and Chase touches my arm. "Do you want me to give you a ride tonight? It might be nice to have some alone time."

Part of me wants to say yes because this is my boyfriend. The guy I'm supposed to be making out with. But the other part of me doesn't know what to think or which way is up.

Was it a coincidence Damon hit the boards when Chase and I were going to kiss? What's his plan with all those videos of me? My world's been flipped upside down.

I want to pretend living with Damon isn't real, so I can't let Chase give me a ride home. Not if I want to maintain the illusion that nothing has changed. That I won't go home and end up sleeping in practically the same room as Damon.

I don't have any way to lock him out, unless I also lock him out of his room. Interior door locks wouldn't keep him out. The image of Damon looking down on me while I slept plays through my head. Did he do that last night?

It's terrifying I didn't know he was in my room. He could have done anything to me in my sleep. My body heats, but I ignore it.

If I tell Chase what's happening with moving and Hawk, Damon, and Cam, what would Damon have to hold over my head? Sharing the video with the school? Nothing really happened.

Fuck, what were Chase and I talking about? Driving me home. Yeah, that's not happening until I figure out what's really on the line. Of course, the longer I keep the fact I'm living at Damon's a secret, the more Chase might be hurt when it comes out.

"Mia can get me home. I know you like to hang out with your friends later than I usually want to stay." I touch his hand. "Besides, I might be coming down with something and I'd hate to get you sick."

"Yeah, with the play, I can't afford to get sick." He pulls away from me. "I'll make sure you have some vitamin C to keep you well."

"Thanks." I'm so fucking confused. This is my boyfriend, but why does it feel like I'm cheating when I'm touching him, and not the other way around? I definitely feel guilty.

As we eat dinner, they talk around me while I'm spinning out thinking about the Devil's trio and how they have me ensnared in their web. They'll be there tonight at the party. I've watched them disappear with girls before. It's what they do.

My chest burns and I resist the urge to rub at it.

I have no right to say anything about them hooking up with other girls. I'm dating Chase and they're single. Besides, it's not like I could date them all. Even if that was an option, they don't date anyone. That's part of the allure for most girls.

But me? Could I be with guys with no commitment or fidelity?

All three of them? Has any girl been with all of them? That hasn't happened from what I've heard. I might live under a rock, but even I hear about their sexual conquests.

Mia told me about the time she fucked two guys at once. Have they thought about sharing a girl between them? And now I'm thinking about all three fucking me. I mean, three could be possible, right? My brain stalls out, because they're intense, even one-on-one. All three of them would be overwhelming.

Mind-blowing.

Shivers crawl down my spine. That's not normal, right? I shouldn't be considering how to fuck three guys, when I haven't even fucked one. But they make me curious and ache for more. My cheeks flush when Chase touches my arm and smiles at me.

Does he know what I'm thinking about? Is it written all over my face? I should tell him and get it over with, so we can figure out where to go from here.

But I don't.

We finish up dinner and head out to the vehicles. I ended up driving the BMW over to Mia's and leaving it there. She won't question why I have that car, because she doesn't really know me that well.

Chase starts to wrap his arm around my waist and then decides against it as we walk to his truck. I resist rolling my eyes.

"What happened to your car?" I ask as we climb in. Mia and Tanner wouldn't have to drive separately if he had his car. We also could have fit in Mia's car, but Chase refused to sit in the back seat.

"In for repairs. The parts are taking forever to get in. There were scratches all down the side. Hit some animal, probably."

My brow furrows as I put on my seatbelt. "You didn't go back to see what you hit and if it was okay?"

Chase glances my way before starting the truck. "It was dark and late. I doubt I could have found whatever I hit anyway. Probably ran off. It's not a big deal."

He turns on the radio like he always does when he doesn't want to continue the conversation. I've noticed it before, but now it bothers me.

What kind of person hits an animal and doesn't go back to check on it?

The party is at Fletcher's house. He hosts a lot of parties. We've come here a few times during the summer. Chase parks the truck, sighs, and turns to me.

"I'm sorry, babe. I'm stressing over this part in *Othello*. Maybe I should have gone back, but I can't do anything about it now." Chase looks like he's actually sorry, but something inside me doesn't believe him.

He is an actor and he's a good one. How much of everything he gives me is an act?

Does Damon have proof Chase is cheating on me? Or is he just playing with my head?

Chase reaches across the console and touches my jaw. "I wish you were feeling better. It feels like we have even less time to be together now."

Technically, we didn't have to do anything today. If he wanted alone time, we could have hung out instead of going to the hockey game, and we certainly don't have to go to this party. It was a choice he made. If he wanted alone time, maybe he should try scheduling that instead of tacking it on at the end of other plans.

My door opens before I can say anything.

Mia smiles. "Come on, bestie. I'm ready for my first party as an ant."

"Ant. That's stupid." Tanner leans against the side of the truck with his hands in his pockets. He's an attractive guy, which isn't surprising given he's Mia's twin. He gives me strange vibes though. If he weren't her brother, I don't think I'd want to hang out with him.

"You're stupid." She sticks her tongue out at him. "At least I don't have to deal with the horsemen. I still don't understand why you didn't transfer to Deimos. You could have played football here."

Tanner looks away from Mia. "I have plans for this year."

Mia rolls her eyes and takes my hand to help me out of the truck. Chase has already walked around the back.

"Careful, Mia. Evan's coming down with something. You don't want to get it." Chase jerks his chin toward the house that's all lit up. We can hear the music from two houses away.

"Are you sick?" Mia leans in as Tanner falls into step with Chase.

"Maybe a little." I hate lying. My gut twists as I say it. I don't think you get anywhere you want to be by lying, but right now, there's so much at stake. Kissing my boyfriend shouldn't be an issue. I should *want* to.

"We'll get you a screwdriver. Orange juice and vodka. The perfect cure-all." She hooks her arm in mine. "We're going to have so much fun."

The party is in full swing when we walk in. Mia keeps ahold of me, but the minute we step inside, the crowd swallows Tanner and Chase. I'm not worried. Chase usually heads to the pool area where they play beer pong. He knows I have Mia to hang out with this time.

"Mia!" Abby separates from the mass of dancing teens and walks over to us. She gives me a once-over before saying less enthusiastically, "EvanAnn."

I have on jeans and a t-shirt with a jacket. It's nothing fancy. Or slutty, which I did judge Mia's outfit a little when we met up. She's in a skirt that barely covers her ass and a crop top that hugs her breasts. But she's my friend and can do whatever she wants.

"Hi, Abby." Mia doesn't release me. "What's good tonight?"

"They've got a keg, but you need to dance with us." Abby grabs Mia's other hand. "Come on."

Mia turns to me with hopeful, excited eyes. "Evan?"

"I don't dance." I shrug, like it doesn't matter that I'll be left alone at the party. "You should go ahead."

Mia turns to Abby. "Let me grab a drink and I'll be back, okay?"

Abby glances at me, but then grins at Mia. "Yeah, I'll see you over there."

She disappears into the bodies on the dance floor.

"Come on." Mia drags me toward the back of the house.

"You should go dance. I'll be okay." I'm used to being left to my own devices at parties. Chase tends to play beer pong, leaving me to people watch. It works out.

Mia pulls me into her side as people surge around us. "You're my bestie. That means I stick to you like glue. Unless I'm hitting on a hockey guy, then we'll figure it out."

"You can dance, Mia. It doesn't bother me. Chase plays beer pong and I don't. I'm used to standing on the sidelines."

"Maybe." She shrugs. "After we get a drink and find somewhere you'll have fun too."

We walk into the kitchen where bottles cover the huge island and counters. It's a lot of choices.

"Welcome, ladies." Liam stands beside the island. Besides being on the hockey team, we've had classes together. "What can I make for you tonight?"

Mia smiles and twirls her hair around her finger. "I loved watching you play today."

"Yeah? You came to watch me?" He gives her a crooked smile, showing off his dimples. He's a good-looking guy. Not as hot as Hawk, Damon, or Cam, but he's tall and muscular with brown hair and brown eyes.

"Yeah. I've never been to a hockey game before. I'd love to learn more about the sport." Mia maintains eye contact with him the whole time. It's kind of fascinating to watch.

I don't really know how to flirt, but this is like a masterclass. The eye contact. The knowing smiles. The interest.

Liam nods. "Let's get you two some drinks. Then we can find a spot to sit and talk by the pool."

"That sounds amazing. I'd love a sex on the beach." She arches her eyebrow.

He chuckles. "Of course you would." His gaze falls on me. "What are you having, EvanAnn?"

Mia looks at me expectantly. I want to be this girl's friend, but I also don't drink much. Okay, I don't drink at all.

"She'll have the same." Mia decides for me.

Liam bobs his head as he grabs bottles and solo cups, mixing two drinks. "So, transferring your senior year either means you've got huge balls or you worked your way through your last school and need some fresh meat."

Mia's laugh is high-pitched and delighted. "Definitely looking for fresh meat."

He gives her a crooked smile. "You're in the right place."

He hands us the drinks and grabs a beer, gesturing for us to follow him. Mia squeals excitedly to me as we wind our way through the party to the door. The cool night air is much better than the stifling air inside.

My senses are on high alert, waiting for one of the Devil's trio to pounce. But so far, I haven't seen any of them. I'm not sure if they'll do anything to me here. They seem to like to get me alone before striking.

I glance around looking for Chase and Tanner, but I don't see them either. They must be inside. Liam leads us over to some couches.

"Here we go." Liam sits and pats the seat next to him. "Time to get to know the new girl."

Mia sits down and drags me down beside her. She takes a sip of her drink, but I just hold mine. It smells fruity, but I need to keep my wits about me. Somewhere at this party is the trio, and there's no mom to stop them from doing whatever they want. I'm not reliable when I'm sober when it comes to them. They stir something wicked in me.

Liam and Mia flirt and drink while I watch the other people at the party. There's a couple making out beside the pool. In the water, a few people swim and play in their underwear. It's pretty low-key out here, but music spills out the doors, keeping with the party mood.

Through the windows, I can make out the bodies moving in the dimly-lit rooms.

A game of beer pong is set up in the corner and I recognize some of Chase's friends, but he's not over there with them. I haven't seen the Devil's trio anywhere either, and I don't know if that's a relief or a disappointment.

DAMON

The party is packed tonight. We're all on a mission to find Evan on her own and drag her into a room. We're supposed to text when we find her, but I haven't seen her inside.

I do see a familiar head of dark hair as Chase walks towards the bedrooms. I follow with my phone out, ready to catch him in the act.

It's considered a party foul, but fuck this asshole. It's time Evan learned the truth, so her loyalty can switch.

He walks across the party and stops to say something to Hawk. Hawk smirks as Chase talks.

Fuck it.

I walk over to join them.

As I close in, Chase says, "No one would blame you for quitting, man. Especially now, before the play begins. Jason could slot right in there. He's been working on his lines with me. He'll do a great job."

Hawk glances at me and holds out his fist for me to bump.

Chase turns and smiles warily. "Hey, I thought you were supposed to be out this year. Going pro or some shit."

I lean against the wall next to Hawk. "Plans changed."

"That's a shame." His gaze lingers on the almost-healed scrape on my jaw. He looks away quickly. Fucker. He knows.

"You getting a piece tonight?" I ask, like I don't know he's dating Evan.

Chase smirks and looks out over the sea of dancing girls. "I've been hoping to find something quick before I go hang out for the rest of the night."

Hawk meets my gaze with a look before turning to Chase. "I'll see you Monday at the cold read."

Hawk walks away. Chase shakes his head.

"I don't know why EvanAnn cast him, but he'll definitely bring an audience." Chase blows out a breath. "What about you? You going to find a girl tonight? Olivia's been eyeing you."

My smile widens as a movement over Chase's shoulder catches my attention. Evan comes in through a door and turns up the stairs. "I have another girl in mind."

Chase is already looking at the crowd. "Me too."

He taps my arm like we're fucking friends before heading to the dance floor. He grabs a brunette and pulls her in tight against him, whispering in her ear. I snap a few pictures on my phone of them talking with his hands on her ass, before turning toward the stairs.

EvanAnn

After a while and a lot of flirting, it's clear something is happening between Liam and Mia. I should leave so they can get to know each other without a third wheel.

I touch Mia's arm. "I need to find the bathroom."

"Want me to come with?" She glances at Liam. Her cup is empty and her eyes are a little darker.

"No, I'm good to go alone." It's an excuse anyway. I do have to go, but I want to find Chase. We should spend some time together. Maybe that will help rekindle some of those initial sparks.

Liam points toward the door in the shadows. "There's a bathroom on the second floor. If you go through that door, you'll be at the stairs, and the door's at the top."

"Thanks."

Mia grabs my hand and squeezes it. "Come find me in..." She looks over Liam and he gives her a cocky smile. "Thirty minutes, okay?"

I nod and lean in. "I'm riding back to your place with you tonight. Is that okay?"

"Of course." She smiles. "I won't leave you here."

I look down into my still-full cup and offer it to her. She smirks and takes a sip. I step away and walk around the pool to the door Liam pointed out. When I glance back, Mia and Liam are talking. Her hand is on his knee as she leans in close.

He's focused on her and only her. It looks easy. I'm happy for her.

At least she's not hitting on Hawk, Cam, or Damon. Yet.

I haven't seen any of them, even though I've seen other hockey players around. Maybe they've already found girls to fuck. My stomach clenches. Just because they're trying to blackmail me doesn't mean they want me. And I don't have a right to be jealous.

I shake it off, open the door, and walk upstairs. There are a few people waiting for the bathroom, so I join the line.

Pulling out my phone, I text Chase.

ME:

Where'd you go?

I'm on the second floor

Waiting for bathroom

I look down the hallway. Those are the bedrooms everyone knows are available for sex. It seems kind of impersonal and weird to use someone else's bedroom for sex, but I guess it's better than the back seat of a car.

By the time it's my turn, Chase hasn't answered me. I open the conversation with Hawk. He hasn't texted me since yesterday. I should erase his messages so Chase doesn't see them, but he never looks at my phone.

Chase isn't worried about me straying. Why would he? I'm loyal and don't do anything but stay home. Apparently he should be worried, because my home now includes a guy who doesn't mind if I watch him masturbate.

And that kiss. A shiver rolls through me as my knees weaken. Fuck. I need to put it out of my head. Damon is toying with me. I don't know why, but I'll find out.

I wash my hands and head out into the hallway. The last person in line disappears into the bathroom, leaving the hallway empty. The music reaches up here, but it's quieter than it was on the first floor.

I could find somewhere quiet to hang out until Mia is ready to leave...

Instead, I take a breath and turn to head down the stairs.

I run right into someone tall and they grab my arm to keep me from falling. That dark and earthy scent makes my eyes widen and my insides combust. My gaze shoots up to meet piercing blue ones. His smile is wicked.

"Evan."

CHAPTER 25

EvanAnn

Keeping hold of my arm, Damon drags me forward and opens a door before shoving me inside, shutting the door behind us. I blink, confused as to how this happened. How I, once again, find myself alone with Damon. This time at a party, where anyone can find us together.

Fuck. Would anyone really believe I was having sex with Damon in a bedroom at a party? Probably not, honestly.

I back away from him as he closes the distance between us. My leg touches the bed and I sidestep. He lets me keep that space between us.

Bed plus Damon would be bad. This is bad. What if someone saw us? I mean, it would make for great gossip. Even if he didn't come in here to fuck me. My mind stalls on that thought.

"We need to discuss your rules, little devil." He narrows his eyes and everything inside me goes on high alert.

"Rules? What are you talking about?"

He's between me and the door, but he didn't lock it. This probably isn't like earlier, when he masturbated for me. Thinking about his fist stroking his cock makes something warm swim in my stomach. He wants control of me.

I need to be firm with him. This can't keep happening. I'm with Chase. Chase actually *wants* to be my boyfriend. He likes me. I don't know what Damon and his friends want from me, but it can't be good.

Closing the distance between us, he tips my chin up. His fingers burn me. "I didn't like Chase trying to kiss you earlier."

My cheeks flare hot, remembering him crashing into the boards. Not a coincidence, then. Fuck.

"He's my boyfriend. Out of all the guys I shouldn't be kissing, he's the one guy I should." I shouldn't even be arguing this with him, but fuck him. "You don't own me."

His chuckle is dark. "That's where you're wrong, Evan. I do own you. Maybe the video of you kissing Hawk isn't as scandalous as I would have liked, but you don't want your boyfriend to know about it. Or he wouldn't have been having a casual conversation with Hawk at the party."

I drop my gaze to his t-shirt. I didn't tell Chase about kissing Hawk or Damon. The guilt ties my gut into knots, but I also don't want Chase to quit the play. I'm sure Brandt would find a spot for him if he asked. And then Brandt would gloat.

Damon raises my chin again, forcing me to meet his gaze. "And you probably don't want him to know I have had my hands and mouth on you."

His gaze drops to my lips and I try to come up with something, but my mind goes blank. Hands and mouth on me, while technically correct, sounds a lot dirtier than he had his hand on my ass and his mouth on mine. It felt a lot dirtier than that.

Anticipation floods me. Will he do it again?

What is wrong with me?

"I find that I understand better with pictures. This should help you understand what Chase will be feeling." He holds his phone out to me.

I glance at it, expecting to see us in the bathroom, because of course, he has a camera in there. But instead, I see Chase with his arms around Abby. It's dark and crowded, and they're both wearing the same outfits from tonight. My stomach sinks.

Damon scrolls through a few pictures. This is tonight and he's all over her. Hands and mouth. My heart races like I've been running away from something. Something I should have known.

Damon glances at the phone. "Hmm, not that one? Maybe you'd prefer to recreate this one."

He holds his phone up again, and a video plays of Chase with a girl on his lap, making out. I lean in to see what's happening as she moves up and down on him. Her skirt lifts a little higher and I see Chase's cock sliding out of her.

I turn away and close my eyes. My insides are a riot. It can't be true. Someone would have told me he was cheating.

My stomach sinks. But who? The people I'm friendly with probably wouldn't know.

"He's fucking her, little devil. This was Wednesday, right before you had your pizza party with Cam."

My chest hurts. Chase had brought me home after dinner with his parents and dropped me off with a goodnight kiss. He claimed he needed to head home to do homework. I didn't doubt him. I didn't even think twice about it, because that's what I did that night too, until Cam showed up. From a party... Did Cam take that video?

"Looks like your boyfriend doesn't share your theories on loyalty." Damon glances at the door and slides his phone into his pocket. His fingers grab my chin. He searches my eyes with a wicked smile. "What's it going to be, Evan? Are you going to play by my rules, or am I going to blow up your life? I mean, you have to spend the next three months working with Hawk and Chase together. It could go easy, or it could be pretty contentious for you if Chase knows your other actor is fucking you on the side."

"I'm not fucking anyone." I jerk my chin out of his hand. My heart hurts. I'm not in love with Chase, but I like him. He's my boyfriend, but obviously, he doesn't care about faithfulness. Maybe it's not what I think. Maybe that video is old and maybe he's just dancing with Abby tonight because I don't like to dance.

"But you want to." Damon's voice drags me back to the present. He wets his lips and my stomach flips. "Just like your man is out there fucking some other chick, while you're in here with me."

Tears cloud my vision. Fuck, I don't want to cry. Not in front of Damon, but I need to go break up with Chase. Or at least have him explain... What's there to explain? He's fucking other girls. Is it because I wouldn't give it up to him?

Am I surprised he cheated on me? I was so surprised by his attention when he asked me out, I almost asked him why. It didn't make sense. We don't make sense, but part of me needed to belong to someone.

"I have to get out of here." I try to walk around Damon.

"Evan—" Before Damon can say anything more, the doorknob rattles and we hear a girl's giggle.

Damon takes my arm and pushes us both into the closet, with him pressing me against the back wall of the reach-in closet. He slides the door mostly shut, casting us in shadows. This must be a guest bedroom because the closet isn't filled with clothes.

I blink away the tears in my eyes. Maybe Chase being my boyfriend was all a joke, because he's all up on his ex tonight. Fuck, I just want to leave.

I look up at Damon's face and open my mouth, but his hand covers it before I can get any words out.

"I don't know, Liam." Mia seems uncertain, but in a flirty way.

"I can tell you more stats if that's what will get you there," Liam's voice is clear. "He'll be here in a minute. Why don't you be a good girl, and help me warm up?"

There's still a swath of the room visible. But we're behind the door and no one will look in the closet. Mia walks to where I can see her and pulls her top off. My eyes widen and I shake my head.

We should let them know we're here. I look up at Damon, who's watching out the sliver. I tug on Damon's shirt, but he presses into me. His lips touch my ear. "Shh."

A shiver works through me. He lowers his hand to my throat, sending sparks chasing beneath his touch.

"How do you want me?" She reaches behind her back to unhook her bra.

"On your knees, baby." Liam walks into the frame and undoes his pants, releasing his cock. I shouldn't be watching this, but I can't seem to look away.

Mia sinks to her knees on the carpet. We really shouldn't be here. Maybe we can sneak out while they're occupied.

I whisper, "We shou—"

Damon squeezes the sides of my throat gently. It startles me into shutting up. I can't see the color of his eyes in the darkness, but I feel the intensity of his gaze on me. He leans in, his body pressing into me, his lips against my ear again, sending tingles through my system.

"They'll be done quickly, little devil. Then we can continue our conversation. If you don't want your boyfriend to find out about us, you'll be quiet."

Who cares if Chase finds out? He's a cheater. But if people realize I'm in a closet with Damon Storm, what else will get out? That I'm living with him? Then what? I may not have a reputation at school as anything but a goody two-shoes, as Cam would say, but that would be gone in an instant.

Chase might spin the rumor that I was the one cheating on him. My cheeks burn.

I nod to let Damon know I'll be quiet.

I don't know what's happening with the Devil's trio, but I don't want to upset Chase before the play even begins. It'll be bad enough when I break up with him, but we're professionals.

Chase is the best choice for Iago. I wasn't blowing smoke up his ass. But if he's mad at me and a costar, it could create tension that would be bad for the play. I don't think he would quit, but he could make it uncomfortable for everyone. The showcase is still my best bet to get accepted into a great school.

Can I even break up with Chase right now? What about his father's birthday party where I have the chance to meet Sandra Cox? Fuck. I don't want to use Chase, but isn't that what he's doing? Using me for what? Or is he cheating because I won't have sex with him?

That's definitely not happening now.

Mia doesn't know I'm in here. Would she hate me if she knew? Besides, if I were in Mia's position, I wouldn't want to know my friend is in the closet watching me with a guy. If I don't have Chase, I can't lose Mia.

Damon's hand rests on my neck. My pulse pumps hard. Can he feel it? The sounds of smacking and groans draw my attention back to the room, and my eyes widen when I see Mia taking Liam's cock in her mouth.

She strokes what doesn't fit as she bobs on his dick. When she comes off his cock, she licks the tip. Damon's body touches me everywhere. His heat drives the inferno inside me hotter. I press my thighs together at the unexpected ache forming.

"Is that good?" She continues to stroke him and sits back on her heels looking up. "Is Fletcher on his way?"

"Yeah." Liam looks down at her with hooded eyes. "Suck it."

She takes him back into her mouth, taking his cock so deep her nose almost touches his abs. Her eyes never leave him. She hums around him. Does she like doing that? He groans, so he apparently likes it.

The bedroom door opens and closes. Damon's lips brush my neck above his thumb, causing me to startle against him at the cascade of warmth that floods me.

"Fuck, yeah," Fletcher says.

Lifting his head, Damon curses softly and I look up at him. His face is turned to watch out the slot. His body covers me, hiding me if anyone glances into the open door. His cock is hard against my stomach. I couldn't forget the feeling of him against me if I tried.

But he's seeing Mia half-naked giving a blow job, is that why he's turned on? It can't be because of me. She has great breasts. Not something I should be thinking, but she's beautiful.

His chest rises and falls against mine and his fingers stroke up and down my neck. My skin buzzes with anticipation. His breath brushes my ear. The weight of him rests against my body. I press my hands against the wall behind me and take in a shaky breath.

I don't think this is going to be over quickly.

There's a sucking and then a popping noise. Mia hums. I look out the slot and she kneels between them. It's like a porn. She sucks and strokes Liam while her other hand strokes Fletcher's cock. Then she comes off Liam and turns to take Fletcher into her mouth.

I shouldn't be watching this. That's my friend. This is supposed to be private. But I can't seem to look away. It shouldn't be flooding my body with heat. It's difficult to see sex and not get turned on. I should close my eyes, but I can't look away. The scent of my arousal fills the small space.

My face is so hot. It's also difficult for me to resist the scent and hard lines of Damon's body pressed into me, making me shudder against him.

Damon presses his head against the wall beside mine. His hair tickles my cheek. "You like the look of that, little devil. Does it turn you on?"

I turn my face toward his ear. My cheek brushes against his. "It's just a physical response," I say quietly over the sounds of sucking and groans of pleasure.

"Do you wish it was you between them?"

The noise stops, saving me from answering. Not them. But the Devil's trio? My breath catches. His other hand slides along my side beneath my shirt to cup my breast, tracing his thumb over my bra and the hard tip beneath it. I should stop him, but it's like lightning through my veins. When I make a noise, he tightens his hold on my throat, just enough to quiet me.

No one's touched me like this before.

"Fuck, baby," Liam says. "If you want both our dicks in you, we need to do it soon or I'm going to come."

What? My gaze is drawn to the opening. Mia stands and they both put a hand on her breasts. She reaches below her skirt for her panties. They flutter to the floor as the guys bend down to take her breasts in their mouths. Her moan is loud.

I gasp as my pussy gets even wetter. Damon squeezes my neck slightly and his other hand slides down to grab my hip. My gaze shoots to him, but his head is still next to mine, not watching them. His thumb slips beneath my shirt to touch my bare stomach.

"Fuck, little devil, you smell like heaven." His words are soft in my ear.

An involuntary whimper escapes me. My startled gaze goes to the opening to make sure they didn't hear me.

Mia stands in front of Fletcher in only her skirt, stroking his cock while his fingers disappear between her legs. Both Liam and Fletcher have their shirts off, but their pants are still on. Liam steps up behind her, squeezing a bottle of something over his fingers. He slides his palm over his condom-covered cock, before sliding his fingers between Mia's ass cheeks.

My breath catches.

She cries out softly as her hips move between their hands.

"Fuck, you're so tight. I'm going to come as soon as I push into this tight ass." Liam fucks her ass with his fingers.

"We're going to have to do this another time so we can swap." Fletcher meets Liam's eyes and smiles.

"I'm game." Mia's voice is strained.

They remove their hands, and Mia wraps her arms around Fletcher's neck. She gives a little jump and he helps her wrap her legs around his waist, holding her ass.

My breathing is almost as rapid as hers and all I'm doing is standing here, breathing in Damon and the smell of sex. Of course, Damon strokes his fingers gently across my skin, slowly driving me out of my mind.

Fletcher's cock slides between her legs before he thrusts it inside her. They both make a sound of satisfaction. My pussy clutches at nothing. The button on my jeans loosens and my attention snaps to Damon. My hand goes to stop his on my pants.

My eyes are wide even though he's a shadow against me. I shake my head.

"Damon," I hiss. "What are you doing?"

He grabs my wrists and pulls them above my head holding them there, pressing against me fully. His forehead rests against mine, and I can feel his breath against my lips. Mia makes a guttural moan and I glance away from Damon to see Liam sliding his cock slowly into her ass, working it in and pulling out to slip in farther.

My breath catches and my pussy throbs.

When he's completely inside, they all let out a moan. Mia is suspended between the two men pressed against her. Their cocks are both buried deep inside her. Fuck, what does that feel like? She'll tell me if I ask her, but then I'd have to admit I was creeping on her in the closet with Damon.

She might tell me anyway. She might have already told me at lunch, but I think I blocked it out.

Damon shifts my hands to one of his. He slides his other hand down the front of me. Teasing over my breast. I hold my breath. What is he doing?

He holds my wrists captive, making me helpless to stop him. I should be watching the monster in the closet with me, but my attention is drawn to the three people having sex. I can't look away, even as Damon touches me, making me ache for more.

They begin to move. It takes them a few moments to find a rhythm. My zipper lowers, and Damon slides his hand down the front of my pants, beneath my panties. He rests his forehead against mine, holding my hands above my head.

"Evan?"

The pause is long enough for me to say no. I could tell him to stop. I don't know if it will work. If he'll do it anyway. But I throb as my insides burn. I crave release. I part my legs a little more. It's not like I have a boyfriend anymore. It might not be official, but why shouldn't I have what everyone else has?

His fingers slide over my pussy. I suck in a breath at the sparks that catapult through my system. No one else has touched me like this. It's too much.

My lips part to ask him to stop, I swear that was my intent. But he slips between the folds of my pussy and glides over the wetness, rubbing the center of me. Pleasure spirals through me.

It's rougher than when I do it. His finger's thicker.

"Damon," I whimper. Needing more. Needing him to stop. Fuck, needing him to keep going.

"Shh, little devil, let me give you what you need." His fingers delve deeper, teasing at my entrance, circling it while rubbing my clit. I'm on meltdown. Knowing Chase is probably cheating on me right now gives me the courage to let this happen. This is *definitely* cheating, but fuck, it feels so fucking good.

I've masturbated. Damon's watched me, but nothing bigger than my finger has been inside me and certainly not anything like what Mia is currently taking. This morning was the most action I've ever gotten, and I really only watched Damon get off.

He presses his thick finger inside me, sliding in easily with how wet I am. I gasp at the sparks lighting me up inside. My pussy squeezes around his finger. Oh, fuck.

"Fuck, little devil, you're so fucking wet and tight for me." His voice is hidden by the moans and grunts from the room. But in here, it's only the two of us in the dark. It feels like a dream.

I can't focus on what's happening to Mia when my world is being expanded in this closet. He's not focused on what's happening outside this space. This is so much worse than a kiss on the cheating scale, but I can't do anything to stop it. He's taking what he wants, and he wants me.

He wants me.

I don't want to stop it. I whimper, feeling the fullness of his finger inside me. My body wound so tight it feels like I'm going to explode.

Damon's mouth crashes down on mine as he fucks me with his finger. It's so fucking different than when I do it. I can't control what he's doing as he pushes me faster toward the edge. Everything inside me winds tighter and tighter. Our tongues slide against each other. My hips rock, chasing my release.

He swallows my moans. His thumb rubs my clit while his finger pumps inside me, confined by my jeans. My insides are sparking, igniting, bursting.

"So fucking tight," he says against my mouth.

The noise outside reaches a crescendo as I shatter, clenching around his finger as he works me through the orgasm. My mouth opens against his in a silent scream. His kiss consumes me as my pussy clutches at his finger still buried inside me.

His breathing is heavy. His cock is still hard against my stomach. As I slowly ease back into myself.

Mia giggles. "That was great, guys."

Her voice is like a splash of cold water. What did I do? I tug at my hands, but Damon doesn't release them. He deepens our kiss.

The sound of the guys removing their condoms and the rustling of clothes is the backdrop as Damon lifts his mouth from mine. His eyes search mine in the dark as he pulls his hand from my pants. Little aftershocks ripple through me.

He lifts his finger with my wetness to his lips and sucks it into his mouth. "Sweet."

He doesn't release me. My body is sated from my orgasm. My lips feel swollen from his kisses. But everything feels sensitive and I'm still on edge. Like I need more. I squirm against him, not sure if I want more or if I should run away.

"I want to do this again," Mia says.

"Anytime, baby," Liam says.

There's sounds of kissing while I breathe with Damon hovering over me. His breath is chaotic, a little out of control. Does he want me? My pussy aches. And I can't look away from his eyes. What he did to me... I can't process it. I can't explain it.

The door opens and closes. I jerk on my wrists, but Damon holds them aloft.

"They're gone," I whisper. "We can go now."

Damon doesn't say anything, but his hand slides over my breast. My nipple tightens as his thumb rubs across my tip. I suck in a breath.

"I can't wait to fuck you, little devil. To feel that hot cunt tighten around my cock."

Those words finally break the spell he's cast over me. He doesn't want me. He wants a little fuck toy.

I jerk on my hands. "Let me go, Damon."

The door to the room opens and we freeze.

It closes, and there's the sounds of heavy petting and zippers being undone. My head falls forward onto Damon's chest. I don't know how much more of this I can take. I didn't think I'd be into watching others have sex, but watching Mia with those two was something I could definitely rewatch.

Which is so wrong.

"I need your cock," Abby says as she moans softly. My head falls back against the wall. I don't want to watch Abby with anyone. The picture Damon showed me of Chase and her crosses my mind.

He wouldn't do that while I'm at the party, right?

Fuck, I'll keep my eyes closed while she does whoever she's doing.

"So is it over with the wallflower?" Abby asks.

I stiffen.

"Nah." There's sounds of kissing, but that was undeniably Chase's voice.

"So, what? You just need to get your dick wet? Is that it? Is that all I am to you?" Abby pouts.

"No, babe. It's not like that."

It's exactly like that. Fuck this. Fuck him. Maybe I should charge out of this closet and tell him to go fuck himself.

CHAPTER 26

Damon

"So is it over with the wallflower?"

Evan stiffens against me at the girl's voice. I don't recognize it. Hawk or Cam probably would. My cock is so fucking hard right now and she's so fucking wet. If she had a skirt on, I'd be balls deep in my little devil, but she's wearing jeans and there isn't a lot of space to maneuver in this small closet.

At least, not without bumping elbows and making enough noise to alert the other occupants of the room.

Honestly, if we're going to be in here for a while, I might sink my fingers back into Evan's tight little cunt and keep her coming. Fuck, I don't think I've ever felt anything as good as her pussy squeezing around my finger when she came.

This wasn't the plan, but plans change. The plan was to make her aware of her new rules. Meaning no fucking Chase Chadwick. I wasn't supposed to end up trapped in a closet with her while two of my teammates railed her whore of a friend.

Evan exhales and I'm tempted to release her hands, but I like holding her captive. I like her being helpless for me.

I've never done anything like this with a girl. Most girls are more than willing. I like that she fights me. I like when she caves to the pleasure. I'm going to enjoy having control over Evan.

"Nah." Chase fucking Chadwick.

Evan lifts her head.

"So what? You just need to get your dick wet? Is that it? Is that all I am to you?" the girl says.

"No, babe. It's not like that."

Evan's eyes narrow and her lips press into a thin line. She jerks on her hands and opens her mouth. Fuck, is she going to blow our cover?

I slide my hand over her mouth to keep her from alerting them to our presence. Her eyes blink up at me. I wish I could see them more clearly, to see what she's feeling.

Everything is always written on her face.

"I've missed your cunt." Chase groans with pleasure. "Fuck, I've missed your mouth."

A whimper comes from Evan. Seeing pictures and hearing him cheating on her in the same room are not the same. She trembles against me, and not in a good way. I can't do anything about this. They'll leave when they finish, but I'm sure, until then, this will be torture for her.

Somehow that doesn't make me as happy as I thought it would.

"What about your girlfriend? I saw her with Mia earlier?" the girl taunts.

"Look, my dad—"

The door to the room opens.

"Whoa, guess you guys forgot to lock the door."

I relax. Finally.

I don't know what kept Cam, but I'm glad he didn't interrupt Mia with Fletcher and Liam. I wouldn't have the taste of Evan's pussy in my mouth and know how tight she feels.

"Fuck off, Warwick," Chase growls.

I release Evan's hands and they drop to her sides. I don't know if she can see my eyes, but I slowly remove my hand from her mouth. When she doesn't make a sound, I quickly do her jeans back up.

"Oh, sorry, no can do, Chase Chadwick. See, I reserved this room for right now. So, you and your whore can either continue while I watch, or get the fuck out." Cam must sit on the bed, because I can hear the sound of the mattress settling under someone. "Fair warning, I'll be critiquing both of your performances while you go at it."

"Fine, we'll find another room." The girl's tone is snide.

The sound of a zipper fills the room. Evan shakes against me. Is she fucking crying over that asshat? I don't know what to do with a crying girl.

"Just a little longer, Evan. Hold it together." I run my hand over her smooth hair, drawing her head against my chest before resting my hand against her head. This isn't what I'm good at. I'm good at hockey, fucking, and fighting, not at comforting girls who find out their fucker of a boyfriend cheats on her.

"What the fuck was Chase doing in here?" Hawk's voice. I missed the opening and closing of the door. "Where's Damon?"

"Evan," I say softly.

She shakes her head and her arms go around my waist, clinging to me like I'm her lifeline. Fuck.

"Lock the door," I say loud enough for the others to hear me.

I hear the door close while the closet door opens. Cam's gaze narrows on my back.

"What—" he cuts himself off when he sees Evan huddled against me.

Hawk steps into the opening and raises an eyebrow. The room smells like sex, and it probably smells like it in here too. Next time I make Evan come, I'm going to watch her face as she shatters.

But right now, she needs something I'm not sure I can give her. We can't stay in the closet though. When I lift her, she wraps around me, burying her head in my shoulder like I can provide comfort.

I carry her out and sit on the edge of the bed with her wrapped around me like she rides a motorcycle. This isn't something I can handle.

But it might be something I can use.

"What happened?" Hawk sits on one side of me and Cam sits on the other.

"Chase was getting his dick sucked by Abby when I came in." Cam fills in the blanks.

Evan releases a breath, but she's not even trying to get away from me. I hold her hips against mine. My cock is still hard and pressed against her pussy, but I'm not doing a damn thing until she responds.

"Fuck." Hawk reaches out and slides his hand over her back. "We got sidetracked by Olivia. She's on a rampage to find you after you ditched her earlier."

Evan lifts her head and glares at me. I can do glaring. Her blue eyes are dry and filled with accusation as they narrow on me. Does she think I came to her after being with Olivia? Maybe I should leave that in her mind. The idea isn't for her to get attached to us.

The plan is to use her to destroy Chase, which she might be more on my side right now than his. After Chase is taken care of, I need to remove her gold-digging mother from my house.

When I don't say anything, betrayal sparks in her eyes. When she begins to pull away, I pull her in tight.

"I didn't fuck her, little devil." I brush her blond hair away from her face. "I haven't even kissed her."

"You knew he was cheating on me." Her voice is strong as she attempts to pull away from me. "How long?"

I glance at Cam. She follows my gaze and he nods.

"Saw him at a party fucking another girl on Wednesday." Cam runs a hand through his hair. "Asked around and found out he's pretty much open for business. Sorry, Evan."

She nods. Her lips press together. "I should go find him."

Her eyes meet mine and glance down at my hands on her hips, but I don't release her. From now on, she's ours.

"What are you going to do?" I ask.

"I'm going to go break up with my boyfriend, for starters. And then I'm going to ask Mia to take me home." There's anger and betrayal in her eyes. I can use that.

"We should get out of here." Hawk stands, but his gaze stays on Evan. "Go somewhere we can talk."

"I should talk to Chase." She blows out a breath.

"Did you even like him?" My words aren't as calculated as they usually are.

Her eyes return to mine, and I get caught in the silvers and blues swirled together like a kaleidoscope. What color do they turn when she comes? I'm determined to find out.

She draws in a breath. Her arms rest on my shoulders, but she's not clinging to me like she was. I miss it.

"He was my boyfriend. Of course, I liked him." She looks away, but her gaze meets Cam's.

"Was, goody two-shoes?" He caught that too.

"I'm not staying with a guy who cheats on me." She straightens and realizes how intimately we're pressed together. My cock also realizes and twitches. She bites her lip and her cheeks flush pink. Her eyes meet mine for a second before she drops them.

Is she remembering how good it felt to have my finger in her pussy? I'd love to show her how much better my cock will feel.

"Before you do anything, we need to discuss the rules, little devil."

She lifts her gaze to mine. There she is. There's that fire for me. "What does it matter? It's not like I'm going to stay with a cheater. Are you going to spread those videos around school? I mean, it would be embarrassing for everyone to see me naked, but it was only a kiss, Damon. I used to act. I kind of figured I'd do a nude scene at some point."

I arch an eyebrow. "You know the other video I have."

She laughs. "Everyone masturbates."

Cam sucks in a breath. I'm surprised he doesn't ask me to send the video right then and there.

"Besides, I'm sure you can't see anything." Her eyes search mine. "Why would I want to protect the asshole who was my boyfriend?"

She's clinging to the anger. Good, I want her fighting.

"Hawk's right. We should get out of here." I stand and hold Evan as she lowers her legs and puts her hands on my chest. Our eyes lock and hold as she slides down my front to settle on her feet.

"I'm going home with Mia." Evan looks away as she steps back.

I let her have that space. For now.

"Sorry." Cam chuckles. "She's all over Fletcher and Liam currently. I don't think she's ready to leave."

Hawk steps into her and she turns to face him. He slides his hand against her jaw. "Text her and your asshole boyfriend. Tell them you're sick and getting a ride home. We can discuss this at Damon's, and then you can decide what you want to do about your boyfriend."

"I don't have a boyfriend." She doesn't drop her gaze.

"Fine," I say. Her attention comes back to me. "Don't text him then, but you're leaving with us, Evan."

She narrows her eyes like she's going to argue more. But I know what she feels like when she comes and what she tastes like, I'm not going to let that go. I give her a cocky grin.

When she remembers, she blushes and lowers her gaze. "Fine, I don't care."

"How are we going to get her out of here without someone seeing?" Cam asks.

CHAPTER 27

EvanAnn

I TEXT Mia to say I'm catching a ride with a friend because I'm ready to leave. She responds that she has so much to tell me. The image of her with those two guys is burned into my memory and I'm not sure I won't stammer my way through our next conversation.

I send a quick *heading home* text to Chase. He hasn't replied to my previous texts. But now that he's shown me who he is, I'm not surprised. I hope Abby's worth it. I wish he would have finished the sentence about his dad. It seemed to be his explanation for why he was dating me.

Cam knows his way around Fletcher's house and heads to a side entrance no one really uses during parties. I follow them down the stairs I took to the bathroom and through a dark hallway. Damon keeps a hand on me every step of the way.

I don't know what to feel right now. That picture was from tonight. I knew Chase was all over her on the dance floor, but I didn't expect him to fuck someone at a party I was at. It hurt to hear Abby and Chase together. They broke up before the assignment that put Chase and I together. Now that I think about it, he volunteered to be my partner, which was unusual.

Maybe I should have known it was all a con, but he was so fucking convincing.

He's an actor. I feel stupid for not noticing the difference. Thankfully, I wasn't stupid enough to give him my virginity. Maybe that's what he was after. But why introduce me to his parents? Why talk about a future together? Did he think that's what I needed for him to fuck me?

This whole thing has me so angry and confused.

Damon guides me to Hawk's bike. I let Hawk slip the helmet over my head and fasten it. I even climb onto the bike behind him by myself, wrapping my body around him, leaning into his warmth. At least I have jeans on this time.

I can't focus on the possibility that the motorcycle might crash. In my mind, I'm in that closet hearing Mia getting fucked while Damon has his hand in my pants. His finger buried in my pussy. My fingers curl into Hawk's shirt.

It was intense, but was it because of watching someone else have sex, or because of Damon? I know the truth. If it had been Chase in that closet with me, it wouldn't have been anything like that. Everything about Damon winds me up.

But Abby and Chase sullied the memory of the best orgasm of my life. I can't believe I felt bad for cheating on my boyfriend. Part of me is so fucking proud I didn't do anything more than make out with Chase. He wasn't my first kiss, but he was my first boyfriend.

Fuck him. I never even saw his cock. Definitely didn't touch it.

I didn't recognize the girl in the video from the party on Wednesday. I don't understand any of this. Which is frustrating because I'm supposed to become a great director, but I was blind to the drama happening in my own life.

I drag in a breath. No one talks in the helmets tonight as we glide down the dark streets. It's a little more comfortable riding with jeans on as opposed to a skirt. I snuggle into Hawk's warmth and draw strength from his scent.

I can let myself enjoy this without guilt slicing through me.

I don't want to think anymore tonight. But I guess I need to figure out what the Devil's trio really wants from me. That was why Damon dragged me into that room in the first place.

We pull into the garage at my new home. I was so worried about

Chase and what he would feel knowing I was living here. How stupid am I?

Did he ever care? Did I?

Part of me wonders if I only said yes to being his girlfriend because I was so lonely. He gave me attention when no one else did. Maybe I liked being seen for once, instead of hiding behind a camera.

I was ready for more. I was ready to be seen. He pulled me out of my life that rotated around school and plays. It was good for me. I know that.

Hawk parks the bike. Before I can even attempt to get off, Cam lifts me into the air and sets me on my feet. He helps me take my helmet off and his dark eyes search mine for a second.

I don't know what he sees, but he takes my hand into his large warm one and we follow after Damon. I don't question anything. It doesn't matter anymore. Honestly, I could fuck all three of these guys tonight and not feel an ounce of guilt. It would be satisfying to throw it in Chase's face when I break up with him.

The lights are out in the mansion, making it look ominous in the dark.

"Are our parents here?" I ask as Damon lets us in the side entrance with the keypad. I have that number in my phone now. My insides buzz in anticipation.

"No." Damon leads us down to the basement. He walks over to the bar and sets a few bottles on the counter. His piercing blue eyes meet mine. "Want a drink?"

Normally I would say no, but fuck it. Maybe I need to stop letting everyone run over me. Stop being content to stay in the background and watch life happen around me.

I release Cam's hand and walk over to the bar. "Yes. I'd like all the drinks."

"Do you even drink, goody?" Cam leans against the bar next to me.

"I do tonight." I still don't know how to feel. I liked Chase. At first, it was amazing he noticed me. Maybe I'll cry about the relationship I thought I had and lost later, but it's not like I went into it with both feet. I didn't fall in love.

Maybe I'm incapable of love.

Maybe I saw my mom diving in and out of relationships too much over the past few years to know what a relationship is really like. Maybe I've been waiting for the crash, because it seemed too perfect. The wallflower with one of the most popular guys in school. It's the plot of so many high school dramas. But that's not real life.

No, real life is seeing your boyfriend get a blow job because you haven't given it up to him. And knowing he's fucking around on you, because you won't put out.

Damon sets a shot glass in front of each of us. These guys don't make sense either, but at least they're upfront about wanting to use me. Even if I don't understand why.

Cam clinks his shot glass against mine. "Cheers."

He tosses the shot back and I watch his throat as he swallows. My pulse kicks up a notch. Cam's a nice guy. I can kiss him if I want to now. It doesn't matter if I haven't officially broken up with Chase. It's over.

I lift the shot glass and smell it. My nose wrinkles at the potent scent.

"You aren't supposed to smell it, goody." Cam sets his empty glass on the bar. "Open your throat and take it all down."

I arch an eyebrow, remembering Mia taking Liam's cock all the way into the back of her throat. It was impressive. He wasn't as big as Damon though. My pussy stirs. Are they all that big? Am I going to find out?

Fuck it. The shot hits the back of my throat and burns all the way down. I gasp and put my hand over my heart at the burn. Fuck.

"That's it." Cam smirks and takes my shot glass from me and sets it on the bar.

I drag in a breath and look at Damon. "Now what?"

His smile grows wicked and my insides burn, but I don't look away. Because I don't have to. But I need to know exactly what this is. They don't want me because I'm suddenly available. There's something more at play here, and it's time I know the truth.

"What do you want from me? And don't say everything because we both know that's not true." I back away from the bar and turn to sit on the couch. Obviously, I wasn't enough to keep Chase from cheating on me. The alcohol spreads through my body. I feel warm inside and for once, it isn't because of these guys. "So, tell me why you're fucking around with me when there are dozens of girls who want you?"

"I wouldn't say dozens." Hawk sits near me but not right next to me.

I scoff. He feels closed off from me in a way I don't understand. It can't be because I pushed him away that night. I had a boyfriend then. His green eyes meet mine. There's still interest there, but there's also maybe some anger.

I can almost think clearly when they aren't touching me, but the warmth of that shot is sizzling through me, making me relax. Making me tingle.

Damon pulls the ottoman in front of me and sits down opposite me. His knees on either side of mine. I glance at his fingers tangled together between his knees. Fuck, they're long and thick, and one of them has been inside my pussy. Fucking me until I saw stars.

My insides are boiling and I'm sure my face is red at this point.

If I want him, I can have him. It's still not a great idea to fuck the son of the guy my mom is dating, but fuck it. I can have them all if I want. A dangerous thought to have when Cam sits on my other side on the couch. I'm surrounded by three guys who make my pulse race.

They're intense one-on-one, but all together...

Fuck. I think about them surrounding me, naked, their cocks thrusting into me. My pussy, my ass, my mouth. I cross my legs against the growing need. It's weird. My body definitely wants them in an almost anxious way. What Chase made me feel wasn't a fraction of how much I want these guys.

"Don't break up with Chase." Damon lifts his gaze to mine.

"What?" My brow furrows and my stomach twists. "Why would I stay with him? After what I saw? What everyone knows? I already feel like a fool."

"Evan, you have two choices. We could do this as a collaboration, or I can use the videos I have to encourage you." Damon meets my gaze. Not an ounce of tenderness lingers in his sharp eyes. "Including this morning in the bathroom, in case you were hoping to blow shit up anyway."

My mouth opens and closes. The image of him jacking off while I watched and that kiss play through my memory. I press my lips together. It would definitely look like more happened and it did tonight in the closet.

I cross my legs against the ache in my pussy. I don't know what they want from me so badly that they're willing to blackmail me to get it. But I need to find out before I give them any more of me.

Hawk clears his throat and breaks the stare down between me and Damon. "Obviously, this would be easier with you willing to help us."

"Willing? What exactly am I willing to do?" I cross my arms under my breasts.

"Whatever we want." Damon's words draw my attention as his gaze drops to my breasts. They grow heavy and tight beneath his gaze. He touched me there. Held my hands above my head and touched me wherever he wanted. I was helpless to stop him. It was intense and so fucking perfect.

"Everything?" I ask with an arched eyebrow.

He smirks.

"We need to bring Chase down, but we can't come at him directly. We want to hit him where it hurts, and that's you." Hawk reclaims the floor. "With his cheating, we figured you might be willing to get some payback of your own."

The problem is, Chase didn't cheat just once. According to them, he's cheated the whole time we were dating. Everyone in school probably knew it except for me. How humiliating. But he never considered I'd cheat on him.

Why should he? I'm easy. He takes me out once in a while and introduces me to his parents, and I'm happy to go back into my little box while he's off screwing whoever he wants. Do I want to know why he keeps me, when he could easily be single, fucking everyone in sight? Is it the rush of doing it behind my back? Or do I give him something the others don't?

It can't be the part in the play, because based off his audition, I would have cast him as Iago anyway. And now that I know how devious he is, the part suits him.

"If I was willing?" I lean back in the chair. My gaze locks with Damon's blue eyes.

"Where were you on June eighth?" Cam asks. Damon jerks his head to glare at Cam.

"Probably at home." I shrug. It's where I spent most of the summer, working on *Othello*.

"Not out with your boyfriend?" Cam leans forward with his elbows on his knees. The muscles in his arms grow more pronounced. Fuck.

My heart picks up pace. Why are they so attractive? I focus on the question he's asking. A specific date? "Why?"

"Was Chase in a car accident this summer?" Cam's dark eyes meet mine. "And were you with him at the time?"

I shake my head. "I wasn't there. His car is being repaired. He said he ran into something at night. Maybe an animal. There were scratches on the side. I asked because he was driving his truck instead of his car, which is unusual." I glance at Damon's jaw that's still healing. It's currently clenched and a muscle ticks in it.

What if it wasn't an animal? Fuck, can I believe Chase would hit someone and leave them?

"It doesn't change anything." Damon's eyes lock with mine, and the hate that underlies whatever else is between us rises to the surface, making my heart crash against my ribcage. I don't mind that he hates me. That he holds me down and forces me to take what he has to give. That every moment in his arms wraps me in desire.

Maybe it's wrong to want him like that. Maybe I don't care anymore.

"You don't think it's weird Chase picks a wallflower to date his senior year?" Hawk stands and paces.

"Abby asked. He was saying something about his dad when Cam came in." I'm embarrassed I fell for the actor, when I thought he was showing me who he really was. Did I fall for him? I wasn't in love with Chase, but I thought we had something. He made me feel special. Like he picked me out of all the girls. Now I feel stupid for even considering he wanted me. "He introduced me to his parents."

"Maybe he was looking for an image upgrade." Cam strokes his chin as he studies me. "Date the good, studious girl who's top of the class and has a promising career ahead? Fuck, it's not a bad idea. My dad would love it if I stopped partying and had someone who kept me on track."

Still not feeling attractive over here. It was stupid to think Chase wanted me when he could have any other girl in school.

Damon looks me over. There's still that edge to his eyes, a look that says I don't belong here with them.

"Evan has appeal," he admits, begrudgingly. "He could have just wanted to fuck her."

I almost laugh. "Thanks. I'll make sure to put that on my resume. Appealing enough to fuck. It kind of has a ring to it."

He smirks. "Tell me, Evan. Was it the live porn or my presence that turned you on more?"

My breath catches. With Chase, I was gearing myself up to have sex. With Damon, I would have let him fuck me in that closet and had no regrets.

"The porn," I lie. The live sex show definitely didn't hurt my arousal, but the minute he touched me, I wanted more from him. I wanted it all. He's dangerous. I shouldn't even be left in the same room with him, let alone practically share rooms separated by a bathroom.

The idea that he wouldn't have even needed to be my boyfriend to take me should be appalling. But the attraction, on my side, at least, is overwhelming. I'm confident he knows that and will use it. I just have to be aware when I'm being used.

He chuckles darkly. "You suck at lying."

"Okay, fuck." Cam runs his hand through his hair. "You two need to fuck and get it out of your systems."

My mouth opens to deny it.

"What do you say, Evan, want to reenact your favorite show?" Damon strokes his hand over his cock that strains against his jeans. He didn't come in that closet. But the memory of him pressed tight against me makes me burn. "Where do you want me? Your pussy or your ass?"

I snap my mouth shut. The nerve of this guy. Though my body is definitely listening and interested.

Fuck him, and not literally. I narrow my eyes.

"What do you need me to do?" I ask.

"We need Chase to think you two are still a thing." Hawk draws my attention from Damon, interrupting our stare down.

I meet his green eyes. "Why?"

"Don't you want to know what he's up to?" Hawk asks. "Why he's dating you and still fucking around?"

I narrow my eyes on him. Is this another *Evan's attractive enough* speech? It sounds like they only want me to get to Chase. So, the only reason to stay with Chase would be to help them.

Hawk blows out a breath. "That night he didn't hit some animal. He ran Damon off the road while Chase was getting road head from some blond."

Fuck, that hurts more than it should. My gaze flicks to Damon and the scrape on his jaw.

My heart aches, but I resist the urge to rub it. I know Chase was cheating on me, but we were good back in June. We spent a few days together between his camps, but he withdrew toward the end of the month.

"She doesn't need to know the whole story. She needs to tell us whether she's in or not." Damon catches my eyes. "I could always upload those videos to some sites. You're eighteen."

Fuck. Even if I got them taken down, once something's on the internet, it's never really gone. But I'm not the only one in the most damning video.

"Wouldn't that ruin your NHL dreams?" That's a thing, right? They need to be somewhat free of scandals when they're signed.

"I'm not ashamed of my body, little devil." He leans forward and wets his lips. "I may not be an ant, but I can edit a video to not show my face. And I'm not ashamed of your body, either."

Heat floods me. Yeah, he's dangerous to my sanity. I want to hate him and get him to make me come in the same breath. So fucking dangerous.

But am I just a warm body to them? Do I need to be more? What if I use them the way they want to use me? I've always been curious about sex, but too controlled to let it happen with someone else.

With these three, they pluck my control from me like taking a toy from a kitten. I don't need to impress them or make them like me. But what exactly are they offering?

"Here's the deal, Annie." Hawk drags my attention back to him. "We can't come at Chase directly. Taking you from him would have been our play, but we want it to hurt. For him to know we didn't just take you from him, but you came willingly. Together we can find ways to make him hurt even more, with you on the inside."

"So, you didn't really want me?" I keep my voice steady, because with every word he said, it crushed something inside me. I don't know why I thought some part of them was attracted to me. Somehow, being a game to them hurts worse than knowing Chase cheated and used me the whole time. "It was all a game, then?"

EvanAnn

CHASE DIDN'T REALLY WANT me. Should it surprise me the Devil's trio don't really want me? That I'm a means to an end? I should leave. I look down at my hands as the room falls silent around me.

It's not like my identity is tied to my attractiveness. If I was still trying to be an actress than yes. But not as a director. I need to be smart and commanding. So what if the hottest boys in school don't want to fuck me. I never thought they did before and I went on with my life. But their interest in me has unlocked something I'd tucked away. Fantasies I never thought would come true.

I drag in a breath and lift my gaze to Damon's. He's watching me with an intensity that's almost unnerving.

I raise an eyebrow, because no one has denied it. Yes, I'm a girl and they're boys. They don't need to be attracted to me to fuck me. I'm well aware of that fact.

"Seriously?" Cam asks.

I turn to him confused, but he's looking at the other two and shaking his head like they're disappointments.

His dark eyes meet mine. "Cards on the table, goody."

I brace myself for what he's about to say.

He clears his throat. "Yeah, this started as kind of a game. We wanted to take you away from Chase. To make you both pay for what happened to Damon—"

"But I—"

He puts his finger against my lip, stopping me. "The girl in the car with him was blond. He has a girlfriend that's blond. It was easy to deduce you were the one giving him road head."

My cheeks warm, but I keep silent. They thought I was the type of girl to give a blow job in a car? No one's ever thought of me like that.

"But when we found out he was cheating on you, that opened up the possibilities." Cam takes his hand away from my lips. "He still wants you for some reason. But if you want revenge on him, we can have a good time while we finish him off."

I swallow. "What does that mean?"

"It means you're hot and we want to fuck you." Cam winks and smirks at me. "I would have had my hand in your skirt every day during English Lit if I thought you'd let me get away with it."

My mouth opens and closes. "I'm not like those other girls. The ones who chase after you."

Damon's hand on my thigh jerks my attention to him. "You're not. You're right. Those girls would have been on their knees at the first hint of interest from us."

My lips press together. Like Mia? She would have done exactly what she did with Liam and Fletcher to any of the Devil's trio. Fuck, probably all of them at the same time.

"Why me?" I narrow my eyes at Damon because he'll tell me the truth. He doesn't flirt or play with me like the others. He hated me from the beginning.

Damon grabs the backs of my knees and pulls me closer to him. "Maybe I like the way you smell when you're aroused, little devil." His hands grab my hips and draw me to straddle him on the ottoman. My hands hold his shoulders to help stabilize me. "Maybe I want someone I can play with how I want to, without her making a fuss at me. Or telling all her friends about it."

My insides burn as his hard cock presses against the seam of my jeans. "How do you want to play?"

He smirks and grabs my hair, pulling my head back. His mouth touches my chin. "Did you like being held in the closet while I fucked you with my finger?"

I whimper as his teeth scrape against my jaw.

"Answer me, little devil." His other hand squeezes my hip. "Did you like me holding you down?"

"Yes." The word falls from my lips as anticipation crawls over every nerve. I want to beg him to touch me more.

"That's what we want. We want to play with you. Explore our darker sides without having someone decide it isn't what she wants." Damon lifts my head so our eyes meet.

He wants me to give him my control. I should be terrified, but fuck if I'm not curious. "What's in it for me?"

"Sex with three guys not enough for you, Annie?"

Hawk's voice makes me turn and pulls on my hair in Damon's hand. I hiss at the pain. Damon leans in and bites my earlobe. I gasp at the sparks scattering through my blood.

I drag in a breath and try to focus on the conversation, and not the desire Damon's touch ignites within me.

"What makes you think I want to have sex with you?" I dare to say, even though right now, I'm more than willing. "All of you?"

Hawk smirks. "Check her panties, Damon."

"What?" I turn my attention to the devil I'm currently straddling.

"See if she's wet." Hawk's words make me cringe, because I'm practically soaking over here.

"Why don't you show me, little devil?" Damon releases me, but leans back on his hands. "Put your hand in your pants and show me your fingers."

My breath hitches. This is humiliating and hot at the same time. Maybe I'm broken for wanting this. Maybe they'll humiliate me more. But at least I'm part of the game with them. I know the rules and how to win. They aren't pretending to have feelings for me. They want to fuck me. I just have to keep emotions out of it.

I undo my pants while they all watch. Holding up my hand like a magician to show them it's dry, I meet Damon's heated gaze. Does he think I won't do it? They don't know I'm a virgin. They won't treat me like glass or a trophy to be put on the shelf. They won't be gentle or ease me into anything.

I slide my hand down into my panties and stroke my finger over my pussy. Lust, hot and thick, pours over me at the anticipation in Damon's eyes, knowing these three are completely focused on me.

My pussy gets wetter. I bite my lip and pull my hand out to show them. My fingers glisten in the light.

Damon smirks and grabs my wrist. He puts my fingers into his mouth and sucks my juices off them. I inhale a sharp breath as my pussy pulses in need.

"You taste divine, little devil." Damon catches the back of my neck and his mouth takes mine. I can taste myself on his tongue, something that I never thought I would like, but I also taste Damon. Dark and rich.

He pulls away with a smirk. "You want us. We want you. All we need are some rules."

"Rules?" My pants are still undone, but I don't reach down to fix them.

Damon's eyes are downright wicked. "Rule number one, little devil, you're ours."

"That seems to be a very vague rule." I arch an eyebrow and wet my lips. "What does it mean?"

"It means you don't fuck anyone but us," Damon says. The words are harsh, like he thinks I want to find the next cock to jump on. "Including your boyfriend."

Does he really think Chase is fucking me *and* all those other girls? Hasn't he put it together Chase isn't getting what he wants from me, so he's gone to look somewhere else?

My stomach twists. If I'd known, I still wouldn't have slept with Chase. I wouldn't have gone out with him in the first place.

"What makes you think I'll be fucking you?" I haven't exactly agreed to fuck them. To be their little fuck toy. I meet Damon's sharp blue eyes and try desperately to not show my interest or my fear.

Sex isn't a scary thing for me, but there's still a bit of a size difference here. Mia took those two guys easily, but neither of their cocks were as big as Damon's. And she's done that before. I know because she told me, but hearing about it and seeing it are two different things.

I haven't seen Cam's or Hawk's dicks yet, but something tells me they're not going to be average.

Damon's smile is anything but nice. "We could bend you over that chair and take turns fucking that tight pussy right now, little devil. And you'd come so fucking hard you'd see stars."

Fuck. I could get off to that image right now. That shouldn't appeal to me. But fuck if I'm not curious. I figured I'd lose my virginity to Chase when it felt right, but it never did. With these guys, my body and my resistance melt every time they touch me.

I'm not sure I'll last an hour in their presence before I let one of them put their cock in me. Honestly, part of me wants to stand, turn around, and say *prove it*. I need a cold shower and a few hours away from them to clear my head. The shot of alcohol probably isn't helping my inhibitions.

Even though I didn't fuck Chase, I thought he was loyal. But these guys have no obligation to me. They can fuck whoever they want, whenever they want. If they called any girl, she'd be here in five minutes ready to do their bidding. My stomach twists into a burning knot.

Fine, if they want to fuck me and play little games, I'm down. But if they want to fuck me, I'm not sharing.

"If I'm willing to consider *fucking* as part of this deal, I'm not going to fuck anyone else. I won't fuck anyone who's fucking other people." That was a lot of fucks, but hopefully they'll get the message. I never would have been with Chase if I knew he was with other girls.

Damon narrows his gaze, but he nods. "We'll only fuck you."

Honestly, I figured that would be the end of it. That they'd never agree to that stipulation. Negotiations over, I'd go back to my room and pout because the Devil's trio doesn't want to dick with only me. I didn't expect him to say *yes*.

My panties are soaked. I tighten my thighs around Damon's hips and he smirks.

"No fucking or kissing Chase." Damon rubs his fingers over his lips.

My breath catches. The way Damon kisses me is like he wants to consume me. He got me off in the closet without me doing anything to him. That's not what he'd do for someone he didn't want, right? Or was it his way of seducing me away from Chase?

These thoughts aren't helping, but if he thinks I'd turn around and fuck Chase, it's not happening.

"No problem. I don't want him." Part of me wants to tell them I'm a virgin. But the other part doesn't want to share that with them. They aren't offering me a relationship. Just fucking.

What if my virginity is why Chase didn't really push for more? He claimed he was willing to wait for me to be ready. What if that's why he wanted me, as if my virginity was some sort of prize? He was only willing to wait because he could get what he needed elsewhere.

These guys are used to girls throwing themselves at them. What if the Devil's trio won't want me if they find out how inexperienced I really am? They want someone they can play with. Someone open to letting them try new things. Everything is new to me.

Everyone needs a first time. I'm willing to test my limits and find out what I like with the three hottest guys in our school.

Maybe that makes me a whore.

I don't really care. Maybe I want to be *their* whore. Heat floods me.

Only one problem with the kissing stipulation. Chase has been extra touchy-feely lately. If I continue to be his girlfriend, he's going to continue to touch me and kiss me.

"If I'm his girlfriend, he'll probably try to kiss me," I admit.

"Don't let him."

I narrow my eyes at Damon. "I don't know if you know this, but he's bigger and faster than me."

Damon leans forward and those eyes pierce my soul. "If he kisses you, we'll punish you."

"Punish me?" My voice trembles, imagining whips and chains.

Damon grins. "Maybe we'll spank you or tie you down and not let you come while we fuck you."

Fuck, that doesn't sound horrible. I shift uncomfortably on Damon's lap.

"Fine. So, rule two is you guys are mine." I search his eyes. If they break the rules, I'm out.

His gaze drops to my pants and a shiver works through me.

"No more masturbating, Evan. You need an orgasm, you come to one of us and we'll decide whether you've earned it." He smirks. "The only ones who fuck you are us."

My brain stalls out, like seriously glitches. "You want me to…"

"Ask me to slide my hand into your panties and fuck that pussy until you come on my fingers? Yes, that's exactly what I'm saying."

I can still feel his hand in my pants, stroking me, fucking me. I ignore the aching pulse that demands me to say *okay, how 'bout now?*

"Rule three." Damon slides his hands over my hips and presses me against his cock. "You tell us everything that happens with Chase. We need details. That means no more phoning it in, watching him play beer pong. Pay attention. Remember what he talks about with his friends. We need to know what's important to him, and how to take it from him."

My mouth opens and snaps shut. How long have they been watching me?

Okay, well, I need to make sure to keep my friend out of this.

"Rule four. No fucking Mia," I say. This is non-negotiable.

"Isn't that covered in rule two?" Cam asks. I turn to meet his dark brown eyes.

"Mia wants to fuck the whole hockey team, including you." I try to act nonchalant, but I've already lost my boyfriend. I don't want to lose my friend too. "She's my friend, and I don't want to make her upset when she finds out we're hooking up. She's going to try to get you to sleep with her." My gaze goes to Damon, remembering her fucking those two guys. She's a lot more experienced than I am, and once they realize that about her, they may decide they want her instead. "Even if this crashes and burns, no fucking Mia."

Damon nods slightly and I release the breath I'd been holding.

"Rule five." Damon's smile is dark, and it makes my insides burst into flames. "We get to play with you how we want to. You have a say in it, but you need to be open to experimenting."

My heart skips a beat. They want to do whatever they want to me. I'm in that closet again with Damon pressed up against me. My hands caught in his, helpless to do anything but feel, as he slides his hand into my pants.

Why does that sound appealing? They want me to basically give them free rein over my body. They decide how to play, and I go along with it. Whatever *it* is. I want experiences. I want to be overwhelmed with passion. I want them.

"One caveat." If I'm giving them everything, I need to trust them. "The first time for penetration, I get to say when."

"Not oral." Damon leans back. "We get to fuck your mouth for now, but we'll let you decide the first time for pussy and anal."

Fuck. I've never even given a blow job. There's a first time for everything. I don't know why they want to fuck me, but I'm attracted to them in a way I've never been attracted to anyone else.

If I'm going to pretend to have a boyfriend, why not explore sex with three guys who, according to locker room gossip, know how to fuck. And Damon's already given me one orgasm. A really good one.

"Okay." I can figure this out. How hard can a blow job be? Maybe there's an instructional video out there...

Cam's dark eyes watch me closely. Maybe he suspects I'm innocent. Can I really blame them for not asking what my experience is? My boyfriend is a manwhore. My best friend fucked two guys within an hour of meeting them. My mother... I swallow. My mother hasn't settled for a man until Adam. Yes, he's handsome, but also wealthy.

Guilty by association.

"What are the other rules?" I take a deep breath, preparing myself.

"Have you been tested?" Damon's leading this charge, but I know they've probably already discussed this prior. It makes this whole thing hotter to know they're all on board with fucking me, that they've thought about it more than right this moment.

I'm sure Chase would have fucked me too, but I would have thought it meant something since we're dating. It would have been special. I know with these guys it won't mean anything. It won't hurt emotionally when it ends, because I already know it will. I won't get attached.

"I'm negative." I'm not going to lie and say I've been tested, but I've never had sex before. The only finger I've had in my pussy prior to tonight was my own. And the orgasm Damon wrenched from me was so much better than anything I've given myself.

"Birth control?" Damon searches my eyes like I'm going to lie.

"I started it this summer," I admit. Sex was going to happen at some point, and I wanted to be protected in case the condom broke.

"Did you ever have unprotected sex with Chase?"

I shake my head. I never had sex with Chase. And that makes me happy. He's not worth my time. Going forward, it will be my turn to put on an act for him. To pretend I still want to be his girlfriend.

"Rule six. No condoms." Damon pauses, like he's expecting me to explode or to agree readily.

"Why?" Safe sex is important. Why would they want to forgo that?

"Your cunt is ours, little devil. I want to fill it with my cum and know it's leaking out of you afterwards." Damon's words make my pussy pulse. "I want to own you."

A shiver tears through me.

"Have you been tested?" I search their faces.

"Yes, and we always wear condoms." Damon leans back on his hands.

"What if I get pregnant?" It's a reasonable question. "I'm not terminating a pregnancy, but I'm also not ready to be a single mother at eighteen."

Damon looks at the others before returning his gaze to me. "We'll take care of that if it happens. Don't fuck with us though and stop taking your pills."

My brow furrows. "Why would I do that? I want to go to college and start my career. At some point in the future, I might want kids. Not anytime soon."

That would be a disaster. Pregnant by my potential stepbrother? Or one of his friends? Not knowing which one. Fuck, I'd be asked to leave school if anyone found out. It's not going to happen.

"Anything else?" he asks me.

"That's it?" Six rules and I get to explore sex with three guys. What the hell is happening to my life? Why isn't this freaking me out more?

"For now." Damon smirks. His hair falls over his forehead as he meets my gaze. "Let's go upstairs."

DAMON HELPS ME STAND. I do up my pants, suddenly aware I agreed to have sex with three guys. Cam steps into me and his knuckle tips up my chin. His smile is disarming.

"You owe me a kiss, goody." Cam's gaze drops to my lips.

I wet them as he lowers his mouth to mine. His arm wraps around my waist to drag me into him as he takes his kiss from me. Sparks ignite inside me like mini-explosions. The fire rages hotter inside me at the slide of his tongue against mine. His kiss rocks me to my core, because I didn't know I could be this attracted to three guys at the same time.

My fingers slide into his hair to hold on, as the weight of what I've agreed to begins to sink in.

I'm kissing Cam in front of Hawk and Damon. I've basically agreed to do anything they want. They'll want me to do what Mia did at some point.

But how long will they want me? I have no clue. Maybe only until I break up with Chase. Maybe when they get bored of me.

Hell, maybe it will be after they figure out I'm a virgin. But I want the same thing they do, a way to explore sex without judgment. I don't want someone to take it easy with me for my first time. I don't need them to be tender and caring, or any of those things I'm supposed to want.

I want the stolen moment in that closet with Damon. His mouth hot on mine as he blows up my world. I want them.

"Fuck, goody." Cam lifts his mouth from mine and lifts me against him.

When I put my legs around his waist and my arms around his neck, he smiles.

"I might need to carry you around like this all the time." He jostles me a little and a little laugh escapes me. His dark eyes sparkle as he walks toward the stairs. "We're going to have so much fun."

Those butterflies erupt in my stomach. "Now?"

"Now, little devil." Damon's eyes capture mine over Cam's shoulder. I look over at Hawk, who doesn't smile. His green eyes watch me though.

I pushed him away before. But it doesn't mean I don't feel bad for what I thought was the right thing to do.

Cam carries me up to Damon's bedroom and lowers me to my feet before backing up and sitting on the edge of the bed. The others join him, leaving me standing awkwardly in front of them.

Damon smirks and there's a fire in his eyes that makes me want to run, even though I desperately want to stay.

"Take off your clothes, little devil."

"What?" My fingers twitch next to my jeans.

"Hmm. One more rule. You do what we say," he says. "You agreed to be ours."

I swallow. It sounds like *you're ours* encompassed everything he wants from me. He did say he wanted everything. Do I really want to be under their control? To let them decide how and when to fuck me?

What's the worst that would happen if I broke up with Chase's lying ass? He wouldn't quit the production, and he wouldn't sabotage it if he wants it to boost his career.

But every time one of the trio fucks me, it's my decision. And it's like I'm giving Chase the middle finger for fucking around on me. I can't believe I tried to be loyal to that asshole.

Of course, I didn't know I had options, since he was the only one who was interested at the time. But if I offered sex to anyone willing, I might have a few more options. But none of them would have been like the guys in front of me. Their offer is hard to refuse and not just because of the blackmail.

There's only one problem. They want Chase to find out and he's going to be angry. When things blow up with Chase, it could affect my play.

"If Chase tries to fuck with my play, you'll help me stop him." Knowing they want to fuck me gives me courage. Even if I'm convenient, it's me they want. They could ask any other girl, and most would take them up on their offer. Honestly, they probably could have found a girl to fuck around with Chase and find out all his secrets if that's what they wanted.

But they're willing to give up other girls to have me. Knowing that feeds my ego. A lot.

"Deal." Hawk gestures to my clothes. "Do what you're told, Annie."

I guess this means I'm open for business. My mouth. Fuck. Why does this turn me on?

It's not like they haven't seen everything I have before on video, but it's still difficult to get over the shyness. I take a deep breath and grab the hem of my shirt. After I draw it over my head, I drop it to the floor.

The room is so fucking quiet, but I'm not about to ask for music.

I hope they aren't hoping for a sexy striptease as I toe off my socks and undo my jeans at the same time. I slide my jeans down and step out of them, leaving me in my bra and panties.

A shiver rolls over me as their eyes drink me in.

I have slender curves. I don't think I have a great body. The girls surrounding me at school are the cream of the crop, so it's hard not to feel a little inferior. I accepted long ago that my mind is what's going to take me places, not my body.

"All of it." Damon leans back and strokes his palm over his cock in his jeans. My pussy clenches, remembering those fingers inside me. Will he do it again? Will he make me come while the others watch? Fuck, I get even wetter at that thought.

I try not to question what's happening to me or who I am right now, because maybe this is exactly what I want. Someone to take the decision away from me. Someone to tell me exactly what to do and when. To finally give up the tight control I've had to maintain for years to get to where I am now.

I can't fall in love with one of them if I'm fucking all of them.

My bra has a touch of lace on it, but it's not anything particularly special. I wasn't expecting to get undressed for anyone today or any day really. I take it off and drop it on my pile of clothes. If I focus on them, I'll lose my nerve. My panties aren't fancy, just plain cotton bikini briefs. I don't even own a thong or anything remotely sexy.

I slide them off over my hips and let them flutter to my feet. Stepping out of them, I shiver, feeling totally exposed. Our rules are the only guarantee they won't fuck me today, and I'm not sure how strongly I'll enforce them.

Damon stands and walks over to me. I hold my breath. He doesn't touch me, but his eyes take in every inch of me as he walks around me.

"Are you willing to shave your pussy?" He stops in front of me. When his fingers brush my pubic hair, my breath releases on a shudder.

"I don't know how." I meet his eyes. I'm naked and he's still fully clothed. I guess I'll get used to it. Wetness trickles from my pussy.

"I'll help you," he says.

Fuck. Thinking of him working on trimming my pussy hair makes me want to squirm. I don't know what's happening to me, but I'm ready to shed the parts of me that made Chase Chadwick think I was an easy target.

Damon glances at the bed and then at Hawk and Cam. His blue eyes lock with mine as he reaches behind his head and tugs his t-shirt off with one hand.

Fuck, he's ripped. Every inch molded. I want to explore him with my hands, my mouth. I want to kiss every inch of him.

"Time to get the first hurdle out of the way. Lay down on the bed."

The others stand, making room for me. Their jeans bulge in the front.

"What does that mean?" I ask softly.

"Oral only, little devil, as promised. Now do as you're told." Damon puts his hand on my bare hip, sending sparks throughout me. He guides me toward the bed.

"What if I'm not good?" I look up into Damon's eyes. The worry is real. What if they try me and find out I'm not good at all, and this is over before it begins? They must have considered that, since Chase is off fucking everything that moves.

Damon slides his hand into my hair and grabs it, yanking my head back. I gasp at the sizzle of anticipation that heats my blood. He closes in until my breasts touch his chest. His mouth hovers over mine. My hard nipples ache. I suck in my breath.

"Then we'll work with you until you're perfect for us. Which you will be, little devil. Perfect for us." His lips claim mine and he pulls me in close. My bare skin collides with his. A jolt of electricity chases through my veins and lights up everything inside me.

He kisses me like he has all the time in the world. His hand stays in my hair, holding me how he wants me. His other hand slides between my thighs and teases my clit before he pushes a finger inside me. I gasp. It stretches me, making me full.

I moan into his mouth.

"So fucking wet." He fucks his finger in and out of my pussy, pushing me higher and higher as he presses his body against mine and fucks my mouth with his tongue. I was already so keyed up, it doesn't take much to shove me over the edge. Crying out, I come all over his hand. "That's it, little devil."

He pulls his fingers out of me and shows me my wetness. "Open."

I part my lips, still buzzing in the afterglow. He slides his fingers inside my mouth, and I taste my musky cum.

"Suck them."

I close my lips around his fingers and he fucks them in and out of my mouth, building the need inside me all over again.

"Use your tongue. And mind your teeth. I doubt this is your first rodeo, but you're not here to do the work, little devil. We'll take what we need from your body." His eyes darken as he watches his fingers. My insides are a twisted web of desire.

When he draws his fingers out, he rubs my saliva around my nipple, making it tighten almost painfully. No one's touched my bare breast before. Heat seeps through every inch of me.

"Bed. Now." He lowers his zipper, frees his hard cock, and strokes it.

I wet my lips nervously. Only his word means he won't fuck me. But this whole agreement between us relies on trust. If I can't trust them, this won't work. So, if they fuck me over, I'm out.

CHAPTER 30

EvanAnn

I'm in over my head here, but I'm a quick learner. At least that's what I keep reminding myself.

Cam's hand touches my back and guides me over to the bed. His shirt is gone and he's as cut as Damon. Thicker though, heavier. "Up."

I climb onto the bed and kneel there, unsure what to do next. At some point, he'll fuck me. They'll all fuck me. Maybe all at the same time. My pussy aches. I shiver and wait for him to tell me what to do.

He touches my breast, lifting it. I suck in a breath. Damon's the only one who's touched my breast before. Cam's fingers toy with my nipple, making me even wetter. "Lay down. Head off this side."

I do my best to follow his orders. Lying down on my back and scooting so my head hangs off the edge. My hands clutch into the duvet to keep me from falling. Damon steps in front of me.

"Knees up. Spread them wide. Relax them out to the side."

Instead of overthinking it, I do as he orders. I don't question anything as his cock bobs in front of my face. When I spread my legs, I hesitate for a moment. I'm exposing myself, letting them see everything. I've never felt more vulnerable. They could just fuck me and get it over with. There's not a lot I could do to stop them.

The bed dips between my legs. A hand touches my inner thigh and I hold my breath, waiting for him to thrust deep inside me. It's going to happen sooner or later. I can't see anything but Damon's cock and abs. My thighs tremble with the need to close my legs. No one has been this close to me before. I don't know if I can do this.

They're all still wearing their jeans, which makes me feel a little more secure.

"Relax, Annie." Hawk's words are hot against my thigh as he presses a kiss there. A shiver works through me as he trails kisses up my thigh toward my pussy. I keep my legs open, even though I want to close them.

Is he...? But they're going to use me?

"Oral is on the table, goody. Did you think we only meant you servicing us?" The bed dips next to me as Cam sits.

Actually, I did.

Cam's hands cup my breasts as Hawk parts my pussy lips and his mouth closes over it. My mouth opens at the sensation and I lift my head to look down at Hawk, shocked at how different that feels than fingers. His green eyes collide with mine as he explores my folds with his tongue.

"You have nice tits." Cam's words make me turn to look at him. He smirks as he squeezes them and rubs his thumbs over my nipples. Sparks trickle through me from his touch to pool where Hawk's mouth is. "Great size."

My cheeks flush with heat at the compliment. My thighs fall out to the side as Hawk takes his time exploring my pussy with his tongue. My insides are like a live wire.

Damon's hand slides into my hair and cradles my head. I release the tension on my neck without him asking, letting him take the weight. Fuck, this is happening. They're all touching me. He holds my head up for a second while I pant. This flood of heat is unlike anything I can give myself. The fire inside me rages out of control. They're crashing through firsts of mine and not even knowing it. It will be my secret.

"Open." Damon lowers my head and I meet his eyes as he drops my head down.

I open my mouth and his thick cock thrusts into my mouth. I gag a little, but then he pushes past it and I try to relax and go with it. I keep my teeth away from his cock. Though, he's so big it's not easy. Hawk's finger slides inside my pussy, thrusting in and out, making me moan around Damon's cock.

Damon groans low in his throat. Did he like that? My body shudders as they work me. My fists clench the comforter even though I don't think they'd let me fall. Cam leans over and takes my breast into his mouth. I'd cry out, but my mouth is full of smooth, thick cock. The fire swells inside me.

Damon uses my mouth, thrusting in as deep as he wants, and I take it. I don't hate the slide of his cock against my tongue. The thought that he's using me to get off makes my insides burst into flames.

"Such a good little cum slut." Damon tightens his hand on my hair. "You're going to swallow, aren't you, little devil?"

I can't answer him, but I'm not opposed, especially with Hawk's and Cam's mouths on me. Hawk's finger fucks my pussy as he sucks on my clit, and all that beautiful tension builds to a crescendo.

I moan around Damon's cock as my pussy pulses and clamps tight around Hawk's finger. My hips buck against his mouth. Hawk sucks and licks me through my release. Damon's thrusts into my mouth grow chaotic until he groans and hot cum hits the back of my throat.

I swallow around him and suck as he empties inside me. It's more intense than I ever could have imagined.

Hawk lifts from my pussy, slowly thrusting his finger in and out a few more times, making aftershocks ripple through me. When Damon pulls out of my mouth, I suck in a breath, right before his mouth crashes down on mine. Upside down and a tangle of tongues.

Another aftershock rips through me as Cam sucks on my other breast before they all move away. My head drops to the side of the mattress. I clench my fists in the comforter. My body feels warm from my orgasm, but chilled without anyone touching it.

Well, fuck. That happened. I want to laugh. I didn't even let Chase get that far. Though he asked me to suck his cock, he never offered to go down on me. Maybe if he had, I would have done more.

There's movement on the bed and hands slide beneath my ass. I don't have the energy to lift my head to see who's there. Anticipation sizzles in my veins.

A tongue traces my clit lightly, sending sparks into the fire. Hands cup my breasts and a cock bobs in front of me.

"Open, Annie." Hawk lifts my head slightly before thrusting into my mouth. He's a little thicker, but not as long as Damon. "You tasted so good, baby girl. I'm going to need to taste that pussy daily."

Fuck. A girl could get addicted to these kinds of orgasms.

"I only had a taste before." Damon sits beside me and strokes his fingers over my nipples before pinching them. I gasp. The sharp pain shimmers into pleasure as he strokes his fingers around the tips.

Cam slides lower and thrusts his tongue into my entrance. I moan at the exquisite feel of his tongue fucking in and out of me.

"I love it when you moan, baby girl." Hawk keeps thrusting a little deeper every time. "I'm not going to last long. I nearly came going down on you, feeling you clench around my finger. That tight little pussy. You're going to feel so good around my cock."

Tingles shoot through me as I come on Cam's tongue.

"So fucking responsive, baby girl." Hawk thrusts in and holds it there for a moment, blocking my airway. "That's it. Swallow around my tip like a good girl."

I swallow for him as blackness edges at my vision. The praise makes me want to please him. He pulls almost all the way out, as Cam's tongue explores lower. He lifts my hips and spreads my ass cheeks before tonguing my puckered hole, breaching it. I gasp at the sensation and try not to squirm away from him. I suck on the head of Hawk's cock and tease the tip with my tongue.

When Cam thrusts his tongue into my asshole over and over, Hawk matches the strokes as he thrusts deep into my throat. Moaning, I come again.

"Fuck, baby girl." Hawk thrusts his cock deep and groans his release. It hits the back of my throat as I swallow to take it down. "I love your mouth."

He pulls out. And there's a shift again as Cam leaves me. Damon moves on the bed and he doesn't start slow when he gets between my legs. He sucks on my clit, making me arch off the bed with a moan as my already sensitive pussy shatters.

Cam steps in front of me and thrusts his cock into my open mouth.

I take him, even though he makes me gag. He's thick, and hard, and long, but I'm familiar with having a cock in my mouth now. I relax my throat for him. Hawk moves to my breasts and they start all over again, working me up, using my body.

I never thought it could be like this. I was nervous with Chase, that he would take advantage. But it's not that way with these guys. Oh, they'll take advantage, but to do that, I have to trust them. Which means they need to follow my rules if they expect to have an all-access pass to my body for as long as they want me. I'll take what I can get from them.

I'm not thinking about how long this might last. Not right now.

So far, I'm good with oral. I don't know when we'll move on to the other parts, but this—this I can do. My hands tighten into the duvet.

Hawk takes my nipple between his lips and then bites down on it. I choke on Cam's cock, but he grunts and slides his hand to my other breast, pinching the nipple.

Damon slides his finger into my pussy as he sucks on my clit. It's intense and so fucking good. I moan around Cam's cock. Damon's tongue toys with my clit as he pumps his finger in and out until I can't hold back anymore.

My release rips through me at the same time Cam comes down my throat. I swallow around him.

"Fuck, this pussy is going to feel good wrapped around my dick. I can barely get my finger in there." Damon's words aren't for me, not like Hawk's were. Cam pulls out.

"I'm going to fuck her tits next time," Cam says as he grabs my breast currently not being suckled. "I'll come all over this beautiful neck."

Damon works his finger in and out of my pussy while they discuss what they want to do to me like I'm not here, like I don't matter. I'm just the vessel they're using to get off.

Maybe it's because I'm convenient. After all, I live here now. Hawk switches breasts and his hand slides down my belly to rub my clit while Damon's fingers thrust in and out of my pussy. I can feel the muscles tightening for release. I don't know if I can come again.

My eyes close and I feel the warm splash of something on my belly. I lift my head to see what's happening. Damon kneels above me stroking his cock as he comes on my stomach. My pussy clenches around his finger.

Hawk lifts off my breast and drags his fingers through Damon's cum on my stomach before sliding it down over my clit, rubbing it into me. He has his cock in his hand, stroking it quickly.

He groans as he comes on my breasts. Fuck, why is that so hot? I drop my head back as I can feel another release closing in on me.

"Keep your eyes closed, goody." The first splash of cum on my face surprises me, but then my release takes over and I arch off the bed. It's so strong. My mouth opens but no sound comes out.

I fall back on the bed, panting. I've had plenty of orgasms before. Self-gratification is easy and helps me sleep after a stressful day, which going to Anteros and Deimos is fucking stressful. But I've never had anything like this.

My whole body is exhausted. My legs tremble.

Damon removes his finger from my cunt and Hawk thrusts his finger with Damon's cum on it into my entrance. Damon drags his finger through the cum on my breasts and rubs it over his fingers before sliding down to my asshole.

"Have you taken a cock in the ass before, little devil?"

"No," my voice is scratchy. Anal sex doesn't seem like something I should lie about.

"Good." He presses his finger into my ass. "Relax."

I don't really have any muscle strength left to begin with, so I do as he says and let him ease his finger into my asshole, using Hawk's cum as lube. Hawk slides his finger through more cum on my breasts and stomach, and slips it inside me like they're filling me, even though they aren't fucking me yet.

Hawk's finger in my pussy with Damon's finger in my ass reminds me of watching Mia take both guys' cocks. Just their fingers feel like a lot. Imagining it's their cocks sets me on fire. The buildup sneaks up on me, and I cry out as I come around their fingers, clenching tight.

"Fuck, that's going to feel great on our cocks. Don't keep us waiting too long, little devil."

I already know I'm going to enjoy sex with these guys and there's really nothing holding me back. Maybe a little fear. As soon as I know I can trust them...

Cam lifts my head and uses a warm washcloth to clean my face. Part of me wants to curl up and go to sleep. As soon as Cam finishes, Hawk and Damon take their fingers out of me.

I don't even try to move. Everything aches deliciously.

At some point, the guys took off their jeans and boxers. Damon scoops me into his arms and carries me into the bathroom, where the shower is already running. He steps in and sets me on my feet. When my knees give, he draws me against him, holding me up.

My skin tingles where it touches his. I rest my forehead against his chest and inhale his earthy scent.

Hawk gets in with us and grabs the soap. His hands run all over me, while Damon holds me upright. Damon turns me so Hawk can get both sides. The flames flicker to life with every stroke, but I'm so tired.

"You did well, baby girl." Hawk's praise fills me with pride. I smile, even though I'm exhausted.

Damon tips my chin up and claims my mouth with his. The kiss is hotter and messier than the other times he kissed me. "Don't wait too long to give permission, little devil. I'm going to need to fuck you often."

CHAPTER 31

Cam

I WAIT for Damon to help Evan out of the shower. Hawk takes a minute to wash himself off and steps out to grab a towel. I step in and take a quick shower, watching Damon make sure Evan takes care of herself.

She brushes her teeth and he makes her show him her pill case. They even discuss when she takes it. Controlling bastard.

We discussed the risks of unprotected sex before even offering her our rules. Evan has big dreams. She wants to be a director. She's not going to risk everything to trap one of us with a kid. But it's always a possibility, girls have done worse for money.

Her cheeks flush with color when she meets my eyes in the mirror. The towel is tucked around her tight. Having her naked body stretched out in front of me made me want to thrust into her tight little pussy or that sweet little asshole.

Fuck. I've fucked a lot of girls. Probably more than I should have, but this feels different.

We own her. Exploring sex with her is going to be fun. It's fucking brilliant. I don't need to flirt with her to have sex or have her reject me because she doesn't want to. Sure, she has a say in it, but we'll get to try stuff we normally wouldn't.

Once she removes the limits she put in place.

Other girls talk, and that shit gets out. One guy liked rough sex, and soon no girl would have sex with him even though he didn't always have rough sex. There's a lot of things most girls won't even try, or if they do, they want you to commit to them first.

Damon guides Evan into her room. As I step out of the shower, I hear drawers opening and closing. Their voices rise. I wrap the towel around my waist and head into Evan's room.

"Seriously?" Damon holds up a pair of pink panties, similar to the ones she peeled off earlier. "You wear these to get laid?"

She narrows her eyes on him. "What does it matter? They all come off the same."

"Packaging matters, little devil. As a director, you should know that."

She snatches the panties out of his hand and pulls them on. I lean on the doorway to the closet. I don't know why he can't see her innocence. Maybe he doesn't want to see it.

There's a reason she draws us in. She's a lamb amongst wolves.

He stops her from grabbing a nightgown and lifts her against him. She squeals a little as he carries her past me and into his bedroom, dropping her towel on the floor of the bathroom on his way through.

I chuckle and follow them in. Damon grabs one of his red Devil shirts and pulls it on over her head. She sighs, but it's almost as long as a nightgown.

"Now can I go to bed?" She takes a step toward the bathroom, like she's going to sleep in her own bed.

Damon steps in her way and gestures to his bed. "Climb in."

Her eyes widen as she notices all of us in the room. We're wearing boxers, but nothing else.

"You want me to sleep with you?"

Damon tips her chin up. "You're ours."

I close in behind her and slide my hands over her hips. "Weekends we get to play and sleep together."

She leans back into me and her warmth feels good. She yawns, and all the fight seems to leave her. This is the easiest thing for us to take from her. We'll sleep next to her.

Maybe Chase was her first or maybe there were others before him, but maybe no one's really spent time with Evan, getting her there. Making sure her needs have been met too. But we will.

I don't know if she's really considered what kind of dark desires we have.

She didn't even think to ask. Poor goody two-shoes. We're going to have so much fun together.

EvanAnn

I'm so warm and my bed is so soft. But my pillow is hard and hot. I open my eyes, but the room is dark and I'm completely disoriented. An arm wraps around me, drawing me in tight against a body.

Clips of last night flood my mind. Mia, Liam, and Fletcher. Damon in the closet. Chase. Agreeing to be theirs. Sucking their cocks while they played my body like a finely-tuned instrument. Bed.

I thought it would take me forever to fall asleep, but as soon as Damon pulled me in tight against him, exhaustion took over. I didn't sleep well the night before, and then everything that happened yesterday and last night.

It was a lot.

Cam is snuggled up against my back, curled around me with his hard cock pressed against my ass. My leg is over Damon's. I've never slept with anyone else before, let alone two someones, and I know Hawk is in the bed as well.

This is what I agreed to, but somehow I didn't think cuddling would be part of it.

I blow out a breath. I won't become attached to these guys. They aren't offering me a future or even a relationship. Just sex.

The hand on my shoulder squeezes me lightly.

"You up, little devil?" Damon's voice is sleepy.

"I didn't dream last night?" My words are soft to not wake up the others.

"No. Still okay with your decision?" His other hand slides down my side to where his t-shirt rode up in the night.

My breath catches as his fingers slide along the elastic of my panties brushing against my skin. "Yes."

For better or for worse. I'm all in on this.

"We didn't mention consent."

I swallow. "You said we'd discuss things before they happen."

"I want to be able to make you come while you sleep, little devil." His hand slides beneath my panties and his fingers glide over my pussy.

I bite my lip and hold back my moan at how good his touch feels.

"Will you let me?" His finger teases my entrance.

"Please," I whisper. My hips rock against his, needing him to make me come.

"That's not a yes, little devil." He thrusts his finger into my pussy, but leaves it inside me.

"Yes," I whimper.

Cam thrusts his hips against my ass. Anticipation crawls over my skin as my pussy pulses around Damon's finger.

"Don't you want to know what I'll do to you while you sleep, little devil?" Damon chuckles as I try to move his finger by rocking my hips.

My hand is on his warm skin. I slide it down his body. He doesn't know I've never touched anyone else's cock before. It makes me bolder than I normally would be, because he doesn't want me to be tentative.

I slip my hand beneath his boxers and stroke along his cock.

"You want my cock, little devil?" He chuckles, as he begins to fuck his finger in and out of my pussy. "I can fuck this cunt right now, if you'd like. We could move on to more games."

"Like what?" I turn and press my lips to his chest as my hand closes around his hard cock.

"All the normal positions, of course." His breathing grows harsher when I stroke his cock like he did in rhythm to his finger in my pussy. "Someone could be pounding this sweet pussy while someone else fucks your mouth."

I drag my tongue along his salty skin. He inhales sharply.

"You like that, little devil. You're so fucking wet for me."

My thumb brushes over his tip and he's wet. "You're wet for me too."

He chuckles. "Fuck, take my cock into your cunt and fuck me properly, Evan."

"You could use my mouth," I offer. His cock twitches in my hand.

"Come for me first." He shifts my body on top of his and kisses me as he finger fucks me. My knees fall to either side of his waist. His thumb works my clit and I don't hold back. My orgasm washes over me, taking my breath with it.

"You feel so good when you come." He draws his fingers out of my panties. "Let me fuck your face, little devil."

I slide down on the bed, pulling his boxers down. My hand closes over his cock and I lower my mouth over it. He grabs my hair and I release the tension in my neck as he holds me still.

"You need me to stop, tap my leg three times." He holds my head as he thrusts up into my throat. It's different than last night. The other position helped open my throat up. He hits my gag reflex, but I relax around him. "Suck on it."

I do my best to suck on him as his cock slides in and out of my mouth. It doesn't take long before his cock jerks against my tongue and his warmth floods my mouth. He lifts me off his dick and I rest my head against his hip.

He drags me up his body and his mouth finds mine. It's easy to forget he hates me when he's kissing me. To lose myself in the feel and taste of him. He lowers me to his chest again and breathes out.

"You'll let me make you come when you sleep?" His hand strokes over my hair.

"As long as you follow the rules."

"Deal."

His heartbeat beneath my ear lulls me back into sleep.

I WAKE UP LATER, ALONE IN DAMON'S BED. VAGUELY I remember him shifting me to a pillow. I sit up and look around the room, but the bathroom door is open and no one is inside. This is how I thought things would go.

I take a quick shower and brush my teeth. When I walk into my room, I check my messages on my phone. I have messages from Mia, Mom, and Chase.

MIA

We need to hang out. What are you doing today?

I glance at the open door to the bathroom. *Fucking my future step-brother* probably isn't what I should type. I rub a hand over my face. Probably shouldn't say *I have to check in with my new owners* either.

I could ask what she's up to, but then she might say *Liam and Fletcher* and that's a memory I don't want to keep bringing up. She doesn't know we saw her with them.

If I do get together with her today, she'll likely recap the whole thing. I could let her know I caught the live show, but that would probably be a bad idea. She'd probably wonder why I was in the closet, and who I was with, and then we'd go down the rabbit hole that is my life currently.

Okay, put that one on pause. Next.

MOM:

Staying in the city. Be home tomorrow night.

The time stamp is ten last night. If I thought I might see Mom more by living under the same roof as her boyfriend, I was apparently wrong. I don't get my week of Mom time after a breakup, but hopefully she'll find more time for me when things settle down with Adam.

I have no idea what the guys' plans are for today. The urge to check in with them is strong, but unnecessary. Yes, I agreed to a very weird sexual arrangement with them, but I still have homework and things to plan for the play.

I take a deep breath before opening Chase's text.

CHASE:

Sorry missed you

Hope you feel better

Want to get dinner tonight?

I look at the time stamp on the last one. It's from early morning, probably when I was mid-orgasm. Maybe I should feel guilty for cheating, but I don't. Not even a little.

Every girl in school probably knows Chase is open for business. They must have laughed behind my back, while I thought I had a good boyfriend. Fuck. Now that's all I'm going to see. Those girls knowing they've had my boyfriend.

But what those girls won't have is the Devil's trio.

I dress for the day and figure out my schedule, reviewing what I need to do today.

I know the guys aren't in Damon's room, so that means I have to go find them. My hair is up in a messy bun—it's a disaster after I went to sleep with it wet—and make sure I'm all put together. I haven't really gotten the chance to explore the house on my own.

Fuck, I left my car—er, Damon's car—at Mia's last night. Okay, two things I need to talk to the guys about. Chase wanting to go out and someone needs to take me to get my car. If I show up on the back of one of their motorcycles at Mia's house, there are going to be questions I don't want to answer.

Sure, she's my friend, but she's still new. I want to trust her, but the burns of other ex-friends still linger, making me wary.

CHAPTER 32

EvanAnn

I FIND the guys playing video games in the rec room. Some kind of first-person shooter. They don't pay me any attention as I walk in with the sandwich I got from the kitchen staff. I still don't know how I feel about having someone do what I'm perfectly capable of doing myself.

There's an open seat, so I sit and tuck my feet up under me, taking a bite of my sandwich. I watch them focus on the game. Each of them has taken a moment to glance toward me, but whatever battle is happening onscreen is apparently too important to look away from.

They're all wearing athletic pants and t-shirts. It's weird knowing I slept with them and had their cocks in my mouth and all their mouths on my pussy. Heat washes through me.

Fuck. Hawk said he wanted to go down on me every day. Sign me up.

The sandwich is by far the best thing I've had in a while. I suck the sauce off my fingers as I try to figure out who's winning onscreen.

"Evan, for fuck's sake," Damon growls.

I straighten. "What?"

I'm just sitting here. I wipe my hands on my napkin. He glances toward me.

"On your knees, now. Take off that shirt and anything you have on under it, and suck my cock."

My mouth opens and closes. Really? I glance toward the door. What if our parents come home? Or one of the many household staff come down here?

"Now?"

Damon growls. "If I have to count, you'll regret it."

Will I? I arch an eyebrow, but I need some advice so I put misbehaving on hold. I agreed to this, and they agreed to my terms. If I start fucking with their terms, they might disregard mine.

I swallow. While I know we'll eventually have sex, I'd rather control when the first times happen.

Setting my plate to the side, I peel my top off and watch their soldiers move through the battlefield. When I take off my bra, my nipples tighten in the cool air. As I start to walk toward them, all three start yelling over each other and gesturing at me, like I'm in the way.

I put my hands on my hips and glare at Damon. "You could pause it."

"It doesn't work that way, little devil." He glances at me. "Crawl over here so you don't block the TV."

It's probably not the most humiliating thing they'll have me do, but my cheeks flame with heat as I drop to the floor and crawl on my hands and knees. Someone dies in the game.

I lift my gaze and see Hawk watching me intently. I don't know if kissing is part of our deal, but I'd like to think it is. Because I really want to kiss Hawk again.

Fuck, why does crawling on the floor to Damon turn me on? My jeans rub against my clit as I make my way to Damon's feet. I put my hands on his knees and look up at him, waiting for what's next.

"You're a smart girl, Evan." Damon doesn't take his eyes from the screen. "Do you need me to walk you through it step-by-step, or do you know what to do?"

Each word strikes at my confidence. Seriously, I don't know what I'm doing here, but they think I do. I hate to think it, but how did Mia do it? She seemed so fucking confident when she was down on her knees and working two cocks.

If Damon's body hadn't distracted me from the show, I might have paid closer attention. Taken notes.

It's not like I haven't had Damon's dick in my mouth already, but there was very little I had to do other than open my mouth and suck.

Fuck. Maybe a manual would be good. I reach for the waistband of his athletic pants. It's stretchy enough and he doesn't act like he's going to stand up, so I can draw them down. In the few romance novels I've read, the cock just magically gets freed from his pants.

I don't have that kind of power though. I slide my hand down the outside of Damon's boxers over his warm solid cock. He hisses and I jerk my gaze up to his face. Did I do something wrong? He's not looking at me.

"If I wanted a hand job, I would have asked for one." Damon glares down at me with impatient eyes. "Give me your mouth, little devil."

I squirm, but then admit defeat. "Could you stand so I can pull these down?"

He arches an eyebrow but doesn't look back at me. "Lift my cock out of my pants and take care not to crush my balls."

Hawk must have revived in the game because he's no longer paying attention to me, but he does make an *obviously* noise. Maybe there's a guidebook on the internet, *How to Play the Whore When You Haven't Done Much Yet.*

I slide my hand into Damon's boxers and work his waistband down so his cock is free. Somehow, I don't think it'd be appropriate to hold my hands up and say *ta-da*. My hair is at least back and out of my way as I lean over Damon's lap.

Taking a deep breath, I hold his cock upright with my hand at his base before trying to mimic what I've seen in porn and last night. I immediately take way too much into my mouth and gag, jerking back.

"Lick it, goody."

My watery gaze darts to Cam. He gives me an encouraging smile and a wink.

"Pretend it's your favorite ice cream cone."

Acting. That I can do. It's what got me into Anteros to begin with. Well, not sucking cock, obviously, but acting. When it was clear I was going to be typecast by everyone as the best friend or the snobby bookworm, I changed to directing. That way, I was in control of who did what.

I slide my tongue along the underside of Damon's cock. After all, ice cream melts. When I get to the tip, I wrap my lips around it and swirl my tongue over it.

"Fuck," Damon hisses and I taste his cum. Not a lot, but enough to know this is working.

With renewed confidence, I set to work, stroking his base like Mia did as I work the tip with my mouth and tongue. I slide a little more into my mouth and hollow out my cheeks as I suck and bob up and down, never taking him as deep as that first time.

It doesn't seem to matter if I take him deep. His hips thrust up occasionally and I hum around the little tastes of him when precum emerges. I drag my tongue through his slit. My breasts rub against his legs. I press my thighs together against the building ache there.

I could slip my hand into my pants and make myself come. It's not like Damon hasn't seen it, but would that be against the rules? After all, he's here. He just wouldn't be doing it himself.

An explosion goes off on the screen behind me, and suddenly Damon's hand is on my head. He doesn't press me down, but holds me there as his hips thrust up into my mouth.

"Fuck. I don't know whether to thank you, little devil, or to thank Cam. I was worried you didn't have any skill and I'd always have to fuck your mouth to come." He breathes out a harsh breath as I suck a little harder. "Fuck."

He pushes me down and thrusts up, but I relax my throat as he comes into my mouth. I swallow the best I can, but giving head is messy.

He lifts my head off his cock and drags me up onto his lap to straddle him. His fingers quickly undo my pants. His mouth captures my nipple and sucks as his hand slides into my panties and his finger thrusts inside.

"Oh, fuck." I don't try to stop the need to rock my hips with his thrusting finger. My fingers tangle into his hair to hold his head to my breast. My head falls back, giving in to the pleasure, letting him wind me tight again. I whimper. "Don't stop."

He chuckles darkly before switching to the other breast and thrusting his finger deep and curling it to touch a spot that makes me moan and tremble in his arms.

Each tug on my breasts makes my pussy clamp down on his thrusting finger until I can't think anymore, and I ride out wave after wave of pleasure. My breath crashes into me as I come down.

Damon's hand tucks into my hair and brings my head to his as our mouths collide. His fingers continue to work me until I shatter again. He draws me against him. His wet cock rests hard against my stomach. I breathe him in as I work to regulate my breathing.

My pussy clutches around his finger in tiny aftershocks.

Yeah, my virginity isn't going to last long with these three. I'm already contemplating standing and divesting myself of my pants and more, but fuck, it's way too soon to trust them.

Maybe it's wanton of me to enjoy going down on Damon. To enjoy being used by him. But they already think I'm a whore, which is freeing. No one is setting me on the shelf because I might be breakable.

Nope, they'll take me out of the box and play with me.

"You made me lose, little devil." Damon kisses my neck, sending a fresh wave of sparks through me. "Why are you down here?"

I straighten and try to drag my thoughts out of sex, but his finger is still inside me and his lips are sucking on my neck.

"My car. I need to get my car. I mean, your car."

He sits back and raises an unimpressed eyebrow at me before rubbing my clit. "You left my car?"

I nod, trying not to roll my hips against his finger. "At Mia's yesterday, before the game."

"Is that all, little devil?"

I shake my head, but I'm losing the battle of where the blood flows in my body.

"Words, Evan."

I bite my lip, not wanting to say his name while feeling any pleasure. Fuck. I pull my phone out of my pocket and open Chase's text.

"Hawk," Damon says.

Hawk takes my phone from me and reads the text. Of course, he also scrolls back and reads the other texts. What few there are.

"He wants to have dinner with her tonight." Hawk sets my phone on the end table beside him and sits back. His hooded green eyes study my face. "Is that what you were going to ask about, Annie?"

"Yes," I bite out with a gasp as I tremble, so fucking close to coming around Damon's fingers again.

Damon drags his fingers out of my jeans before I come and paints my wetness on my lips. "On the floor, kneeling, Evan. I want to see what you would have looked like in Mia's place."

Heat courses through me as I stand and lower to my knees. I don't bother doing up my pants.

Damon leans back on the couch and gestures to Cam and Hawk. "This is interactive time. See, we watched Mia suck two guys' cocks at the same time. Didn't we, Evan?"

I nod and swallow. "Yes."

"You had the better vantage point." Damon's blue eyes are lit with wickedness as Cam and Hawk both pull out their cocks for me. "Show me what I missed, little devil."

These guys are both bigger than the ones Mia did this to last night. I reach for them and slide my fists down their cocks and up again, finding a rhythm. I turn my head toward Hawk first. I meet his green eyes as I lean forward and lick his cock, remembering what Cam said, before sliding him into my mouth and sucking gently.

Hawk keeps his eyes locked with mine as I explore his cock with my mouth and tongue. His eyes darken and something raw tugs at my insides. This is both degrading and powerful in the same breath. Yes, I'm on my knees for them, but they need me to make them feel good.

I pull off and turn to meet Cam's dark eyes. I lick and suck on his head until he thrusts in a little deeper. My pussy gets wetter as he slowly fucks my mouth. My legs are spread and my jeans are tight against my clit.

I work with him as our gazes remain locked. Someone could walk in right now and I wouldn't even notice it. So focused on giving them pleasure. I pull off and gasp before turning back to Hawk. With no hesitation, I take him into my mouth and slide him in deep, relaxing my throat. My eyes water as I meet his, but I suck and lick his cock and see that facade he holds so tight around him start to slip.

He grabs my hair, pulling it. I relax into the pain, knowing he wants to take, and fuck, do I want him to. I want him to take everything. He growls and fucks my mouth as he tugs me closer and closer, until my nose brushes his abs. He's so deep inside me, I can barely breathe.

A flush of heat spirals through me and I moan at the ache between my legs. The need to have him this deep somewhere else.

"Fuck, baby girl." He comes with a roar, flooding my throat and making me choke as I try to swallow it all. "Finish off, Cam."

I turn and take Cam deep, following his lead. Hawk kneels beside me and slides his hand into my jeans and panties.

"So fucking wet, baby girl. You like the feel of our cocks in your throat."

I moan as he works my clit.

"You need to let us fuck this pussy soon." He growls in my ear as his finger fucks into me. "Then you can suck cock while your pussy gets the pounding it needs."

My moan is muffled around Cam's cock as my release gushes out of me, all over Hawk's hand.

"You like that, dirty girl." He chuckles as he leans down and sucks my breast into his mouth, laving at my nipple with his tongue. Aftershocks ripple through me, my pussy pulsing around his finger.

Cam groans as he comes in my mouth. Exhaustion weighs on me. I'm going to need to nap to keep up with these guys. My gaze meets Damon's.

"Think about when you want to give that pussy up, Evan." He leans forward and tips my chin up. His gaze falls on my naked breasts. "Don't hold out too long."

CHAPTER 33

Hawk

SINCE ANNIE IS MOST comfortable on my bike, Cam and I take her over to Mia's. We're careful not to actually ride past Mia's house. She knows we ride and it's not like our motorcycles are quiet.

Cam parks behind Damon's car and comes over to help Annie. She really needs to figure out how to get off a bike on her own.

I don't know how to feel about Annie. I want to make her beg. I understand she was loyal to that dickhead of a boyfriend of hers when she pushed me away. But it doesn't take the sting away.

But fuck, seeing her on her knees is fucking empowering. Her mouth was made for my cock and watching her take the others was exquisite. I'm not going to kiss her again until she begs for it though.

"I'll see you back at the house?" She holds the keys and her eyes meet mine, but not like when she held my eyes as she blew my fucking mind. Her eyes are more uncertain again.

"We've got schoolwork." Cam tucks her hair behind her ear. "Try to stay out of Damon's way if you can."

Her cheeks glow red. "It's not like I can lock him out."

"If you figure out a way, don't." Cam tips her chin up and he's one hundred percent serious.

Damon wants access. He's already determined to make her his whore. He gave her the time to come to terms with it, but he'll keep pushing on those boundaries until he breaks through them. One way or another. But right now, we need her to trust us and that means allowing time to let it build.

She swallows.

"If you think he's bad now, you wouldn't want him riled up and coming for you." Cam steps back. "Go on, you need to get ready for your date."

She sighs. "I still don't think this is a good idea."

"He's your boyfriend, Evan." Cam climbs on his bike. "You need to treat him how you always treated him."

"Without the kissing and fucking," I add. Though the idea of punishing her sounds like fun. Tying her up and spanking that firm ass before thrusting deep inside it. Will she like anal or hate it? Either way, I'm willing to fuck her ass until she comes or as punishment.

She opens her mouth and closes it with a shake of her head, before sliding into the driver's seat. The car starts and she pulls away.

"She's not going to fuck him," Cam sounds certain as he lowers his visor.

"She would have kicked his ass to the curb last night." I lower my visor and rev my engine as we pull back onto the street. She's done with the fuckboy.

"He deserves to be kicked in the balls." Cam chuckles.

If he touches her, he'll wish we'd let her kick him in the balls. It won't be just Annie who I punish if he touches her.

---

*Evan*Ann

I take a shower and blow-dry my hair, glancing at Damon's door the entire time. It's not like he's in his room or that he'd know what I'm doing currently. But part of me craves his attention. The other part dreads it.

I don't bother with makeup. As I look into the mirror, I drag in a breath.

I'd rather not go tonight. What Chase did... What he's doing... If he didn't want to wait, why bother dating me? He could have been with all those girls without dragging me into it. He could have not cheated on me. He would have gotten the part in the play by proving he was the best for it.

That's the thing I don't get. Why me? And because I'm going along with the plan to stay with him, I can't even ask. I can't throw in his face while I'm *not* sucking his dick, I've had three in my mouth already today. And I liked it.

My cheeks flush as warmth floods me. Yeah, I liked it. There's no denying that.

But I don't get to throw anything in Chase's face because I have to pretend nothing's wrong. As far as he knows, I'm still his loyal director girlfriend and I don't think he's the biggest asshole in the world. Which is saying something, because I'm living with Damon Storm.

Earlier, I texted Mia that I needed to catch up on homework. And Chase wanted to take me out tonight. She understood and promised we'd spend so much time together this week we'd get sick of each other.

I don't know that I would have been able to look her in the eye after watching her have sex with two guys last night. I'll work on that for Monday.

"You remember your rules." Damon's voice makes me drop my phone on the counter.

I turn and his gaze roams over my body, assessing what I have on. Maybe imagining me naked, since he's seen and felt everything. The furnace inside me kicks up the heat.

What's it going to be like after we start fucking? Will some of this tension when he's around dissipate? Or will it be worse, being around him and knowing what he can do to my body, but not being able to?

When his eyes finally settle on mine, he cocks his eyebrow.

He said something. Rules.

"Ah, the rules. Don't do what I do to you with my boyfriend." I flash him a cocky smile. Worst thing that could happen is he'll tell me to get on my knees and suck him off. That would take my mind off this stupid date.

"You're into acting, Evan. This should be a simple assignment. Do what you've been doing without touching Chase's cock. I know that might be hard for you, but we don't want to waste your talent."

My lips press into a thin line, but then I let them soften into an easy smile. Ah, yes, I'm the whore. He wants to see me act?

I loosen the tension in my body and stroll over to him as he leans against the doorframe. My heart is beating a hundred miles a minute, but he won't see it. I rest my hand on his chest and look up at him.

"You don't want me to seduce my own boyfriend?" I hold his eyes as I let my hand trail down his hard abs to his waistband. Teasing my finger beneath the edge, I give him a slow lazy smile. "What will he think when I don't beg for it?"

Damon's smile is equally lazy, but his eyes have darkened. "Don't worry, little devil. When you get home, I'll let you suck my cock until I can't get it up anymore."

I bite my lip, because I don't know how long that would take.

He steps into the bathroom, forcing me back until he has me trapped against the counter. His hands rest on either side of my hips. My breath catches and I press my thighs together.

"Maybe..." He leans down and his cheek brushes against mine. "I'll have you suck it all night with you in my bed, naked. We could fall asleep like that. My cock warm and wet in your mouth all night long."

Why does that not sound awful? What is wrong with me? Why does he tempt me when I know he hates me? I know he's not doing this because he likes me.

"Maybe I'll keep my finger in your tight little cunt." His lips kiss my jaw. "Because as soon as you open up that pussy to me, that's where my cock is going to be all night long. Buried deep inside you, so if I need to fuck, you'll be right where I need you."

He kisses down my jawline and neck and pulls my shirt to the side before his mouth latches on and sucks. I'm so out of my league with him. Sparks are dancing through my veins.

I slide my hand down over his hard cock, imagining it inside me. Damn it, I don't want to be a cliché in my own head, but seriously, it's so much bigger than his fingers. Hypothetically, I know it will fit, but my brain short-circuits every time I think about what it will feel like.

His hands slide along my waist to my belt. I whimper as he undoes it. I'm already his to do with as he wants. And he's mine to do with as I want, kind of. Fuck it. I slide my hand into his pants and boxers and grip his hard length.

He grunts as he flicks open my jeans and pulls down the zipper.

"I have to go soon," I whisper.

He bites the tender skin he's been sucking on. I gasp in a breath and he shoves down my jeans and panties over my hips.

"You want to play the seductress, little devil?" He lifts his head.

I get a glimpse of the desire burning in his eyes before he spins me. My hands land on the counter and he shifts behind me. His hot cock slides between my legs. My eyes widen in panic and meet his in the mirror.

He smirks as he presses his cock lengthwise against my pussy. "Just because I can't penetrate your cunt yet doesn't mean I can't use it to get off."

I want to ask what that means, but then he begins to thrust his hips, sliding his cock between my pussy lips against my clit. I suck in my breath as heat floods me.

"So fucking wet, Evan." He pushes my back making me lower, changing the angle. "You want me in this pretty little cunt?"

"No," I manage to get out. My breathing is chaotic as he uses my body. That tension is swelling in me. Each stroke pushes me higher.

"I want to come inside you, little devil."

My pussy gets wetter and those sparks are combining. "What do you mean?"

"Meaning I'm going to put my tip against your entrance and come inside you. I won't fuck your precious pussy. Yet."

I'm on fire. Am I worried about him saying fuck it and thrusting in deep? A little, but it's going to happen. I need to be able to trust him.

I meet his eyes. "Okay."

He smiles. "Good girl. I need you to come all over my cock first."

He holds my hips as he thrusts between my thighs and pussy. His gaze lowers to watch what he's doing to me. I never imagined sex would be like this. I'm in this for the wrong reasons. He'll crush me with those videos and the one he's probably recording right now. I don't look to see where he might have hidden it.

"I want to watch this video later." My hips follow his until the intensity gets to be too much.

He smirks. "I'll make sure to have it available when you get back from your date."

I cry out as my release takes me under. He slides back and I feel the tip of him against my entrance. His hand bumps against my pussy as he strokes himself with his tip pressed tight against me.

His eyes meet mine in the mirror as he groans his release, bucking against my entrance as warmth floods me. He pulls back and his finger fucks his cum deeper into my pussy, pushing me over the edge again.

"That's it, little devil. Take my cum into your cunt. I want you to feel it dripping between your legs while you sit across from your fuck-boy. So you remember who you belong to." He pulls his finger out of me and holds it in front of my mouth. "Clean them. Taste how good we are together."

I part my lips and he thrusts his finger inside. As I suck on it, tasting Damon and me, a little aftershock ripples through me and I moan.

He draws his fingers out and wipes his hand on a towel before putting away his cock and straightening my pants. He pulls me back against him.

"If you forget yourself, Evan, you're going to have to explain to your boyfriend how you got cum in your cunt." He pulls my shirt to the side to show off the reddish bruise forming. "And who gave you a hickey."

He pulls away from me, leaving me chilled after the heat of him. I narrow my eyes on him in the mirror. The only reason he marked me and fucked me was to put a claim on me.

Fuck him. He thinks he knows who I am. But he doesn't know the first thing about me.

CHAPTER 34

EvanAnn

"Hey, babe." Chase walks over to the booth and sits across from me.

He's fifteen minutes late, which is typical and wouldn't have bothered me before today. Okay, it would have bothered me, but I wouldn't be as annoyed as I am now. Is he late because he's a dick or because he was getting his dick wet?

"Hi." I cough into my sleeve and give him a smile. I'm leaning into the cold because that shit can cling to me for at least a week and then I'll have to figure out another way to keep him from kissing me.

His smile falls a little. "Damn, are you getting sick for real?"

I nod. "It's only a little cold. Should be gone in no time."

Or you know, a week or two.

The server stops at our table and takes our order. I want to be out of here as quickly as possible. My panties are damp with Damon's cum, and I don't want to risk getting a UTI.

When she disappears, Chase leans back. "I couldn't find you at the party. I looked all over."

I doubt he looked at all. But I can't really go into that.

I lean forward with my elbows on the table and put my chin on my hands. "Oh, you looked? I texted you and told you where I was at one point. Before that, I was out talking with Mia and Liam by the pool, near your friends playing beer pong."

Not even hidden away or clustered with a big group of people. Nope, just sitting and watching everyone. He was probably hitting on Abby at that point, knowing I wouldn't be on the dance floor.

"I must have missed you." He runs his hand through his hair and looks toward the server. "I went outside to play beer pong and didn't see you or Mia."

Probably because you just fucked Abby. I pick up my glass of water to help douse the flames burning inside. How could I have been so stupid to believe he'd be happy with me?

I have nothing to offer him except, what? Being a virgin? Being smart and capable? He has never even tried to cop a feel of my breast. What's making him hold onto me?

What makes me think the Devil's trio is going to be happy with me?

Fuck, I don't want to think about them.

"I didn't see Tanner at all either." I unroll the fork and knife from the napkin to keep my hands busy.

"He was with me most of the night. Good guy." Probably as his alibi. Chase reaches his hand across the table and I reluctantly give him mine. His hands are warm. They always are. But I don't feel any sparks or even a hint of him wanting more. "I think Mia is good for you, babe. You two seem to get along. I'm glad that you didn't have to stand on the sidelines and watch me get drunk with my friends."

Or was he glad I was distracted so he could get some.

"I do like Mia." And I'm trying desperately not to think about him and Abby recreating what Mia did with Liam. It twists my stomach. At least I didn't see anything, only heard them. I can't believe I'd been considering losing my virginity to Chase.

I've already gone further with the trio than I've ever gone with Chase, which makes me smile.

"Are you ready for your big day tomorrow?" Chase smiles easily like everything is okay. Maybe he was worried I saw something at the party. He doesn't normally sneak off during parties if I'm there. This might have been a one-time thing. At least while I was there. There's the video of him with another girl on Wednesday night. Who parties on a school night?

The temptation to blow this up, right now, is almost overwhelming.

Tell him I know about him hooking up with Abby. Would he grovel? Would he laugh at me? My insides twist. It doesn't matter.

If I don't want to be called a whore—by anyone besides Damon—then I need to keep up this charade.

You're into acting. I really don't need Damon's voice in my head, but he's right. This is just an improv scene where I'm playing Chase's girlfriend. Easy enough.

"Yeah, we have read through in the afternoon. I can't wait to hear the cast perform the whole play." This is easy to talk about. Safe. And it's the exact reason I don't want to rock the boat. I need my actors to be in their prime, not pouting about getting caught fucking someone else at a party. Or about me kissing other guys. Though I've kind of taken that to the next level.

A smile tugs at my lips. Fuck, the orgasms these guys give me are beyond anything I imagined.

"You really think Hawk was better than Jason for Cassio?" Chase rubs his thumb against the webbing of my thumb. I resist tugging my hand away from him. "Can the guy do Shakespeare or is he just another pretty face? I mean, he's probably as good-looking as I am, which makes sense for the play, but I'd hate for it to fall apart due to bad acting."

Wait a minute. I arch an eyebrow. *He's* questioning *my* choices? Fuck him and the horse he rode in on.

"I only picked the best for the parts." I pull my hand away and put my napkin in my lap, resting my hands below the table. "If you'd really sucked and stank up the stage, I wouldn't have cast you as Iago."

His face reddens. His ego is huge and he's never taken criticism well. Oh, he'll take it and be nice to your face, but once you leave, he'll rip you to shreds. I've heard him do it to Mr. Watson and other teachers many times. Chase's mouth opens, but before he can say anything, the server puts our meals in front of us. I thank her with a smile, and she checks if we need anything before she leaves.

His color is normal again and he smiles easily. "I know you only cast the best, babe."

I give him a tight smile before eating my veggie burger. This date could end any minute and I'd be happy. What's the point of dragging out my relationship with Chase? How does that help the guys get revenge? Unless they plan to reveal what we've been doing behind closed doors.

I consider it for a moment. As long as Chase doesn't get access to the actual videos, I don't have a problem with him seeing them. It better not fuck up my play though.

Chase chats about classes this week. He really doesn't need me to comment at all. It works for me, because I need to think this situation with the Devil's trio through now that I'm not being kissed or given orgasms. Those tend to be very distracting.

Damon didn't deny he was still filming in the bathroom. For all I know, he has the whole house set to record. Why keep recording me? They have me. He has damning video already, but things will just progress from here. I guess I'll see tonight if the one in the bathroom looks like he's actually fucking me.

My pussy clenches remembering his thick length sliding against it. I glance at Chase, but he's already talking about something else. I honestly don't feel anything for him. Especially now. Before this, what I felt wasn't lust. Maybe awe? The hottest guy in the drama department wanted me. How could I say no to that?

Of course, he wants every other girl too. Which begs the question, why ask me in the first place?

I pick up a fry and drag it through the ketchup. "Do you want to fuck me?"

I bite the fry and chew while he looks at me like I grew a second head. It's not like I haven't cussed in front of him before, but I haven't been blunt about sex.

"Of course, I wouldn't be with you if I didn't." Chase runs a hand through his hair and leans forward on the table. "I thought you wanted to wait. But if—"

"I do." I tilt my head while I study his blue eyes. "I want to wait, but that has to be hard on you, right?"

I lean forward and he gives me a wry smile.

"I can handle waiting until you're ready to have sex, babe." He reaches out and brushes his knuckles against my jaw. "I don't mind waiting."

"Hmm." I pop the rest of the fry in my mouth. He isn't exactly going without while waiting. "What if I said I wanted to wait until I got married?"

"That's your choice, EvanAnn." He straightens. "I want to have sex with you when you're ready, but I'm not looking at this relationship like it's a race to the finish line. You're the real deal. A lot of these girls are so fucking fake, but you're not. I know you're going to excel in this industry, and I just want to be there to support you while you do it."

And fuck all the women who happen to be around me.

"Do you really think our relationship will last past high school?" I lean back. I really just want to dig into his mind and see what his thought process is, because maybe this is how he works with girlfriends. Maybe he's always cheated, even when he was with Abby.

Maybe she was okay with that, but he has to know I'm not.

"I hope so." He smiles. "Honestly, I don't think I'll ever find anyone better than you, babe. My dad's right about you being the smartest girl with the brightest future. I know a good thing when I find it, and intend to hold on with both hands."

Fuck. I mean shit like this would have made me want to end our relationship even if he wasn't a cheater. I'm eighteen years old. My brain isn't even finished forming yet. He's a fucking liar and a cheater, so that's a dead-end road I don't plan to walk down.

But he mentioned what his dad said about me. I'll have to remember to tell the guys about that.

What I'm doing with Damon, Cam, and Hawk is also a dead-end road, but at least they aren't pretending it's something it isn't. They'll get me off and I'll get them off. Besides, I'll get to lose my virginity in some epic way, instead of the backseat of Chase's car.

"Look." Chase leans forward and places his hand over mine. I leave my hand under his, even though I want to pull away. "I'm your first boyfriend. I'm not going to be a dick and force you to do something you don't want to do. If you want to wait forever, then I'll wait forever." He smirks. "I hope you don't want to wait forever though, because you and I will be stellar together."

He glances down at his almost empty plate and squeezes my hand. "Why don't we get out of here? We can go for a drive. Maybe park somewhere and make out. Let me show you how good I can make you feel."

I squirm in my seat, not because of his words or even the look he gives me, but because Damon's cum is not staying inside. If he wanted me to think about him, he definitely found a way for me to have a constant reminder. And a way to make me not want to have Chase's hand in my pants.

Of course, Damon wouldn't believe me if I said I didn't want Chase's hand in my pants, because in his mind I'm just a whore who can't get enough. Which, fair. With Damon, Cam, and Hawk, I can't.

I cough a few times, pulling my hand from Chase's and use the napkin to blow my nose, because there's no way I'm going to make out with his cheating ass. But I will be Damon's whore.

"I think I should go home and get some rest, so I don't get too sick." I give him a disappointed smile. "Maybe next weekend we can find some time together. The play is going to take all my energy this week."

He grins, but there's an edge to it. "Yeah. You need to get better for the play."

THE HOUSE IS QUIET WHEN I RETURN HOME.

"Honey, is that you?" Mom comes out of the living room as I head up the stairs.

I stop and wait for her to catch up to me.

She smiles. "How are you doing? Settling in okay? I know we were gone, but I assumed you'd be out with your boyfriend most of the weekend."

"I'm good, Mom." I smile and tuck my hair behind my ear. Strands keep working their way loose from my bun. "I need to study tonight."

"You know, you can use any room to study. There's plenty of space." She glances behind her. "There's the library and the downstairs rec room. You don't have to disappear into your room, unless you want to."

"All my stuff is up there." I shrug. It's easier, but I don't tell her that. "Did you have a good date night?"

Mom beams. "The best. I should have told you about Adam sooner, but I didn't want to jinx it. I'm happy."

I release my breath. "I'm really happy for you. I should..."

I point upstairs. She steps back and nods.

"Okay, if you need anything, let me know." Mom looks at my clothes. "I'd hoped to take you shopping this weekend. Maybe this week—"

"Rehearsal starts this week."

Mom nods. "Maybe I'll order some clothes online to help fill out that closet."

I think of my too-short skirts and bite my lip. "Maybe a new uniform skirt. My old ones are kind of short."

"Of course." Mom turns and walks away. "I'll see what I can find."

"One skirt," I call after her. Fuck. I should have told her nothing. I really don't need anything. Casual clothes, dress clothes. I'm set. Mom seems to think because we live here, I need an upgrade. I hope that's not what she's thinking.

I climb the stairs and startle to find Damon at the top of the steps.

He's looking at me like I'm the problem.

"Mom can afford a skirt with her job, since she doesn't have to pay rent." I brush past him.

"I like your skirts, Evan." He follows me down the hallway and into my bedroom, closing and locking the door behind him.

It's not like I can lock him out, so I ignore him. At least, as best as I can while his earthy scent clings to everything. Even in this huge room, he makes it feel small and tight.

Ignoring him is probably the best course of action if I don't want to end up with his dick in my mouth. My traitorous body hums with anticipation, but I sit down at my desk and pull my books out of my backpack.

"I like them best when you have to go up to the board during calculus." He lays down on my bed. We haven't exactly discussed the sleeping arrangements, but he did say he wanted me to suck his cock all night, so I'm assuming it will be a his bed or mine situation. "You tug at the back of your skirt like that's going to make it longer. Those bare thighs beg for a cock to slide between them."

My pussy pulses, but I open my laptop and sign in, determined to pretend he isn't here.

He stands and stretches before going over to my closet. I pull up my assignments. Honestly, I'm ahead and don't have much to do, but it's easy to fall behind during a production. I can't afford to have any of my grades drop.

"It's this one, isn't it?"

My skirt lands on the desk next to me. The one I need to retire. I lift it off my book and set it to the side.

He leans his ass against my desk next to me. "Put it on."

I glance up at him. "What?"

"Put it on, Evan." His hand cups my jaw and he presses his thumb between my lips. "You wanted to watch the show. I want you to wear this and nothing else while we do."

My tongue darts to taste his thumb. Salty. His eyes narrow.

"Do what you're told."

I push back my wheeled desk chair. The sooner this is done, the sooner I can get back to working on my homework. I take off my shirt and undo my pants.

Damon straightens and I freeze. His hand brushes over the mark he left on my shoulder.

"Mmm, I should mark you more often. There's something satisfying about knowing you bear my mark." His blue eyes meet mine. "You can't strip for your boyfriend or he'll know I've been here."

Every inch of me buzzes, waiting for him to touch me, to make me come. Fuck, I'm already addicted to the feel of his skin against mine.

I push my pants down, including my panties, and then reach behind me to undo my bra. Damon's hand skates over my stomach, leaving goosebumps in its wake, before sliding between my legs.

"After this, we're going to shower, little devil."

I lift my gaze to his as he slowly strokes me. His eyes remain on his fingers between my legs.

"How much of this is from me and how much is from you?" It sounds like a rhetorical question as I drop my bra on the ground.

I pick up the skirt and step back from his touch to put it on. He puts his finger in his mouth and sucks on it. My pussy throbs with need.

"Definitely some of me still in there." Our eyes lock. "I like the way we taste, little devil."

He lowers into the chair and pulls his cock out of his pants, stroking the hard length.

"Turn around, Evan."

I turn my back to him.

"Fuck, that is short." He slides his hands up the backs of my thighs and cups my ass cheeks. "Are you ready for me to fuck this pussy, little devil?"

"No." The word is breathy, but solid. It's going to be hard not to give into temptation with him.

"Shame." He draws me back. "Sit on my lap."

I lower myself down onto his lap. His cock rests below my pussy as he arranges my legs to the outside of his.

He turns us so we're facing the desk and slides forward to reach my laptop. He opens a browser and navigates to a cloud drive. "If you want to edit these for us, let me know. I'll make you copies. Something tells me you'll make them look even more amazing than they already are."

"You want me to edit my own blackmail videos?" I lean against his shoulder, relaxing into his warmth.

He's wearing a t-shirt, but his warmth bleeds through to my back. He chuckles. "I could keep them to myself, but I'm a giver."

He presses play and pulls me back with him as he slouches in the chair. The first frame of the video is him standing in the doorway.

"I like having access to you, Evan." His hands splay out on my breasts, sliding his finger over my nipples. I catch my breath and arch into his hands. His cock brushes against my pubic hair, teasing me.

In the video, I walk over to him and put my hand on his shirt, as he watches me with amusement.

Now, his hand slides down my stomach, pulling the skirt up before slipping under. His fingers tease my thighs. In the video, he backs me up against the counter. I look so small compared to him, but the fire between us is obvious.

"Do you know what I like about watching this?" he murmurs in my ear like he doesn't want to disrupt the movie, but there's no sound.

"What?" I ask as he squeezes my breast with one hand and the other begins to rub my clit. He spreads my legs wider with his.

"That you get off on watching." He pushes his finger into me and fucks it in and out. "That your body is so fucking ready to fuck, I could bend you over the desk and slide deep inside you. Do you know how good that's going to feel, Evan? My cock stretching out your tight little cunt?"

I whimper and he adds another finger to stretch me, but I know it will feel fuller, deeper with his cock. A part of me aches to find out, but another is worried that once he finds out I'm a virgin, he won't want to play with me anymore.

"Stroke my cock, little devil," he whispers before sucking on the back of my neck.

I slide my hand between our legs and find his length. My hand barely fits around him.

"See, that cock is going to feel so good, isn't it?"

I whimper as he pushes me higher. Onscreen he has me bent on the counter, his cock between my thighs.

Now, he takes my other wrist and forces my fingers into a fist with two fingers out with his. When he takes his fingers out of me and smears my slick on my nipple, he puts our fingers on my wet clit, rubbing firmly against it.

"Damon," I whisper, because I no longer care about anything but the fire he spreads through me.

"It looks like we're fucking in this video, Evan." He licks the side of my neck as he moves our fingers lower. The slick entrance of my pussy slides beneath our fingers.

I gasp at the sensation. He rubs our fingers over my clit again.

"Oh, fuck." My pussy clenches needing more.

"Do you know how much control it took not to fuck my cum into your dripping wet cunt, little devil?" He bites the corner of my jaw. "Look at us. Look at how much you wanted it."

He rubs my clit fast and hard with our fingers as I watch him on the screen, pushing me over the edge, making me come all over his cock before he lines up against me.

My fingers tighten around his cock as he begins to work me faster in tight little circles. I cry out my release, drenching our fingers as he strokes me through my orgasm and I watch him come against me on the screen. He angled the camera perfectly to get this shot.

Now, he kisses my shoulder and an aftershock tightens my pussy. I slide my other hand over his cock, rubbing the slick that leaked out of me over it.

"I want your mouth this time, little devil." He pushes back from the desk and takes our fingers off me. "On your knees."

I stand and turn before dropping to my knees. I don't hesitate to take his cock into my mouth. He drags the hair tie out of my hair and tosses it to the side. His fingers gather my hair into a ponytail in his fist.

"Relax, Evan, give me your throat." His other hand strokes the side of my neck.

As soon as I give him control, he fucks into my mouth, pushing deeper than I would take him on my own. I brace myself on his thighs as he thrusts hard and deep, over and over again. I can almost imagine him doing this to my pussy.

An aftershock goes through me again, making me clench around nothing.

Damon groans as his cum hits the back of my throat. I swallow around him. He goes still and I suck and lick his hard cock in my mouth. He makes an appreciative sound.

"You're a good little cum slut." He lifts my head and wipes the sides of my mouth. "Shower, and then you can study. I want you in my bed tonight."

I know better than to argue. Besides, I like the idea of sleeping in that big bed with him.

CHAPTER 35

Hawk

I GAVE up trying to sleep at around five o'clock in the morning. I should go for a run or workout. Instead, I get on my bike and head to Damon's. It's easy to slip into the house. We've been doing it for years.

The only difference is, Damon's and Annie's doors are locked. It takes me a few seconds to unlock it because I brought an interior door key with me. Locking the door behind me, I stare at Annie's made bed and grin.

That's about right. I leave my shoes behind. Shedding my shirt and coat, I walk through the bathroom and into Damon's room. Damon lays sprawled on his back, naked. Annie is naked and wrapped around his leg with his cock in her mouth.

They're both sound asleep, neither moves when I walk in. Annie sucks a few times on his cock. It's semi-hard, but he's not currently getting off on it. I quickly undress the rest of the way before moving to the end of the bed.

Much as I'd love to slam my cock into her cunt, we have boundaries for now. But oral is definitely on the table. I slide her legs apart and suck in a breath. Her soft curls are gone. Damon had mentioned shaving her, and they must have done it last night.

Her pussy is bare and glistens with wetness. My cock pulses with need, but I'll fuck her mouth after I get a taste of her pussy. I move slowly to not wake her up.

I've always wanted to fuck a girl while she slept. All soft and warm. This time, I'll likely wake Annie up during, but next time... I kiss her inner thigh and move onto the bed between her legs. She's still asleep and suckles on Damon's cock.

I slide my tongue along her slit, gathering her wetness. She tastes so fucking good. With light movements, I lick her pussy. She grows slicker with my ministrations. When I suck her clit, she whimpers and sucks on Damon's cock.

When I slide a finger inside her cunt, she moans softly. I look up and meet Damon's eyes. His cock is fully hard now, and his fingers are in Annie's hair. He smirks at me.

We maneuver Annie so she's on her side with Damon's cock in her mouth. I slide her leg up and over my shoulder, opening her up more to my mouth and finger. Damon fucks her mouth slowly, while I suck her clit and thrust my finger in and out in rhythm with him.

She moans as her pussy tightens around my finger and her hips buck against my face as she finds her release. Damon groans as he unloads into her mouth. She swallows and he releases her hair.

Her sleepy blue eyes find mine and she crawls down the bed to me. Her wet pussy slides against my cock, but before she can kiss me, I turn my head. It takes every ounce of control I have not to notch my cock at her entrance and thrust deep inside her.

"No kissing, baby girl."

Her blue-gray eyes meet mine with confusion.

Damon pulls her hips away from mine so she's kneeling over his face. She whimpers as he brings her down and takes over where I left off. Annie meets my eyes before kissing her way down my chest and abs. Her warm mouth sinks over my cock.

Fucking heaven.

I let her explore for a few seconds before sliding my hand into her hair and thrusting my hips, fucking my cock into her throat.

Her release was gentle, but this time, it's about claiming. She keeps her throat open for me and doesn't push me away as I fuck into her mouth. She might have rejected me before, but she can't now.

Growling, I lift her head off my cock as she pants from Damon licking her clit. "Beg me for my cum."

Her darkened eyes open and focus on me. "Please, Hawk, give me your cum."

I tighten my hand in her hair and she winces, but Damon must do something she likes because she moans softly. "You can do better, baby girl."

"Fuck, please come in my mouth, Hawk. Fuck my mouth. I want it. I need it. Please." She wets her lips and tries to lower her head even though it pulls her hair.

I thrust up and lower her onto my cock, pushing past her gag reflex. She swallows around my tip and moans as she shudders from whatever Damon's doing, or maybe from having my cock in her throat as I fuck in and out. Whatever it is, it's enough to push me over the edge. My release shudders through me. When I come in her throat, she swallows me down.

We all collapse on the bed. My hand strokes over Annie's hair.

"What time is it?" Damon asks.

"Almost time to get up for school." I rub my other hand down my face. "You need to show Cam your pussy, Annie."

She buries her face in the blankets next to my hip. "It wasn't at the top of my list of things to do this morning."

"That one's a priority."

CAM

First period B day is my class alone with Evan. We can't change our behavior at school because she's still dating the asshole, but I want to slide my fingers under her short skirt and finger fuck her to orgasm before class begins.

Fuck, I wanted to do that last week too, but now I have permission.

It's not an option, but it's what I want to do. Especially after the text from Hawk that Annie has a surprise for me. If they got her to give it up, that would be reason enough to skip first and find a closet to feel that tight little cunt squeezing my cock.

She's sitting at the table like nothing happened this weekend. Her focus is on her books and whatever she's scribbling on her paper. When I sit next to her, her gaze flicks up at me and her cheeks turn pink.

I smirk. Interesting.

"Tell me, goody. Do anything interesting this morning?"

Her mouth opens and closes, and I swear I see her brain glitch. "We're supposed to act normal."

I chuckle. "I am. Last week I was trying to get into your pants, or rather, under that skirt. Now is no different."

Except I know what she feels and looks like under that skirt now. How her mouth feels around my cock and what that pussy tastes like.

"How do you feel about skipping classes?" I ask, leaning into her to drag in her woodsy scent.

"I'm against." She straightens. "I need to keep my grade point average high to get a good academic scholarship for college. Besides, don't you think people would talk about us disappearing?"

"Fine, but you need to tell me what Hawk wants you to share with me, otherwise I'll pull you into a closet to find out."

Her cheeks grow pink and she glances around the classroom, but the teacher isn't even here yet. She leans in and her lips brush my ear when she says, "Damon shaved me."

She pulls away and faces the front of the classroom. I mean, it's weird that he would shave her, but then my slow-ass brain catches up. It's not that he shaved her, it's *where* he shaved her.

"I want to see."

Her eyes widen and she crosses her legs. "No."

"Then let me feel." I arch an eyebrow at her.

Her blue eyes narrow on me. "Cam, this is school. This is a classroom with twenty other students. I'm not going to let you put your hand in my panties."

I narrow my eyes on her. "After class."

"My schedule is super busy today, Cam. Can't it wait?" She sounds a little resigned, which means I'm wearing her down.

"Damon and Hawk have already seen it."

Her cheeks turn bright red. "I'm not a contest."

I chuckle. "We've never shared a girl before, goody. I want to keep everything fair. After all, you live with Damon. He's got full access to that tight little body. I have to grab it when I can."

That doesn't seem to impress her.

Hmm, maybe I should do this another way. "What if I take you somewhere no one will find us or know?"

She turns and considers me. We have five minutes between classes.

"And I promise to make you come in under a minute. And I won't make you suck me off."

She glances over her shoulder to the others in class. I'm being quiet enough, they won't hear.

"Come on, Evan. This must be a pretty stressful day. Don't you want a stress reliever before..." I glance at her stack of books. "Ew, calculus."

She bites her lip, making me want to lean into her and kiss it better. "Fine."

The teacher comes in and I slide back to my side of the desk to avoid the temptation of sliding my fingers under that skirt. I didn't mind her pubic hair. But the idea of all that soft, wet skin to play with, to suck on...

By some miracle, I manage to stay erection-free during literature. But as soon as class is dismissed, I pass a slip of paper to Evan and leave the classroom. Otherwise, I'll herd her to the location and get us both in trouble.

There's a hallway between our class and Evan's next class. It's an older part of the school that isn't currently being used. They have funding to work on it, but that's not starting until later in the year. It's never good to be doing construction when new donors might come in for tours.

One of the classrooms has a lock on it. Fortunately, I know how to pick locks, and it's out of the way enough that no one should notice both Evan and I went this way.

I unlock and open the door, slipping inside, but leaving it open a little for Evan. For a moment, I'm worried she isn't coming, but then the door tentatively pushes open. Her blond hair shows as she peeks in.

I grab her and pull her into the room, closing the door behind her.

"This seems like a bad—"

I kiss her as I back her into the door and lock it. My hands hike up her skirt to draw her panties down.

"Cam," she mumbles against my lips as her panties drop down to her ankles.

"I've only got a minute, goody." I drop to my knee, slip her panties off one ankle, and hike her leg over my shoulder. "Fuck, look at that. So fucking pretty."

Her head hits the door as she looks up at the ceiling. "I was promised an orgasm, not commentary."

"Lucky you, you get both." I cup her pussy in my hand. "You're already wet for me. Were you squirming during class, anticipating my mouth on you?"

Her gaze drops to mine. "This all counts toward your minute. Tick-tock."

I slide my finger into her tight cunt before sucking on her clit. Her hands clench in my hair as she gasps in a breath. The only sound in the room is her panting and the wet sound of her pussy as I fuck her. I bite softly on her clit.

"Cam," she whimpers and I work her faster as her cunt tightens around my finger. I promised under a minute. "Oh."

Her cum floods my mouth and I drink her up. I draw my finger out of her and stand to grab some tissues from the desk. Evan leans against the door exactly how I left her.

"Good?" I arch an eyebrow as I pat her dry between her legs.

She reaches up and grabs the back of my neck dragging me down for a kiss. If we didn't have to get back to class, I'd do it all over again. She pulls away.

"Thank you, Cam."

"I'm sure you'll repay the favor later." I step back and suck her taste off my fingers.

She straightens her panties and skirt. Suddenly, nervous. "Do I look okay?"

"Good enough to eat." I smirk.

She shakes her head. "I'll see you tonight?"

"Count on it."

CHAPTER 36

EvanAnn

DAMON ACTS like I don't matter in calculus, which I'm too high from my midmorning orgasm to care about. Besides, Mrs. Conrad talks fast today, and I'm too busy taking notes. When we walk to history, Damon follows me, matching my pace. The hairs on the back of my neck stand on end waiting for him to do something.

The feel of his cock in my mouth all night was oddly pleasant. Maybe not pleasant, but soothing. Waking up to Hawk and Damon was not something I'd thought about before. But hell, it made for a very relaxing morning.

I drove Damon's car to school and parked it toward the back of the lot so no one would notice the BMW. Otherwise, it shouldn't be hard to keep my move into Damon's house a secret.

No one usually comes to my house. As soon as my Honda is back, I'll return Damon's keys and everything will go back to normal.

I sit in my chair and Damon sits at his spot across from Mia's seat. He pulls out his phone to ignore me, which is what he would have done last week. I'm glad we're maintaining this. It would be weird for him to be cornering me between classes. Or worse, inviting me to eat with them at lunchtime.

I give an involuntary shudder. Nope, I'll eat inside like the good little nobody ant I am.

My phone dings, and I'm curious if maybe Chase is texting or Mom.

SEX GOD:

When are you going to open for business, little devil?

I stare at my phone. I didn't put that number in there, and *definitely* wouldn't have used that name. The only one who calls me little devil is Damon.

Wait? Is he flirting with me? Is this his idea of flirting? Or does he just want to fuck me? My pussy pulses, totally onboard. But fuck that.

When I narrow my eyes at him, Mia comes in with Hawk. They're chatting, and part of me shrivels. Yes, he sucked my clit and fucked my mouth this morning, but that's all I am to these guys. A hole to fill.

He wouldn't even kiss me. Morning breath? Or the fact I just swallowed Damon's cum?

The guys won't fuck anyone else while they're with me, but we never set an end date. They could end it when they decide to fuck someone else and use the blackmail to make me compliant again.

After all, there's new blackmail now. Not that I care about hurting Chase, but the fallout from a sex tape can linger.

Mia's gaze collides with mine and lights up. She hurries to our desk. "Oh, my god, I have so much to tell you. I didn't see you this morning."

"I went to Mr. Watson's classroom." What I don't say is that I didn't want to run into Chase this morning. Avoiding him might be the only way I can stay his girlfriend, because he makes me so fucking mad. Also, I really didn't know how to approach Mia after the show I caught.

"Oh, I didn't know that was an option." Her gaze turns scheming for a moment before she smiles. "I can't wait for lunch to tell you about the party."

My gaze darts up to Damon and he smirks at his phone. My phone buzzes.

I don't think I want to know what he sent me this time. Hawk sits across from me.

"Hey, Annie," he says. Those green eyes catch mine, and for a second, I forget myself. A rush of arousal spreads through my body like wildfire.

"Oh, when are we going to get together to work on the project?" Mia leans her arms on the table, which presses her breasts together and shows her cleavage in her unbuttoned blouse. She definitely has bigger breasts than me.

My face reddens and I look down at my lap. I can't help that I saw her with Liam and Fletcher, but it doesn't make it easy to look at her and not picture her half-naked and sucking on their cocks or them fucking her together.

It's what Damon wants to do to me. Am I ready to be fucked like that?

I must have missed a discussion, because Mia touches my arm. I meet her blue eyes.

She grins. "I know you have a million things on your mind with the play starting, but we're going to try to work on the report this week during lunch if that's okay?"

My mouth opens and shuts. I glance up at Damon. His face is passive and aloof. But his eyes are heated as they drop to my mouth. I cross my legs against the ache forming.

"Yeah, lunch works." I tuck my hair behind my ear and turn to meet Mia's beaming smile.

"Awesome."

Apparently, Liam and Fletcher were just the appetizer. She's looking at Hawk and Damon like they'll be her main course. I swallow down the bile that rises at the thought of them taking Fletcher and Liam's places. It's not that hard to imagine.

She's everything I'm not. Beautiful. Confident. Sexually experienced.

The teacher comes in and begins today's lecture. After a few minutes, I feel another buzz on my phone. Curiosity has me glancing down at the locked screen. Two new messages from Sex God.

I blow out a breath and make sure Mia isn't watching me as I open my phone.

SEX GOD:

Can't wait to recreate the final part of that scene

Look at your phone, Evan

I roll my eyes and close it. When I lift my gaze, Damon glances at me, almost like my movement drew his attention. His eyebrow raises a little like he's asking *how about it?*

I don't even know what to think about one guy fucking me, let alone two guys fucking my pussy and ass at the same time. At least they know I haven't had anal sex before.

Right now, Damon just wants in my pussy, but as soon as we start fucking, he's going to want my ass. I don't know what to think of any of this. I thought I'd lose my virginity to Chase Chadwick, and it might be okay. Now there's Damon, Hawk, and Cam, circling like vultures.

My phone buzzes and I want to resist looking, but I don't.

SEX GOD:

Giving head will get old

We could fuck that pussy while you work on homework and barely disrupt your flow

A little hard to work and have your mouth fucked

Think about it

My cheeks stain with heat. I thought Hawk's messages were bad. If I didn't think he'd find a way to punish me, I'd block Damon's number.

For the rest of class, I try to ignore Damon and Hawk and just take notes. When class ends, we gather our things and Mia talks logistics with the guys.

"We could meet inside. It might be easier to talk." She twirls her blond hair around her finger.

"Or we could go out to lunch?" Hawk smirks. "We can ride to the burger place and be back in time for afternoon classes."

This doesn't sound like a good idea. But when I turn to say that to Mia, she's practically giddy about riding with the Devil's trio on their motorcycles.

"I texted Cam." Damon jerks his head. "Come on, Evan. You can ride with me."

My whole body pulses to life. Mia goes up on her toes and squeals silently as she squeezes my arm.

"I can't believe this is happening," she whispers.

Shouldn't she be thinking about Liam and Fletcher? Not the Devil's trio?

We stop at our lockers, and I try to figure a way out of this. I know Hawk has a spare helmet, but I never noticed one on Damon's bike. Maybe I won't be able to go and Mia will spend an hour with the Devil's trio on her own.

My insides churn with jealousy.

Damon's heat engulfs my back at my locker. I try to control my breathing, because I probably look like a needy bitch right now. It's not my fault he's training my body to anticipate his needs in just a few days.

"Turn around, Evan."

It's not like we're alone in the hallway. There are stragglers who haven't made their way to the cafeteria yet. But I do what he asks.

He lifts a helmet I haven't seen before. It's not the one Hawk rides with.

"I keep it in my locker." Damon holds it over my head, and I help him guide it on.

I tip my chin up so he can buckle it for me. I hold my breath as his fingers brush the underside of my jaw and neck. The place he marked me throbs, and I have no doubt he plans to keep a mark on me.

If only to ensure I won't be taking my shirt off for Chase. It's not like he wants me to actually be more than his fuck toy.

"Good?" he asks, lifting the face shield.

Our gazes collide, and all I can think of is the slide of his cock in my mouth.

He smirks as if he can read my thoughts. "Come on, little devil. We'll have time for those thoughts later."

My heart skips a beat as he leads the way out to the bikes. Mia pays attention to Hawk as he gives her the rundown on how to ride as a passenger. Her helmet is already on, so I don't have to watch Hawk touch her.

It's in the rules. No fucking Mia. But maybe I should have been clearer. I don't want them to even touch her. Or talk to her. Or flirt with her.

Damon straddles his bike and brings it upright off the kickstand. His bike is similar to Hawk's, but it has a smaller seat which will force me to sit pressed up against him. I step on the peg and slide my leg over the back.

Damon turns with his helmet open. "You going to be able to get off without me carrying you, little devil?"

His eyes sparkle with amusement. I'm tempted to tell him to fuck off.

"I'll manage." I slide my hands around his waist to hold on.

"To turn on the Bluetooth, press the button on the inside." Damon rubs his hand over my thigh. "I'm going to fuck you on this motorcycle, Evan. Not today, but soon."

I release a shaky breath before reaching up and turning on the Bluetooth.

"You good, Annie?" Hawk asks.

"Yeah." My thighs clench around Damon's hips. I haven't ridden with him, but this isn't my first time on a motorcycle. I relax into Damon's earthy scent mixed with leather. He's familiar, the smell and touch of him. My body craves it.

"You good, Mia?" Hawk asks.

"Oh my god." Her voice is in my helmet. "This is so exciting."

"Just hold on. It'll be a quick ride," Hawk says as they start their engines.

Cam straddles his bike and puts on his helmet. "I didn't know I was supposed to bring someone."

My insides churn, but Cam laughs.

"I could take Evan from Damon easily." Cam starts his motorcycle and we all pull out.

"I doubt that." Damon's voice is wicked in my helmet.

Cam laughs. "How do you like riding, Mia?"

"A lot. I like it a lot."

"I bet you do." Hawk's comment is thick with innuendo.

I definitely should have been more specific. No fucking, no touching, no flirting. The motorcycle vibrates between my legs as I try to cling to Damon for all I'm worth. The burger place they were talking about is only five minutes away.

Some students even walk there for lunch.

I don't usually leave campus, even though it's a privilege for seniors and honor roll juniors. The cafeteria has better food than the fast food options available nearby.

I can feel Damon's breathing against my chest, like I could when I slept with him. He pulls up to a stop sign and rests his hand on my knee.

My breath catches. He has to know Mia is seeing this. She might tell Chase. Maybe he's hoping she'll tell Chase so he breaks up with me. And then, what? We don't have a deal anymore?

My chest tightens. Would Damon be done with me so quickly? I don't know why he wanted to make this deal with me, of all people. Just to get back at Chase? Or to punish me for moving into his house?

We drive into the parking lot, and Damon stops his bike. The others rumble to a stop next to us.

"Give us a minute." Damon's voice is gruff in my helmet.

"What?" Mia sounds confused.

"Yeah, we'll head inside." Cam cuts out next.

I haven't opened my eyes. That weight still presses uncomfortably on my chest. What am I doing? This could blow it all up.

"Evan, what's going on?" Damon rubs his hand over mine still clenched in his shirt.

I'm going to ruin everything if I don't start acting normal. "Sorry."

I release him and climb off his motorcycle pretty easily, and then work on removing my helmet while Damon sets his kickstand and gets off. He has his helmet off already and reaches for mine.

"I can do it." I step away, even as the buckle evades my fingers.

His eyes narrow on me and he steps in close. "Let me."

I drop my hands to my sides and tip my chin up. He quickly unbuckles the helmet and lifts it off my head. I try to turn to head inside after the others, but Damon grabs my hand. The sparks that scatter through me every time he touches me cascade up my arm.

"Wait, little devil." He draws me back toward him. "What's wrong?"

He tips up my chin to look into my eyes, but I avoid him. "Nothing.

This isn't a good idea. This isn't normal. I should be eating a salad in the cafeteria."

"It's a project for class."

I finally meet his eyes and arch an eyebrow at the stupidity of that statement.

He smirks and glances toward the restaurant. They parked in the back, and there's no window facing us. "Maybe I just wanted to get between your legs again."

I roll my eyes. "We're going to get caught if we stay here."

"No one would assume anything is going on." He sounds so confident.

I search his eyes. "You really think no one will believe you and I are doing anything but studying?"

Is that really what he thinks of me? That I'm not a sexual being?

"I thought you thought I was a whore? Maybe you want to prove it to people." My eyes widen. "Is that it? Are you going to make me suck your cock, so everyone knows what a dirty little slut I am? Should I drop to my knees here?"

"No. Fuck, Evan, I just wanted to make sure you were all right."

"That doesn't make sense." I step forward and put my hand on his side. "No, I think you want someone to see you with your little fuck toy. You want to prove to Chase I'm just as big a cheater as he is."

His sharp blue eyes search mine. For a second, I think he's going to pull me closer and kiss me. My fingers tighten into his side in anticipation of his kiss.

His gaze drops to my lips and then jerks up toward the restaurant. He turns me and pushes me toward the entrance. It takes me a few seconds to recover, but then I move away from his touch and enter the restaurant.

Damon's on me like a shadow as we walk up to the counter. The others already have a booth, and Cam entertains them with a story. Damon stands too close, but I don't want to push him away or tell him to back off.

Too much of my life has been spent toeing the line. Coloring inside the boxes. Even with Chase, I let him put me in a box to keep me whole and untainted. He let me stay in my box.

Damon refuses. He's torn open the box that kept me safe from everything else. Safe from being ridiculed or teased. But now it's like he wants to expose me to everyone else.

I don't know if I'm right, but he does like to call me a cum slut. It doesn't sound like an insult, and I like it when he says it. It doesn't make sense why something so offensive would turn me on, because he doesn't even like me.

We step up to the counter and I still haven't figured out what to order. I could just get fries. They have a garden burger, but it isn't one that I like.

"What can I get you?" The older woman at the counter looks us over.

"Two burgers, everything on them, fries, and a Coke." Damon touches my hip.

I shy away from his touch. "Just fries and a Diet please."

When she tells us the cost, Damon taps the credit card machine before I can even get out my debit card. I press my lips together, but she moves away to grab our order.

"Is that all you're going to eat?" he asks quietly.

I take the two drink cups she set on the counter and hand him one. "Burgers aren't exactly my favorite, as a vegetarian."

"We could have gone somewhere else." Damon follows me to the drink station.

I shrug and get my Diet Coke with vanilla in it. I'm putting the lid on when Damon moves in close to me. If only he didn't stir something inside me, if I could just ignore him, even with the way he towers over me.

Our order is called and he goes up to the counter, while I head to the booth. Mia sits next to Hawk, across from Cam. If I sit next to Cam, Damon will sit next to me. No, thank you.

I squeeze in next to Mia. When I lift my gaze, it runs into Damon's knowing look. He sits across from me and slides my fries over. Even though it's not a lot of food, I'm not sure I would have been able to eat much at this awkward lunch.

Mia clears her throat as she puts down her cheeseburger. "So, we should probably schedule a time to meet each week outside of class to work on our project."

"This is about a project?" Cam rolls his eyes. "Man, I was hoping there was a party we were planning or something."

"When do I plan parties?" Damon asks.

Cam shrugs. "It could happen."

Hawk leans back in the booth. "Yeah, we can arrange something around Annie's play schedule and hockey practice."

"Maybe we could just do lunch once this week." Mia glances at my fries. Her lips purse like she's going to ask if that's all I wanted.

"Sure," I say. "The library is open during that time."

"We can't eat in the library." Damon lifts his gaze to mine.

"We'll eat before, then." I pop a fry in my mouth and chew it while his focus centers on my lips.

"We could meet twice, then we'd only need half the period." Mia blows out a breath. "I just don't want to fall behind in any classes. They didn't talk about how difficult the Deimos classes were in the Anteros brochure."

"Annie's the smartest person in our schools. Seems like you picked the ideal best friend."

I look around Mia at Hawk, but he's scrutinizing Mia like she's some sort of mole. I narrow my eyes on him. "She didn't know who I was when I met her in the office."

"What?" Mia seems to pick up on what Hawk is throwing down. "Ann—I mean, Evan tied my tie that first day."

"Seems pretty lucky to me." Hawk still gives her a side-eye.

"It was just a coincidence." I shake my head and eat my fries. "Yes, we can meet Tuesday and Thursday during the second half of lunch to work on the project."

"Now that that's settled..." Cam grins and wipes his hands on his napkin. "When are the 'rents out of town, Hawk?"

"No, Cam. Not this year." Hawk takes a drink from his soda.

"What are you talking about?" Mia asks, twirling her hair.

Damon glances at her then looks away like she bores him, but he does that with all the girls. So, is he interested in Mia? He's so fucking unreadable. I want to dive into his head and figure everything out.

"Hawk usually throws at least one banger every year. His mom is out of town off and on, but his dad likes to spend a week in Cabo this time of year, leaving him all alone in his huge mansion." Cam frowns, like it's devastating to him that Hawk will be all alone.

"Sounds like he needs company in his huge mansion," Mia says, catching on.

"I knew I was going to like you." Cam grins at her and a stone drops in my stomach as Mia beams. "What he needs to do is throw a rager, because it's our last year."

Hawk glares at Cam. "If you start the speech—"

"What speech?" Mia asks.

"It's not important." Damon finishes off his second hamburger and his fries. He glances at my half-eaten fries and frowns. "That's not enough."

I arch an eyebrow at him.

"So... party?" Cam asks Hawk. Fuck, Mia wouldn't be holding out on them for pussy or ass if they wanted her.

Hawk shakes his head. "He isn't leaving for a couple of weeks. So, no rager anytime soon."

"But there will still be parties, right?" Mia looks at Cam who grins.

"Of course. I'm sure you'll be on the party list, since they're almost always at Fletcher's."

My cheeks heat and my eyes collide with Damon's. I push my food away, no longer hungry for it. Because suddenly I'm back in that closet, pressed between the wall and his hard body. His finger inside me while moans echo in the room outside of our hiding space.

"Come on." Damon stands and puts our trash on the tray.

"We still have time, don't we?" Mia glances at the others. And then she looks at me.

"Evan." Damon's voice is commanding. As much as I want to disobey him, because we do have time, I don't in front of Mia. I get up and follow Damon.

"Should we... ?" Mia asks.

"No, we've got time." Cam glances and meets my eyes before I head out the door.

CHAPTER 37

Damon

EVAN WANTED TO DENY ME, but fuck that shit. I help her put on her helmet. I climb on my motorcycle and wait for her to get on the back. As soon as she presses against me and wraps her arms around my waist, I take off.

We've got time, but if we're late to our next class, no one's going to fucking care. If they do, I'll say she started her period and needed supplies. The office knows she lives with me now. Evan doesn't question when I don't head toward the school.

There's a small grocery store that has a lot of organic crap not far from the burger place. I don't give a shit if she eats it now, but I know she's got shit happening after school. She needs to fucking eat.

We pull into the lot and I park.

"What are we doing here?" Evan steps off the bike like she's been doing it for years.

"Getting you food." I set the kickstand and climb off, removing my helmet and then hers.

Her brow furrows, but I take her hand and drag her behind me into the grocery store and over to the take-and-go section.

She stands next to me, still looking up at me incredulously. When I meet her eyes, her cheeks flush with color. She glances around to see if anyone is nearby. "I thought you were taking me somewhere to…"

I smirk. "Then you'd better hurry up and pick something if you want to get off too."

"I didn't—" She stops herself and blows out an exasperated breath. "I really was fine with the fries."

"You have rehearsal after school. When's the next time you're going to be able to eat, Evan?" I study the food in front of me and reach for a salad. "This?"

She takes it from me and puts it back. Then she grabs a different one, along with a bag of nuts.

I take both from her and go to the self-checkout. She's still trying to get her card out of her wallet as I finish the purchase.

"I could have bought it," she says. Her blue-gray eyes meet mine like a stormy sky. I can almost see the thunder in them.

I ignore the kick in my chest she causes and steer her out of the store. I open a saddle bag and drop her food into it. She has her helmet on and her chin lifted. I buckle it for her and put my own helmet on.

"How far does the Bluetooth range go?" Evan asks as she climbs on behind me.

"Not far, and definitely not with buildings between us." I start my motorcycle and ease us out onto the road. "You want to talk dirty to me?"

"Thank you for lunch."

"That seems like something you could have said in front of Mia." I noticed Evan's discomfort at lunch. Like her friend was invading her territory. Usually I'm not keen on girls getting jealous, but I liked it on Evan.

I take off for school. We might actually make it back before the others.

"I would have been okay if you'd taken me somewhere else." Evan's voice is quiet and her fists clench into my shirt.

"Were you horny, little devil?" My cock twitches.

"Maybe." Evan's voice is breathy and her body presses close to mine.

"One of these days, I'm going to fuck you on my motorcycle. Somewhere quiet, where you can scream as loud as you want as you ride my cock." Fuck, thinking about it is getting me hard. "What's keeping you from letting us fuck that pussy, little devil?"

She doesn't say anything.

We're close to school now. When I pull in, Cam and Hawk's bikes are already parked. If I could be positive we wouldn't be seen, I'd risk kissing her, but this can all be explained away. We went to lunch with our history partners, and the food wasn't appealing to Evan. So we went to the grocery store to get her food for later.

Nothing nefarious in that statement, except the fact I want to bury my cock wherever Evan will let me put it. Mouth, thighs, pussy, ass. It doesn't matter. I want them all, but will settle for whatever she'll give me.

Even if she wants to dole it out piecemeal.

After we dismount and store the helmets, I get her food out of the saddle bag and hand it to her. When we walk into school, people are hurrying to their next class.

When we reach the hallway where she needs to turn to go to Anteros, she lifts those pretty eyes up at me like she really wants a kiss. I'd drag her into the nearest closet if I thought we could get away with it, but there are too many people around.

"Later, little devil."

EvanAnn

"Babe."

Wincing, I stop gathering my things after our seminar on dialects ends and look up at Chase. I came into class almost as soon as the final bell rang. Chase had a seat on the other side of the auditorium, but Mia had saved me a seat near her.

"Hey," I say and lift my books against my chest.

"Where were you for lunch?"

Fuck, I forgot to text him. "Mia and I went out with our history partners to discuss our project for class. I meant to text you."

He straightens. "Who are your history partners?"

"Hawk and Damon." Mia smiles. "But this is the only time we'll be going off campus."

"You went off campus with Hawk and Damon?" Chase gives me a

once-over, and now I'm glad Damon didn't decide to take me some-where to ravish me, because I would have looked it.

I shrug and turn to walk to our table read. "We needed to discuss the project."

"Are you sure they aren't targeting you for something, babe?" Chase puts his arm around my shoulders and drags me into his side.

I cough violently and he steps away from me. "Why would they target me?"

Chase rubs the back of his neck before shaking his head. "I don't know. I just don't like them paying you more attention than normal."

Now that I know he's the reason Damon got hurt, I recognize the twinge of guilt.

Mia laughs. "We have a project with them. It's not like Evan snuck off to have sex with them."

I cough again to hopefully account for my reddening cheeks. I didn't sneak off to have sex with them, but I did sleep in Damon's bed twice this weekend—naked the second time—and I'll probably get off a few times before bed tonight.

"You should get some cough drops, babe." Chase now has two feet between us.

I push open the door and Hawk smirks as we walk in. "I'll get some when I go home tonight."

"You're going to get some when you go home, Annie?" Hawk's smile turns lewd.

Get some. Ha, ha. I should tell Hawk to stop saying shit like that in front of my boyfriend.

"Cough drops. For my cold." I arch an eyebrow at him.

He steps closer and puts his hand on my forehead. "You don't feel sick to me."

His green eyes twinkle down at me.

"Hey, we should run lines. Since we're mortal enemies and all that." Chase comes up beside me and Hawk.

I pull away to go to the head of the table, where Keira sits, and set my stuff down beside her. She already has the nameplates and scripts set up around the table.

"Thank you." I sit down.

She shrugs. "I was here early with Hawk Wilker. Alone. I had to do something."

Nervous energy. I get that. Every time I'm near one of the Devil's trio it hits me too.

Chase and Hawk stand together talking. Mia throws heart eyes at Hawk, but he seems oblivious. After a few seconds of being ignored, she comes over and sits next to me.

"Are you okay?" She puts her hand on my arm. "I wasn't sure where Damon was taking you, but it didn't look good."

"He knows I'm vegetarian, so he wanted to make sure I had food since rehearsal starts after school." There are so many holes in that, but hopefully, Mia doesn't poke at them. It's the truth, but why would Damon care if I ate and how would he know I'm a vegetarian? Maybe he'd know about rehearsal through Hawk, but it's all a pretty flimsy house of cards.

"That was sweet of him." Mia smiles.

Keira's eyebrows go up as she looks at me. She knows better. Damon is not sweet, but hopefully she keeps that to herself.

"So, I know we have rehearsal tonight, but maybe we can grab a coffee after?" Mia leans in. "I have to tell you about the party and my weekend."

I take a drink from my water bottle. I hope I can pretend it's all new information and I didn't see her take a guy's cock in the ass. Though I might ask for pointers. "Yeah, we can do that."

The room fills with my actors, and they all find their way to the table and their spot. Mia stands to go find her seat, which is next to Mark Green. He smiles at her and shakes her hand as they introduce themselves.

Crystal sits next to Chase, since their characters are married. And Sophia sits next to Hawk. He leans over to say something to her and she giggles.

None of this is new. Hawk flirts with everything in a skirt. We're just lucky the guys don't wear kilts at this school. But this churning burn in my stomach is new. I have no legitimate claim on Hawk. Or Cam or Damon, but we have an agreement.

Seeing them act normal is going to kill me.

I stand and clear my throat to get everyone's attention. "Before we get started, I just want to congratulate all of you for being chosen to be part of the production. And I'm really excited to see what we can make together."

We manage to keep the read through to the time we have for today. Keira helps me pass out schedules. They'll also be emailed.

"We want to be off-book in three weeks. Tech week will be on week eight, with the full productions the week after. If you have any conflicts, please resolve them prior to that week." I stand at the head of the table. "We have seven weeks to perfect this. If you can't be at a rehearsal, please let me know ahead of time. All rehearsals are mandatory."

I look around at the faces at the table and breathe.

"We have rehearsals starting after school. Check the breakouts, because if you aren't in the scene you don't need to be here. You are always welcome to come and observe so long as you don't distract the actors. I can't wait to pull this together with you. I'll see you in two days for our next full cast meeting."

The bell goes off at the perfect time. Hawk stands and walks over to me. My heart quickens. I managed to shift him to the back of my mind.

Mia and Chase are also heading my way. Hawk gets there first.

"Hey, I need to talk to you about something." Hawk gestures and turns to look at both Mia and Chase. "It's kind of personal. Do you mind?"

I glance at Mia and Chase who step away, but are clearly still in hearing distance. Hawk lifts an eyebrow and Keira clears her throat.

"There's the sound booth." She gestures toward the door.

"Perfect." Hawk takes my elbow and guides me that direction. I yank my elbow away and open the door.

He steps in and I follow, closing the door behind me. A window faces out into the room. While this isn't the black box room, it's a smaller version of it. Brandt and I will be swapping rooms every other day for rehearsals. Each is fitted with a sound room.

Hawk glances toward the window and turns his back to it. "What did Damon do to you?"

I arch my eyebrow. I don't know what I thought he was going to say, but that wasn't it. "Why?"

Hawk steps toward me, but I cross my arms and glance out at the remaining people who are here for rehearsal, including Mia and Chase.

"Because Damon can be a dick."

I laugh a little, because he's not wrong. "He took me to a grocery store to get food so I wouldn't starve this evening. Don't you have to get to hockey practice?"

"I can be late." Hawk glances over his shoulder. His green eyes darken when he looks back at me. "Cam said he likes the new look."

My eyes widen, but I know they can't hear us out there. "Not here. Okay? We can't play here. This production means the world to me and I'm not going to risk it for whatever this is between us."

He nods. "That's fair. But we need to find somewhere it's safe for you to let down your guard, baby girl. We can't have you wound so tight all the time."

My mouth opens. Is he talking about...? He wets his lips. My pussy clenches because his mouth and tongue are perfect.

"I'll see what I can find." I open the door and step out of the too-small space because I'm about to overheat.

"Thank you, director." Hawk bows to me before gathering his stuff and heading out.

He's going to be trouble.

CHAPTER 38

EvanAnn

It's seven o'clock when we wrap up for the night. Mia helps me close up and waits for me to leave with her. Chase comes over and kisses the top of my head.

"Feel better, babe." He heads out. Hawk waited for me after auditions to make sure I got out to my car all right, but not Chase. How did I not notice he was a huge dick?

Tonight was his night off from football practice, but he won't be able to do this every night. Some nights, rehearsal won't start until after sport practices. I don't know how long the cough thing will hold him off from kissing me in front of Hawk.

And what will that mean for Damon's punishment?

"If you want to skip tonight..." Mia hesitates. "You do look a little peaked."

I blow out a breath and turn to Mia with a smile. Even though I've been avoiding this discussion, I really want to keep her as a friend. "I'm good. I want to go grab coffee with you. You drove?"

"Yeah." She smiles.

"Okay, how about we meet at the coffee shop? Nickle's Black Coffee is open late."

She arches an eyebrow. "Nickle's Black? That's the name?"

"Yes, like the band, but not." I shrug. "They have good coffee and they're open late."

She chuckles. "All right. Let's do it."

We walk out and her car is parked much closer than mine.

"Mine's out there." I gesture to the only car remaining in the far parking spaces. I could have moved it closer after school, but I couldn't risk Chase asking me about it if he decided to walk me out. I should have guessed he wouldn't. Especially since we wouldn't be able to make out with this pretend cold. "I'll meet you there."

"You sure you don't want a ride to your car?" She opens her car door and smirks as she meets my gaze over the roof.

"It's my exercise for the day." I wave her off.

She gets in her car and starts it, but I don't hear her drive off. I continue walking over to the BMW and climb in. There's a note on the steering wheel.

Be good, little devil.

My cheeks burn. I shake my head and start the car. As soon as I pull out, so does Mia. I lead her over to the coffee shop, which is filled with Nickelback memorabilia.

When I get out, Mia parks next to me and steps out. When she sees the inside, she laughs.

"It's the only late-night coffee shop." I hold my hands up in defense.

She laughs. "At least they lean into it."

We go to the counter and order our coffees and some pastries before sitting at a booth in the corner. We chitchat about homework a little while we wait for our orders, but once we're settled in, Mia leans forward with a smile like the cat that ate the canary.

"So. The party."

I swallow my coffee and put it to the side. I'm an actress. I can pretend I've never heard the way she moans when she comes. Or seen her naked breasts and ass while she fucked two guys.

"Yeah, sorry I ditched you early at the party. I wasn't feeling well." To be honest, I *wasn't* feeling well. Finding out Chase was fucking other girls made me nauseous.

"I fucked Liam and Fletcher."

"Yeah?" I ask, as if I want more details. And not because I have the image of them burned in my head as Damon made me come on his hand.

Mia grins. "Seriously, it was amazing. I've fucked two guys at the same time before, but these two were awesome at it for their first threesome."

"Oh?" I take a sip of my coffee, hoping the steam will account for my flushed cheeks. She's telling me sex stories which *should* make me blush, right?

"I had to convince them to give it a go, but once they were in? They were in, if you know what I mean." Mia wiggles her eyebrows.

Unfortunately, I do. At least visually. "So, are you going to see them again?"

She runs her finger around the rim of her coffee mug. "Yes, but today was a total game changer."

My brow furrows. "How so?"

"Hawk seemed extra flirty, and Cam..." She makes a humming noise. "He seems down to play. I don't know about Damon though. I heard someone call them the Devil's trio."

"Mm-hmm." I'm trying to keep my cool and not tell her to back off. How could I? I'm technically dating Chase while I'm sleeping and messing around with the others.

"Can you imagine, Evan?" Her eyes are bright as they meet mine. "The three of them together. My god, I would love to be the middle of that clusterfuck."

I clear my throat and look at my coffee. I don't need to imagine. There are so many ways they can take me. But I need to get Mia to back off, somehow. Because they agreed to never fuck her. I don't want her to get her hopes up only to be let down. "I've never heard of them doing that with a girl before."

Not before me. Who knows if this is something they do regularly, and no one is ever the wiser? I don't know how the girl would keep quiet about it. Unless they always choose someone like me. Something tightens and twists in my gut at that thought.

"I bet I can get them to do it." Mia flicks her blond hair over her shoulder and winks to the cute guy behind the counter. "Guys can be experimental at this age. Especially with a willing girl."

"Maybe." My face is almost as hot as my coffee. I can't share what I did with the three of them with Mia. Maybe they'd be more than willing to accept her proposal if I hadn't made not fucking her part of our deal. If I told them what she wanted from them, would they want her more than me?

My insides shrivel a little. They say they want me, but they don't really know me.

"Oh, definitely." Mia's gaze gets that far-off look. "Riding with them today was amazing. All that power and danger." Her gaze cuts to mine with a knowing smile. "I think Damon likes you."

"What? No. I'm dating Chase." My heart ricochets in my chest. Is it obvious we've been together? That I've spent nights in his bed?

"There's something. He went out of his way to feed you. Guys don't do that. At least, not without getting something in return." She leans forward and wiggles her eyebrows. "Are you secretly sucking Damon's cock?"

"Mia!" I glance around to see if anyone we know is nearby. Fuck, is it written all over my face? Maybe I could tell her he's going to potentially be my new stepbrother, and that's why he's being nice. That opens a whole new line of questioning I'm not prepared for, even if it would explain a lot.

Chase is using me. I don't want my new friend to use me too.

"Yes, you're dating Chase. But if I were dating someone and Damon Storm wanted me on my knees, I'd say yes please." Mia winks. "It's not like anyone needs to know."

"I'm not that kind of girl." I would never have cheated on my boyfriend. Maybe something in me always knew Chase was cheating on me, but I felt horrible about those kisses. It never would have gone past kissing, and I would have told him about them, because they were eating me up inside.

I'm only in a relationship with him now for revenge. For the Devil's trio, I'll be what they want and I'll get the experience I desire without developing an attachment to any of them. I'll be loyal to them.

"All of us are that girl under the right circumstances." Mia leans forward and gives me a grin. "You can't tell me you haven't thought about any of those three in a sexual way. They exude sex."

I drop my gaze. Dirty dreams don't count. And she doesn't know I've been with the three of them in a sexual way.

She laughs. "The curse of the teenage girl. To be horny and not allowed to be slutty." She shakes her head. "If he offers, you should do it. I would, in your place."

"I have a—"

"Yeah, yeah, you have Chase." She waves it off like it isn't a big deal. "I'm sure he loves your mouth as much as he can, but there's something thrilling about being with someone like Damon. They remind me of the kings of our school." She slides her finger through the whipped cream on her coffee and sucks it off. "I've sucked their cocks. Luke, Caden, Jack, and Eli. It doesn't really count toward your body count, so why not?"

I'm trying not to let my mouth gape open at her reasoning. Body count? "We just think differently on this."

Mia shrugs and sits back with a killer smile. "More for me. Maybe you've never felt the power of grabbing a guy by his dick and sliding your mouth over it. Taking control of their pleasure. Knowing what they want most in that minute is you. Your mouth. Your body. It's fucking powerful stuff, Evan."

I don't know what to say to that. Have I felt it? Yes. Is she right? Also yes. But I can't talk about what I'm doing with the guys with anyone. Not even Mia. Especially not Mia.

"It's okay though." Mia leans forward again and her smile softens. "Someday you'll understand. Then those guys better watch out."

I sip my coffee and Mia decides to go into more detail of her night with Liam and Fletcher. Apparently, I only caught the first showing. There was apparently an encore.

By the time I park Damon's car in the garage, I'm afraid my cheeks are permanently red. The amount of detail she went into wasn't necessary, but maybe she wanted to empower me. To give me the confidence to suck a cock and broaden my sexual experiences?

I'm all for female sexuality and the freedom to express it, but I don't know. For some reason, it's never felt like the right time to have sex.

Granted, I'm loving coming on their tongues and fingers, and I like the feel of their cocks in my mouth.

Have I imagined how it's going to feel when they fuck me? I clench my thighs together at the aching need pressing there. It doesn't help that once I'm in that house, I'll be under Damon's command again.

I guess I could have talked to Mia about what they want from me. To explore the darker sides of their sexuality? How would I even look that up? What would I look up? Being held down?

What I know is they have full control over me. If Damon wants me, he just has to command me. My pussy throbs. Yeah, that's not as distasteful as it should be.

The house is quiet downstairs. I haven't received any texts from Mom today. She's disappearing into this house and this life, and I don't know if I like it. Usually we have a night where both of us are home and don't have anything better to do than sit and talk and watch a movie.

But I haven't really had a chance to talk to her since school began. Even this summer, she was gone a lot. Maybe Adam is the real deal for her.

I climb the stairs to my bedroom and the bed I've slept in once so far. I glance toward the open door to the bathroom, but there's no light coming from the other room.

It's not like we have anything scheduled for tonight. The guys might not be here yet. I drop my backpack next to my desk and go to my closet to grab some leggings to change into. When I open my closet, I have to blink to make sure I'm not imagining things.

Mom went crazy. There's more than twice as many clothes in here. New uniforms that look the proper length. Dresses I have no place to wear. Jeans, and sweaters, and t-shirts.

"Your mother went shopping."

My heart skips at Damon's voice. I spin to face him.

Sweat drips off him, and he's only wearing a pair of shorts.

"Guys should be here in twenty." He steps into the closet with me.

I breathe him in. That earthy scent of his is richer when he's sweaty. It's not like when Chase sweats, I can't stand to be near him. But Damon smells fucking good. I swallow as he closes in on me.

I take a step back and he smirks as he pulls open my underwear drawer. "I got you something too, little devil."

He pulls out a pair of delicate lace panties and hands them to me.

"You bought me panties?" I arch an eyebrow at him.

"Packaging matters, little devil." He dangles the panties in front of me. When I take them, they're soft between my fingers. He takes hold of my arm and pulls me into the bathroom.

I set the panties on the counter and drag in a breath as he leans in to start the shower.

"Take a shower with me." He kicks off his shoes and takes off his socks. There's a lot of skin already showing, but then he takes off his shorts.

My mouth waters at his hard cock. Fucking Pavlovian response. He already has me trained to want it.

He closes in on me, trapping me against the counter, and undoes my tie. I try to ignore the pulsing inside. The need growing and expanding.

"I need to do homework." My words are quiet. My fingers clutch the counter as I watch him. My breathing is erratic.

"You'll have time." He tosses my tie into the hamper and works on the buttons on my top. "This would go quicker if you'd help."

His blue eyes flick up to mine. I swallow down the lust that floods my body. It's a command. It's a rule. I unhook my skirt and pull down the zipper to let it fall to the floor. My panties follow. He takes off my shirt and I undo my bra as he tosses the shirt in the hamper.

"You have great tits, Evan." He takes them into his hands and slides his thumbs over the tips.

I suck in a breath as my bra falls to the floor. Being naked with Damon is becoming normal and addictive. He tips my chin up and his mouth crashes down on mine. When he lifts me against him, I put my arms around his neck and legs around his waist to steady myself. His sweaty, hot skin brands mine.

His cock presses lengthwise against my clit. I gasp at the heat of him against me.

"Hmm, I like the way you feel against me." Damon steps into the shower and under the warm water. "I want to bury my cock in your pussy, little devil."

"No." I'm pressed tight against him. Every inch of me touched by him.

"Shame. Good thing I love this mouth."

My back hits the tile as his fingers dig into my ass and his mouth captures mine. His cock throbs hot and hard against my clit. It would be so easy to just give in. Let him fuck me. My fingers tangle into his hair. The kiss seems to go on forever, and not nearly long enough at the same time.

"You want to pretend to be the good girl?" He slides his fingers between my legs and thrusts one into my pussy.

I bite out a cry at the sudden fullness.

"Tell me what good girls like, little devil," he whispers in my ear. "Do they like watching their friend have sex with two guys?"

I whimper as he fucks me with his finger, sliding his cock against my clit, winding me so fucking tight as he surrounds me in his scent and heat.

"I already know you like that. Do good girls like my finger in their aching, tight cunt?" Damon scrapes his teeth along my jaw, making a shiver course through me at the sparks igniting everywhere. "Answer me, Evan."

"Yes, Damon." I can feel him smile against my jaw.

"Do good girls like my mouth on their pussy?" He kisses his way to my mouth again, but hovers there not kissing me, teasing his lips against mine.

"Yes," I whisper, trying to close the distance between our lips as he pushes me closer and closer to the edge.

"Do good girls like to come?" He licks my lips.

I gasp in a breath as my insides tighten to the breaking point. "Fuck."

My release cascades over me, pulsing around his finger.

"Sounds like they do." He chuckles. "Good girls like to suck cock, don't they, little devil?"

I lean my head back against the tile as I catch my breath. He pulls his finger from me and releases my legs. I lower them until they touch the wet tile, then I sink to the floor on my knees before him.

My eyes lock on his as he strokes his cock. I open my mouth for him.

"Such a good girl." He thrusts his cock into my mouth. "Touch your pussy for me while I fuck your face. Be my good girl."

I don't think about it. Every time he calls me that, it lights something up inside me. His touch, his scent, his warmth, all ignite me into flames I don't want to resist.

I get what Mia was saying. Yes, I want to suck Damon's cock. I want him to sink into me and claim me as his. All the way. But what happens when he gets what he wants? Does it mean he'll be fucking me all the time? Or will he grow tired of me?

I slide my finger over my clit and all those thoughts buzz away. He's not gentle with me. He doesn't take his time, but uses my mouth as I strum my clit, feeling little aftershocks ripple through me.

His groan is the only warning I have as he pushes in deep and his warm cum floods my throat. I swallow as best as I can. His blue eyes lock with mine. My mouth is wrapped around his still hard cock. His hands rest on the wall above my head.

"Get off for me, good girl. Make yourself come. I want to watch you shatter." His words make me moan, but I don't pull off his cock. He didn't tell me I could.

I slide two fingers into my pussy, wishing they were his, before using my other hand to stroke my clit. I suck on his cock as I work myself.

"Imagine it's my cock in that pussy stretching you out. My body pressed against yours as I slam into you over and over again. Your pretty little cunt milking my cock for everything I have. It's yours, little devil. For now, this cock is all yours."

For now. I try not to focus on those words as my release washes over me. It's not as strong as when he had his finger in me, but it's still good.

He pulls his cock from my mouth and lifts me to stand. My knees are shaking. He takes my hand from my pussy and sucks my fingers in his mouth. Our eyes lock and hold. His blue eyes are darker with lust.

My eyes are drawn to his mouth. What it can do to me. But it's hard to focus on anything but Damon when he's naked in front of me. He takes my fingers out of his mouth and grabs the back of my neck. His mouth claims mine as our bodies press together. Our tongues slide against each other. I can taste both of us.

"Tell me, little devil," he says softly against my lips. "Did you kiss your boyfriend today?"

I shake my head, opening my eyes to meet his. "I told him I had a cold."

"Good girl." He pulls me back under the shower and hands me the bottle of soap. He leans his head back in the water and slides his hands into his hair. Every muscle ripples in his body, and fuck, there are a lot of muscles.

I squirt some soap into my hand and slide it over his hard chest.

He chuckles and looks down at me. "I've got something for you."

I lift my eyes to his but I continue to wash his body. His muscles twitch beneath my fingertips.

"Let's finish in here and I'll show you before the others get here."

Tingles chase down my spine as he puts soap in his hand and begins to wash my body. By the time we leave the shower, I'm ready for more. I pull on my new panties. I need to grab some clothes. When I step toward my bedroom, Damon blocks my path.

"I need clothes."

He backs me into his room and reaches into a drawer, pulling out a t-shirt. He puts it on over me. "I prefer you naked, little devil, but my clothes will do."

My cheeks flush red. After he grabs a pair of sweatpants and pulls them on, he walks to his nightstand. My heart clatters as he opens the second drawer full of sex toys. I squeeze my thighs together.

He grabs something and then opens the top drawer to retrieve the bottle of lube.

"You've never had anal sex, so we need to do some prep." He sits on the bed and pats the spot beside him. "Don't worry. I won't bite."

His blue eyes capture mine and I don't resist. I join him on the bed I've slept in for two nights. His intentions definitely aren't pure, but he's building my trust. Or maybe he's only being kind to get me to end the restrictions.

"We'll wait until the others get here to play with it." He holds out a blue rubber plug about the size of his finger. "Take it."

I take it and study it before offering it back. "Has that been in some—"

"No. It's new. It will help get you ready for anal play."

My cheeks are hot as I lift my eyes to his. He seems to be in a good mood tonight. The toy is new? Did he plan for this or does he just have an unlimited supply of new butt plugs for each girl? Maybe he labels them.

"There's a base, so it won't get lost in there."

I wrinkle my nose. I definitely don't want to end up in the hospital with something wedged inside me.

"Did you eat dinner?" he asks.

He's all over the place tonight. I give him a curious look. Why does he care? I'm just his toy.

"I had a pastry with my coffee after rehearsal, but I ate the lunch you bought me after school." It's more than I usually eat.

"I'll go get you something."

"I don't need anything, Damon."

He grabs my waist with his hand. "You barely weigh a thing, Evan. You're going to be burning more calories with us, so you'll need to eat more."

My mouth is still open when he closes the door and leaves me alone. I don't understand what's going on. He left the lube and the plug on the bed. I give a little shiver and stand.

I walk into my room and glance at my closet. Leggings would be okay to put on, right? It's not like he told me not to wear them. But I decide not to bother as I head to my desk and pull out my laptop and books.

I'm just getting into my homework for tomorrow when there's a knock on my door. It's probably the other guys. Damon definitely wouldn't knock. I open the door a crack and my mom smiles at me.

My heart skips a little. She's still checking on me. That's good.

"Hi, honey. I just wanted to make sure you got the clothes." Mom glances down at what I'm wearing. Damon's t-shirt is huge on me, but I'm not wearing anything but panties under it. Did she see the panties he bought me in the drawers?

"I was getting ready for bed." I gesture to my perfectly made bed.

"Of course." She doesn't really know what I wear to sleep, so this could be one of them. "Well, if you need anything different or want more options, let me know."

"Thank you. It's more than enough, Mom. I'm fine. I really don't need anything. Just the skirt would have been enough."

Damon saw all the things my mother bought me. It's too much. It cost more than she was paying in rent. She should be saving money in case we need to move again. Would it be mean to tell her I don't think we'll be here long? I could see us moving again in a few months?

Damon passes behind my mother, heading to his room. "Good night."

"Night." Mom beams at him. She notices he carries a plate of food. "Did you not get enough for dinner?"

"I worked out." He glances at me.

She turns back to me and shakes her head. "I honestly don't know where he puts it all. You never ate that much."

I shrug. We didn't have much to eat. I made do with what we had.

"You let me know if you need anything. Okay? I want this to be a fresh start for both of us. You're such a pretty girl." Mom touches my damp hair.

"I'm good. I have everything I could possibly need. Thank you for the clothes."

"Anything for you, honey. Good night."

"Good night." I close the door and flick the lock. My head thumps against the door. She wants to believe this is her fairy tale ending, but it's kind of a nightmare for me.

"Little devil."

Is it a nightmare? Mia's words come back to me about how any girl would be crazy to not go after Damon Storm. I'm definitely winning the breakup. If I was allowed to tell my boyfriend we're broken up.

Hands sweep up my thighs as Damon's heat closes in on me. My insides soften and my panties grow wet. What is he doing to me? Who will I be when this is over?

"Come eat."

CHAPTER 39

Damon

EVAN SITS at my desk with her feet tucked up on the edge of my chair. The lacy edge of her new panties shows a little, but I'm sure she's unaware of it. She's eating the food I asked for from the cook. Her large, blue-gray eyes watch me.

I have my textbook open on my lap, reading a chapter for class. The plug sits on my bed, waiting.

All that's left is for Hawk and Cam to get here. We agreed at hockey practice to do this together. After all, we haven't played like this before. I have constant access to Evan, but I don't want to monopolize her.

It was hot watching them go down on her and suck her breasts as she took my cock. I'm not possessive of girls. That's not fucking healthy. I fuck them, and if they go fuck someone else, that's their prerogative. I'm not about to go caveman on a high school girl. Fuck that.

I've managed to stay a free agent, even though Olivia seems possessive of me. She's in a few of my classes and sat near me at the beginning of school. I don't trust her. I don't have to trust a girl to fuck her, but there's something about Olivia that's just fucking off.

Which means I'm not going there. Not that I can with our deal with Evan.

I'd rather have full access to Evan than fuck around anyway.

Cam texts me that they're both here. I go to my door and open it, waiting for them to come up the back way. Evan takes a drink of water while she watches me.

It's taking everything I have not to fuck that pussy. She's ripe for the taking and so fucking ready, but she's holding back. She could be testing us. Every time I ask, she says no. What would she do if I took it anyway?

This deal between us means she needs to trust us. If I take her, she wouldn't trust me. Like today at the restaurant, thinking it was a trap. She needs to trust me not to do stupid shit to blow her up.

Honestly, going to the restaurant at lunch today could have been a move to out the good girl. It's one I'll keep in my back pocket. But I'm not done enjoying my blackmail yet. I want her to forget where we are so she goes down on me. Not force her to.

I've given her all the promises I can. I'll fuck only her. But fuck, she needs to let me fuck her properly. I shouldn't have agreed to her deciding when we get to fuck her.

She takes a bite as she continues to contemplate me.

Of course, taking her out today was jabbing a knife into Chase's back. He needs to know I'm all over his girl. Maybe he'll believe her pretty lies.

"Hey," Hawk says as he and Cam walk down the hall and into my room. "Hey, Annie."

Cam smirks as I lock the door. "Show me your panties, goody."

She drops her fork and stands to lift my shirt to show off those lacy panties I bought for her. They're still fucking innocent looking, but hotter than the cotton ones she had. The cotton ones were utilitarian.

"Good choice." He bumps his knuckles against my arm.

"Are you done eating?" I ask, and sit on the edge of the bed.

Her eyes widen. "Yes. May I go brush my teeth?"

"We're not animals, Annie." Hawk chuckles.

She still hesitates and looks to me. I nod slightly and she hurries into the bathroom. She doesn't close the door. Good. She's learning how this is going to go moving forward. No barriers between us.

"We need to figure out how to spend more time with Evan." Cam sits on the other side of me and picks up the plug with a smirk. "Who's going to do the honors?"

The water shuts off and Evan stands in the doorway, watching us. I meet her gaze but talk to the others.

"She needs someone to suck on while the other two take care of her pussy and ass." I love that I get to be blunt with her, though I don't sugarcoat anything for other girls either. Some girls get mad with that kind of talk, but not Evan.

She doesn't drop her gaze from mine, waiting for me to tell her what to do. I love that she gives me this.

"Hawk." I gesture to the bed. "She can suck your cock until you come. Then Cam can go next."

Hawk undoes his belt and kicks off his shoes.

"Come here, little devil."

She crosses the floor to stand at my feet. I lean back with my hands propping me up on the bed. My cock is already rising to attention, and her gaze drops to my pants. Yes, girls generally do what I tell them to, but having Evan obey me fills me with lust and power.

"Take off the shirt."

Her gaze jerks up to mine, but there's not defiance there. She takes the hem and lifts the shirt off over her head. This is what she's giving us. The trust we won't take it too far, that the rules we've set in place will hold.

Her arms drop to her sides. Her blond hair is almost dry and falls around her shoulders in soft waves. Cam reaches for her breast, cupping it.

"I can't wait to suck on these all night long." Cam leans in and kisses her nipple.

Evan sucks in a breath and presses her thighs together. Her stormy eyes stay on mine.

"Lose the rest, Evan." My words are a command.

She slips her thumbs in the sides of her panties and lowers them down. Hawk steps up behind her and slides his hand down her stomach.

"You're going to ride my face after that plug is in your ass, baby girl. I need the taste of you on my lips to sleep tonight." His fingers slide between her legs and she releases a little moan. "So fucking wet for me."

He draws his hand back and sucks on his fingers.

Cam and I stand with Evan between the three of us. We're all taller and larger than she is. Honestly, we're bigger than most girls and Evan is not particularly tall. She shivers slightly. Naked in a pack of devils.

"Hawk, lie on the bed. This might take some adjusting once we get Evan in position."

Her eyes widen and I slide my hand over her jaw.

"Don't worry, little devil. We'll get it right." I lift my gaze to Hawk's. "I want her kneeling on the edge of the bed, ass up with her mouth on your cock. Legs spread open."

She gasps a little. I stroke my thumb over her bottom lip. These fucking lips. I've never been obsessed with a girl's mouth before, but I want these lips on mine.

"We're going to fuck your pussy with our fingers and tongues only."

Her eyes darken with desire. I'd be more than willing to fuck her pussy with my cock.

"Unless..."

"No." The word is soft, but firm.

"Hmm." I glance at Hawk as he settles on the bed. "You know how I want you."

She takes a deep breath and moves to the bed, kneeling between Hawk's knees. She takes hold of his cock and meets Hawk's eyes.

"Make me come, baby girl."

Evan bends over to take him into her mouth. She's gotten better at blow jobs, at least. She's downright enthusiastic.

"Suck and lick, little devil, that's it." I pick up the lube and offer it to Cam.

He grins and takes it.

"Prep first." I put my hands on her thighs and spread them a little wider, opening that glistening pussy for me. "Let's get her ready to take it. We took a shower, and I made sure she's clean."

She whimpers. I rubbed her asshole with the soap, teasing her until her breathing hitched, but I didn't let her come again.

Cam smirks and squeezes her ass cheeks, pushing them together and spreading them open, revealing her puckered hole.

"Such a pretty little hole." Cam spreads her ass cheeks and bends to lick her asshole. "I'm surprised no one's fucked it before."

She moans around Hawk's cock.

"Maybe she was saving it for us." Cam slides his tongue against her hole before pressing the tip of his tongue in.

She makes a startled noise.

"Lift her," I tell Hawk. When he does, I ask, "No one's played with this ass before us, little devil?"

"No." The word is breathy as Cam continues to explore her ass with his tongue.

I slide my fingers against her clit. "Has no one tried, or were you worried?"

Her hips rock against my fingers. "No one tried."

"Chase must have been a lousy lay." Hawk rubs his thumb against her lips. "Basic fucker. Don't worry, baby girl, we'll make that ass feel real good."

He lowers her back down on his cock. Cam begins to really work her ass with his tongue and she makes these little noises like she's getting close. I kneel below Cam and slide my finger into Evan's pussy, before leaning in and sucking on her clit.

She moans hard as I fuck her pussy with my finger and suck on her clit while Cam's tongue fucks her asshole. She comes all over my tongue as her hips rock against us.

"She definitely likes her ass played with." Hawk groans. "That's it, baby girl, suck that cock. Such a good girl."

Cam straightens and wipes his mouth on his t-shirt before grabbing the bottle of lube and spreading it on his fingers. I lift my mouth from her to watch. My finger circles her clit while I fuck my finger in and out of her pussy.

Fuck, this girl gets under my skin. I want to take out my cock and sink it deep inside her and keep it there while we fall asleep. Having her mouth on my cock while I slept was amazing, but being buried deep in her, with her naked body draped over mine, is going to be even better.

Cam slicks the lube over her puckered hole before sliding the tip of his finger inside. She moans.

"Easy, goody. Relax and let me in. I need to get you nice and slick for the plug." Cam rubs her ass cheek.

I slow my finger to gently fuck in and out of her pussy until I feel her relax around me. I give Cam a nod, and he slides in a little deeper before coming all the way out and sinking in a little farther. He works his way into her ass until his finger is buried to his knuckle.

She moans softly as I curl my finger to stroke that spot at the front of her cunt.

"Fuck her mouth, Hawk." I meet his eyes and he smirks as he gathers her hair into his hand. I don't want to tell Evan what we're doing, but we're going to give her a taste of how it will feel to take all of us.

Cam and I alternate fucking in her holes and pulling out in rhythm with Hawk fucking her mouth. She trembles between us. I can feel the press of Cam's finger through the thin membrane separating us.

"Can you imagine when this is our cocks, little devil? Sliding in and out, filling your cunt and ass with our thick cocks?"

She moans as she comes all over my fingers again. Fuck, I want to feel that pussy clamp down on my cock.

"So fucking tight," Cam says. "Relax, goody, so I can pull out."

Hawk groans and Evan swallows him down between panting. "Trade me, Cam."

"Fuck off." Cam's lubing up the toy.

"You don't want your dick sucked?" Hawk arches an eyebrow, but he hasn't taken his cock out of Evan's mouth.

I chuckle. "Put the toy in her ass, Cam, then Hawk can fuck her with it while she sucks you."

Evan whimpers, but still sucks on Hawk's softening cock.

Cam presses the tip against her asshole and pushes in steadily. Evan groans and I fuck her with my finger while teasing her clit.

"Relax, baby girl, you're doing so good taking that plug for us. We'll be fucking that ass in no time. Then we won't have to fight over this pretty mouth." Hawk arches an eyebrow at Cam.

Evan takes little hitching breaths between sucks.

"Almost there." Cam thrusts in the widest part and she shatters again, clamping down around my finger and the toy.

I stroke her through it and then pull my finger out. "Need to cum, little devil. I'm going to do what we did yesterday."

She whimpers as Hawk slides out from under her. Her head rests on the bed. He walks around to watch.

I pull my cock out of my sweats and place the tip against her entrance. It would be so easy to slip in, to say it was an accident and fuck her properly, but... fucking trust.

I stroke my cock pressed firmly against her opening. My fist wrapped around the tip to keep her from taking me as her hips want to rock. Her entrance kisses my tip like a wet mouth. She's a little out of it, so I hold her hip. We have an agreement. As long as she doesn't hold out forever, I'm willing to wait to sink my cock into her cunt if it means she'll trust us.

Hawk grabs the base of the plug and twists it in her ass. She groans and buries her face in my blankets. Her hands grip the fabric tight. Fuck. She's so sexy when she's drowning in lust.

Groaning, I press my cock against her as my release shoots out of me. She eases back a little to take me in just slightly. My hand trembles with the urge to pull her onto my cock.

"Fuck, little devil." I release my cock and slide my finger in my warm cum to bury it deeper inside her. Her cunt pulses around my finger.

"Fuck, man." Hawk runs his hand down her thigh that's shaking like a leaf after her orgasm.

"She needs a breather." Cam slides his hand over her hip while he strokes his cock. "Turn her over and I'll fuck those tits instead of her mouth."

I step back and let the others take over. I run my hand through my hair, uncaring that the mix of my cum and hers is still on it. I'm going to need her to give in sooner rather than later. She wants it. I know it. She knows it.

They flip her onto her back and Cam straddles her waist. When he drizzles lube on her breasts, she gasps at the chill. Cam chuckles as he rubs it between her breasts. Hawk tugs on the plug and she lets out a little huff.

I straighten my sweats and lie down next to her on the bed.

"Can you feel me warm inside you, little devil?"

"Yes." She rolls her head toward me and those stormy blue eyes meet mine. I brush her blond hair off her flushed face, behind her ear. When I rub my thumb over her swollen lips, she parts them.

She moans, but I don't look to see what the others are doing to that hot little body. Hawk is either fucking her with his finger or mouth or maybe both while playing with the plug in her ass. Cam has her tits pressed around his cock as he shuttles it between them, rubbing her nipples as he strokes himself.

But right now, her eyes are on me. They're blue with streaks of gray through them. Almost silver. I don't know how I ever thought they were dull. I move in and press my forehead against hers.

"Do you feel how much we want you, little devil?" I say it softly. "This isn't for anyone else's benefit except ours. Yours and ours. Your body belongs to us as soon as you're ready."

She cries out as she comes and I surge forward to capture the sound in my mouth. She moans as our tongues collide. I slide my hand into her hair and hold her while I explore every inch of her mouth, learning her.

I plan on keeping Evan as my pet for a while. Which means I have to make sure her mother doesn't go anywhere until I'm ready to be done.

CHAPTER 40

EvanAnn

THIS YEAR IS DEFINITELY NOT GOING AS expected. I'm at my locker, but I can't seem to focus on what books to grab.

I slept in lacy panties with the guys, who wore their boxers. I was surprised they stayed over on a school night. While Hawk mentioned making me sit on his face, he didn't because I was exhausted by the time they finished coming on me.

My neck and breasts. My stomach.

Tingles chase through my system. Why does it feel good when their warm cum hits my skin? Marking me as theirs? I'm curious how sitting on Hawk's face will feel, since it's already amazing when he goes down on me.

My problem right now is that my curiosity is running away with my thoughts.

I want to feel them inside me. Not just their fingers. Virginity isn't special to me. I just haven't had sex with anyone before. There's a little fear of the pain some women feel, but the bigger fear is what they'll think if they find out I'm a virgin.

It's not a guarantee they'll even notice. But if they do...

Will they treat me differently? They treat me like their whore, and honestly, I like being their whore more than I ever liked being Chase's girlfriend. I scrub my hand down my face. This is crazy.

Last night, I almost fell asleep in the shower as they washed me afterwards. Damon didn't make me suck his cock while we slept, but Cam's mouth was on my breast the whole night, making me keyed up in the morning.

I don't know what to think about last night as I put my books in my locker. I lost count of the times I came. The feel of their warm skin pressed against mine as I woke up wrapped around Cam, with Damon pressed up against my back. Cam's mouth on my breast. Damon's finger in my pussy. I shattered for them with a cry.

Even though I masturbated in the past for stress relief, this is a whole new level.

They're going to fuck me. It's only a matter of time and my consent. It would have been so easy to say yes to Damon last night, but I'm not quite ready to be "open for business." I can't get enough of them as it is. I'm afraid of falling behind in classes because I'm too wrapped up.

We haven't really discussed their desires yet, and maybe that's what I'm afraid of. I'm supposed to be open to exploring, but I haven't even done the basics yet.

"Hey, babe." Chase crashes back against the locker next to mine. I jump a little. "New skirt?"

My face blooms with heat.

"Um, yeah, the old ones are all a little too short now. Mom got me a new one." I almost put on a whole new uniform, but instead just opted for the skirt. It might have been too suspicious if I wore a whole new uniform and anyone noticed the BMW I'm driving. My old skirts were worn and way too short. Though apparently not too short for Damon. He stood behind me while I brushed my teeth and tsked the length of my skirt. He wanted me to roll it up at the waist, but I ignored him.

He did lift my skirt to make sure I wore the new panties he got me. And slid his hands beneath to cup my ass cheeks. When he asked if I enjoyed the butt plug, I didn't lie. It felt good. Different. A little weird, but good.

I close my locker and look up at Chase. If I didn't know he was probably fucking someone else last night, I would have been ashamed to face him after what the Devil's trio did to me. Instead, I feel relaxed and ready to face the day.

I didn't get back to my homework though, so I'm a little behind where I want to be. I'm already ahead, but things tend to get harder as the performance draws closer. I'm going to have to mention to the guys that homework needs to come first.

The problem is I can't tell Damon I need to do schoolwork, because he'll just mention fucking my pussy or ass, so I can do other things while they use me.

A shiver goes through me. I don't think he understands how distracting they all are. There's no way they can fuck me and I can just work on my homework. Maybe after a while, but how long are they really going to keep this up? When will they get tired of me?

"I like your skirt." Chase smiles. His fingers brush my hair, bringing me back to the here and now. "How are you feeling?"

I blink up at him. What is he talking about? And then I remember… the cold. I cough slightly and rub my throat. "A little sore, but I'm getting better."

He frowns and reaches into his backpack. He pulls out a bottle of vitamin C tablets and offers me one. "I'd kiss you, but it's not worth the risk, babe. Guess we'll have to save all our loving for this weekend."

"This weekend?" Chewing on the tablet, I walk toward my first period and wonder where Mia is. Chase falls into step with me. I can only hold him off from kissing me for so long. But what's the worst that happens? Chase kisses me and then Damon punishes me. I don't even know how he wants to punish me. Spanking? Orgasm denial? Those just make me more curious.

"Party at Olivia's house." Chase stays close to my side. "It's always a blast. We can spend some quality time together, if you know what I mean. Saturday night. You and me."

"And Mia." I manage not to grimace at the thought of him touching or kissing me. I'm not planning on going anywhere alone with Chase. Even though I'll eventually have to kiss him again, there's no way I'm letting him touch me any more than he already has.

Again, it's acting. I can pretend to like Chase for a night.

"Yeah, sure, we'll bring Mia." Chase runs a hand through his hair and smirks. "People are going to think we're a throuple."

I narrow my eyes at him. Yeah, I'm not cool with him even making jokes about fucking my friend. Not when I know he's probably had his dick in at least a few of the girls we just passed in the hallway. I don't know what I'd do to him if he touched Mia.

He chuckles, thinking I'm jealous.

"I don't need anyone but you, babe." He leans down and kisses my forehead. "See you in second."

What a fucking liar.

He wanders off. When I turn to slip into my class, I catch Damon watching us. He leans against the wall, talking with some other guys. A girl stands close to his side, but his sharp blue eyes are on me. My breath catches. He turns and walks down the hallway.

Is he worried I'm not being truthful about my interactions with Chase?

Fuck him. I shake my head and go into the classroom. Like I want to do anything with that lying piece of shit. The only reason I'm still dating him is because Damon told me to. If I had my way, we would have broken up on Saturday night.

Maybe Damon, Cam, and Hawk like fucking me right under his nose.

Maybe I like it a little too much too. I don't know what their time-frame is, but I'm not looking forward to the end. I need to start getting information on Chase. Figuring out why he holds onto me.

It's certainly not for our sex life.

"You doing okay?" Mia slips into her seat next to me.

"Just tired." I smile. "It's going to be a long month."

"Yeah, I've looked at the schedule. Between classwork and the play, I'm so booked. I can't imagine what your schedule must look like." Mia rests her chin on her hand. "If you need help, put me in coach."

I laugh. I wish it were that easy. I'm the only director and the only one the Devil's trio can play with. And I wouldn't want it any other way.

DAMON

I take my seat next to Olivia in first period. She leans my way with an inviting smile.

"You're coming to my party Saturday, right?" She bats her thick eyelashes at me. "I was sad we couldn't party before school started. We need to make that right."

"We'll be there." I turn my gaze to the front of the classroom. Weekend parties are the places to be seen and fuck girls. Though now I have Evan, so I could just stay home and fuck her all night. If she'd fucking let me.

It's only been a weekend, but fuck, feeling her cunt kiss my cock makes me want to bury myself deep inside her until she comes all over me. She's tight and always so wet for me.

"Megan said she saw you with EvanAnn on your motorcycle yesterday at lunch time." Olivia is fishing. I don't even bat an eyelash.

"We have history class together. A group project. Mia Lewis was on Hawk's bike." I need to downplay this shit because Olivia gets territorial even though she has no right to be. She's scared off girls I wanted to fuck before. I've never laid a finger on this chick, and she wants me all to herself. Fuck that.

The only girl with a claim on me is Evan. I just need to fully claim her.

There's no world where Evan wins a bitch fight with Olivia. Olivia would bury her.

"I know I said EvanAnn is probably a virgin, but I could be wrong. She probably puts out, but only to certain guys. She's too good for most guys." Olivia taps her nails on her desk and glances toward the front of the classroom. Is she trying to say Evan is too good for me? "I don't think you'll get what you need from her, but I'm more than willing to take care of any pressing concerns."

She puckers her red lips. She wears too much makeup. Not like Evan, who barely wears any. I like her scrubbed clean and aching for an orgasm.

"It's a class project." I turn to her. "What makes you think it's anything more?"

"You don't let anyone ride on your bike with you." She pouts. "I'd be more than happy to ride with you."

Fuck. "That's why I chose Evan to ride with me. She has a boyfriend. If I'd let Mia ride my bike, she might get the wrong idea."

Olivia nods and looks thoughtful for a moment.

"The new girl is making waves." Olivia's eyes narrow. She must have heard about Liam and Fletcher.

"Not interested." It was bold of Mia to go after two guys after a week of school. She's not familiar with our gossip mill around here. Nothing is off-limits, especially a girl being slutty. But maybe she doesn't care. She was hardcore flirting with Hawk.

She tried to engage me, but I'm not flirting with the friend. Not if it's going to make Evan shut us out longer.

"In Mia? Interesting." Olivia stretches her legs out. "You don't have to worry about other girls this year. I can be the girl you need. You can focus on hockcy, and I can take care of all your desires. Besides, you wouldn't want to break up the happy couple."

Back to Evan and Chase. Fuck. This girl is like a terrier. She can't seem to let it go.

"Happy couple?" I scoff. I've already stolen Evan out from under him, even though he doesn't know it yet. He never should have thought he'd get away with a quick fuck while Evan was at the party. The video would have been damning by itself, but he had to go and fuck his ex. What an asshole.

"Even if you were interested in EvanAnn, which you aren't, she must be lousy in bed because Chase is getting his dick wet in a different girl practically every night." Olivia smirks. "They probably have some sort of agreement though, or else she's really stupid."

"Right, because every girl knows when her boyfriend is a cheater." I shake my head. Fucking Chase. It was only a matter of time before Evan found out about his exploits. She's not completely cut off from everyone else. Or is she?

The only friend she seems to have is Mia, who's new. I haven't noticed her talking with anyone else.

"I heard they talked about it, and she is fine with an open relationship on his side." Olivia watches me out of the corner of her eye. Fuck, this bitch won't quit. "It doesn't go both ways though. He's horribly possessive over her. His little director."

If Olivia presses this hard about a ride on my bike, I need her to see Evan isn't her competition. To keep Evan out of Olivia's crosshairs. Olivia may want me, but I don't want her. Nothing about her plastic persona appeals to me. Girls like her become clingers once they get what they want.

"For fuck's sake. It was a project, Olivia. That's it. I don't want the little ant." I run my hand through my hair before turning and giving Olivia a flirty smile. "Besides, I'm sure we can find a project of our own on Saturday night."

She perks up, thinking she's won, and leans in, showing off her tits. "I can't wait."

I'll deal with this mess Saturday.

WHEN I WALK INTO SECOND, HAWK AND CAM ARE ALREADY seated around Evan. She's focused on her tablet. When I walk by, her eyes lift to mine and her lips part slightly. Fuck. My cock stirs. If she wasn't "dating" Chase, I could pull her into a supply closet and fuck that pretty mouth before third.

Her cheeks flush and she looks down at her tablet. Maybe she's thinking the same thing.

I'm not ready to blow up her relationship with Chase. Not until we have enough to take him down. However I do it, I want to cause the most damage. He wants her, but why is he fucking around? And last week when she was home alone, why wasn't he there fucking her?

Maybe Olivia is right. Maybe Evan is a lousy lay. I don't need her to be an expert though. And if her blow job skills keep improving, she can be taught. Fuck, last night I should have taken her pussy with the plug buried in her ass.

We agreed, though. It's not about consent, it's about trust. I want to use her tight little body how I want, and she won't let me if she doesn't trust me.

Chase walks in early for once. He sets his books down and comes back to Evan's desk. She looks up at him in surprise. He squats down beside her. He's avoiding looking at any of us surrounding her.

"Hey."

"Hey." Evan sounds confused, but she doesn't look at any of us either.

"I was checking out the schedule and it looks like you have dinner off on Wednesday. Do you want to have dinner at my house with my parents?"

Her cheeks get pink and she looks down at her desk for a moment. "I have to eat with my mom Wednesday night. She wants to make sure everything is going well this semester. Sorry. But you and I have the party Saturday night."

"And my game is home on Friday." He grins at her. "You're going to come watch?"

"Of course. I'll see if Mia can come with me."

He chuckles. "Maybe people will think you and Mia are a couple and I'm the third wheel. My parents are going to be at the game. They'd love for you to stop by and say hi."

"I can try."

He smiles. "Good. They think you're good for me. They're right."

The teacher comes in and Chase stands to head back to his chair. Hawk leans in and trails his fingers down the back of Evan's neck. She shivers.

Chase is still dating her even though she isn't giving him anything. But he was cheating on her this past week when she was available.

What isn't Chase finding in Evan? She's warm and willing. She comes easily. Sure, she didn't really know what to do with my cock the first time she put her mouth on it, but once Cam talked her through it, she did fine.

She's a fast learner.

I study Chase as he pays attention in class. Or rather, pays attention to his phone during the lecture. He obviously wants to spend time with Evan. With his parents. Does that have anything to do with us taking her out to lunch yesterday?

Was he coming over to stake his claim in front of us?

She doesn't belong to him. Maybe on paper, but when it comes down to it, she belongs to me. To us. Even if she's a means to an end. I can't beat up Chase for what he's done, but I can take his perfect relationship and twist it to my needs.

Twist her into my little fuck toy. Show him how far she'll go for me. Ruin his little good girl. Because I have her. He may think he has her, but he doesn't. She's in my bed at night.

I've had my cock in her mouth, and I'm determined to get into that tight little cunt of hers. To stretch her out and make her moan so fucking hard as she comes all over my cock before I flood her with my cum.

"Mr. Storm?" Mr. Ridgeway says.

"Yeah?" My tone borders on belligerent. I was supposed to be done with this bullshit. Sitting in classes, taking notes, answering teachers. I was supposed to be training daily to get to the next level. To make my way onto one of the best college teams. To have the recruiters in the NHL see me. To sign a fucking contract.

"Did you not hear my question?" Mr. Ridgeway looks like he swallowed a lemon.

"Obviously." I arch an eyebrow, waiting for him to ask me again.

The room twitters with quiet snickers and chuckles. Mr. Ridgeway glares at me. I wait because what's he going to do to me? Abso-fucking-lutely nothing.

Just like Chase is going to get nothing from Evan. I may not be where I'm supposed to be, but I'm going to rule this fucking school while I'm forced to be here.

THE LIBRARY IS quiet when Mia and I walk in. I might have eaten a little slower than normal, knowing she would flirt hardcore with Hawk and Damon during the half hour we have to work on the project.

Chase practically pouted when I told him where we were going. When he tried to come along, I told him we needed to focus.

Mia's gaze bounces around the room. The librarian behind the checkout desk. The rows of books. Our library has two floors, with steps in the back leading to shelves of more stacks.

"Where are we going to meet them?" Mia whispers.

I blow out a breath and look around. There are a few nooks and crannies to hide from the librarian in, but I figured since we were working on a project, we'd be front and center. I could text them, but I shouldn't have their numbers.

I gesture to Mia and start walking. "Let's do a quick sweep."

Ten minutes later and there is no sign of them anywhere.

"This was a waste of time." I walk back to the doors because I'm done. I push out into the hallway and start for the theater wing. If they think I'm going to sit around and wait for them like a good little pet, they can figure out when we can work next. I have things to do.

"Wait. We can at least check to see if they're in the cafeteria." Mia grabs my arm and I let her bring me back to the cafeteria. Chase isn't at our table, but I'm no longer worried about Chase's dalliances. I glance out toward the courtyard and see the guys sitting at Olivia's table.

"They must have forgotten." I shrug as Olivia puts her hand on Damon's chest and he smiles at her. It's not like he's going to fuck her. Resisting the urge to rub at my heart, I turn on my heel.

"Where are you going?" Mia asks.

"To get ready for my afternoon classes."

"Well, I'm going to go talk to them." She straightens.

"Have fun with that." I walk away as Mia marches out to the court-yard. Maybe I should stay and support my friend, but I'm having trouble breathing. My chest tightens as I go to my locker and switch out my books.

What I have with the Devil's trio isn't anything more than sex and revenge. I shouldn't be surprised they're keeping up appearances by flirting with other girls. If they stopped, it would raise questions.

I slam my locker shut and head into the Anteros section. I have better things to do than hang out with guys while my friend tries to get into their pants. She won't succeed, but I can't tell her that. Am I a horrible friend?

It's not like Mia is professing her undying love for the guys. She wants to fuck them. Not even long-term. Nope, I'm done thinking about that.

I head into the empty black box theater and climb the steps to the back row of the audience. Drawing in a breath, I sit and stare at the space. Tomorrow after lunch, we'll be in here for rehearsal. I'll have all my actors available to me.

I pull out my tablet and take notes on how best to use the time we have. We'll have full run-throughs closer to performance, but right now, we need to either do exercises to work on memorization or work on cadence of speech.

A few actors in the cast are familiar with Shakespeare, including Hawk. I could divide them up and have each of them run their lines. The actors with experience can help with pronunciations and delivery.

It'll also mean I won't need to spend any time with Chase or Hawk. I send a quick message to Keira to let her know what I'm thinking. After a minute, the door to the theater opens and she walks in.

She looks around and spots me, climbing the steps before dropping into the chair next to me. "What's going on?"

"You could have just texted back. How did you know I'd be in here?" I turn to look at her.

She smiles. "Because this is where I'd be. And if you're reworking our plan, something else must be going on. So, what's wrong with what we already had?"

Keira puts her feet up on the chair in front of her and crosses her ankles as she stares out at the black box.

"Nothing's wrong. The whole cast together this early just isn't as effective as it will be later on." I slide my tablet and phone into my backpack. "I just want to make the best use of their time."

She nods. "It'll work. But is it the best use of our principals' time?"

I tip my head back against the wall and put my hands over my eyes. "Probably not."

"So, what can we do to utilize everyone according to their talents?" Keira turns her face toward me.

"You and Jason can help the extras with their lines while I work with the principals." And suddenly, I have both Chase and Hawk in my group again.

"Or we can do it the other way. It's early on and we have time." Keira smiles softly. "But if something else is bothering you, you can talk to me."

I give her a surprised look.

She laughs lightly and holds up her hands. "This school is stressful. Everyone wants the best roles and best positions, but there aren't enough for everyone. It's cutthroat, but right now, you and I are on the same team. I don't see that changing in the future. So, if you need someone to talk to, I'm here for it. I won't judge, but I'll listen."

"Why haven't we been friends before?" I ask.

"Probably because I'm right below you, hoping to take your spot when you graduate." She bumps her shoulder against mine. "This place messes with your head. Honestly, I don't need to use you to get a leg up, I'm doing fine on my own. I appreciate you taking a chance on me for your assistant. And I know you've got stress outside of the play. Who doesn't?"

I draw in a breath and release it.

"It's an open-ended offer." Keira stands. "We've got a long road ahead of us, and if you need help focusing by sorting through whatever's in your head, I'm here."

She heads out, leaving me to mull over her words. I need to prioritize. The Devil's trio could easily consume all my time if I let them. But they were never part of my strategy this year. The play, schoolwork, college. Those are my three priorities. Everything else has to come below those. Including the Devil's trio.

CAM

"And then she said she wanted to lick my feet." Brad sits across the table in the courtyard from where Hawk, Damon, and I sit, telling a story about his weekend.

Olivia leans into Damon and says something quietly. He hasn't fucked her and isn't going to, but she thinks she has him wrapped around her finger.

A girl clears her throat behind us and for a second, I wonder if Evan finally grew a pair and is coming to confront Damon. Fuck, I'd pay good money to see that. A girl fight between Olivia and Evan would sell out.

We turn and Mia Lewis stands there. She straightens, but she isn't looking at me. She's got her sights on Damon and Hawk.

"We were supposed to work in the library today for our history project." Mia arches an eyebrow and crosses her arms. All she needs now is to tap her foot.

I grin, because I'm interested in how this is going to play out. Damon looks around like Evan would be anywhere near this shit show. Is he really surprised she isn't leading the charge?

"Slipped my mind." Damon shrugs.

Hawk smiles. "Sorry."

"You do realize Evan's time is valuable. She's scheduled for practically every second of the day. And we need to get this history assignment done." Mia arches an eyebrow.

She was flirty at lunch yesterday. But today, she's all righteous indignation on Evan's behalf. Fascinating.

"I'm sorry, but who are you?" Olivia stands and puts her hands on her hip. "Do you even know who you're talking to?"

I lean my elbows on the table behind me. Okay, Mia and Olivia catfight. I can get behind that.

"I wasn't talking to you." Mia looks her up and down with a bitchy attitude.

Olivia taps her finger against her lip and gives Mia a fake smile. "You're new, so I'm going to go easy on you, Mia. See, everyone's already heard about you, Liam, and Fletcher this weekend."

Mia's smile is vicious. "Are you trying to sex shame me?"

Olivia shakes her head, but her smile doesn't fade. "I don't think you know how this school works yet. Which is a shame. There are levels here, but they aren't quite the same as the levels at normal schools. Our cream of the crop aren't the jocks and cheerleaders." Olivia turns and runs her hand through Damon's blond hair. "They have money and popularity."

"And if someone doesn't have money?" Mia asks.

"Then they don't matter. So, your little pet project with the charity case isn't going to win you any bonus points at this school. I talked to your brother Tanner this weekend." Olivia closes in on Mia. Mia's taller by a couple inches. "Your family has money, don't they? They made a huge donation to the school to help you get in."

Mia's lips tighten, but she smiles. "Are you going to get to your point?"

"Oh, I'm already there." Olivia smiles and sits next to Damon. "You may have money, but you're never going to be popular here. Maybe as a slut who likes to get around, but that's all you'll ever be."

Mia smiles. "I didn't ask you, did I? You offered like I wanted your little rant. So hear me now, I don't give a shit if you think I'm a huge slut. What I care about is doing my best at this school. And to do my best, I need someone like Evan, who's clued in to what's important." Mia looks at Damon and Hawk. "Such as our grades, so when you're ready to work on our school project, let me know and I'll see if we can squeeze you in."

She storms off. I'm grinning because that was awesome.

"Can I slow clap?" I glance around at the others. "That feels like a slow clap moment."

"Fuck off, Cam!" Olivia crosses her arms and glares after Mia.

Yeah, those two aren't done with each other. And when their showdown happens, I want front row seats and some popcorn.

DAMON

"Hey, you got a minute?" I stand in my coach's doorway after practice.

"Come in, Storm." Gary Young rocks back in his desk chair as I walk in and take a seat on the edge of the chair in front of his desk. "What can I do for you?"

I run a hand through my hair. Practice was rough, but I'm ready for the next level. "What's it going to take?"

Coach Young rocks forward and clasps his hands on the desk. "How's the leg feeling on the ice now?"

My leg had to be cast for a few weeks this summer when they were concerned it was a break. I'm still working on restrengthening the muscle. Even though it was a bone bruise and not a fracture, the leg still aches.

"Good enough." I lean back in the chair, trying to appear confident.

He nods. He knows what I want. I want what I had before that accident took it all away.

"Enough people have heard about you that I might be able to send off some tapes to draw recruiters to games this year. But you need to be in peak performance when they show up." He sighs. "They'll know you had to drop from the USHL for the year."

"Is there any way to get back on the roster?" I rub my thigh. "If someone else gets an injury, or someone drops out?"

He shakes his head. "I'm sorry, Damon, but it's too late this year. It might be too late for college hockey this round. We could possibly get you back on the USHL team for next year. I know you had hopes to go to the Northeast for school, but they'll be scouting at the premier boarding schools. If you'd been able to go to the summer camp at least…"

I blow out a breath. The accident ruined everything. The injury meant I wasn't able to go to development camp. My father suddenly couldn't let his only son head out of state for my final year. I'm lucky he didn't sell my bikes and still lets me ride.

"Whatever I need to do, I'm willing." I lift my gaze to Coach Young's. "Anything."

He nods. "Let me see what I can do. I might have a string or two left to pull."

He opens his drawer and pulls out a brochure. "It's not in Boston, but they've been making waves with their hockey program."

He passes it to me, and the Crowne Mawr University logo stands out in the corner. "It's a few hours away. They pulled in a new coach a few years ago, and the team is finally NCAA qualified. He's building a team to showcase their skill. He might be interested if you're willing to work for it."

"Work for it?" I'm one of the best hockey players this school has ever seen. What more do I need to do?

"You need to fix your grades, Damon." Coach Young clasps his hands together and gives me a look. "Everyone at this school knows you can make the grades, but you keep fucking it up. No fucking up this year."

"Got it." I stand and head for the door. Keep my grades up and make sure my game is flawless.

"I know you can do this, Damon. That accident was a fucking tragedy, but there might be another way." Coach stands and gestures to my leg. "Focus on school and getting better. You want this? No partying this year. No girlfriends. Just focus on the prize."

My jaw tightens. No issue on girlfriends. I have Evan to warm my bed. But I won't be able to fully focus on my future until I destroy Chase Chadwick's.

CHAPTER 42

EvanAnn

I SPENT the afternoon focusing on my classes and then working with my actors at rehearsal. Not once did the Devil's trio interrupt my train of thought, but now that I'm home... I grab something from the kitchen before heading up to my room to work on homework. I'm determined to get as much done as possible before Damon finds me and makes me do whatever he wants tonight.

A shiver flows through me. I should tell him no, but I won't. While I can't let this consume my life, I can take a break.

Does he work out every night? Will he pull me into the shower with him again? Make me go down on him? Fuck my pussy with his fingers until I come?

I cross my legs. I've changed into comfortable clothes for the night —leggings and a sweatshirt. I even put my hair up in a ponytail. I'm hoping to put it in a bun if he wants me to shower with him again.

It's going to get dry if I keep washing it this often.

Focus. Fuck, I need to focus on homework and not the door to his bedroom. I was fine at school. Able to put them all out of my mind. But now, in this room, it's like he's everywhere. I've never had this level of distraction in my life before. Even Chase didn't exist outside of the space I allowed him in my life.

Maybe that's where I went wrong. Compartmentalizing Chase. If

I'd been more enthusiastic about spending time with him, would he have still cheated on me? Probably. Fuck.

Chase doesn't really want me. He wanted something from me sure, but not Evan. Damon wants me more than Chase ever did.

I eat the ratatouille the chef made for me. It's good, and I hope there will be leftovers for the next several meals.

I texted my mom I'd be home for dinner on Wednesday. She can't wait to hear what I've been up to. I check my phone to see if Chase has texted, but he hasn't. Today was weird. Chase has been clingy, but today was a lot. At lunch he sat closer than normal, while making sure he wasn't close enough to get whatever sickness I have.

Does he suspect I'm pulling away? I need to figure out why he's with me and what makes him tick. Things I probably should have known as his girlfriend, anyway. Chase hasn't really pushed sex with me. He brings it up, but doesn't actually try to coax me into it.

Not like Damon. I resist the urge to look toward Damon's dark room again.

Even though Mia brought up me giving Damon head last night, I don't think she actually thinks I would do it. And I know Chase would never believe I had it in me.

We were supposed to work on the history project earlier, but now I need to get ahead on the project. I hope they don't think I'm going to do the project without them. But I can't afford to let any of my grades slip.

The door in Damon's room slams shut and I startle, turning in my chair. I press my lips together, even though my body softens. I'm still upset they ditched us at lunch. Mia said she went out there to let them have it, but Olivia got in her face.

I turn back to my homework and ignore Damon. But tingles crawl up my spine knowing he's near. If he wants me, he'll let me know. We don't have a friendship. I can't go ask if he's had a bad day and expect him to open up to me.

The shower turns on. I squirm in my chair. He doesn't say anything. When he doesn't come in and pick me up to take me in with him, I drag in a breath and release it. Good. I need to do work, anyway.

I'm making headway on my homework and finally calmed down

when the shower shuts off. I turn and see his back as he heads into his bedroom. He drops his towel, so he's completely naked as he walks away. His back, ass, and legs are chiseled.

He hasn't said anything to me. I turn back to my work, trying to focus, but I can hear him moving around in his room.

When he doesn't initiate anything with me, I figure he's not coming in and finish my homework for class and make an outline for our project. I stretch and go into the bathroom. I close his door quietly before going into the toilet.

When I'm washing my hands at the sink, Damon walks in in a pair of athletic pants and no shirt or shoes. He stops behind me, puts his hands on my hips and drops his head to rest between my shoulder blades.

I rinse off my hands and turn off the water. After I dry my hands, I rest them on the counter. He hasn't moved.

I don't know what to do. Do I ask him what's wrong? Or will that make him upset?

"Fuck," he whispers. He straightens and turns me around. He tips my chin up and his mouth is on mine before I can say anything.

I don't want to sink into this kiss. This should mean nothing. But his kiss claims me in a way Chase's never did. It's like Damon couldn't resist, no matter how hard he tried. It's intoxicating. His hands slide beneath my leggings and panties and shove them down over my hips.

My hands remain by my sides, even though my fingers itch to dig into his hair and pull him closer to me. He lifts me and sets my bare ass on the counter. I gasp at the chill and he deepens the kiss.

My leggings and panties are stripped off me. His hands are on the insides of my thighs, spreading me as he closes in until I feel the hardness of his cock against my pussy through his pants.

He drags my head back by my ponytail and meets my eyes. Both of us are breathing heavily.

"Now?"

"No." I'd push him away and tell him to fuck off if I wasn't so weak. I want whatever he's willing to give me, but I don't want him to fuck me like this. Something's upset him.

He grabs my sweatshirt and lifts it over my head. His eyes take in the lacy bra before he unhooks it and leaves me naked on the counter before him.

"You haven't fucked your boyfriend, have you, Evan?" He takes my breast into his hand and slides his thumb over the tip.

I suck in a breath. Feeling a little bratty, I say, "Not today."

His eyes narrow on mine. He pushes a finger deep inside me. I cry out at the intrusion, but his kiss made me so fucking wet.

He drags his finger out and licks my slick off it. "If you let him fuck you, I'll know."

"How?" I can't take any more of this bullshit. "What if we used a condom? It's not like I'd let that manwhore fuck me without one."

"But you'll let us?" He slides his finger back in slowly, dragging his thumb against my clit. "How do you know I didn't fuck someone today already, little devil?"

I try to control the desire spiraling through me mixing with my rising anger. It's like he wants to fight. I meet his steady gaze. "Then our agreement is null and void."

He brushes his cheek against mine as he says in my ear. "Good thing I didn't. Let me fuck you properly, little devil."

His tone has turned coaxing. Fuck.

"No." There's no way I'm letting him in when he's in this mood. I don't deserve his anger.

He growls, sending shivers through me. He carries me into his bedroom and tosses me on his bed. I don't have time to scramble away before he comes down on top of me and kisses my neck. It's like he's trying to incinerate me with lust.

I grab onto his sheets to resist grabbing onto him. He rocks his hips into mine, still wearing his sweats. A whimper of need escapes me.

"I want to feel you come on my cock, Evan." He bites my neck and I hiss at the sting of pain. He kisses down my chest until his lips close over my nipple.

I arch up into him as he sucks on my breast, flicking the tip with his tongue. My heart is beating so hard and my pussy aches to feel his finger or his tongue in it. Anything to relieve this ache.

"I could keep this up all night."

I whimper as he spreads kisses across my chest to my other nipple and begins to suck it. My pussy pulses. Empty, needy.

"I don't even need to touch that precious pussy to get what I want." He lifts over me. Our eyes lock as he straddles my hips and holds himself up with one arm. "I don't need your pussy to come, little devil. But you need me to touch it, don't you?"

He dips down and takes my mouth in a carnal kiss. His cock brushes my stomach, but otherwise he holds himself away from me. I groan in frustration as he pulls away.

He strokes his cock in his hand, but holds my eyes captive. My fingers clench into the sheet. Fuck this. I can get myself off. Just not without him in the room.

I slip my hand down between my legs. He gives me a wicked smirk.

"That's cheating, little devil."

"You're here." I give him a little shrug like it doesn't matter, as I slide my finger over my clit and release a sigh. Pleasure surges through me. I'd prefer it to be his hand, but it's not like I haven't gotten myself there before.

He chuckles and grabs my wrists, pulling them above my head and binding them with one of his large hands. "No."

I squirm beneath him, but he straddles my waist and strokes his cock.

"If you want to get off, I can fuck you." He slides his knuckles across my breast on the next stroke. Why is he doing this?

I press my lips together and narrow my eyes on him. Fuck him. "Why were you angry when you came in?"

"That's none of your business, Evan." He quickens his strokes. His lips part as he stares at my tits. "You have fucking fantastic tits. I could come on them or come inside you. Your choice?"

"Did something happen at school? Practice?" I consider the possibilities. I haven't seen him since lunchtime.

He doesn't want to talk about it. Fine. But I can still ask. If he's going to make me lie here and watch him come without getting me off, he can be annoyed with me too.

"You want this dick, little devil?" He leans down and flicks his tongue against my lips. His hand strokes his cock against my stomach.

I squirm beneath him. "Do you think this is going to work? That I'll say yes because you're getting off without me?"

His smile is wicked. "You get off on watching, Evan. You're so wet right now I could probably fist that pretty cunt."

My eyes widen in horror. "No!"

Apparently, I do have limits.

"No fisting!"

"Pretty sure you only mentioned cocks." Damon releases his cock and reaches behind him. His fingers touch my clit.

I struggle to knock him off and get my hands away. "No, Damon."

He chuckles and strokes his finger over my clit. "It would take a lot of time to get that tight cunt to take a fist, little devil. I could barely get two fingers in it."

Every inch of me burns and as much as I want to get off, I don't want him to touch me. Not with the imminent threat of his whole fist in my pussy.

He slides his finger inside me. "So fucking tight."

"Please, don't," I whimper. My hips rock against his finger, chasing the release I know he can give me, even if I'm scared he'll take things too far.

"I'm not going to fuck you with my fist, Evan. At least, not until after I can get my cock in there." He flicks my clit and I shudder, but then he stops touching my pussy and returns his hand to his cock. "I'm also not going to make you come tonight."

I blow out a frustrated breath.

"The only way you're going to come is if I thrust my cock deep inside that pussy."

I close my eyes as he continues to jerk off. He groans and I feel his warm cum on my breasts. It still feels good, but I need more.

"I'd like to go back to my room now." I open my eyes and glare into his determined blue eyes.

"Might be a minute before I can get it up again." He rolls to his back on the bed and chuckles. "Keep those fingers out of my pussy."

I roll off the bed. In the bathroom, I stop and use a washcloth to clean his cum from my skin and grab my clothes from the floor before going to my bedroom and redressing.

What an asshole. So he's upped the game to not give me an orgasm unless I let him fuck me? How long will I last that way? My pussy aches with the need to come. It's gotten a little too much love lately. I've gotten greedy.

I sit at my desk, waiting to hear him come back through and decide to fuck my mouth. Or start all over again.

My phone buzzes. I glance and see the notification of a text from Chase. I don't even want to look at that right now.

But it does give me an idea. I don't need Damon to give me an orgasm.

ME:

Need to come

HAWK:

Where's Damon?

ME:

Not helping

HAWK:

Be there in 5

I have no idea where Hawk lives in relation to Damon's house. If he can get here that quickly, awesome. I guess that's the benefit of having three guys who want to fuck me instead of just the one dick.

I glance toward Damon's room. *Might be a minute*? Wonder if Hawk can get here before Damon gets it up again.

There are ways of getting off without using my fingers, but if Damon wants to push me tonight, there are two other guys who won't.

I go through my homework to see if I have anything else I can get done. After a few minutes, my door opens. I turn and see Hawk locking the door. Glancing toward Damon's room again, I smirk.

Fuck him and his *come on my cock* rule that isn't in the agreement.

"Why does this feel like the beginning of a cheesy porn?" Hawk runs a hand over his dark hair and glances toward Damon's room. "Is he denying you, baby girl?"

I release my breath and stand. "Yes."

He crosses the room and grabs the back of my neck, dragging me into him and kisses my pulse. I melt into him. I'm ready to come.

He drops his jacket on the ground. He must have taken his shoes off downstairs. Keeping hold of my neck and kissing everywhere but my lips, he backs me up until my knees hit my bed. I don't need him to kiss my mouth to come.

"Strip, Annie. I'm going to suck your clit while you suck my cock."

Thank, fuck. I'm still worried Damon is going to storm in and ruin my fun, but so far, he's a no-show. I take off my clothes while watching Hawk strip. He's built stockier than Damon. When he takes his boxers off, my mouth waters with the need to taste him.

"How do we do this?" I ask and sit on the bed.

He looks at me like I said something wrong, but then whatever thought he has passes. "You'll straddle my head and face my cock. From there, it's pretty self-explanatory."

He lies down and I carefully put my knees on either side of his head. He drags my hips down and sucks on my clit. Sparks flood my veins and I moan, but cut it off, worried it might get Damon's attention.

I stretch out over Hawk and take his cock into my mouth. My nipples rub against his stomach. He thrusts his finger into my pussy making me moan again. I rock against him, racing for my orgasm before Damon comes in and ruins everything.

Hawk sucks my clit, and bright lights explode behind my eyelids as my pussy convulses around his finger. I moan my release around his cock.

A hand grabs my ponytail and pushes my head down onto Hawk's cock, almost making me take him too deep.

"Evan, Evan, Evan." Damon's voice pushes me over the edge again.

Hawk chuckles against my pussy before he groans his release. I swallow his cum. When I stop swallowing, Damon lifts my head from Hawk's lap. I gasp in a breath.

"Did I give you permission to get off?" His sharp blue eyes cut through me.

"Hawk did." And if he keeps thrusting like that, I'm going to come again.

Fucking hell, if looking into Damon's eyes while Hawk's tongue thrusts into my pussy isn't going to get me there, I don't know what will.

"Besides, it's part of our deal." I close my eyes as I shatter again. My hips rock against Hawk's face. "Oh, fuck. If I need to come, I have to ask one of you."

Damon's eyes narrow on me. He knows I've won this round.

Hawk lifts my hips and slips out from beneath me. He wipes his mouth with a smirk.

"If you don't want to take care of her, I'm sure Cam can sneak out tonight." Hawk slides his fingers over my clit and it pulses greedily.

I gasp as Damon's hand tightens in my hair. "I want to add limits."

"You want to renegotiate, little devil?" Damon searches my eyes.

"Yes."

"Good, so do I." He releases my hair. "Call Cam."

CHAPTER 43

EvanAnn

WHEN I GO into the closet to grab pajamas, Damon stalks off to his room. Before I can pull out a nightgown, he comes back and puts one of his t-shirts on over my head.

"I have pajamas," I mutter.

"You also have a pussy you don't want to use." Damon turns and leaves before I can say anything.

I don't know what to say about that. Cam is on his way over, so we're waiting for him. I can imagine what Damon wants to change in our arrangement.

"Is that why you're angry?" I stalk after him, shoving my arms through the sleeves of his shirt. "Because I won't let you fuck me."

He spins and I skid to avoid colliding with him. "Maybe I don't understand why you're so precious with your pussy when everyone else has already had it."

My lips press shut and I narrow my eyes at him. I knew he thought I was a whore. I just didn't expect to feel hurt when he threw it in my face.

"Maybe you two should go to separate corners of the house until Cam gets here." Hawk sits on the end of my bed. He's dressed again, but he gestures for me to come to him.

I search Damon's eyes for a second longer before turning away.

When I step in front of Hawk, he pulls me down onto his lap. The things I've done with these guys make my head spin. I know Damon doesn't understand that they've taken so many firsts already. But they took me from zero to sixty on the first day.

Yes, I'd been kissed and Chase grazed my boob once, but other than that, this is all new to me. But I don't want them to know that. I'm not sure I like that they think I'm a whore, but I don't want to be treated like a virgin anymore.

It's freeing to know they believe I'm something I'm not. I can let go of my preconceived ideas of what I need to lose my virginity. But it doesn't release the fear of the unknown. The fear of potential pain.

With Chase, I felt like a trophy to be put on his shelf. Yes, I'm his girlfriend, but obviously he doesn't need me to meet his sexual needs. Even if I fucked him the first time we talked about it, I have no doubt he would have still cheated on me.

I don't think these guys will cheat on me, because we have an agreement. But these guys probably wouldn't look at a virgin twice. Maybe they would be worried a virgin would read too much into sex.

Cam comes in through Damon's room and runs a hand through his hair. "Okay, I'm here. What are we discussing?"

"Renegotiating. Apparently, Annie has limits." Hawk rubs his hand down my back.

"Don't we all." Damon lowers himself onto my desk chair. Is he reaching the end of his limit with me? Does he want this to be over?

Cam looks at all of us. "What did I miss?"

"Damon tried to convince me to fuck him by withholding orgasms, so I asked Hawk to come over and help me out." I spill it because I don't know how Damon would try to spin it.

"It's not like you're a fragile virgin who needs to be wooed." Damon jerks his hand toward me.

I glare at him. I'm not fragile. Fucker.

"Okay." Cam walks across the room and sits next to Hawk and me. He puts his hand on my bare knee and a little bolt of awareness shoots through me. "So, what's on the table to renegotiate?"

"No fisting or other new stuff without prior permission." My cheeks are hot. "You can't just command me to do something like that and expect me to obey."

"Are we going to have to discuss everything, Evan?" Damon leans back in the chair. "Or can we just assume once you let us fuck your pussy and ass, you'll be okay with us filling all your holes with our cocks? What's the limit on discussing things?"

"You want to explore your darker sides, but I don't think I want your whole hand up there." Wincing, I realize my mistake.

"You don't think?" Damon leans forward. "Fine, I'll allow discussion of things that might fall under the category of kink, but group sex is definitely in our agreement."

"Fine," I snap back.

"But..." Damon stands.

My heart flutters with nerves.

"I'll allow that. If we discuss your hold out strategy." Damon walks over and tips my chin up. "I want a time limit. You can give it up before then, but I don't want this to drag on for months with you protecting your cunt like it's fucking gold."

I swallow hard. His eyes are dark, and that tension that sizzles between us is still there.

"We've already agreed to your other terms, Evan." His thumb trails down my throat, like he can't help himself. Fire dances beneath his touch, making me shiver. His eyes give me a knowing look. "You get all of us. So give us all of you."

"I—" Have no idea what to say. They think I've probably had tons of sex, so I can see why they wouldn't want to hold off. But I can't tell them the reason is because I haven't had sex before... with anyone. Not unless I want to confess. Would they even believe me at this point?

What virgin would agree to this insanity?

"Two weeks," Cam says. "We've all gone without sex for longer than a month before."

"Speak for yourself." Damon scoffs and walks back over to my desk chair to sit and glare at me some more. I miss his touch.

Two weeks? I squirm on Hawk's lap. I've been dating Chase for four months, and they've gotten further in a weekend than he ever did. I might never truly be ready to have sex with three guys, but they're circling, and eventually Damon will win in this tug-of-war.

Much as I might want to deny him, I want him in a way that's slowly taking over everything. The anticipation of them touching me has me tied in knots.

"You'll be getting head whenever you want." Hawk runs his hand between my legs and settles his hand against my pussy. It throbs beneath his touch. "It's not like you're going without."

I swallow and lift my gaze to Damon's. "Two weeks."

"Or less." He runs his fingertips over his lips.

"You agreed to take care of Annie's needs too, Damon." Hawk slides his finger against my clit through my panties. I bite my lip. "She can't masturbate to take the edge off. So, no making her call us to take care of her."

"Wait," Cam says. "Feel free to send Evan our way. You get her to yourself far too often. If you don't want to make her come, I'm happy to be on standby." He turns and nudges my chin up. "I'll take whatever I can get."

He slides his lips against mine, making me needy for more.

"So we're all in agreement?" Hawk says as his finger slides beneath my panties and strokes my wet clit. "If it's not fingers, tongue, or cock, Annie gets a say in if it happens. And in two weeks, we get this pussy if she hasn't already caved before then."

I drag in a breath as Cam's hand slides beneath the shirt to cup my breast and stroke my nipple. My eyes lock with Damon's as the others work me, winding the string tight inside me.

"Two weeks. No fisting." Damon runs his fingers over his lips. "You need to get off, I'll get you there. And same goes for me."

Cam tilts my head his way and kisses me while Hawk shatters me again. I'm fully aware of Damon watching this, of how much I get off on him watching them make me come.

We play for a while longer, kissing, sucking, licking until we've all found our releases. But Hawk and Cam can't stay tonight, so at some point they have to leave.

I say my goodbyes and slip into the bathroom to use the facilities and clean up again. I'm still wearing Damon's t-shirt. When I walk out of the water closet, I wash my hands and brush my teeth.

When Damon doesn't request my presence, I go into my bedroom. My bed is huge and cold, but I guess it's mine, and where I should be sleeping. I crawl under the covers, feeling relaxed. I don't think that went exactly how Damon hoped it would go.

Maybe he thought he could break me. The truth is, he probably can. There's a lot of things I want in my life, but I never thought Damon Storm would be one of the things I could have. Definitely not all three of the Devil's trio. Cam and Hawk were off-limits too.

Girls like me don't date guys like them. Hell, those guys don't even date. They just fuck. And they don't fuck girls like me.

I pull up the covers and open my phone to read the latest episode in a Dramoine fan fiction. Okay, maybe I can see why I might have a thing for a bad boy who hates me.

I plug my phone into the charger and set it on my nightstand, turning off the light. Glancing toward the bathroom door, I blow out a breath and try to relax into my bed without a warm body next to me. It takes me a while to fall asleep. The next thing I know, I'm being carried.

"What?" I'm not fully awake.

"Can't sleep." Damon's voice. He hasn't turned on the lights. He's just a dark figure carrying me into his room.

He lowers me onto the bed and crawls in next to me, drawing me in tight against his body, curling around me. I drag in his earthy scent and release a sigh as I sink back into sleep.

I SPEND EVERY SPARE MINUTE ON WEDNESDAY MORNING reviewing what we're going over during rehearsal this afternoon. It's the only time I'm guaranteed to have my full cast, so I don't want to waste anyone's time. Keira was right though our original plan was good, but if we want to work on accents, I need the principals working on something else.

Mia clears her throat when she sits down in history. I glance up from my notes. Hawk and Damon sit across from me. I'm not even sure when they got there. Well, that's not true. Damon followed me from calculus.

"We need to work on the project for this class." Mia narrows her eyes on the guys. "I'm not going to carry your weight on this, so let's figure out some time that will work, since clearly lunch won't."

"We have play practice tomorrow night after hockey." Hawk's green eyes meet mine for confirmation.

"We can meet at my house after your practice." Damon's words catch my attention. He means *our* house. "Would that work?"

His gaze is on Mia. She nods.

"Yes, it would."

"Evan?" Damon turns to meet my eyes and I swallow.

Is he going to out me to my friend? But what purpose would that serve? We haven't really talked since he carried me into his room last night. He woke early and was gone by the time I was getting ready.

We ignored each other in calculus, which was fine with me.

"Does my house work for you?" Damon asks.

"Yeah." I open my phone and add it to my schedule as the teacher comes in.

After class, we go to the cafeteria. I grab my salad and head to the end of the table, instead of where I normally sit. Chase stops Mia when she tries to join me.

"She's working." At least that's the part of Chase I actually like. He understands my manic energy when I'm preparing for things.

I barely notice Mia and Chase talking down the table from me. As soon as I finish eating, I get up and head to the black box theater. We'll be in the large one after our afternoon acting studio lecture.

On my way there, I'm caught up rereading a part of *Othello*, and considering if I should make the actors not add inflection as they rehearse, when I realize I'm not alone. There are footsteps behind me, which isn't unusual.

But I need to be aware of my surroundings, so I turn and find Hawk stalking after me.

I stop walking and finish turning toward him, but he grabs my elbow and leads me into a closet near the black box. He crowds me back against the wall.

"Hawk, what are you—"

He lifts me against him and his mouth is on my neck. Oh. My body bursts into tingles. I reach out and feel for a flat surface to put my phone on as my other hand slides over his velvet hair. His hands slide up my thigh under my skirt.

I set my phone down and grab for his belt. I have his fly open as he pushes my panties to the side and slides his finger deep into me. My breath comes out in a little moan as he begins to finger fuck me.

As soon as I have his cock free, I stroke it.

His forehead rests against mine. "Fuck, I've been thinking of this pussy all morning."

His eyes are unreadable in the dim light of the closet. My breath quickens as he pushes me closer and closer to the edge.

"Fuck, Annie."

I can't hold back, shattering all around his finger.

"That's it, baby girl." He pulls his finger out of me and I drop to my knees to take him into my mouth. He sucks his finger in his mouth, taking the taste of me. "Such a good girl."

He strokes my jaw as I suck and lick his cock. He grabs the back of my neck and holds me still as he comes in my throat. When I pull off after swallowing, my breathing is ragged.

It was quick and frantic and so fucking good.

He lifts me to my feet and slides his thumb over my lips. "I could do this all afternoon, baby girl."

I drag in a breath and groan. "I have to go."

He tucks himself away before straightening my panties. "I know. But I'm going to be tasting your pussy on my tongue as I quote Shakespeare this afternoon."

My pussy throbs and I lean in for a quick kiss. He turns his face at the last minute and I kiss the corner of his lips. For a second, I think it's a mistake, but I don't think he's kissed me since that first night when I pushed him away.

My insides feel off, like I've just gotten off a carnival ride.

When he steps away, I grab my bag from where it dropped on the floor and walk out of the closet. Fortunately, the hallway is empty. I tug my skirt to make sure it's in place and pop into the restroom to rinse out my mouth and clean up a little.

I've noticed he hasn't kissed me, but I didn't think it was intentional. Now I'm not so sure. It doesn't matter right now. I have to focus on the play, so I head to the black box for a few minutes before class.

When I slip into the auditorium, the bell is about to ring.

"Where were you?" Mia asks in a whisper.

"Black box." I hold my breath, hoping she doesn't ask too many questions. That was where I was. Just not the whole time.

"You must be under so much stress right now." She frowns. "Can I help with anything?"

I smile thinking of how Hawk helped me only moments before. "I'm good. But thank you. It means a lot."

"I'm your bestie." She preens. "I have to make sure you have everything you need."

Chase leans over and kisses my head. "Do what you gotta do, babe. We'll support you."

The class starts and I relax into my seat. Some of the tension I was feeling earlier is gone. But when the lecture starts covering material I already know, I slip back into my work and all my thoughts are, once again, on *Othello*.

When class ends, I rise and walk to the black box theater. Keira comes in after me. I'm sure Mia and Chase are taking their break.

Hawk walks in shortly after we begin our discussion. He walks over to us and we stop mid-sentence to look up at him. His presence is commanding and my breath catches.

With a nod to both of us, he holds out my phone. "You left this behind in class."

"Thank you." My cheeks redden because I must have left it in the closet.

"Anytime, Annie." He flashes me a grin and walks over to the chairs.

My skin tingles, but I try to shake it off. Did he kiss me last night? Or this weekend, at all?

"Good job on casting Hawk." Keira smiles as her eyes dance between us. "He's exactly the right guy for Cassio."

I glance up and he gives me a smirk. He is perfectly wicked. I swallow, but get back to business.

CHAPTER 44

EvanAnn

Tonight means dinner with Mom at home. Dinner is a surreal experience, entering into the dining room to a set table with a server standing to the side, ready to serve us. I don't know if I'll ever get used to this.

I appear to be the first one to make it to dinner. Mom didn't really say there was a specific time for dinner here, but I figured it would be the normal time we've always had it.

I sit in the same chair I sat in last Monday and lay the cloth napkin over my lap, trying not to gape at the server. She stands quietly in the corner of the room like a statue. It's a little unnerving.

Damon walks in and takes the seat next to me. Awareness threads through my body. But it's probably not appropriate for him to sit there.

When I open my mouth, he lifts my chin and says quietly, "I didn't ask you to open your mouth, Evan."

My cheeks flare with heat as I snap my mouth shut. My eyes narrow on him. That's when we hear my mom and Adam talking on their way in. Damon isn't touching me when they walk into the room with huge smiles.

"I feel like I haven't seen you in weeks, Evan." Mom settles in the seat across from Damon without a word about him sitting next to me.

"It's been a busy week so far," I admit.

As soon as Adam is seated, the server comes out with plates of food and sets them down in front of us. It looks like eggplant parmigiana. My mouth waters. This kitchen spoils me. I'm used to grilled cheese and frozen pizza for dinner. Maybe some microwaved veggies.

"How's the play going?" Mom asks. Her blue eyes shine. She's so different now than in the past few years. Everything about her is more relaxed. She's so fucking happy we're here and it shows.

Right now, I'm thinking it's not so bad. I'm just glad we can have a dinner together.

"We started rehearsals on Monday, but it's going well. I got my dream cast." I smile thinking of Hawk in the closet and later him bringing me my phone.

"When are you going to have Chase come to dinner?" Mom asks.

My heart stops. Damon's hand slides over my thigh and I'm glad I thought to change into jeans and a t-shirt instead of keeping my uniform on. Even so, my skin burns beneath his touch.

"Do I know Chase?" Adam asks Damon.

"Chase Chadwick," Damon fills in with no tone to his voice.

"Ah, Thomas's boy. Thomas brought him to dinner a few times. I'm surprised you haven't had him over before." Adam takes a bite and turns to my mother. "Thomas Chadwick is one of my business partners. When we have our dinner party, he'll be here with his wife, Jessica."

I bite my lip. Okay, so yeah, my mom is going to meet Chase's parents. Will they talk about me? I kind of feel bad, because they were really nice. I should have broken up with Chase, so this wouldn't be an issue.

"We'll definitely have to have Chase over to dinner." Mom turns her gaze back to me.

I toy with my food. "Uh, with play practice and his football practice, that might be a big ask before the showcase."

Hopefully I won't have to continue this charade past then.

"Well, any time you want to have him over, feel free." Mom smiles sweetly, but Damon's hand squeezes my thigh beneath the table.

I don't think Damon will be thrilled about having the enemy in his house, but what can I do? He's my boyfriend to everyone else. It would be weird if I didn't have him over at some point. Not that I've even told him I moved.

I try to focus on eating while Mom and Adam carry on a conversation without either of us needing to participate. Mom's going on about how this school was a stretch, but I got in with a scholarship, so I'm making the most of it.

"Evan's competing for Valedictorian."

"I wish Damon would put forth more effort into his grades." Adam smiles for my mom's sake. "All he seems to care about is hockey. He would have given up his senior year for a chance to be selected for the more competitive schools, but then the motorcycle accident happened."

Damon's hand slips away from my thigh, but I barely notice. I know about the accident, but what does he mean?

"Did they ever figure out who did it?" Mom asks.

Damon's jaw tightens. My heart clenches with the need to... what? Comfort him? Sleeping together is messing with my brain.

"Hit and run. No idea. The police are still looking into it." Adam shakes his head. "But it gives Damon another chance to get into a good school, which is what he should be focused on. Plenty of good schools have hockey teams. Maybe you can help him see the benefits of studying and college, EvanAnn."

Adam smiles at me and I force a smile in return. What the hell?

"She doesn't have to show me anything." Damon pushes back from the table. "I know what I need to do for my future."

"We're not done with dinner, Damon." Adam glares at him as Damon stands. "Return to your seat."

"Why, so you can piss on my dreams some more?" Damon's gaze narrows on his father's. "The recruiters talked to you. You agreed I could do this, but then I get in one accident that clearly wasn't my fault, and suddenly this is *my* fuck up. It's too far away. Too soon. I need to stay at this fucking school for one more year."

"Watch your language." Adam's face grows stern.

"Why? You control my life, but you can't control what I say." Damon walks toward the door.

"Come back and finish dinner." Adam's voice is loud.

I curl in on myself. It's been a long time since my father was with us, and he rarely raised his voice at me.

I keep my gaze on my dinner, feeling awkward about being here. Yes, I'm privy to a lot of Damon's life, but this is too much. I wouldn't want my mom to yell at me in front of other people. Definitely not her boyfriend and his son.

"I'm so sorry about him. He's eighteen and really good at it." Adam draws in a breath and releases it. "It's refreshing to have someone at the table who's trying her best to make sure she has options."

I lift my gaze to his.

"Your mother says you're going to college." He smiles like that says it all.

"For theater," I say, wondering what he's implying.

"But you'll have a college degree in case that doesn't work out."

My insides twist. The infamous backup plan. That's not why I'm going to college. And yes, some people should really have them, but not Damon. "You've seen your son on the ice, right?"

"Of course." He smiles like he's proud.

"I don't need to be a recruiter to know he excels at it. And when you have talent, you do everything to develop it." I don't know why this is working me up so much. Maybe the implication I'm going to college to get a backup degree, in case being a director doesn't work out.

I know how hard it's going to be and I'm doing everything I can to mitigate the risk. But when you have talent, you lean into it. And fuck the naysayers.

Mom makes a soothing noise.

"Adam didn't mean Damon doesn't have talent. Just that you can't put everything into a career that might not happen." Mom smiles at him like she understands.

"You do know it's going to be a lot harder for me to make it, even with talent. Right?" I set my fork down and take a drink of water. "But I have to try to live my dream, even if it might not work out. I'm sorry, but I'm not hungry anymore. I also need to study for a test coming up. Excuse me."

I leave the dining room without another word. My insides are in a whirlwind. There's a lot I don't understand about Damon's dynamic with his father, but to crush his dream before he even starts—I can't accept that.

My mother has always been my number one fan. Without her support, I wouldn't have made it into Anteros Conservatory. To hear her side with Adam on having a backup plan hurts my heart.

I walk up to our rooms, but Damon isn't there. Part of me knows he doesn't want to talk to me about this, but I want him to know I'm here for him. I'm not sure why. What's between us isn't anything more than physical.

When I go down to the gym, it's dark, and the rec room is empty. I head out to the garage to see if he took off. I can hear music blasting as I walk up to it.

When I enter the garage, I shut and lock the door behind me, just in case. My mom might come looking for me after that exit. I doubt she'll look for me here though. Damon sits on a low stool next to a bike, with tools spread out on a mat beside him.

Part of me settles at seeing him.

There's a couple of stools beside a table nearby, so I sit on one and watch him. He continues to work on the motorcycle with scratches along the side from skidding across the pavement.

My heartbeat stutters. How bad was it?

A helmet that's also scratched up sits next to it. The face shield is torn off. What if he hadn't been wearing it? I can't even imagine how frightening it must have been to be hit. Going down, knowing there's nothing between the ground and his body.

"If you're going to stare, grab the socket wrench."

I hop off the stool and walk over to the toolbox. My dad used to make me get tools for him when he worked on the car. My memories of him are fading, but I remember the tools. I bring over the socket wrench and hand it to Damon.

He glances at it and makes a noise that must mean I did okay.

"Is this the motorcycle?" I don't ask if it's the one Chase hit or the one that changed Damon's future. Fuck, maybe that's the bike that changed my future, because without it, I wouldn't have been on Damon's radar.

I still would have moved in with him because of my mother. Maybe he still would have tormented me. I know he wants to use me to get to Chase, but is there any other reason?

He glances at me with those eyes that definitely ask if I'm stupid. But then he returns his focus to the motorcycle. His jaw is healed, but the skin isn't smooth there. I can't believe that was his only injury with how damaged the bike and helmet are.

"Where did you get hurt?" I have to talk fairly loud to be heard over the music.

He releases a breath and says, "Volume four."

The music turns down.

"Did I ask to talk about it, Evan?" He works on the bike without looking at me.

"No, but talking might help." I shrug. I want to help, but I don't know how.

He glances at the door before his gaze rests on me. "Come here."

I swallow and do as he asks. Is he going to make me suck his cock again? I don't mind if he wants to. He scoots back on the stool and flicks his eyes to the space he created. I swallow, preparing to kneel.

"Sit."

Huh. I sit between his legs and he puts his arms around me to reach the bike.

"See this?" He grabs hold of something on the bike.

I nod, awareness flooding me from being close to him.

"Hold it like this."

"Like this?" I take hold of it.

"Good girl." His earthy scent is heightened by the smell of oil and gasoline. He reaches around me and works on the bike. Every now and then, he asks me to hold something else. The damage to the bike is more obvious close up. There's a brown stain on the chrome I try not to consider might be his blood. My stomach flips.

What if the accident had been worse? What if instead of walking away, he didn't? My heart drops at the thought.

"Why won't you let me fuck you, Evan?" It's been so long since he spoke, I startle a little in his arms. My brain takes a moment to register what he's talking about.

"Why do you want to fuck me?" Heat spirals inside me.

"I find you attractive. It doesn't take much for a guy to want to fuck a girl." His breath flutters my hair next to my ear, sending a shiver through me. Attraction definitely isn't the problem.

"Maybe I'm worried I can't trust you yet." I blow out a breath.

"Pause music." The music stops. "What do you need to trust me?"

"Time." I shrug and lean my head back against his shoulder. "It's not like we started any of this with the best intentions. You want revenge against my cheating boyfriend. I'm done with the asshole. Maybe you don't like me invading your space in your home."

"I like you in my bed, little devil," he says quietly. His voice is dark, like being wrapped up in his arms under his covers. It's one of my favorite things about this whole situation. I don't have to be alone anymore.

"Why me?" I turn a little to look up at him. I need to see his eyes.

He lowers his gaze to me. "You're something I can take away from him."

My heart skips. That's his surface motivation though. He could do that without making me continue to date Chase.

"If that were the case, you should have had me break up with him on Saturday." I sigh and look down before meeting his blue eyes. "I don't know what it will take to let you in. Trust is an issue, especially after you threatened to fist me last night."

He smirks. "I wouldn't have. My fist would probably break you, and then you'd never let me fuck you."

I shake my head. "But in that moment, I couldn't trust you wouldn't. I didn't know what you were going to do." Fuck, I need to make him see what I need. "What you want from me..." My breath hitches. "I need to know you don't always see me as a sex toy available for your use. I need to know you aren't going to hurt me. That I'm not disposable."

He looks away. His jaw clenches and I want to reach up and soothe it. I couldn't at the dinner table, but now, when we're alone, I can. So I do. My fingers feel the rough skin still healing on his jawline.

His gaze drops back to mine.

"You can use me whenever you want, but I need to trust you'll take care of me when I need you to." I stroke my finger along his jaw, loving the buzzing feeling swirling inside me from being close to him. "I need to know you see me as a person, and not just an object to use. I'm okay being used by you, but that can't be the only thing between us."

His eyes narrow and I almost laugh.

"For fuck's sake. I'm not looking for love." I shift my gaze to his lips, not able to look him in the eyes. "I don't even know if I need to like you. But I do need to trust you."

I look up at his eyes. Fuck, they're a beautiful shade of blue. He lowers his head until his nose brushes mine. My breath catches, and the ache that was an undercurrent from sitting close to him erupts into flames.

"I can do that." He captures my mouth.

A tool drops on the concrete, shattering the silence. I jerk away, but he follows me. His hands take hold of me, turning me, and soon I'm straddling his lap, wrapped around him. My hands find their way into his hair, holding him to me as our lips and tongues explore.

Any control I might have had shatters.

His cock is hard between my legs, but we have jeans between us. I rub against him and he groans into my mouth. I don't want to give up his hands on my hips or my hands in his hair. This kiss, I don't want it to end.

I rock on his lap and he slowly begins to help me move against him.

He pulls away, pressing his forehead against mine as we continue to grind against each other. Our breathing chaotic. "I'm not going to ask again, little devil. But when you want me to fuck you, tell me."

I nod as the pressure builds inside me. He takes my mouth again, like he can't get enough of me. It's possible I'm just convenient or uncomplicated. Maybe this is something more. He's in my blood. I'm more attracted to him, Cam, and Hawk than I ever was to Chase. Every time they touch me, they lead me a little deeper into the dark forest of desire, and I don't think I ever want to leave.

His hand slides up my back and into my hair, cradling my head. His cock rubs against my clit with every rock of our hips, until I'm trembling with the need to shatter. So close.

I cry out into his mouth as my release takes me under.

"So fucking sexy when you come, little devil," he murmurs against my lips. He holds me against him and kisses me. I don't think I ever want this to end.

CHAPTER 45

Cam

I OPEN the door and close it softly behind me. It's late, and I should be at home, but I've been avoiding my house tonight. Dad's on a new tear about me not doing enough to get into college. He keeps pointing to Hawk and saying look at what he's willing to do. Why can't I be more like Hawk.

I spent the last hour at Fletcher's because I didn't want to wake up Evan, but now I just want to crawl into bed with her. Using the light on my phone, I navigate through Damon's room to his bed. She's curled up against him. Her face soft in sleep.

That constant pressure in my chest releases. I set my phone on the charger and pull off my clothes, leaving my boxers on. I don't need to fuck tonight. The need I have is deeper. When I'm with Evan, I don't feel as lonely. Hawk and Damon are my friends, but they have their own lives.

Evan is mine. Ours.

When I slide under the covers and my cool skin touches Evan's warmth, she wakes up.

"What?" she mumbles.

"Shh, goody. It's me." I press up against her, knowing I'll warm up soon.

"Everything okay?" she says and wiggles her ass back against me to get comfortable.

"Yeah." I release my breath and kiss her behind her ear. "Everything's good now."

***

HAWK

I get off the ice thirty minutes early to give myself enough time to change for play practice. Thursdays are going to be rough, but it was the compromise I made to be in the play.

Chase also has football practice, but they get out earlier than us, which is why I need to leave early. We're still pre-season, so Coach is okay with it.

I walk into the classroom and Annie looks up from the table. We're in the smaller room this time. It's only me and Chase going through a few scenes. She smiles at me.

"You're early." She looks back down at whatever she's scribbling on. Her brain is constantly working. I'd love to pick it apart. I want to sit and discuss Shakespeare more with her. The lunch where she got into it was amazing.

I sit across from her and glance at the door. "Where's your partner?"

"Keira?" she asks as she pushes a strand of hair behind her ear. It immediately falls back into her face. "She's got a lesson tonight."

"So it's just you, me, and Chase?" I ask. Fuck.

Her blue eyes lift to mine. "Yes, but it won't be a problem, right?"

"It won't be a problem for me, Annie." I reach out and brush the strand of hair behind her ear.

Her breath catches and her eyes darken. It would be so easy to kiss her. I've done everything but kiss her lips again. I don't know what I'm waiting for. She can't take back the night she rejected me, but she wants me now. She even called me the other night to help her out.

But still, I can't kiss her. Has she noticed? Does she burn for it yet?

The door opens, and I slowly remove my hand from her face to turn and watch Chase walk in. His eyes are narrowed, but he smiles when his gaze falls on Annie.

"Hey, babe." He sets his bag on the floor next to her and leans down like he's going to kiss her.

When she coughs a little, he sighs and kisses her hair instead.

"I brought more vitamin C." He sits down next to her and reaches into his bag. He hands her the vitamin.

"Thank you." She gives him a smile and avoids looking at me. She puts it in her mouth and chews on it.

"This weekend, my parents want to take us out on the boat." Chase brushes her hair out of her face and I want to rip his arm off. "Don't say no, babe. The fresh air will do you good. You can wear that little bikini you wore to my house this summer."

Annie's cheeks grow redder. "Chase!"

He smiles. "What? You looked hot in it. Forgive me for finding my girlfriend attractive."

Her eyes narrow on him.

"We need to get started." When she stands, Director Evan takes over. It's like a switch. I find it fascinating.

"Okay, let's start with Act 2, Scene 3." Annie strides out to center stage. "I'll read the other characters in the scene. We'll go up to when Othello comes in."

"Hey, guys, sorry I'm late." Mark Green walks in a little out of breath.

Annie grins and walks toward him. "I thought you couldn't make it."

"I rescheduled." Mark glances at me and then Chase. "We'll get more done with me here."

Mark's a decent guy. Keeps to himself and manages to stay out of trouble. He's a serious actor. Most actors at Anteros are, but some, like Chase, got in more on their daddy's wallets than their talent because their grades weren't up to standard for Deimos. Not that Chase isn't good, but Mark has a hunger for it that Chase will never feel.

We run through a few scenes. Annie gives us notes. Stops us occasionally to ask us to do it slightly differently or to move one of us on the stage. By the time our hour is up, Annie is almost ecstatic.

"This was amazing. Thank you so much." She's packing up her stuff.

Chase glances at his phone. "Hey, babe, I've got to go." His gaze darts to me. "You going to be okay to get to your car?"

She gives him a look as if to ask if he's serious, but then she shakes her head. "I'll be fine. Hawk and I are headed over to Damon's to work on our history project."

Mark grabs his bag and nods to me. "See you all tomorrow."

When the door shuts behind him, Chase closes the distance between him and Annie. "I don't like this, babe."

"It's a school project." She rolls her eyes and continues to pack her bag. "Mia is going to be there too."

He glances at me with suspicious eyes. I grin and wink at him. I don't give a shit what he thinks.

"I thought you were meeting at lunch." Chase looks at Annie.

"It didn't work out." Annie stops and puts her backpack on. "You know what, I'm not going to say it counts for my grade. Because you know that." She looks Chase dead in the eyes. "What's the problem, Chase? Don't you trust me?"

He swallows. "Of course, I trust you. I don't trust them."

"Then you have nothing to worry about." She grabs her phone and glances at me. "Are you ready to leave? I need to lock up."

"Fuck." Chase glances at his phone. "I trust you. I'll see you tomorrow, babe."

He leans down but she coughs again. He releases a sigh, but kisses her on top of her head.

"Get better soon." He gives her a look, like she can fight off a cold for him, and then he takes off.

When the door shuts, Annie releases her breath. "Think he's going to fuck someone?"

She toys with the keys in her hands.

"Probably." I shrug and glance toward the door before moving in closer. "But you could fuck someone too."

She arches an eyebrow. After Damon's hissy fit the other night, I don't blame her.

I laugh and hold my hands up. "I wasn't referring to that part of the act, but we manage to find ways to get off."

She motions for me to follow her out. As she locks the door, she looks over her shoulder at me.

"Why won't you kiss me?" she asks softly.

"Do you think you deserve a kiss, Annie?" I glance down the darkened hallways.

She moves away from the door, and I fall in step with her as we walk toward the parking lot.

"I was doing what I thought was the right thing at the time." She blows out a breath and our footsteps are the only sound in the hallway. "I had to push you away."

Logically, I know this, but something keeps bothering me. "Did you push away Damon?"

Her mouth opens and closes.

"It's okay, baby girl." I smirk. "We all know you like Damon the most."

"What?" She turns and pushes me. It surprises me and I stumble a little. "I don't even like Damon *most* of the time. And he definitely hates me."

Her stormy eyes glare up at me. But it's bullshit.

I close the distance between us, backing her up until her back is against the lockers. I drop my bag next to her feet and put my hands up beside her head, caging her in. "You can't tell me if Damon offered you the same deal but only with him, you wouldn't have taken it."

"I wouldn't—"

"Don't lie. Fuck, Annie. I get it. You're attracted to all of us. And you'll fuck all of us, but Damon's always been it for most girls. He's the bad boy." I slide my fingers along her jaw. "I kissed you first, but he's the one you didn't push away."

Annie's eyes narrow on me. "Do you know how hard it was for me to push you away?"

"Don't—"

"I'm not lying." Annie grabs my tie and pulls me down so our eyes are on the same level. "You changed everything for me. You blew up my world. I didn't know that kisses could feel that way. And yes, I was loyal to my fuckboy boyfriend, because I didn't know better."

"You don't have to—"

"I don't have to what? Explain myself? Because obviously I do." She blows out a breath across my lips, but she's so riled up. "I wanted you. I wanted to keep kissing you that night. If I could have, I don't know that I would have stopped at kissing.

"Damon…" She struggles to put together what she wants to say. Her eyes flash up at me. "Damon is complicated. But I want all of you. It's not a fucking competition."

"It could be." I flash her a cocky smile.

"Stop." She fights a smile. "I'm being serious. You knocked down the wall. Once I kissed you, I was so fucking confused. And then Damon kissed me and… he's not easy. I was angry at him for humiliating me, and that tangled up with lust. But he hates me, and you were so fucking nice to me and flirty and everything. You blew up my world with that kiss. He just finished tearing down the ruins."

"Annie…" I don't know what to say. Damon, Cam, and I could have easily competed against each other our whole lives. But Damon chose hockey, Cam chose to party, and I chose academics. We balance each other out, but a part of me knows Damon is just as good as me at everything.

If he wanted to, he could beat me at everything and he chooses not to.

But Annie…

"Kiss me, Hawk." She leans her forehead against mine and closes her eyes. Her nose brushes mine. "Please. I want your kiss so bad. I need it, please."

Her hand curls around my neck and she tugs on my tie as she continues to whisper *please*.

Fuck. My hand threads into her hair and pulls her head back as my mouth crashes down on hers. She gasps into my mouth and I take everything she has to give me. I lift her and her legs wrap around my hips, bringing our mouths in line as I press her back against the lockers.

She whimpers as her hands cling to my neck. Her tongue brushes against mine and I'm lost. How I managed to not kiss her for so long is beyond me.

CHAPTER 46

EvanAnn

I PARK in the garage and Hawk rides in next to the car. My lips feel swollen from his kisses and I want nothing more than to pull him back down and kiss him again. But Mia is going to be here soon to study.

I get out of the car and grab my things to carry inside. The plan, at least on my side, is to pretend I don't live here. Which might be hard if my mom comes in. If it happens, it happens.

Mia won't have access to the guys through me because they aren't allowed to fuck her while we're doing whatever we're doing. I don't know if Mia will take the *don't fuck my future stepbrother* as a rule or a challenge. I'm trying to trust the Devil's trio, and that means trusting they won't cross that line.

Hawk walks behind me into the house. His hand brushes the small of my back. I shiver at the flood of tingles he ignites and look up at him. We didn't do anything but kiss because there wasn't time. But I desperately want to do more.

His gaze drops to my lips. Anticipation buzzes through me. He leans in.

"How'd practice go?" Damon asks. He has on jeans and a t-shirt.

I step away from Hawk and tuck my hair behind my ear. Damon smirks at the two of us.

Hawk laughs. "Fuck off."

"Where are our parents?" I ask. Suddenly nervous because Mia is coming here.

"Out." Damon closes in on me and drags his thumb across my lips. "Have you been kissing your boyfriend?"

"You want to call me your boyfriend, baby girl?" Hawk leans against a side table and winks at me.

My heart ratchets up a beat. "You guys don't do girlfriends."

I glance at my phone. Mia could be here any minute. Do I have my books? Do I need anything from my room?

Damon slides his hand into my hair, drawing my attention. "If I'm going to have to endure your friend—"

"You're the one who invited her here."

"Give me your panties, little devil."

My eyes widen. "What?"

"You heard him." Hawk rubs the corner of his lips. "Do what you're told, baby girl."

"I'm wearing a skirt." I try to back away, but Damon tightens his hold, drawing me in against him. At least this is one of the newer skirts.

"And I want to know that you're bare under there." Damon drops his lips to mine and talks against them. "It'll be our secret."

"He won't stop pestering you until you do it." Hawk chuckles.

"Fine," I whisper.

"Good girl." Damon kisses me briefly before pulling away. He spins me around and lifts my skirt.

I roll my eyes but slide my thumbs into the sides of my lacy panties and push them down my thighs. When I bend over, he slides his thumb over my entrance. Liquid heat flows through me.

"Try not to stain your skirt, little devil."

I step out of my panties and hold them up. "Happy?"

"Immensely." Damon snags them from my hand and shoves them in his pocket.

The doorbell rings. Damon grabs the back of my neck and kisses me properly before releasing me.

"Behave." He heads to answer the door.

He's the one who needs to behave. Mia is going to flirt with both of my guys, and I can't do a damn thing about it. But they don't need to flirt back.

I hear Mia's voice in the hallway and pick up my backpack. They come around the corner.

"Oh, good, everyone's here." Mia smiles. She's wearing jeans and a t-shirt that clings to her figure. "Where are we setting up?"

Damon nods his head toward the stairs down to the basement. "Why don't we go down to the rec room?"

"So, Damon, do you ever throw parties here?" Mia looks at me with a sly grin.

I return her grin with a shrug. I don't know what she expects to happen tonight. It's not like I'm going to leave her alone with the two guys. Or maybe she'll hit on Hawk because she thinks Damon is into me.

"No." He leads us down the stairs and over to a table the perfect size for playing games. "We should be able to work over here."

"I thought you three ran in a pack. Where's Cam?" Mia takes a chair and I sit down next to her. It's a four-person table so Damon sits next to me and Hawk takes the seat across from me, next to Mia.

"He's not in our history group, why would he be here?" I ask.

Mia shrugs. "The more the merrier, I always say."

An image from the night she took Liam and Fletcher comes unbidden to my mind. My cheeks heat. Is that what she's hoping for?

"Let's focus on the project. I have something I need to do later." Damon's knee brushes mine under the table.

Am I the something he needs to do? I try to keep the heat that pours through me from my cheeks.

"I made an outline the other day." I take it out and pass it to Damon.

He looks it over and grabs a pen. He edits it before passing it to Hawk. Hawk does the same thing before handing it to Mia. She looks it over.

"So do we want to split this up? How do we want to do this?" Mia returns the paper to me.

I glance over their notes, and they're good additions. We split up the work and it grows quiet as we all dig into the text or research on the internet. I cross my legs and focus on my section.

After a while, Mia stretches, drawing everyone's attention. "I could use a drink."

Damon gets up and heads over to the bar. He opens the fridge. "Soda or water?"

She stands and walks over. She stops very close to Damon to check out the contents by bending over.

Damon steps away from her and leans against the bar. His gaze meets mine behind her back, and he arches an eyebrow. They know she wants them, but she's my friend. Mia takes a bottle of Sprite and glances toward me.

"Do you want something?"

"A water." The sooner she finishes, the sooner we'll be done.

"Hawk?" She smiles his way. "Can I get you something?"

"I'm good." Hawk turns the page in his text and continues to write notes.

She glances up at Damon.

He shakes his head.

She brings my water and her soda back to the table and sits down. Everyone falls silent again while we work. Damon leans my way to ask me a question. His breath is hot against my neck, but he maintains a respectful distance.

Mia clears her throat and turns to Hawk. "Can you show me where the bathroom is?"

She winks at me as she and Hawk stand and head toward the other end of the room.

My cheeks heat. Is she trying to create alone time for me and Damon? Or alone time with her and Hawk? Damon watches them go.

"What's her game?" he asks softly. His fingertips touch my thigh. No matter how many times he touches me, sparks ignite.

I meet his blue eyes, keeping my voice low. "She might have mentioned she thinks you like me, and that if you want me to give you a blow job, I should."

Damon chuckles. "Maybe Mia isn't so bad."

I roll my eyes. "It isn't going to happen while she's here."

"Do you think she's offering a quickie in the bathroom to Hawk?" Damon's fingers slide up my thigh.

I open my mouth and close it as I look toward where they disappeared. I release my breath. "Probably."

Do I think she'll offer? Yes. Do I think he'll accept? No. Not after that kiss.

Damon's knuckles brush against my pussy. "How long do you think we have?"

I wet my lips and press my thighs together. "Not long enough."

"Shame." His blue eyes sparkle. "We know you like to watch, but do you like being watched, little devil?"

My breath catches at the teasing touch. "I didn't have a choice to watch or not."

"I could make you come while she's at this table and she'll never know, unless you make it obvious." Damon leans in. His lips brush my ear as he says, "If you can stay quiet."

"Damon." My tone isn't as chastising as I'd hoped. It's almost a plea.

His chuckle races through me as he straightens, taking his hand from under my skirt. Hawk is talking to Mia as they head back to the table. His green eyes meet mine.

Damon wouldn't actually touch me with Mia at the table, right? She takes her seat, and I cross my legs away from him to prevent Damon from doing anything. Mia sighs and looks at me with a pout.

I'd ask what's wrong, but Hawk probably rejected her advances. Hawk clears his throat and our gazes collide. He winks before he settles back into reading.

We discuss the paper more, and come up with a solid plan to finish it this weekend. Before Damon can offer our house again, I suggest we meet at the library.

"Evan." My mom's voice drifts down the stairs. Fuck.

Mia's brow furrows. "Who's that?"

"Uh, my mom." I blow out a breath. Should I come clean? "She gave me a ride here."

"Oh, I was wondering where your car was." Mia smiles. "Do I get to meet her?"

I glance at Damon. He's not looking at me, which is probably good. I turn back to Mia. "Not tonight. I've got to go."

Mia leans back in her chair. Her smile is smug. "Could I use the bathroom again before I go?"

I want to say no, but I also don't want my mom coming down here and telling Mia I live here now. I don't want it to be awkward between us, and I really don't want the rest of the school to find out.

"I'll walk you up." Damon stands and I gather my books into my backpack.

Mia stands and gives me a hug before heading to the bathroom.

"What do I do?" I don't want to leave them alone with Mia, but I don't really have a choice.

"You don't have anything to worry about, Annie." Hawk tucks my hair behind my ear.

Damon guides me to the stairs. When we reach the top, Mom is there with a smile.

"I'm glad you're exploring the house more."

I gesture toward the main stairs up. "How about we go to my room? I wanted to ask you some questions about my clothes."

"Of course, honey." Mom smiles at Damon. "Did you guys get a lot of studying done?"

"Group project. I need to go make sure our guests find their way out." Damon disappears down the stairs as I lead my mom away from meeting my new friend.

DAMON

When I get back downstairs, Hawk has his things packed up. He glances at me, and then toward the bathroom.

"Did she try anything?" I ask quietly. She's already offered Hawk a blow job last week, but he rejected her offer.

"Just flirted and wanted to stay out of the room." Hawk narrows his gaze at me. "She thinks you have a thing for Annie and wanted to give you two time alone."

I shake my head. I didn't think I was being too obvious about my obsession, but if Mia got the impression I want Evan, then who else has noticed? Fuck.

I don't give a shit about Chase finding out, but I don't need Olivia being a bitch to Evan. How would I protect her at school without claiming her? That can't happen for my plan to work.

Then again, Mia is new and doesn't know me that well yet.

"Well, boys, it's just us now." She puts her hands on the back of the chair and glances toward the stairs. "Unless you have parents who will interrupt us?"

Her smile is predatory. Even if Evan hadn't told us she wanted us, it would be obvious.

"I've got that thing I need to take care of." I gesture to the stairs.

"Cards on the table, boys." She straightens and pushes her breasts out. Her blue eyes take us both in. "I'm not looking for a boyfriend, just a good time. And I've been hearing you guys are the best."

Hawk shakes his head and looks to me.

"Does this usually work for you?" I ask her, crossing my arms over my chest.

She shrugs and smirks. "The direct approach gets me what I want most of the time."

"We've heard what you did with Liam and Fletcher." I lean back against the wall. "It's impressive, but not something we're interested in with you."

She arches an eyebrow and glances toward the staircase. "The offer is always open, boys."

"We're not interested," Hawk says.

She shrugs and gathers her things. "We'll see."

She lifts her eyes to meet mine.

"Experience tells me eventually you'll be curious enough to ask." Her smile is subtle. "I don't have many scruples when it comes to sex."

That's been made obvious.

"So if you change your minds, let me know." She moves toward the staircase. "One thing though."

She meets my eyes and I narrow mine on her.

"Evan isn't the girl for you. Not only is she loyal to her boyfriend, she's now loyal to me." Mia smiles. "She knows I want you, so she's not about to jeopardize our friendship or her relationship to do anything with you. When I told her she should give you head, she was insulted. So when you're ready for a real woman, call me."

I almost laugh in her face because Evan is mine. Mine to play with. Mine to tease. Mine to control.

Mia sweeps out of the room. Hawk watches me with a curious look.

"She's going to be a problem," he says softly.

I nod. She's got a mission. "Evan hasn't trusted her with a lot."

"Noticed that too?" He shakes his head.

Evan hasn't even told her friend about what's happening with her home life or the roles we're playing. Mia is new, but does Evan confess to anyone?

"Tell Cam we have to make sure we look available this weekend." I rub my jaw, feeling the rough stubble growing there. It means I need to play Olivia, so she doesn't suspect anything.

"And Evan?" Hawk asks.

I smile. "She'll be where she needs to be."

In my bed when the night is over.

"I need to go home tonight. Dad's at the house." He steps closer to me. "You good?"

I blow out a breath. "I will be."

"Tell her goodnight for me." Hawk claps me on the shoulder and heads out.

I gather my things and walk upstairs to my room. Evan is still talking to her mother. Their voices carry through our shared bathroom. I sit on the edge of my bed and pull Evan's panties out of my pocket, rubbing the soft material between my fingers.

The plan is to use the girls to divert attention from Evan. But we also need to start attacking Chase's confidence in his relationship. It's a delicate balance that could shift at any moment.

"Love you, Mom. Good night." Evan's voice strikes at the core of me.

"Love you, Evan. Sleep well." Her mother. What kind of dumb fate had their partners die and our parents find each other. I'm not even sure how they got together. There's no crossover in their worlds I can find besides Evan and I attending the same school.

The door opens from the bathroom and she stands there. Barefoot, but still in her uniform. That skirt. She puts her foot on top of the other as she stands there waiting for me.

Our eyes lock.

"Come here, little devil."

She doesn't hesitate to cross the room. Tucking her panties back into my pocket, I tap my lap and lean back. She straddles my lap without me saying exactly what I want. Her stormy blue eyes lock with mine as her fingers sink into my hair.

"Kiss me, little devil."

Her lips capture mine. I slide my hand behind her neck and my other hand slides up her thigh to her bare ass, and I take control. Because she's mine. I don't care what anyone else thinks.

Evan is ours.

CHAPTER 47

Cam

WE DON'T NORMALLY GO to the football games, but we know Evan is going to be there. There's also a party afterwards, but for once, I'm hoping we'll skip it and just go back to Damon's and fuck around.

If not, I plan to get white girl wasted. This week has been rough, trying to balance everything. Including dinners with my dad, where he tells me all the things I should be doing to get into college.

I need a night to lose myself. Sex or booze are my favorite options.

The stadium is packed for the first home game, but the student section still has space as we close in on it. Evan and Mia must have arrived early, because they're near the front. That'll make it hard to do anything to Evan.

We're still a secret. I can't pull her onto my lap at the party tonight and make her come. So, might as well get drunk and let her take advantage of me later. I smirk, thinking of Evan kissing me all over.

Her blue eyes meet mine with a blush before she returns her attention to Mia. After Hawk told me about the closet in the drama hallway, I followed his example and tasted that sweet pussy during lunch today, getting her off before she returned the favor.

Evan has been diligent about working on the play. It's almost her whole life right now.

So when I noticed her heading to the drama wing alone, I took full advantage. The girl is stressed, and I'm willing to help her relieve it.

Hawk, Damon, and I head up to the top of the bleachers where Fletcher and a few other guys from the hockey team are sitting. As soon as we sit down, Fletcher offers me a flask. I open it and sniff it. Bourbon.

Pre-gaming the party. Nice.

I take a sip and pass it to Hawk. He offers it to Damon who waves it away. Hawk gives it back without taking a drink. I take another sip before giving it back to Fletcher.

"Watch out, Damon. Incoming," one of the guys mutters.

On the stairs is Olivia Carmichael. Her sights are set on Damon as she and her two friends, Megan and Gemma, follow her to the seats directly in front of us.

"I didn't know you planned to be here." Olivia coos, putting her hand on Damon's knee.

"Why would you?" He arches an eyebrow, but she releases a delighted laugh like it's their own personal joke.

"I'm glad you are. Otherwise, tonight might have been boring." She takes the seat in front of Damon.

Gemma gives me a smile and winks. We fucked sophomore year. It was a party and both of us were wasted. She wanted another go, but I turned her down. I don't need someone who wants more than a fuck from me. And Gemma definitely wants more.

I nod respectfully and almost ask for Fletcher's flask back. But I need to ride my bike to the party. Hawk is willing to take my keys if I drink too much, but there's no way I'm riding bitch seat tonight.

Blake slaps Fletcher on the chest. "Hey, man."

"What?" Fletcher glances at Blake.

He smirks and nods down toward Mia. "I hear she wants to get with hockey players and is good to go. She nice and tight?"

Fletcher smirks. "She's definitely worth the ride."

Olivia turns around. "Are you guys talking about Mia or EvanAnn?"

Fuck, she's got claws. Evan hasn't so much as looked at the hockey players here tonight. Mia gave all of us a once over as we passed.

Fletcher looks at her like she has a screw loose. "Mia."

Olivia makes a little noise of displeasure.

"You know, girls generally stick to their own kind, so if Mia is a whore, that must mean EvanAnn is a whore too." Olivia glances at Damon as if looking for confirmation.

A muscle in his jaw ticks but he doesn't look at Olivia. Fuck, this girl is going to make him explode, and not in the fun way. Fuck it, I'm here for it.

Fletcher laughs. "So what does that make you and your friends?"

The rest of the guys laugh while Olivia's cheeks turn pink. These girls have all gotten around. Maybe not with the dedication Mia is showing, but they've had years to make their way through the guys.

"Are you jealous you haven't taken two guys at once, Olivia?" Blake nudges Fletcher. "We could go right now and help you level up."

"I don't need to level up," she hisses at him. Her gaze goes back to Damon like he might defend her, but his attention appears to be on the game.

"Don't be jealous of the new girl, Olivia." Fletcher taps her nose with his finger. "She's only following in your footsteps."

Olivia opens her mouth, but then closes it. Yeah, she's gotten around to almost all the guys in our school and a few from Anteros. But she doesn't brag about it. The problem is she's never gotten Damon, and she almost missed her opportunity.

She's always wanted him. And she's used to getting what she wants.

"Maybe you should branch out, Olivia. Riordan is down there talking to Mia. Maybe you can get there first too."

I ignore whatever else Olivia says as Jackson Riordan, from our rival team, stands in front of Mia and Evan. I don't need to look at Damon to see where his focus is. I don't know why they hate each other, but Jackson pretends he's okay with Damon. Damon doesn't give a shit about appearances.

EVANANN

"Hey there, pretty girl." My heart stops as I lift my gaze to Jackson. His dark eyes take in all of me. My flight or freeze reaction goes haywire.

I want to run, but I'm locked in place. I wish I had a fight reaction, but he's the reason I know I don't.

"Oh my god, you're Jackson Riordan." Mia captures Jackson's attention, and I can breathe again for a second.

He's only gotten bigger, more built, in the two years since I saw him last in the apartment complex. We went to the same elementary and middle school. I didn't think he even knew who I was until Mom and I moved into the same apartment complex as his family.

A shiver goes through me. That instinct to flee presses on me. He only caught me unawares once. That was when he stole my first kiss. I'd frozen in place. If it hadn't been for my mom calling for me, I don't know what else would have happened. What else he might have done to me.

The intent was there and I was terrified.

I inhale and exhale. We're in the middle of a football game. The stadium is packed, and there's no way he can get me alone. I clue back in to Mia talking with Jackson.

My eyes meet his dark ones. He smiles and gives me a wink while Mia recites his stats. He's a good-looking guy, but when I look at him, it makes me cold inside. All I feel for him is fear.

"I haven't found a lot of open seats." Jackson turns his attention on Mia. "Do you mind if I sit with you?"

Mia nearly squeals with delight. "Of course, here."

Thankfully, she scoots closer to me and leaves room for Jackson on her other side. My heart races and my hands are cold. Damon, Hawk, and Cam have done more to me than Jackson ever did, but I've always wanted them and I agreed to most of it.

Jackson was willing to take what he wanted from me, but that was almost two years ago. We were only sixteen. Maybe things have changed. Whatever he felt for me then should be gone by now.

No matter which way I try to justify it or rationalize it, I can't relax. I sit ramrod straight as Mia flirts with Jackson.

You ride a motorcycle? I love motorcycles. Hockey is my new favorite sport. We're definitely going to the party tonight, especially if you're going to be there.

I'm going to be sick. "I need to go to the bathroom."

Lurching to my feet, I ignore when Mia calls after me. Her voice is lost when the crowd goes wild for a touchdown. I disappear down the walkway behind the stadium. There are still people around. I'm safe.

My chest loosens and I hurry into the bathroom. I stay in there as long as I can get away with before washing my hands.

As I'm walking past the underside of the bleachers, a hand grabs my arm, dragging me under. I try to scream, but another hand covers my mouth and I'm drawn back against a hard body. My panicked mind can only process that Jackson has me again.

This time, no one will be around to stop him. I whimper and tears roll down my cheeks.

"Evan." Damon's voice breaks through my panic and the frozen world I was sinking into. I gasp in a breath. It's him. I'm safe.

I turn and wrap my arms around his waist, burrowing into his warmth. The tears don't stop, but now they're from relief. If I have to be caught by someone, I want it to be one of the Devil's trio.

"What's wrong?" His hand cradles my head as his other hand rubs my back.

It's stupid. A boy stole a kiss from me years ago, and seeing him now turns me into a scared girl all over again. But it wasn't the kiss that frightened me all those years ago. It was something about him that told me I was caught by a predator.

But he was just a boy then too. Maybe I read it wrong.

For a second, I breathe Damon in, grateful for once he's my monster. When I realize Damon's holding me underneath the bleachers where anyone can walk by, I jerk away.

His gaze narrows on my tears. His thumb brushes them away. "What's wrong, little devil?"

"We shouldn't be here," I whisper. The stands go wild again. I turn to leave, but Damon grabs my arm.

"Evan, what happened?"

I open my mouth, but then I realize I can't tell him. Not about Jackson, or the real reason I'm terrified to trust someone. At first, I was definitely enjoying the attention Jackson showed me. The candy he gave me. The smiles we shared. The talks we had. But I didn't see the warning signs.

The Devil's trio are full of warning signs, but my alarm doesn't go off with them. It makes me not trust myself, like maybe my warning system is broken.

"I need to get back," I say softly, looking away from him. His hand squeezes my arm, just enough to draw my attention, and I look up at him.

Damon's face is hard. "We're talking about this later."

"It doesn't matter." I swipe at my cheeks and fan my face with my hands, trying to force a smile. "I'm not your problem. Unless you want to get caught, you should let me go."

At this moment, I don't care either way. I could be done pretending to be Chase's girlfriend. I could finally yell at him for fucking around on me and throw in his face what I've been doing with the Devil's trio. Things I've never wanted to do with him.

For a moment, Damon's blue eyes search mine and I think he's going to press the issue.

But then Damon releases my arm. I make sure the coast is clear when I step out from beneath the bleachers. I hurry back to the bathroom and rinse the tears from my cheeks. Thankfully, I'm not wearing makeup tonight.

I head back up, skirting wide of the area where Damon grabbed me.

When I get back to our seats, Jackson is gone. I release the breath I'd been holding and sit down next to Mia.

"You feeling okay?" she asks.

I nod. "Just too much soda."

"Jackson Riordan, Evan." Mia shakes my arm as the band marches out for halftime.

"Yeah?" I look at her and her cheeks are flushed. She's grinning.

Maybe Jackson has changed. Maybe I didn't know what was happening at the time and misread the situation. A cold chill runs through me.

"How did I not know about hockey?" Mia looks at me like I might have the answer.

I shrug, still feeling off. When halftime is almost over, Damon walks past us. He doesn't look at me and I don't look at him, but I take comfort in his earthy scent.

"I feel like I'm in a candy shop and can't decide what candy to try next." Mia sighs. "Maybe I should lock down a boyfriend so I won't have any more temptation."

"Which one would you choose?" I ask, needing to take my mind off Jackson and get back into the game. I try not to look around to see where he is. Why was he even here? Are we playing his school?

"That's a tough call." Mia starts spouting hockey stats of all the players she's looked up.

I breathe a little easier as the game continues and there are no more surprises. Our team wins, which means Chase will be wanting to party tonight. Part of me is wiped out and wants to go home, snuggle into Damon's bed, and forget this whole week happened.

"Where's the party tonight?" Mia asks.

I look at my phone and Chase has texted.

CHASE:

I'll meet you at Fletcher's

We're celebrating tonight

"Fletcher's." I tense up. That's where I caught Chase cheating on me last weekend. Fuck.

Mia takes my hand so we won't get separated in the crowd as we make our way out to her car. She's seen my car, so I drove to her house and let her drive here. I don't know how I'll get home tonight. Hell, I don't know when I'll get my actual car back. I didn't see Mom at home, so I haven't been able to ask her about the repairs. It's been a week. Surely, it's fine now.

I try not to search the crowd for the Devil's trio or Jackson. I'm sure the guys will be at the party, but I'm hoping Jackson won't. It's not common for someone outside of our schools to be invited to a party, but it's not outside the realm of possibility.

Mia chats the whole way about the Devil's trio and Fletcher and Liam and Jackson and some other hockey guys until I'm ready to drink and dance just so I don't have to hear about hockey anymore.

When we pull up, we're obviously early. There are only twenty cars here. Usually there are around a hundred by the time the partying really begins. I'm wearing jeans and a Devil's shirt Damon threw at me earlier. He didn't like the sweatshirt I had on.

His scent clings to it. His way of marking me for tonight probably. At least the only visible mark. The hickey on my shoulder never gets a chance to heal before he's sucking on it again.

Mia is wearing a pair of short shorts and a crop top that clings to her curves. I can see why guys are drawn to Mia. We may have similar coloring: blond hair and blue eyes, but she has the curves to go with it.

Main character energy.

As we enter the house, the dance floor is already dark and lights swirl around the area. A few people are already dancing. I honestly don't know what room this is in the house, besides the dance space for parties.

"Oh, I love this song." Mia swings her hips in time with the music.

I laugh. "Come on, I'll dance one song."

"Hell yeah!" She pulls me onto the dance floor and she's doing all sorts of moves while I try to stay in rhythm. I've had some musical theater experience, so I can do some dancing, but it's never been my strong point. Just enough to get me into Anteros.

She grabs my hands, and we dance together through that song and into the next.

"I need something to drink," I yell after the third song.

She nods and we walk into the kitchen where the drinks are. The house is more packed now. I wonder where the guys are. Someone grabs me from behind and everything stills in me again.

"Babe!" Chase. Fucking hell, he scared me. "We won."

I turn and his mouth is on mine before I can even cough. Fucking hell. The rest of the room is chaos, but all I can think is I'm in fucking trouble. I don't want to kiss Chase—not that he cares or notices that I'm not kissing him back.

He pulls back and draws me into his body as he whoops and hollers with the rest of the football team. He didn't even notice I didn't kiss him back.

I resist the urge to wipe my mouth and hope none of the Devil's trio saw that. I don't know what Damon meant by punishment, but it doesn't sound like fun. I guess I'll find out soon enough.

CHAPTER 48

EvanAnn

CHASE DRAGS me farther into the room and grabs a Diet Coke and a beer from the cooler. He keeps his arm wrapped around my shoulder. Before I know it, we're outside walking around the pool. I have no idea where Mia is.

Chase sits with his friends and pulls me down onto his lap. My cheeks are red as he hands me my soda. Technically I'm still his girlfriend. This is completely normal behavior for a girlfriend, if she doesn't know her boyfriend is a lying cheating whore.

The problem is, most of the guys around me probably know he's a whore. But will they tell me? No.

Assholes.

I try to relax, but the party is moving outside since it's a nice night. So unlike last weekend when it was quiet outside, everyone is out here now. The music even moves outside, and at least twenty people are in the pool in their underwear.

Chase keeps a hand on my hip as he talks to the guys around us. His friends. I'm supposed to be paying attention, but tonight has been rough. Besides, they're just talking about the game. I'm sure that kiss didn't go unnoticed. Which has me on edge, because I'll eventually have to go home.

Olivia's sharp laughter fills the air. She has Damon by the hand as she tugs him toward the house. I stiffen. Is this my punishment? It's not like I even enjoyed the kiss. It was sloppy and unexpected with way too much tongue.

Hawk sits on the side of the pool with girls swarming around him, mostly in their wet underwear. One of them curves into his side, whispering in his ear. A smirk lifts his lips at whatever she's saying.

When cheers erupt at the other end of the pool, I turn to see Cam doing keg stands while a group of hockey players egg him on. Is this really my life now?

Forced to pretend to be with a guy who doesn't even have the courtesy to keep it in his pants for me. When I lean in to tell Chase I need to go to the bathroom, he pulls me in for another kiss. The guys around us make *ooh* noises.

I pull away, embarrassed. I just want to go home. I wish I still lived in my little house and not Damon's huge mansion. I need somewhere I can lock myself inside and deal with all this.

"Bathroom," I say to Chase, and point toward the house.

He grins and pushes me up to my feet by lifting my ass. My cheeks are hot, but not from anything close to lust. I'm embarrassed and don't know how to stop him from touching me. I don't know what's gotten into him, but whatever it is isn't good.

I walk a couple of steps, dragging in a breath, grateful to be away from him, when Chase's arm falls over my shoulders.

"I'm not letting you out of my sight tonight, babe. I haven't been able to kiss you all week. We've got a lot of making out to do." He smiles down at me and pulls me in for another kiss.

Fuck, I haven't been coughing all day. Because he hasn't tried anything lately, I kind of forgot about the cold today at school, and now that's biting me in the butt. We go into the house and Chase leads me upstairs to where the bathroom is. There's a line.

I lean back against the wall, and he hovers above me with his hands beside my head.

"This week has been amazing." He smiles and glances at the girl next to me before returning his attention to me. "The rehearsal. Fuck, Evan-

Ann, I thought you cast Hawk for his looks, but he's amazing as Cassio."

I arch an eyebrow, but don't say anything as we shift down the hallway closer to the bathroom. He doubted my ability? This is the second time he's mentioned this. It's beginning to piss me off. I'm so over pretending to be his girlfriend.

"You know, when you get done in there, we could find a bedroom and mess around for a while." He arches an eyebrow and smirks.

I lift my wide eyes up to him. Is he serious?

He lowers his face to mine. "Come on, EvanAnn. It's been a long week. You and I need some time together. We don't have to take it all the way, but I'd really like to make you feel good."

The door to the bathroom opens and I slip inside before Chase can kiss me again. I stand there for a moment, completely panicked. What the hell do I do? I have no idea where Mia is. From all appearances, the Devil's trio has completely forgotten about me.

Fuck, that hurts more than I want to think about. But it's also possible Jackson Riordan is somewhere at this party, which means staying with Chase is my best option. I use the toilet and wash my hands.

I pull out my phone and text Mia.

ME:

Where'd you go?

MIA:

Entertaining a very well-endowed hockey guy

Yeah, good for her, but not helpful for me. Of all the guys, I would normally go to Cam to get me out of here, but he's been drinking. I'd hate to interrupt whatever Hawk and Damon have going on.

After all, I'm not their girlfriend. I'm Chase's.

There's nothing I can do to claim them. Would they just laugh in my face? Is that what they're hoping for?

I slip my phone into my back pocket and join Chase in the hallway. He stops talking to the girl who's next in line. She flashes me a tight smile before going into the bathroom. Has he fucked her, or does he want to fuck her? What's his criteria for a fuck buddy?

Chase smirks and grabs my hand. "This way."

He pulls me down the hallway, away from the stairs and toward the bedrooms. I really don't want to go into a bedroom with him.

"Let's go back outside, Chase. I don't feel well."

He stops at a door and tries it, but it's locked. "We can sit in a room for a little while and I promise to make you feel better."

I snatch my hand away, but right then the door next to us opens. Damon walks out. My heart lurches. He steps into the hallway and nods to Chase.

"What's up?" Chase says.

A lead stone falls in my stomach and I put my hand over it as Olivia steps into the doorway. "Damon, come back inside."

I can't look at him. I can't even breathe. Nothing has ever felt like this. It's like my insides are crumbling.

Chase wraps his arm around my shoulders. "Busy up here tonight."

"Yeah." Damon runs his hand through his blond hair.

I want to run, but I'm stuck here in this moment. My stomach twists into knots. I turn and look up at Chase. "Chase, I don't feel well."

He looks down at me and frowns. "You look pale, babe." He glances up at Damon. "Guess we need to get some air."

He drags me away from Damon. I'm not aware of anything as Chase leads me outside. I just go through the motions of getting into Chase's truck and buckling my seat belt. How could Damon do that? Are we done, then? Is he finished with me?

My phone vibrates but I ignore it. Chase drives.

"Can you take me to Mia's? My car is there."

"Sure, but I want to show you something first."

I wish I could care more, but I stare out the window because I can feel tears starting to choke me. What did I really expect? That Damon would keep it in his pants for me? Even my boyfriend cheats on me. Why would I think a guy who wants revenge on my boyfriend would not fuck around, especially when all he gets from me is blow jobs?

I don't even know if I'm doing that right. Maybe I'm horrible at it. Olivia probably gives him everything he needs. Why have I been so stupid when it comes to boys? Jackson, Chase, then Damon, Hawk, and Cam.

All I am is a trophy to be passed along or used.

The city lights fade and I look up. Chase has taken us out of the city.

"Where are we going?" I ask, suddenly alert.

"There's this spot I want to take you to." Chase smiles. "You can see all the stars. It's really beautiful. You're going to love it."

"I just want to go home, Chase." I breathe out. My heart races. This is bad. Chase has always been respectful and kind. But he's also been really grabby tonight. "Just take me home."

"Ten minutes, babe. I swear. We'll look at the stars and see if you feel any better." Chase reaches out and takes my hand, squeezing it lightly.

"Fine." All I have to go home to is my empty bed, which is right next to Damon's. God, I'm such a fool. At least I didn't give it all to any of them. They can go to hell. I don't need a guy or three in my life.

Chase pulls off the road onto a scenic overlook and shuts off the truck. "I know this week has been crazy for you."

It's been intense and wonderful and devastating all in the same breath.

"We just need a moment to breathe." Chase opens his door and gets out.

I should end this charade. I climb out of the truck and remember how it felt to find out he was fucking Abby. Not to mention the other girls he's fucked while he's been with me.

Chase lowers the tailgate of his truck and lifts me to sit on it. He sits next to me and points up at the sky. "There's a million stars we can't see in town, but up here, we can see everything."

I look up and for a moment, just feel the awe. I don't get out of the city very much. Where I live, there are too many lights to see the stars, but tonight, it's clear and there are so many sparkling in the sky. It's breathtaking.

Chase takes my hand. "I know I wasn't around much last weekend. I'm trying to do better by you."

"Chase. I don't think this is going to work out with us." I look down at my lap. "I think maybe we both wanted something different from this relationship."

"EvanAnn, the only thing I ever wanted was you. It's like my dad always says, if you want the best, you date the best. You're the best for me, EvanAnn."

What am I supposed to say to that? Should I tell him I know about his cheating? Will he get mad? How far are we away from town?

He runs a hand through his hair and looks away. "Is this about Hawk?"

When he looks at me, there's anger and accusation in his eyes.

"What about Hawk?" I pull my hand away. Technically, I cheated with Hawk before I knew Chase was cheating on me.

"I see the way he watches you." His eyes narrow on me, like it's my fault anyone looks at me. Like I can control how people look at me.

I slide off the tailgate and wrap my arms around myself, wishing I'd worn my sweatshirt instead of Damon's stupid shirt. "I don't know what you're talking about."

"I've been distant. Not attentive. But this is it for me, EvanAnn. You're it for me. I know it in my bones. But I'm not going to let you make a fool out of me by fucking Hawk Wilker." He grabs my arm. Hard.

"You're hurting me." My heart races and my mind struggles to find a way out of this.

"Why won't you be with me? Fuck, I'll do anything for you." He tries to pull me in but I jerk away from him. "Just let me show you how good we can be together. I've held back because I thought that's what you needed, but maybe I should have pushed you more."

My anger rises and burns away part of the fear, holding me in place. Fuck him and every other guy. They're all assholes. "If you really want to be with me, maybe you shouldn't be fucking other girls."

He freezes for a second. Something like panic crosses his face before it clears. He stalks toward me, but I back away. He's large and scary. There's not a lot of places I can go, except into the woods. "Who told you?"

Dumbfounded, I stop and meet his eyes. "You aren't even going to deny it." Why am I surprised? "I saw you with Abby last weekend."

"We've been dating for four months, and I haven't even seen your tits. Why should I wait for you to be fucking ready when you're a virgin who won't even know what to do?" He glares at me. "But I'll show you what I like."

When he grabs for me, I bolt into the woods, running like the hounds of hell are on my heels. Flight or freeze. I don't know what would happen if I froze now, but I remember what happened with Jackson. No one is taking anything from me again.

"I'm not fucking up my knee chasing you into woods in the dark, EvanAnn. Come out. We can talk this through."

I duck behind a tree and rest my back against it, trying to catch my breath. My pulse races and my chest is tight.

"Fuck!" he yells and he must kick something. "Come on, I'm not going to wait all night for you to come out. Yes, I'm fucking around on you. Are you happy? I confess. And I could be getting some right now, but I'm here with you. I want to fuck you."

"How fucking chivalrous!" I yell.

A bitter laugh comes from him. "Maybe if you'd let me under that skirt or sucked my cock, I wouldn't have needed to go find someone else. I'm a teenage guy. I want sex, and when my girlfriend won't even consider touching my dick, what do you fucking expect?"

"For you to keep it in your pants." I rub my clammy hands down on my jeans. I don't know how to get out of this. Where are we? How far outside of town? He's my ride. I have to get back in that truck with him or stay out here and what? Freeze?

Chase laughs. "You want me to yourself? Come out and suck my cock. Prove to me that waiting is going to pay off. If you do a good job, I'll eat you out."

"Are you fucking kidding me?" I look around, but we're truly in the middle of nowhere. My heartbeat is so loud. I'm trapped.

"Come on, EvanAnn." His tone turns coaxing, but it isn't getting closer. Maybe I can talk him down. "Everyone has to have a first time. I'll make it feel good, babe."

My heart pounds and my feet are stuck to the ground, but I don't answer that. Would he actually force me if I come out? How did I get myself into this situation? And how do I get myself out of it?

"Fine! Enjoy the fucking woods, you frigid bitch. I'm going to go fuck my way through the party."

My stomach drops. He wouldn't actually leave me, right? The truck door slams and the engine starts.

Wait, I'll be stuck out here with no way home. I hurry to the edge of the trees to see his truck backing up. He floors it down the road, leaving me alone in the dark.

My throat closes, and I crumple onto the ground. I'm back to where I should be. All alone.

CHAPTER 49

Hawk

"HAVE YOU SEEN DAMON?" I ask Cam after shedding the hangers-on from the pool. The girls are relentless tonight. Must be something in the water.

Cam smirks. "Went upstairs with Olivia."

He sways a little and his smile is sloppy.

Fuck. "Are you drunk?"

He salutes me and chuckles.

"For fuck's sake." I glance around, but there are too many people here to talk openly about Annie. I haven't seen her for a while and I'm starting to worry. Her I trust, but that fucker Chase... not even a little.

Damon might be pushing the Olivia thing too hard.

"You need to drink and relax, man. One more year." Cam belches and cheers rise from the others sitting around. He raises his hands in the air like he won. "To the seniors!"

I snatch his keys out of his pocket while he's not paying attention.

"You need to sober up." I shake my head. Chase took Evan inside like twenty minutes ago. If she knows Damon is with Olivia, maybe she decided to have her own revenge. Those two know how to press each other's buttons.

My phone rings. It's Annie, but when I pick it up, I can't hear anything over the music.

"Hold on a minute." I walk away from the party and stop at the edge of the backyard where no one is around.

"Yeah?" I ask, running my hand through my hair.

"I didn't know who to call. Mom's not answering her phone." Her voice is small and panic surges inside me. Where the fuck is she?

"What happened?"

She sniffles. "I wanted to leave, and Chase took me to a lookout spot, and things went wrong, and I hid—he left me here."

My chest tightens. If she's hurt, I'll kill him.

"Do you know where you are?" I pocket Cam's keys and pull mine out. I can't head to my bike until I get off the phone with her. The party is too loud.

"No." She sniffles again. "Outside town. Near woods."

Fuck. I'm definitely going to kill him. "Okay, baby girl, I need you to send me your location. I'll be there as soon as I can, okay?"

"Okay."

I hang up, and it takes a minute, but her location pops up in my notifications. Anger rages through me. Fucking Chase. What the hell was he thinking? Leaving her all alone in the middle of nowhere. Anything could happen to Annie out there.

I glance over at Cam, but he can barely stand. He sways on his feet as he tells the guys a story. I'm not letting him ride. As I head into the house, I grab Fletcher by the shirt.

"What's up?" He looks at me startled and a little drunk.

I pull Cam's keys out and push them against Fletcher's chest.

"Take Cam's keys. He doesn't leave tonight, do you understand me?" I narrow my eyes on him. I'm not losing Cam because he rides drunk and gets himself killed.

Fletcher's head bobs up and down as he takes the keys. "Yeah, cool. Cam gets to sleep it off. Got it."

"Good. I'm out." I release him and head through the house. It's fucking crowded and it takes longer than I want to work my way toward the front door.

In the living room, Damon stands against the wall with Olivia pressed into his side. Olivia has her fingers on Damon's waist as he leans down to listen to what she says. Fuck, if Annie saw that, no wonder she wanted to go home.

If he's fucked this up, I'll kill him.

The rage that started with her call bubbles up and I zero in on my target. Because Chase isn't here, I shove Damon.

"What the fuck?" Damon growls, ready to punch me.

I grab his collar and pull him in close so no one else will hear. "The fucker abandoned her out in the fucking woods. I'm going to go get her. You clean up here."

Damon goes still. "What do you mean?"

"I don't fucking know yet. She called me crying. I'm going to get her. Make sure Cam doesn't ride." I search his eyes, and he seems completely sober. "Stop fucking around with the whore."

I push him away from me and his mouth tightens. He saw Annie and Chase kissing. We all did, but Chase kissed her. From the panicked look on her face afterwards, she didn't want it.

But Damon's a territorial bastard when it comes to her, even if he doesn't realize it. I'm sure this is his way of getting her back, but fuck that shit.

I get to my bike, thankful it's a good time of year to ride, because most cars are blocked in at this point. Usually Fletcher's parties don't get busted, but if it's going to happen, it will be tonight. I can't worry about that shit right now.

Annie is all alone in the fucking woods. I notice Chase's truck pulling up to the party as I head out. I don't have time to fuck him up, but I guarantee I'll find him later. And destroy him.

Damon

"Ignore him and let me take care of you, baby." Olivia has been glued to my side since I showed her a little attention.

The fire that burned in me when Chase kissed Evan had me wanting to annihilate everything. He gets to kiss her as much as he wants because she's his girlfriend. Meanwhile, I signed up to be the side piece.

The way I wanted to claim Evan in that moment struck me hard. No girl has had that kind of power over me. Ever.

So when Olivia begged me to take her upstairs, I figured what the hell. I needed to clear my fucking head, to prove to myself Evan doesn't control me. But the minute we were in that room, while Olivia went on about what she wanted to do with me, all I could think about was Evan's wide stormy eyes. The way her lips mold to mine. How she fits me perfectly when we sleep together.

So I left. But when I left the room, of course, I run into Chase fucking Chadwick dragging Evan down the hall, looking for a room to fuck her in. She looked sick, but she's not mine to take care of. So she left with him.

Fucker.

He took her out and dumped her somewhere? What the fuck? I wouldn't even pull that shit with Olivia, and I don't like her. That's what he does to his girlfriend?

Olivia touches my jaw and I jerk away from her.

Startled, she blinks up at me, but immediately adapts and gives me a seductive smile. "Let me make you feel good, baby. I promise you've never had someone like me before."

I look away and see Chase fucking Chadwick walking back into the party without Evan. Fuck. I unlock my phone and pull up the app that tracks her phone. She's in the middle of fucking nowhere, and he's back here to party. Probably to fuck some random.

He touched what's mine. My vision goes red. I shove away from the wall and spin him around.

"What—"

He doesn't get another word out as my fist hits his jaw. The pain feels good. Girls scream and guys move people back as I swing again. Chase is ready and moves out of the way.

"What the fuck, man?" He holds his hands up, but I'm no longer thinking rationally. He dumped Evan out in the middle of nowhere like she's fucking trash. My fist connects with his jaw again.

She's not fucking trash.

"Fuck." He comes at me low and hits me around my center, tackling me down to the ground. "Not my fucking face, asshole."

I bury my fist in his stomach, and he collapses to the floor. I'm on my feet, ready to inflict more damage. This is the asshole that took away my future because he was fucking around on Evan.

She's mine now, but I don't throw that in his face. As much as I want to, it's not the right time to blow this up.

There's a whoop of a police siren outside, Chase must not have heard it as he crashes into me again.

"Police!" someone yells. People start to scatter, but I land another punch on Chase's side and he gets me in the jaw.

I roll him onto his back and just as I'm about to hit him in his nose, I'm dragged off him.

"You're both coming down to the station with us."

Chase rubs his jaw as his eyes narrow on me. But he keeps his mouth shut. Yeah, this isn't over. It's just beginning.

———

Read the completion of the Lust & Liars Duet in
Brutal Little Secrets

<h1 style="text-align:center">Meet C.S. Berry</h1>

C.S. Berry is a combination of my love for writing and my love for reading. She began as an experiment and took off into something I absolutely adore. It's not often you can do what you love and it works as a career. As for me, I love reading and romance and heroines seriously getting railed. I assume since you've read my books, you do too.

If you want to discuss books or anything with me, come join my Facebook group, C.S. Berry's Spicy Executive Suite. And you can always catch me on Instagram @csberry.

Oh and me, I have a lovely family who aren't allowed to read my books. But are so proud, they keep leaking my pen name. My dog and cats don't care about my writing as long as I sit still long enough for them to snuggle.

XOXOXO,

C.S. Berry

Keep up with C.S. Berry
View the shop: csberrybooks.com
View the Patreon: patreon.com/csberry
Join her Newsletter on her website
Join the Facebook Group:
https://www.facebook.com/groups/csberryreaders
Checkout her Website: csberry.com